LOKI'S DECEIT

DONOVAN COOK

Boldwood

First published in Great Britain in 2023 by Boldwood Books Ltd.

Copyright © Donovan Cook, 2023

Cover Design by Head Design

Cover Photography: Shutterstock

Every effort has been made to obtain the necessary permissions with reference to copyright material, both illustrative and quoted. We apologise for any omissions in this respect and will be pleased to make the appropriate acknowledgements in any future edition.

A CIP catalogue record for this book is available from the British Library.

Paperback ISBN 978-1-80483-820-4

Large Print ISBN 978-1-80483-819-8

Hardback ISBN 978-1-80483-821-1

Ebook ISBN 978-1-80483-817-4

Kindle ISBN 978-1-80483-818-1

Audio CD ISBN 978-1-80483-826-6

MP3 CD ISBN 978-1-80483-825-9

Digital audio download ISBN 978-1-80483-822-8

Boldwood Books Ltd
23 Bowerdean Street
London SW6 3TN
www.boldwoodbooks.com

To my brother, Shaun, and his wife, Emma. And their two amazing sons, James and Luke. Who have all supported from afar.

CHARACTERS

FRANKS

Charles – son of Torkel and grandson of Sven the Boar
Hildegard – mother of Charles and abbess of Fraumünster
Bishop Bernard – bishop of Paderborn
Duke Liudolf – duke of Saxony
Roul – spy for King Charles of West Francia
Father Leofdag – priest from Hedeby
Gerold – former slave and spy for Duke Liudolf

DANES

Sven the Boar – former jarl of Ribe, grandfather of Charles
Thora – former shield maiden
Rollo – son of Arnbjorg
Oleg – former hirdman of Sven the Boar
Oda – wife of Arnbjorg
Guttrom – nephew of King Horik

Jorlaug – daughter of Thora's cousin
Sigmund – son of Rollo
Audhild – Thora's aunt
Alfhild – thrall

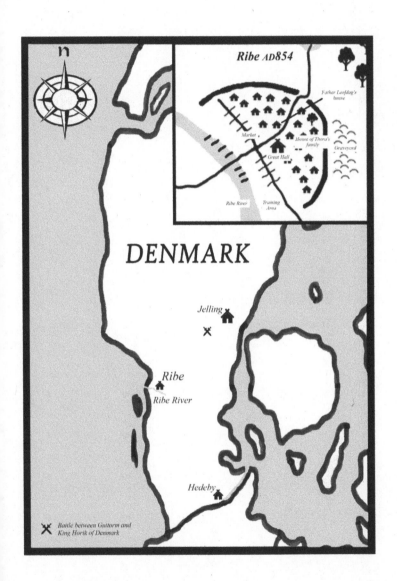

Ribe AD854

Father Leofdag's house

Market

House of Thora's family

Great Hall

Graveyard

Ribe River

Training Area

DENMARK

Jelling

Ribe

Ribe River

Hedeby

Battle between Guttorm and
King Horik of Denmark

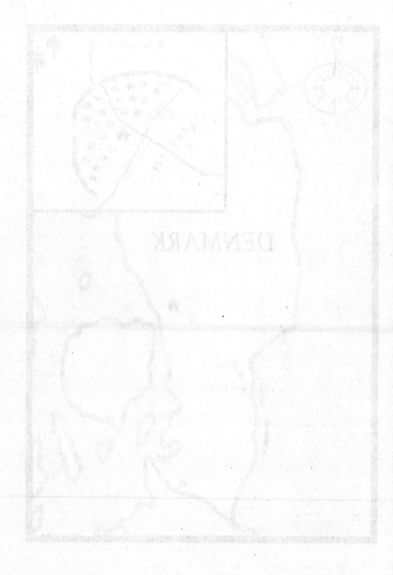

HISTORICAL NOTE

If you have watched the *Vikings* TV series, then you might remember King Horik from seasons one and two, where he initially joined forces with Ragnar, only to betray him and meet a grisly end. But there is far more to Horik, a king who seems to have been forgotten or ignored by the Icelandic writers when they wrote about the kings of Denmark in the thirteenth century.

Horik was one of the five sons of Gudfred, who was king of Denmark between AD 804 and AD 810 when he was assassinated by one of his housecarls. This led to Hemming, a cousin of Horik, being declared king, but his reign was short-lived; by AD 812, he was also dead. After a brief civil war, Harald Klak and Reginfred came out victorious and named themselves the new kings of Denmark. But neither were popular kings and, in AD 813, when they had to travel to the north to deal with a rebellion, Horik and his brothers seized their opportunity and took the throne of Denmark for themselves. This marked the beginning of a troublesome reign for Horik, one where he first shared the crown of Denmark with his brothers and then with Harald Klak to avoid war with the Franks to the south. In AD 824, he became the sole king of Denmark and reigned until AD 854. During his forty-one-year reign, he fought off two invasions by Harald Klak, one of which was supported by Louis the Pious of Francia, and allowed for the first Christian church to be built in Denmark, even though there was no evidence that he loved the Christians. All Horik seemed to have wanted was peace with the Franks and he even went as far as punishing jarls who raided their neighbours to the south. This did not make him popular, which might explain why there's barely a mention of him in the sagas or why the Icelandic writers who wrote about the kings of Denmark did not even mention him. Because of this, there is no record of when he was born or how old he was when he first became king with his brothers in AD 813. Ansgar, the famous monk who was sent to Scandinavia to convert the Norse pagan to Christianity, was said to have become a close friend of Horik's, but even he only mentions him in a few lines, where he refers to him as Eric, and this is only to tell of his death. In *Life of Anskar, the Apostle of the North*, we learn that Horik had become unpopular with his people and along with most of his chief men, Horik died after a three-day battle. Some sources suggest that his nephew, Guttrom, led the uprising against him and also died in the battle, and even though I can't confirm if this is true, I had to use it for my novel. I've been unable to find any mention of this battle or where it might have taken place, which again makes me believe that Horik was very unpopular and that not many people wanted to remember him after his death. I feel that this is a tragedy because, to me at least, he came across as a king who did what he could to stop the mighty Frankish empire from swallowing Denmark up and destroying their gods, much like Charlemagne had done to the Saxon people in the past. Even if it meant allowing churches to be built. If you want to learn more about Horik, I recommend reading *Vikings at War* by Kim Hjardar and Vegard Vike. They give a more detailed explanation of Horik's reign as well as the complicated history between Francia and Denmark.

On a side note, the infamous Ragnar who raided Paris in AD 845 and who many believe was the legendary Ragnar Lothbrok, did play a part in Horik's story. But not like what was shown in the *Vikings* TV series. In AD 845, Horik gave in to the pressure from his jarls and sent a large expedition, about 150 ships led by Ragnar, to raid the Franks. This Ragnar was believed to be a member of the royal family, so most likely kin of Horik, and died soon after returning to Denmark.

Most of this novel takes place in Ribe, a town in the east of Denmark and with a rich history. Ribe is the oldest town in Denmark and is the first town to be mentioned in written sources. Dendrochronological dating of a piece of oak wood from a well shows that Ribe was founded around AD 705 when it might have started as a seasonal marketplace before developing into a permanent settlement. The first church in Denmark was built in Ribe in AD 855 on land granted to Ansgar by Horik I, although some sources say it was Horik II who permitted the church to be built. Although I have to admit, I knew none of this when I first decided that Ribe was to be Sven the Boar's home town in *Odin's Betrayal*. I guess we can call this a lucky accident that my story takes place in such a fascinating town.

1

SUMMER AD 854, THREE WEEKS AFTER SVEN'S
RETURN TO RIBE

Gerold looked up when the cell door opened and braced himself for the beating he knew was coming. He had lost track of how many days he had been in the cell in the tower at Ehresburg, the capital of Saxony, and he often wondered if this was what hell was like. He thought he had been lucky when they escaped Ribe, that cursed town in Denmark, even though they had lost Charles, the little bastard he wished he had never met. When Charles had stabbed the leader of the group sent to capture him, Gerold had thought of nothing else but to flee. With a storm brewing, he and the two remaining spies had made it to the dead leader's ship and had to threaten the captain to sail before the Danes got hold of them. The man had not wanted to, not at night when he did not know the waters well enough. And not with a storm coming. But a knife at the throat from one of the spies had convinced the captain to change his mind. As soon as they left the river and made it out to open waters, the storm erupted and Gerold had been convinced he was going to die as the ship was tossed around by giant waves and lightning lit up the sky. One of the spies had died during the night from an injury he had picked up while fleeing the Danes, and

Gerold had not understood why the other claimed he had been the lucky one. When the ship had docked in Hamburg two days later, Gerold – weakened from constant vomiting – and the remaining spy had been greeted by warriors sent by the Duke Liudolf of Saxony, who escorted them back to Ehresburg, his capital. And that was where hell had started for Gerold.

He had thought that God was smiling on him when he first spotted Charles hiding under a stall in the market in that small town on the border. Only that morning his mentor, an old spy for Duke Liudolf who pretended to be a trader, had told him to be on the lookout for the red-haired son of a Danish warrior in Duke Liudolf's employ. The Danish warrior had been killed, but not after he had slain a few of the duke's men and the boy had disappeared. Gerold had found the small boy who had told him that he needed to go to Denmark to find his grandfather, a jarl in the north and Gerold had convinced him to go with them as they were also headed there.

Everything had gone according to plan and they had made out of Hügelburg with the boy hidden in their cart. His mentor even kept up his role as a drunk and belligerent trader the following day so the boy would not suspect anything. The only thing that had surprised Gerold was when his mentor found the pouch on Charles and took the large golden cross out. The way his mentor's eyes lit up when he saw it made Gerold think he had not been told everything and he sensed they were after more than just the boy. Not that he had known why they were after Charles. His mentor had never told him. Things then went wrong when those bastard bandits had turned up and killed Gerold's mentor.

Gerold and Charles had managed to escape, and he had done his best to convince Charles to go to the nearest town. He knew there was a man there his former mentor had trusted, another spy for Duke Liudolf who would know what to do with Charles. But

Charles had been too stubborn, and Gerold had been forced to improvise. He left a note on the cart in a hidden compartment that only other spies would know about and had done his best to leave a trail for anyone who might be searching for them. But none of that mattered. They had returned to Francia without Charles or the cross. Gerold and the other spy had been brought to Ehresburg and separated. Gerold did not know where the other man was or why they had been held captive, but since he had been here, he had been subjected to daily beatings and given only gruel to eat and dirty water that tasted like piss to drink. So Gerold was confused when the guard grabbed him and dragged him out of the cell. He tried to see where they were taking him but struggled to see clearly through his swollen and blood-covered eyes. The warriors did not like his kind, he had been told, and Gerold wasn't sure if they meant a slave or a spy. Not that he knew which one of the two he was any more.

The warriors took Gerold up some stairs and threw him into a clean cell that did not reek of shit and piss. There was a window as well, a small hole in the wall, and Gerold had to screw his eyes shut because of the light. His stinking clothes were ripped off him before he even adjusted to the light in the room. Panic gripped him as he feared the worst, but he did not want to believe that that was about to happen to him. The men had access to women; he was sure of it. Before Gerold could turn around to defend himself, the warriors emptied a bucket of freezing water over his head. Gerold gasped as the air was taken from his lungs and was rewarded with another bucket of cold water. The warriors laughed as he spluttered before one of them threw something on the ground.

'Get yourself cleaned up. You have a special visitor and the duke doesn't want you to stink like the pig you are.' The warrior laughed and walked away, leaving only one to keep an eye on him.

Gerold sat there, naked and shivering, as he struggled to understand what was happening. He would have prayed, but he had learnt a long time ago that it did not help. God did not care about people like him. He saw that there was another bucket in the cell, this one still filled with water. Gerold crawled to it and rinsed the dried blood from his eyes and the rest of his face. When that was done, he stared at his reflection in the water. His dark hair had grown long, and it was dirty and matted. Gerold knew that no matter how hard he tried, he would not be able to clean it. His eyes weren't swollen as badly as he had thought they would be, but most of his face was covered in bruises.

'You better hurry. Duke Liudolf is not a patient man,' the warrior left in the cell said as he stood there, his arms crossed and looking bored. Gerold wondered if he could kill the guard and escape, but then thought against it. He had been taught to kill people in the shadows where they couldn't see him. And in his weakened state, he would be dead before he got his hand on the warrior's sword.

'Who is my visitor?' Gerold struggled to form the words properly because his jaw was sore from all the beatings and he had not spoken for a long time.

The warrior ignored his question. 'Get dressed or I'll take you up there naked. Up to you.'

Gerold looked at the bundle on the ground and saw it was clothes. Not very clean clothes, but cleaner than what he had been wearing. Seeing no other choice, he got dressed. The trousers were too small and the tunic too large, and it smelt of stale vomit, which made Gerold's empty stomach churn. When he was done, the warrior led him out of the cell and up some stairs until they reached a larger room that was empty apart from the tables and benches. In the room's corner, a large pot sat over an unlit fireplace, and Gerold's stomach growled loud enough to make the warrior laugh.

'You behave yourself and the duke might let us feed you something nice.' The warrior showed Gerold where to sit and then left the room.

Gerold looked around and guessed this was where the warriors ate their meals. He was tempted to piss in the pot that was in the corner, but before he could even think of getting to his feet, the door opened and Duke Liudolf walked in. Gerold had never seen the man up close before and thought he looked older than he had presumed him to be. Grey hair had invaded his dark hair and short beard, but the duke had broad shoulders and thick arms. His eyes scanned the room like a warrior accustomed to seeking threats and, when he was satisfied the room was empty, he stepped away from the door and a woman walked in. Gerold frowned as the woman whispered something at the duke, who nodded, before she removed the hood that covered her face and Gerold gasped. The woman had a stern face and hard eyes, and to Gerold she looked like someone used to being in control. But it was the shape of her eyes and her nose that made him realise who she was. The woman removed her cloak and Gerold's eyes widened when he saw the long black dress and the large gold cross hanging around her neck. It was not as beautiful as the one Charles had, but it was enough to tell him that this woman was very important. Gerold had travelled all over the Frankish kingdoms with his mentor and had seen King Louis of East Francia and his sons enough times to recognise their features on the woman's face.

The woman walked towards him, scrutinising him as an old man walked into the room. The old man, with his grey tonsure and heavily lined face, wore a black cassock with a purple cincture around his waist and a large golden cross hung from his neck, and like the woman, his face was stern and eyes judgemental. He recognised the old man as Bishop Bernard, a man his old mentor had often spoken to. Gerold frowned as he wondered what these three wanted from him. Since he had arrived in Ehresburg, he had been locked in his cell while an old warrior questioned him about what had happened to his dead mentor and in Denmark, after his daily beatings. Gerold had told them everything, from meeting the old, fat drunk in Hedeby who turned out to be Charles's grandfather to their journey north to Ribe, but that never seemed to be enough. So he was curious about why the woman wanted to speak to him.

The woman sat down and stared at Gerold as if she was trying to decide something.

'Are you sure—' the bishop started, and was silenced by the woman before she rubbed the cross around her neck.

'Do you know who I am?' she asked him, her voice firm and used to giving commands.

Gerold studied the woman, the way his old mentor had taught him to. She had the same eye shape and nose as Charles. 'You are his mother. Charles's.'

She nodded and Gerold understood why there were no warriors in the room with them. This was something no one was meant to know, and he worried about what they would do to him after this conversation.

'Tell me about him.'

Gerold frowned, and the woman said again, 'Tell me about my son.'

Gerold glanced at the duke and the bishop behind the woman. Trying to work out if this was real or a trap.

'Answer the abbess,' the duke said, his brow creased.

Gerold looked at the abbess and sighed. 'Annoying.' The duke growled and Gerold continued. 'He is stubborn and too curious. Kept asking the heathens about their gods.' The woman frowned at this, but Gerold carried on. 'But he is also a devoted Christian. I guess it runs in the blood.'

'Why do you say that?' the abbess asked him, her brown eyes scrutinising him.

'Because he was constantly praying. He did his best to say all the prayers during the day and kept talking about how he wanted to be a priest.'

The woman smiled as Duke Liudolf asked him, 'Why did you take the boy to Denmark and not to Bremen, like you were supposed to?'

Gerold glared at the duke. 'I tried to, but he refused to stay in East Francia. He insisted on going to Denmark to find his grandfather.'

'You could have convinced him otherwise,' Duke Liudolf said.

Gerold laughed, surprising himself as much as the others. 'Charles is as pig-headed as his heathen grandfather. Nothing I said could change his mind and I was told not to harm him.' He saw how the abbess flinched when he compared Charles to his grandfather. It was quickly hidden, but he had still spotted it.

'Why?' Bishop Bernard asked with a pained expression on his face.

Gerold raised an eyebrow and glanced at the duke and the bishop. Both men were staring at him and he wondered how much these people really knew. 'His father had told him to.'

'Why would Torkel do that?' the abbess asked.

Gerold shrugged. 'I guess because it was the duke's man who had attacked them, so his father thought it was better to send a young boy to the heathens instead of his mother.' Gerold could not help throwing that last part in. He was getting angry at having to sit here and answer the questions when he had been tortured for the last few days.

'My son believed I was dead. We thought it was safer for him that way.'

Gerold leaned back, surprised by her honesty.

'But why did he not send the boy to me?' the old bishop asked, his head tilted to the side.

Gerold glared at the old man. 'Charles believed you were behind the death of his father. I think he heard something that day in the church that made him think you wanted his father dead.'

'That is ridiculous!' The duke's face went red and Gerold had to hide his satisfaction at angering them. 'Why would the boy think—'

'Because your chatelain attacked him and my son in their home!' the abbess snapped at the duke without looking back. Her hard eyes were fixed on Gerold and he shivered at the anger he saw in them.

Duke Liudolf flinched before his face reddened. 'Not on my orders!'

'Then whose?' the abbess asked as she glanced at the duke over her shoulder. Duke Liudolf opened his mouth to respond, but then closed it and looked away from her. Gerold had to resist the temptation to smirk at the duke as the abbess said, 'Your man attacked Torkel and my son without your knowledge or permission. That means only one thing. Lothar had a different master. One more powerful than you.'

'King Charles of West Francia?' Gerold asked, and knew he was right when he saw the shocked stares of the others.

'How do you know that?' Duke Liudolf asked as he took a step towards Gerold. Bishop Bernard glanced around the room as if he believed someone was listening to them while the abbess scrutinised Gerold.

Gerold wondered if he should have kept silent, but it was too late for that now. 'The other two argued on the ship before one of them died. I heard them mention the king of West Francia.'

The abbess looked at Gerold and he felt nervous under her stare. 'This is not the place for that discussion, but you are right,' she said, surprising him. 'That my uncle, the king of West Francia, has been searching for the cross is no secret.' She glanced at the two men behind her. 'We just never realised he was also after my son or that he even knew about Charles.'

'Why not do more to protect him?' Gerold asked before he could stop himself.

'I was led to believe that both my son and the cross were safe.' The duke and the bishop fidgeted behind the abbess as she said that and Gerold got the feeling they had argued over this already. But there was another thing he did not understand.

'Why now? If Charles had the cross all these years, why is the king of West Francia only after it now? And why did King Louis never take it back from Charles and his father?'

The abbess stared at Gerold and he thought she might refuse to answer his questions. From the looks on the faces of the duke and the bishop it was clear they wanted her to refuse, but then she took a deep breath. 'Because, Gerold. We might be heading to war.'

'War?' Gerold's eyes widened.

'Yes,' the abbess said. 'It's no secret that neither my father, King Louis, or King Charles were pleased to have to sign the Treaty of Verdun. Both men wanted to be the new emperor. That was why they started the whole civil war against Lothar, their older brother, so many years ago.'

'But that was a long time ago. What changed?' Gerold ignored the glares he was getting from Duke Liudolf as he tried to make sense of what he was being told.

'That is none of your concern,' Duke Liudolf said, but then the abbess held her hand up.

'No, he deserves to know. He risked his life to keep my son safe.' She looked at Gerold again. 'What changed was that now my father has a reason to invade West Francia because some of my uncle's dukes were unhappy about him and they went to my father asking him to remove my uncle as the king of West Francia. King Charles found out about this and knows he cannot fight a battle against my father and King Lothar of Middle Francia won't help him either. We think that is why he seeks the cross. He believes it will protect him from my father.'

'And what about Charles? So he could blackmail you?' Gerold asked, and knew he was right when he saw the slight twitch in the corner of the abbess's eye.

'That you don't need to know,' she said. 'Now, Gerold, tell me everything. From the moment you first saw my son to the last.'

'I already told the duke's men everything.' Gerold crossed his arms and looked away.

'And now you are going to tell me.'

Gerold thought about refusing, but then he would only be thrown in his dirty cell again and most likely be beaten. So he told the abbess everything she wanted.

She listened patiently, all the time holding on to the cross around her neck. When he had finished, the abbess let go of the cross and asked him, 'He still has the cross?'

Gerold nodded. 'What is so special about that cross, anyway? The old heathen believed it was the reason his son was killed.'

The abbess nodded while she thought, and then she said, 'Tell me about the old man. Do you think he will protect my son?'

'You will leave your son with the heathens?' Gerold asked before he could stop himself, his eyes wide.

The abbess's eyebrows creased. 'My son will not be raised by heathens!'

Gerold was taken aback by the change in her tone and decided it was best to answer. 'I think he will kill anyone who tries to take Charles from him.'

The abbess composed herself and nodded. 'You did well, Gerold. I thank you for everything you did to protect my son.'

Gerold shrugged. 'To be honest, I wish I never ran into him.'

The abbess was about to get up and then sat down again, her eyebrow raised. 'Why do you say that?'

'Because before that, I had a purpose, a future. My mentor had been hard on me, but he was teaching me to be a good spy. Now the duke and his men think I killed him and even though I just survived the heathens, I came back here just to be beaten and tortured every day. I had believed that finding Charles had been a blessing from God, but I know it was a gift from the devil.' He looked at the abbess. 'Charles will live if you leave him there. His grandfather will make sure of it, but they will also make sure that he forgets about the God you both cherish so much.'

'Don't you dare speak to the abbess like that!' The duke took a step forward with his fists clenched by his side. 'I will make sure you are punished for your insolence.'

'No,' the abbess said, surprising both Gerold and the duke. 'He spoke his mind and I believe him. Torkel had told me enough stories about his father for me to believe that he would not want his grandson to be Christian.' The abbess stood and turned to leave. She walked to the duke and then turned to look at Gerold again. 'Do not take him back to his cell. Get him proper clothes and make sure he gets a good meal, not the gruel you've been feeding him. And I don't want to see him in this keep again. He will stay in your house and you will make sure that no one touches him again.'

'But why?' The duke's eyes widened and even the old bishop looked startled.

The abbess glared at the duke. 'Because your chatelain attacked my son and his father while you were in Hügelburg. If you had paid more attention, then Torkel would still be alive and my son would still be safe. So this will be your penance.' The abbess turned and left without another word, and Gerold could not hide the smirk on his face. The duke, though, turned red as he glared at Gerold, before he too left the room, leaving only the bishop behind.

Gerold could hear the duke shouting orders through the wall and then frowned at the bishop, who stared at him. 'I'd be careful if I were you while you stay in the duke's house. He has many men who can make you disappear, but still seem alive.'

Gerold's eyes widened as the bishop turned and left and, once again, he wished he had never met Charles.

2

A FEW WEEKS LATER, NEAR RIBE IN EASTERN DENMARK

Sven glared at the enemy as they formed their shield wall about thirty paces away. There were about a hundred and fifty men facing the warriors of Ribe, all of them carrying black shields with white bears painted on them. Helmets and brynjas glinted in the late morning sun as ravens and other scavenger birds circled above the two armies, while banners carrying the same emblem fluttered in the wind. Sven had no banner, and neither did his men carry his emblem on their shields. He had been too busy fending off raids to his lands from those who had been loyal to his brother Bjarni, and none of these men had sworn any oaths to him. They were the men of Ribe and while he was the town's jarl, they were fighting to defend their town and the surrounding lands, not for him. The thunderous echo of their shields locking together echoed across the field, and Sven winced as the noise rang in his ears. The gods knew it had been a long time since he stood in a shield wall and he had to grip his spear tightly to stop his hand from trembling. But it wasn't fear that coursed through his veins and heightened his senses. It was his rage at having to battle one of Bjarni's sons-in-law, a young jarl from the north, that chased his

fear away, just like the morning sun banished the darkness of the
night. The young bastard had been plundering the farms north of
Ribe, seeking to punish Sven for killing Bjarni and turn the people
of Ribe against him. Sven had managed to draw the arrogant shit
out for this battle, and today the bastard was going to pay.
'Forward!'

The rival jarl echoed Sven's order, and the two armies marched
across the field to meet each other in grim silence. No man enjoyed
fighting in a shield wall. You had to remain calm, and disciplined. It
was easier to give in to your rage, to forget about everything as you
charged at the enemy with a sword in your hand and screaming for
his death. Sven glanced at Rollo, who was wearing his deceased
father's old war gear, beside him. An old brynja, its metal links fixed
and polished, and a helmet with an eye guard that had to have a
few dents knocked out by the town's smith. The giant warrior's face
was pale under his helmet, and Sven saw his jaw muscles clenching
through his blond beard. He would have wondered how many
shield walls the young warrior had stood in, but there was no time
for that now. The enemy was getting closer.

'Is that a bearded child?' Jarl Asger, the son-in-law of Sven's
dead brother, shouted. The enemy warriors laughed, and more
insults came about Sven's height. But he did not care. Sven knew he
was short and that most men stood taller than him. And that he was
standing between Rollo, a man taller than most, and another
equally tall warrior made him look even shorter. He rolled his
shoulders, which had broadened in the weeks since he killed his
treacherous brother. His arms and legs had lost their softness and
strengthened after weeks of training hard. Even his rotund stomach
had reduced in size, although not by much. Sven wore a brynja, the
same one Oda, Rollo's mother, had given him that night many
weeks ago, and a simple helmet which had a nose guard and a
chain mail curtain around the back to protect his neck. A leather

cap protected his shaved head with the faded tattoo of a raven from the metal of his helmet and helped to keep it in place.

'No, that's a dwarf. They got a dwarf fighting for them!' another shouted. Sven gritted his teeth as he soaked up the insults and used them to stoke his rage.

'I think you made it angry,' Jarl Asger said, which made the enemy shield wall cheer. They were only ten paces away now, close enough to see the faces of the men they needed to kill.

Sven had been a powerful jarl once, a warrior of great renown. But that had been a long time ago and, for the last eighteen winters, most had believed he was dead. That was until Sven had returned to Ribe, the old trading town he used to be jarl of, to ask for his brother's help to protect the grandson he never knew he had. Sven soon learnt that it was because of his brother's greed and treachery that his only son had been taken by the Franks after a failed raid twenty winters ago. That had started a downward spiral for Sven, which led to the death of his wife and him fleeing the town he had fought so hard to get. Bjarni, Sven's brother who became jarl after Sven had left, was dead now. Sven had killed him when he had learnt of his part in that failed raid and now he had to fight one of his sons-in-law who sought to avenge the treacherous bastard.

The two shield walls stopped a few paces away from each other. Warriors from both sides still shouted insults while Sven glared at Bjarni's son-in-law. The man wore a confident grin on his face, and Sven knew he had reason to be confident. Asger's men outnumbered his and his ranks had been filled with some of Ribe's warriors, those who had refused to fight for Sven because he had killed their jarl. Sven looked at his rival's light-coloured beard, kept loose and wild, and his face devoid of any lines. He knew little of this jarl, only that he was the son-in-law of Bjarni, and guessed the young upstart was trying to make a name for himself and earn the favour of Horik, the king of the Danes. Sven's knuckles turned white as he gripped his spear. His Dane axe was slung on his back and he wore his sword around his waist. His spear would start the killing and his sword or axe would finish it, hopefully by taking the young bastard's head from his shoulders.

'Sven the Boar,' Jarl Asger said, his voice strong enough to be heard over the shouted jeers from the warriors. 'Thought you were dead.'

Sven hawked and spat. 'And who are you supposed to be?'

The jarl grimaced. Fame was everything to the Danes, and no man wanted to be told he was unknown. 'I am the one who's going to kill you and avenge Jarl Bjarni.'

Sven glanced at Rollo and saw the giant warrior smirk. 'Aye, but I still don't know who you are.'

The jarl bristled at that. 'I am Jarl Asger, the mighty bear of Denmark!'

Sven grunted. It was a bold claim to make. The jarl might have been taller than Sven, but he was shorter than Rollo and not as broad. But then these young men were full of shit. Sven had been the same once. He glanced at Rollo. 'A good time for killing bears, don't you think?'

Rollo grinned. 'Aye, they're nice and fat this time of the year.' The surrounding warriors laughed as Asger's face turned red.

'We'll see if you are still laughing when I gut you like a pig.' The comment was weak, but his warriors still cheered.

Sven felt the emptiness in the pit of his stomach, even as he traded insults with Asger. His last battle had been against the Franks on the beach so long ago and had been a failure that had cost him everything. And Sven could not afford to fail now. He had to survive this battle because his grandson depended on him. What also made him nervous were the warriors of Ribe. He did not know many of the hundred or so warriors who were fighting for him. He knew they could fight, but wasn't sure that they would fight for him.

Only half of Sven's men had brynjas, the rest wearing leather jerkins or thick woollen tunics, but all had helmets and carried either a sword, axe or spear. Sven had split his army into three groups. Oleg, the old warrior who had aided Sven in his fight with Bjarni, commanded thirty men on the right flank, and Sten, another of Sven's old hirdmen, had thirty on the left flank. The rest of the men were under Sven's command in the centre. Sven's shield wall stood three men deep. Jarl Asger's was five men deep.

Sven wanted to grip the Mjöllnir around his neck, the one that had belonged to his father before him, but he couldn't. Neither of his hands was free, and it would only make him look weak. So instead, Sven clenched his jaw and nodded at Rollo.

'Charge!' Rollo bellowed, and both Oleg and Sten echoed the order. As one, the warriors of Ribe rushed forward, each man keeping pace with the men around him so the shield wall would stay intact. The men in the second row lifted their shields over the heads of the men in the first rank, while those in the third rank had their spears ready to stab at the enemy over the shoulder of those in front of them. Sven had about a dozen archers who sent arrows over their heads and forced the enemy to duck behind their shields.

'Attack!' Jarl Asger's orders echoed along his wall. 'Archers! Shoot!' Asger had more archers than Sven and he gritted his teeth as he tried to ignore the arrows raining down on his men.

Sven grunted as the two walls crashed together, and the echo of the collision reverberated over his head. His shoulder felt numb, the muscle still weak from a recent injury, but Sven forced that from his mind as he stabbed his spear at Jarl Asger. The younger jarl twisted his head to the side, and the spear missed before Asger jabbed with his sword, its sharp point finding nothing but wood as the man behind Sven blocked an axe aimed at his head. Rollo hacked at the shield in front of him with his hand axe and used his larger size to force his opponent to his knees. Men were screaming war cries and threats as they hacked and stabbed at each other while the archers on both sides kept the men in the rear ranks under their shields. Sven stabbed with his spear again, and again Asger ducked out of the way. As Sven's spear went past Asger's head, he twisted it to the side and felt it strike someone. He did not hear the man scream as the tip of the spear sliced his cheek open but saw the blood on the blade as he pulled the spear back.

Asger roared as he stabbed with his sword again, but Sven blocked it with his shield as he struggled to control the rage that coursed through him, knowing that he could not give in to the flames that heated his blood. He had to remain calm and stay alive. But Odin whispered in his ears, telling him to grab his Dane axe and split the younger jarl in two. Blood sprayed over Sven as Rollo killed his opponent, which only made Odin's whispers louder. But Sven ignored the god of chaos as he blocked a spear that came from over Asger's shoulder. Asger used this moment to duck and cut Sven's leg under his shield, but Sven's lack of height worked to his advantage as Asger could not get low enough. Sven punched out with his shield and caught Asger in the face. The younger jarl cried out and both of Asger's warriors on either side of him died as they looked at their jarl. Rollo and the tall warrior on Sven's left wasted no time and punished them for their mistake. As those warriors died, Sven stabbed at Asger with his spear one more time, hoping to kill the younger jarl as his men pulled him to safety, but then one of Asger's warriors grabbed hold of the shaft and tried to pull Sven out of his shield wall. He felt his heart skip in his chest, but Sven refused to allow himself to panic. Instead, he let his instinct take over. As the warrior tugged on the spear, Sven broke the shaft with the rim of his shield, and the warrior fell backwards into the men behind him. Another warrior rushed to take his place, but before he could get his shield up, Sven stabbed him through the neck with the broken shaft. The man's eyes bulged as blood soaked his long beard and he stood there gaping in shock. Sven shoved him back with his shield, which gave him enough time to pull his sword out of its scabbard. Before Sven or Rollo could rush into the breach, a large warrior stepped forward and punched at Sven with his shield, which forced Sven a step backwards.

'Push!' the warrior roared, and Sven felt his entire shield wall being forced back. Asger's bigger force was taking its toll on Sven's men.

'Rollo! What's happening along the wall?' Sven was too short to see for himself and needed the large warrior to tell him.

Rollo was silent for a while and Sven wondered if the huge warrior had heard him. He was about to repeat the question when Rollo responded. 'It's not going well. Both flanks are being pushed back. So are we. Odin knows we need to do something, or they'll surround us.'

Sven was forced back another step by the large warrior in front of him. He wondered who the man was and why he hadn't been in the front rank to begin with. A spear jabbed over the rim of his shield and clanged against Sven's helmet. Sven's head swam, and as he shook it to clear his mind, he realised he had to do something or the battle would be lost. 'Rollo! Are you as strong as your father?'

Rollo was taken aback by the sudden question but quickly composed himself. Even as he was pushed a step back, he smiled. 'Stronger.'

Sven grunted. It was a bold claim to make. Rollo's father, Arnbjorg, had been a close friend of Sven's and had died on the beach in Francia during that failed raid. He had been a beast of a man who could defeat a bear in a wrestling match, and Sven prayed to Odin that the young warrior was right. 'Take my shield. When I give the signal, get out of the way!'

Before Rollo could respond, Sven shoved his shield at him.

Rollo had to drop his axe to take it and then braced himself as Sven took a step back.

'He's running! Their jarl is running!' the large enemy warrior shouted.

But Sven ignored him and the terrified glances of the men around him as he took his Dane axe from his back and allowed his rage to take control of him. His limbs trembled and his heart raced as the world around him slowed down. Sven felt the grin spread across his face as he gripped his Dane axe in both hands.

Rollo glanced over his shoulder. 'What's the signal?'

Sven did not respond, and neither did he notice the young warriors preparing to follow him. Instead, he roared and charged. Rollo's eyes widened, and he stepped out of the way as Sven lifted his axe with both hands and stormed at the enemy shield wall like a rampaging boar. The enemy warrior, who moments ago had been laughing at Sven running away, could do nothing as he stumbled into the path of Sven's axe. The sharp blade sliced through the warrior's neck, splitting the links of his brynja and opening his chest. Blood sprayed over Sven as he barged the dead man out of the way.

Sven swung his axe in a wide arc and severed another man's spine while screaming at the enemy, his sudden anger forcing them back before he heard Asger's voice.

'Kill the bastard! Kill the dwarf!'

Sven looked up and saw the younger jarl standing behind his men, his nose broken and beard covered in blood. He was pointing his sword at Sven, its blade still clean but not wavering. Sven took a step towards Asger when he heard a scream at his side. He turned and used the shaft of his Dane axe to deflect the spear aimed for his side. When Sven had been younger, he could use his Dane axe with one hand, which meant he could hold a shield in his other hand. But he was an old man now, and his arms did not have the same strength they had before. Sven stepped into his attacker and head-butted him with his helmeted head. There was a crunch as he caught the man on the chin and as soon as the warrior hit the ground, his jaw askew, Sven buried his axe in his chest. Sven turned to the younger jarl, his limbs trembling. 'Fight me, you coward!' He twisted out of the way of an attack from a warrior who looked like he had only just started growing a beard and struck the man in the side of the head with the flat of the axe. The young warrior dropped, his eyes rolling in his head as Sven swung his Dane axe in a wide arc and took the arm of another. The man's shriek was enough to curdle the blood of Thor before Sven rushed at Jarl Asger, who was still sending men to deal with the breach in his shield wall. Sven reached the young jarl after a few steps and chopped down with his axe, but Asger twisted out of the way. Just as Sven lifted his axe for another attack, something large barged into him and threw him to the ground. Sven grimaced as his ageing back jolted and his eyes widened when he saw a large warrior looming over him with his Dane axe in the air. But before the axe could come down and end Sven's life, another buried itself into the warrior's chest. The man's eyes bulged as he spat out blood while staring at Sven. But Sven wasn't looking at him.

'Arnbjorg?' Sven muttered as he stared at the giant warrior with light-coloured hair, who freed his axe and danced out of the way of another attack before almost splitting his attacker in two. Sven shook his head as one of his men pulled him to his feet and he realised it was not Arnbjorg he was looking at, but his son, Rollo, who was laughing as he sent Asger's men to Valhalla.

'Jarl Sven, are you all right?' the young warrior who helped Sven up shouted.

Sven shook his head again, just to make sure that it was Rollo he was staring at, before he nodded. He then gripped his axe and turned to Jarl Asger. 'Time to finish this.' He stomped towards the younger jarl as the warrior who had helped him up moved to his right and Rollo appeared to his left. Both younger warriors kept the men sent by Asger away as Sven charged at him. He had expected Asger to turn and run, but the younger jarl roared his own battle cry and ran at Sven.

Sven swung his axe, but Asger jumped out of the way before rushing in and stabbing at him. Sven turned and felt the blade graze his brynja. He chopped down with his Dane axe and Asger twisted out of the way and punched Sven in the face. He then swung his sword at Sven, but Sven used his shorter height to duck under the blade and head-butt the younger jarl in the chest. As Asger staggered back, his face grimacing, Sven swung his axe at the bastard's head. Asger tried to use his sword to block the blow, but misjudged where the axe was going and lost his hand. The younger jarl gaped at the stump where his hand had been only a few moments before as blood squirted into the air. He screamed and, around Sven, it seemed like the air was sucked out of the fight as the warriors from the north stopped fighting and stared at their jarl.

'Protect the jarl!' one of Asger's warriors shouted.

'Fall back!' Another added his voice.

Sven stepped forward and lifted his axe to kill Asger, who was on his knees and still screaming at his missing hand, when Rollo grabbed Sven and pulled him back.

'Shield wall! On me!' the young warrior shouted as the warriors of Ribe rushed towards them and formed a shield wall around Sven.

Sven struggled to free himself from Rollo's grip as he screamed, 'I need to kill him! The bastard must die!'

'No, Sven. It's over. We've won.'

The words were like a bucket of water on the fire of Sven's rage, and as the battle fog cleared from his mind, Sven saw then why Rollo had pulled him away. Sven might have been able to kill Asger, but the younger jarl's warriors would have killed him as they tried to avenge their jarl. The warriors from the north formed their own shield wall in front of their injured jarl, while men behind them pulled Asger away. Sven took a deep breath as he tried to calm his racing heart and his trembling hands.

'Hold the line!' Rollo ordered as some of the younger warriors thought of rushing at the retreating enemy.

Oleg echoed the order in the right flank, but Sten was quiet. Sven tried to spot the older warrior, but couldn't see much because of the taller warriors surrounding him. He took a step forward and was about to step out of the shield wall protecting him when Rollo grabbed him again. Sven glared at the young warrior as he shrugged his hand off his shoulder. He stood in front of his men and watched as Asger's warriors fled. Ravens circled the air above Sven, their cries mixing with the screams of the injured. Sven had to suppress the shiver that ran down his spine. When he was younger, he had relished the shield wall. That was where he had made his name, even before he became jarl of Ribe. But as he stood there, surrounded by death, he prayed to Odin that he would never have to fight in one again.

3

RIBE

Charles closed his eyes, trying to find God while the leaves rustled in the tall tree he was hiding in as he waited for his grandfather to return. He sighed and had to blink the brightness of the afternoon sun away when he opened his eyes again. God was not here. Not in this hostile land where they hated Christians and boasted of killing priests. Where gold crosses were melted in the forges and used to make jewellery, or hacked into lumps which the people used to trade with. It had been a few weeks since they had arrived, and it had not been easy for Charles, especially not after his grandfather had killed Bjarni. But as his grandfather had to deal with the objections of the townspeople, Charles finally got the chance to grieve for his father. That was when he had found this tree and he would climb it every day so that he could be closer to heaven and to his father. Charles missed his father and the way he would ruffle his hair. He had hoped that by being with his grandfather some of that pain would go away, but it didn't. His grandfather was too different. Charles's father knew how to laugh and how to make Charles laugh, but Sven was too serious. Too angry. The breeze picked up again, but this time Charles paid no attention to it as he shifted his position on the thick branch he was sitting on. The tree wasn't far from the house Thora shared with her kin and, like the tree he used to hide in back in his old home town in Francia, Hügelburg, it grew tall and strong, the opposite of himself.

Charles was nine years old and short for his age, something he got from his father and grandfather. He had a mop of red hair which had grown long in the weeks since he had arrived in Ribe. That he also got from his father and grandfather, but unlike them, he was very thin. Charles doubted he would ever be as thick-muscled as his father had been, although he hoped he never got as fat as his grandfather. His blue eyes looked over the roofs of the houses towards the great hall and he bit his lip as he wondered how long his grandfather would be away. From his place in the tree, Charles could see all of Ribe, a large trading town, which sat on the banks of a large river with the same name.

The town was half-moon shaped and had two main roads, one which led to the river from the east and another which ran alongside it. The market, where traders from all over the northern lands and Francia came to sell their wares, stretched along the road which ran alongside the river. Some traders used wooden stalls like in Hügelburg, while others just had small tents, their wares laid out on a piece of cloth which was spread out on the ground. Sven's hall sat next to the road, near the market, and was the largest building in Ribe. Like many of the houses in Ribe, it was longer than it was wide and had no windows, only a small hole in the bow-shaped roof for the smoke to escape from. Smaller longhouses, and some that were square-shaped, were dotted all inside the earth-mound walls that protected the town from enemies that might come from land, or that was what Charles had been told, with many paths leading off the main road to different parts of the town. There was a large grave site outside the walls on the east side of the town, which Charles could not see from the tree because of the wooden palisade on the earth-mound wall, and did not want to see either. The river-banks were covered with wharves where trade ships from other parts of Denmark and Francia would arrive every day. The river was also where the people of Ribe would get their water, which they would use for cooking and cleaning. Most households had a thrall which they would send, but Thora's family didn't. Thora's cousin had to make the journey every morning with two buckets, which took her a while as their house was near the wall on the eastern side of the town, and not near the river. Between the river and the town was a large area where the warriors would train every day and where Charles was forced to go as well so he could learn to fight with the other boys, and a few girls, from Ribe. Charles's grandfather had insisted that Charles went, even though he wanted to be a priest. Something he was not sure how to do here in Ribe.

Charles rubbed the bruise on his left eye as he yawned. The Danish boys were as cruel as the ones in Hügelburg, and they seemed to enjoy hurting him, although he wasn't sure if it was because he was a Christian or because of his grandfather. It did not help that they were all better than him with the wooden swords and staffs they used as spears.

Charles gripped the small wooden cross he wore around his neck as he turned his attention to the main gate and prayed that his grandfather would return. Even if their relationship had been strained, he did not want his grandfather to die. Not before he had atoned for what he had done. Charles had tried to get his grandfather to pray to God, to ask for forgiveness for his sins before he went to fight some jarl from the north, but his grandfather had refused. Sven did not believe in God, something Charles was determined to change, and did not want to confront his mistakes, especially not that one. They had spoken about what had happened to Sven's wife, Charles's grandmother, and Sven had told him everything he remembered a few days after they had first arrived. But since then, his grandfather had refused to talk about it. Charles wasn't sure how he saw his grandfather after learning that he had killed his wife, even if it had been an accident, but he recognised the pain in Sven's eyes every time he glanced at the door which led to the sleeping quarters at the back of the hall.

'Charles!' Thora's voice reached him and Charles looked down and saw her standing below him with a basket in her hands. She was wearing a blue strap dress over a smock, which was fastened by two large egg-shaped brooches. The brooches were just plain metal ones, not like the beautifully carved ones that Charles had seen the wealthier women wear. Thora also wore a necklace made of glass beads and amber, which Charles thought was pretty. Her light-coloured hair was in a thick braid, although as always there were a few loose strands of hair around her face. 'You can't stay in the tree forever.'

Charles sighed and wished he could. Up here, the other boys left him alone and he could forget where he was. But he knew she was right. And besides, the blackberries in her basket looked delicious. His stomach growled as if it agreed with Charles and he quickly climbed down the tree.

'We should call you Charles the squirrel,' Thora said. 'Or Charles Ratatoskr.'

Charles frowned at Thora as he reached the bottom of the tree. 'What's a ratatoskr?'

Thora smiled at him as she sat down and fixed her dress. She had broad shoulders, although not as broad as the men, and had wide hips. Charles guessed she had seen almost thirty years and she had an attractive face, or so Charles had heard some men say, and a scar over her left eyebrow from a past battle. Thora had been a warrior once, something Charles didn't understand, but she had given up on that life after her husband had died in her arms during a battle against the Franks. She had lived in Ribe and had known

Charles's father when they were kids. After Sven had disappeared, her father was forced to leave Ribe because he had disagreed with Sven's brother, Bjarni, and they had moved to Hedeby. That was where Charles had first met her, outside the small Christian church. Charles's grandfather would often visit her father when he travelled to Hedeby and, through God's blessing, the old man had been there when Charles had arrived. Thora had decided to go with them when they were forced to leave Hedeby. Her father had passed and she had nothing else in Hedeby worth staying for. Charles was glad she had joined them. He did not agree with her being a warrior, but she had saved his life and he found it easier to talk to Thora than to his grandfather. 'Ratatoskr is a red squirrel that spends all his time scurrying up and down the great tree to deliver messages.'

'So you think I'm a squirrel?' Charles frowned.

Thora laughed and ruffled his hair. 'Aye, you climb that tree like one and you have red hair.'

Charles couldn't help but smile as he took a blackberry from the basket and popped it into his mouth. He savoured the sweetness before he looked at the branches of the tree. 'I feel safe up there.'

Thora smiled as she glanced up at the tree. 'Your father used to hide in the rafters of the hall when he wanted to get away from the other boys.'

Charles raised his eyebrows. He would never have thought his father would hide from others. He had been a mighty warrior. 'Really?'

'Aye.' Thora nodded as she swallowed another blackberry. 'We never knew how he got up there, but whenever he went missing, I knew that's where he was.'

It surprised Charles that he and his father were so similar. But then, he knew nothing about his father's childhood. His father would never tell him about where he had grown up. Perhaps that was why. Just like Charles had been unhappy in Hügelburg, maybe his father had been unhappy here and was glad to be given to the Franks, where they taught him about God and the wonders of the Christian world. 'Maybe I can find out how my father did it. I'm good at climbing.'

Thora nodded. 'Maybe you could. Just make sure your grandfather doesn't catch you. He never liked it when your father did it.'

Charles scowled at the mention of his grandfather. 'Do you think he'll come back?' Charles had tried hard to ignore the gnawing in his chest after his grandfather had left to fight the jarl from the north the previous day.

'Don't you worry about old Sven. That man is too stubborn to be killed.' She smiled as she offered him more blackberries.

Charles took a handful and popped them into his mouth. He felt the juices running down his chin as he chewed before he swallowed and asked, 'Are you glad to be back here?'

Thora looked at the town, her forehead furrowed, and then said, 'I am. Ribe has changed much since I was last here, but it is my home. My kin are still here and they've been good to us.'

Charles looked at the house where he had been living with Thora and saw her aunt sitting on a stool outside and relaxing in the afternoon sun. The old lady kept calling him thin and was always trying to feed him, but she was nice to Charles. He felt that the rest of the family just tolerated him because of Thora. Especially Haldor, the husband of Thora's cousin. The man was large and fat and spent most of his time sitting around and drinking ale. He would occasionally go out with the fishing boats and spend whatever he earned on more ale. Thora's cousin, Audhild, was a little nicer to him, but only because Charles's grandfather gave them money so they could feed him and that had made their lives a little better. Then there was Jorlaug, the daughter of Audhild and Haldor, who was six years old, short like Charles, with wild red hair and a freckly nose. She liked to scare Charles and would often hide around the corner and jump out screaming at him. Charles didn't like her.

His grandfather had wanted him to stay in the hall, but Charles could not. Not after what had happened that night when they had first arrived in Ribe. Every time he was in the hall and saw the door which led to the sleeping quarters, all he could think of was Gerold laughing at him and him stabbing the Frankish man. So they had decided that he would stay with Thora in her family's house. Charles preferred that as he felt more comfortable around Thora than he did with his grandfather.

'But it's not my home.'

Thora looked at him, and he saw the sadness in his eyes. 'No, I guess it's not.' She chewed on another blackberry. 'It could be. The people are good once you get to know them.'

Charles touched the bruise around his left eye. 'I'm a Christian, though.'

'There are some Christians here. I'm sure they'd be happy to have you join them.'

Charles took another blackberry and stared at it. He had heard of the other Christians in Ribe, but they kept to themselves and he was too afraid to approach them.

'You skipped training today?' Thora asked, which distracted Charles from his thoughts.

Charles nodded and ate the berry.

'Your grandfather will not be pleased.'

'I don't like it. The other boys are all bigger than me and better.' He rubbed the bruise again. 'My grandfather keeps saying that I should fight back harder, but every time I do, they only laugh at me and beat me more. I'm not like my father or my grandfather.'

Thora smiled. 'You are more like them than you know.'

Charles wanted to believe Thora, but he couldn't. The only

thing he had in common with his father and his grandfather was that they were short and had the same eye and hair colour. 'I don't understand why I have to learn how to fight. I want to be a priest, not a warrior.'

'Your grandfather just wants you to be able to protect yourself.'

'God will protect me.' Charles crossed his arms.

Thora sighed. 'Not from the blades of men who want to kill you.'

'That's why He sent you to me. You can protect me from that. And my grandfather, now that he is his old self again.' When Charles had first met his grandfather, he was confronted by an old smelly drunk who was afraid of his own shadow. Thora had told Charles how his grandfather's life had fallen apart and how he had spent many years homeless and wandering around Denmark doing little jobs in different towns so he could buy ale. But as they journeyed north to Ribe, his grandfather remembered the man he used to be. The one Charles had heard about and the Christians in Francia feared. Charles himself was afraid of his grandfather, especially after how willingly he killed people. But Charles knew the only reason he was alive was because of his grandfather and Thora.

'We won't always be around to protect you. That's why you must learn to fight like a warrior, even if you don't want to be one. There are many in Francia who want you dead.'

'All because of that cross?' Charles thought of the large golden cross with the different-coloured gems around its edge and the large red ruby in the centre above the mark of the Carolinians. The cross had once belonged to Charlemagne, the great Frankish king Charles was named after, but he still didn't know how his father had got it or what it had to do with his mother. Charles felt his grandfather knew, though. He saw the way Sven would stare at the cross, his face creased as if a storm was raging in his mind. All he knew was that God had placed the cross in his hands and the kings of Francia wanted him dead because of it. That was why his father had been killed and why he had to live in the land of the Danes.

'The cross is important to the kings of Francia. They believe it will make them great emperors like Charlemagne,' Thora said. 'And as long as you have it, you are in danger.'

'But it is all I have of my mother.' Charles did not know who his mother was. He believed she was still alive, even though his father had told him she had died. He sensed that was another secret his grandfather kept from him.

'And that is why you must learn to fight,' Thora repeated. They had forgotten about the blackberries as they stared at the houses of Ribe.

'But the boys are better than me. They keep hurting me. Even the girls fight better than me.'

'They have been learning to fight longer than you have. They will be better. But you shouldn't let that deter you.'

Before Charles could respond, a boy came running towards them, waving his arms above his head. 'They're back! The warriors are back!'

Both Charles and Thora looked towards the main road and saw the warriors walking along it, some singing songs and others laughing. Charles recognised his grandfather sitting uncomfortably on the horse and the giant beside him. None of the townspeople gathering along the road to the hall were cheering, and Charles remembered another reason he didn't enjoy living in Ribe.

'They don't like him, do they?'

'No, they don't,' Thora responded. 'He killed their jarl and took his place.' Thora stood and picked up the basket before she made her way to the hall. Charles jumped to his feet to follow her.

'But Bjarni had betrayed my grandfather.'

'Aye, he did. But he also made Ribe rich and the gods know the people care more about that. Many here also remember what your grandfather was like as a jarl.'

'He wasn't a good leader?' Charles asked as they reached the hall. He smiled when he spotted his grandfather, covered in blood and dirt, and grimacing as he got off the horse. Charles resisted the urge to cross himself, but he still thanked God when he saw no fresh injuries on the old man.

'No, he wasn't. The gods blessed old Sven with the ability to fight, but not to lead.'

'Then why does my grandfather want to be jarl again?' Charles frowned as Sven scowled at the crowd that had gathered around the hall. The people did not smile or cheer like the returning warriors did, and some even glared at Charles's grandfather. Charles felt the tension in the crowd, like a storm gathering in the clouds above them, and prayed nothing bad would happen.

Thora remained silent for a while as she, too, watched old Sven limp into the hall. 'I don't think he does, Charles.'

4

Sven limped into the hall, wincing because of the old injury on his left leg. Inside, it was dark, even as the hearth fire burnt fiercely in the middle of the hall and torches were lit along every column that supported the large bowed roof. Old shields and weapons, swords, axes and spears, hung on the walls, stained dark by the smoke from the hearth fire and the torches and covered in dust. Reminders of battles long past and of the might of Ribe's men. Sven smelt the smoke in the air, mixed in with the sweatiness of old men who had spent the entire day sitting on the benches that filled the hall and drinking his ale. He eyed those old men, farmers from the nearby farms and the grey beards from Ribe, who had been nothing but a thorn in his side for the last few weeks. They were all glaring at Sven, and he felt his anger at them in the back of his throat.

'Ale!' he ordered as he walked towards the raised seat at the rear of the hall. Sven eyed the wild boar's head mounted on the wall above the seat and, as before, wondered if Bjarni had put it there to mock him. There had been two seats before, one sitting higher than the other, but after Sven had killed his brother and sent his young bitch of a wife away, he had used the smaller chair as kindling for the hearth fire. Behind the raised seat was a door which led to the sleeping quarters at the rear of the hall. That was where the jarl of Ribe would sleep, but Sven had not opened that door since that night when he killed the Frank and learnt the truth about his grandson. There were too many terrible memories in that room, one worse than the rest, and Sven could not bring himself to sleep in there. Instead, he slept in the hall, on the rush-covered floor with the young warriors who had nowhere else to sleep.

'Sven the Boar returns then,' one farmer said, before taking a sip of his ale. Sven glanced at the man, but said nothing. He was tired and his old body ached.

'Is it a victorious return?' another farmer asked. The other men grunted, but again Sven ignored them.

'Aye, we were victorious,' Oleg responded as he followed Sven into the hall with Rollo by his side. Both men were grim despite their victory over the younger jarl from the north. 'We sent them running back to the north. Your farms and your families are safe.'

'Safe?' One farmer, a heavyset man with a long scar on his forehead, put his cup down and glared at Sven. 'Our farms and families were safe before Sven returned and murdered Jarl Bjarni.' The other farmers nodded and grunted as they agreed with the man.

Sven reached the raised seat and collapsed into it, still ignoring the farmers as Alfhild handed him ale. He thought of the first time he saw her, during the feast thrown by Bjarni when Sven and Charles had first arrived, when she had stirred something in him.

'Aye, none of this would have happened if you had not returned and cursed us!' one of the old grey beards said. 'Odin is punishing us for your crimes!'

Sven emptied his cup. 'More,' he said to Alfhild, who took his cup and hurried away. She had become his personal thrall, although Sven was not sure how or why. He found her attractive, even with her boyish face and short dark hair, and if he had been a younger man without the memories that plagued him, he would have bedded her. But she was too young for him and, after Eydis, Sven had found it hard to be with other women. That did not stop the young thrall from following him like a shadow, always handing him his ale and food. Alfhild also cleaned his clothes and looked after his weapons.

It had been a few weeks since Sven had killed Bjarni and became jarl of Ribe again, although none of the townspeople called him that. But it had not been an easy few weeks. The people of Ribe had protested, and many had left after that night, including some warriors who refused to fight for the man who had killed their jarl. Rollo had convinced many to stay, claiming that Sven had only sought revenge, which was his right according to the gods. But what had really persuaded them to stay was the gold and money Sven had given them from the many chests in Bjarni's sleeping quarters. Sven had been surprised by Rollo then. After the young warrior recovered from his injuries, he had become an ally of Sven and rarely left his side. Thora had explained that he wanted to be Sven's champion, like his father had been. Sven had no energy to argue with that, so he let the young warrior do what he wanted. Oleg, his old hirdman and the man who aided him in his fight against Bjarni, had also become an ally, although Sven wasn't sure if he could trust the man. He had already betrayed Sven in the past, and he had also betrayed Bjarni by bringing Sven his old axe and ordering the warriors of Ribe to step back. But Sven kept him close because many of the older warriors were loyal to Oleg, something else Sven did not like, and he needed those men to defend his lands.

Alfhild brought Sven another cup of ale, which he emptied and handed back to her as Thora and Charles walked into the hall. Thora's leg had completely healed, and she walked without a limp. Sven glanced at his grandson and wondered if he had ever seen the boy without a bruised face.

Thora and Charles were followed by some of Ribe's warriors, who were cheerful because of the victory and because they still lived. They filled the benches not already taken by the old men and farmers and called for ale and a feast. Sven turned his attention away from them, even as the grey beards and farmers glared at them. The warriors were allowed to be happy. They had fought well and Sven knew he should reward them for winning the battle they should have lost. After the battle, they had found Sten, one of Sven's old hirdmen, on the ground, a broken spear in his chest and his empty eyes staring into the void as Rollo ordered the men to deal with the dead. The warriors of Ribe were taken to one side and Sten's corpse had been burnt along with those who had died in the battle, while Asger's men were stripped of anything valuable and left for the ravens and the wolves. They had also found Asger's hand, with two gold rings on its fingers, which they paraded around before one of the young warriors threw it on the ground and pissed on it, much to the cheers of the other young warriors. The older warriors had just turned away from the sign of disrespect.

Sven glanced at Rollo, his face cleaned but still smudged with some dirt and his blond hair hanging loose. It surprised him how much the young warrior reminded him of his father, Arnbjorg. Even the way he fought was like his father, but what had impressed Sven the most was how the young warrior took control of the situation. He showed he had what it took to be a leader, something Arnbjorg never had, and Sven guessed the boy got it from his mother, Oda.

The farmers and grey beards were all glaring at Sven, waiting for him to say something. He sighed. 'Your farms are safe, as Oleg already said. Now return to them and leave me in peace.'

'Leave you in peace!' the heavyset farmer said, his face turning red as he jabbed a finger towards Sven. He was the leader of the group, and Sven clenched his fists as he resisted the urge to gut the man. 'Our farms were only in danger because of you, you thick-headed bastard!'

'Do not talk to your jarl like that,' Rollo growled, and took a step towards the farmers. The warriors fell silent and watched as the farmer glared at Rollo.

'He is not my jarl!' the heavyset man said, showing no fear of Rollo, who towered over him. 'Bjarni was our jarl and this man,' he pointed at Sven again, 'killed him.'

'Aye,' another farmer added. 'And now our farms are being attacked by those who seek to avenge him. All my livestock stolen, my son killed trying to stop them.'

'My crops burnt!' a dark-haired man said.

'Then plant more!' Sven slammed his fist on the armrest of his chair.

'Plant more!' The man stood up and took a step towards Sven. 'The end of the summer is near. I should be harvesting those crops soon. There is no time to plant more!'

'And what of my son, my livestock?' the other farmer said again. 'Should I just get more?'

Sven jumped to his feet, his face creased as he ignored the pain in his leg. 'What do you want from me? I marched my men out and defeated the bastard who had been raiding your farms and killing your children!'

'Asger wouldn't have been doing any of that if you hadn't killed Bjarni in the first place!' the heavyset man said. 'His father had an agreement with Bjarni!'

Sven clenched his fists as his anger built up inside of him. The voices of the farmers complaining were drowned out by the blood throbbing in his ears, and it took all of Sven's will to stop himself from attacking the fat farmer. He glanced at Thora and saw her shake her head as if telling him not to react. He also saw the fear in his grandson's eyes, but try as he might, Sven could not control his anger.

'Get out!' he roared and silence filled the hall so that the only things Sven heard were his panting and the flames of the hearth fire. 'Get out of my hall!'

'Even Loki causes less problems than you.' The heavyset farmer glared at Sven before he spat at Sven's feet and walked out of the hall. The other farmers and the grey beards followed him, but the warriors stayed, some jeering at the farmers.

'Bastards,' Sven muttered as he sat down again and tried to ignore the fact that he had been compared to the god of mischief. Alfhild handed him more ale, and Sven nodded his thanks.

'You can't blame them for being angry, Sven,' Thora said as she walked towards him, with Charles behind her. Sven growled, but said nothing as Thora continued. 'And you know they are right.'

He clenched his fist as Rollo gasped and Oleg shook his head. Both men looked at Sven as if expecting another outburst from him, but Sven just sighed and drank from his cup. Thora was the only person whom he allowed to speak to him like that and only because she had seen him at his worst. Drunk and covered in his own piss and puke while wearing clothing that hadn't been cleaned for many winters. That was the person Sven had become after he had fled Ribe. A drunk who was ashamed of himself and afraid of his own shadow, but only because he feared Loki was in that shadow. Sven had hated the gods because Odin refused to let him die, no matter how much he wanted to or how badly others had beaten him. He had survived when he should have died many times over. He had been attacked by wild animals and outlaws and spent many nights sleeping on snow-covered ground. But Sven still lived because Odin wanted him alive. Or perhaps it had been Loki all along, tormenting Sven to amuse himself. Sven glanced at his grandson, seeing the uncertainty in the boy's blue eyes, and thought he understood why. The gods were bastards and mysterious, but there was a reason for everything. Sven thought of the large golden cross Torkel, his dead son, had given Charles. That was the reason for what was happening, and he still struggled to understand why the boy's mother had taken that cross. She must have known how important it was to her family. Or maybe that was the reason. Maybe she believed Charles would be safe as long as he had the cross of Charlemagne.

'They should be grateful that Jarl Sven took his army out and defended their lands.' Rollo defended Sven when he said nothing.

Thora faced the giant warrior with a raised eyebrow and hands on her hips. 'Would you be grateful to the man that caused the death of your children and livestock or for your crops to be burnt?'

Rollo opened his mouth to speak, but then closed it and looked at Oleg for support. Oleg only shrugged before he asked Sven, 'So what do we do now? You defeated Asger, but there is still another son-in-law to deal with. Gunvald has been raiding farms to the east. The farmers there are already refusing to pay the landgilde because of the raids.'

Sven looked away from his grandson and rubbed his forehead. This was not what he had hoped for when he returned to Ribe. If he had known that it had been Bjarni who had betrayed him so long ago, then he never would have returned here. But despite Thora telling him that Bjarni had been behind everything, Sven had refused to believe that his brother would go against him. That mistake had almost cost him his life and that of his grandson. 'This is all Horik's doing. The bastard does not want me to be the jarl of Ribe.' Horik, the king of Denmark, had never liked Sven. Bjarni might have been the one who had ultimately betrayed him, but he had only done so at the behest of the old bastard king. All because Sven went against his orders not to raid Francia. He had not been the only one, though. Many other jarls had wanted to take advantage of the chaos caused by the civil war between the Frankish emperor and his sons and raid one of the wealthiest nations on Midgard. Horik had wanted to avoid a war with the Franks and so he had many of the jarls who had raided Francia killed, but Sven had been too powerful. His army had matched Horik's and so the king of Denmark had to resort to trickery and betrayal. Loki must have been proud of Horik for how he had played Sven.

'No,' Thora said with a shake of her head. 'This had nothing to do with Horik.'

'Thora's right,' Oleg said, and earned a glare from Sven. 'Both Asger and Gunvald are married to the daughters of Bjarni. They would want to avenge their father-in-law and take back what they believe is theirs.'

'Odin knows you would do the same,' Thora agreed with Oleg. Sven frowned as he drank his ale, refusing to admit that they were both right.

'And Asger is a young jarl. His father passed last winter, so he's eager to make a name for himself.' Oleg scratched his bearded chin. 'What better way than to kill the man who had murdered one of the king's closest allies?' Sven scowled at Oleg. He had not murdered Bjarni. He had killed the bastard for betraying him and causing the death of Eydis and the loss of his only son.

'And he left the battlefield with only one hand!' Rollo said, loud enough for the other warriors in the hall to hear him. They all raised their cups and cheered at their victory. Sven watched them laugh and clap each other on the backs while drinking their ale. They would be drunk soon, and Sven would need to provide them with food and more ale to celebrate. He saw the young warrior who had fought by his side during the battle. The blond man, with his hair braided, was almost as tall as Rollo and just as broad at the shoulder. He had fought well, and Sven was sure he was still alive only because of Rollo and that warrior.

'You!' Sven called to the young man. The warriors went quiet as the warrior paled and pointed at himself. 'Aye, you. Come here.'

'Sven?' Thora asked as the warrior stood up and walked towards him and Sven held a hand up to silence her.

'Jarl Sven?' the warrior asked, his forehead wrinkled.

'What's your name?'

'Alvar Gunnarsson, jarl.' Alvar looked at his feet, and Sven scowled at him. The man looked to be about the same age as Rollo and had a scar on his left cheek.

'Your father was Gunnar Halfdansson?' Sven remembered Gunnar fighting for him. The man had been loyal and a great warrior, and one of the few who had made it back from that ill-fated raid in Francia.

'Aye.' Alvar nodded.

'Your father still lives?'

'No, jarl. He died about seven winters ago.'

Sven stared at the warrior as he remembered the man's father. 'He was a great man, your father. The gods know I couldn't have asked for a better man to fight by my side.'

Alvar nodded, but remained quiet.

Sven looked at Oleg. 'Give me one of your arm rings.'

Oleg looked like he was about to protest, but then took one of the silver rings from his wrist and handed it to Sven. Alvar's eyes widened, and both Rollo and Thora smiled when Sven stood up.

'You fought well today, Alvar Gunnarsson. You followed me through Asger's shield wall, and the ravens will thank you for the feast you have provided them.' Sven looked at all the warriors in the hall. 'All of you did.' The warriors cheered as Sven looked at Alvar again and handed him the arm ring. 'Your father would be proud of you.'

Alvar took the ring from Sven and slipped it over his hand and on to his wrist, his cheeks red. 'Thank you, Jarl Sven.'

'Now, go celebrate with the rest of the brave men of Ribe.'

The warriors chanted Alvar's name and slammed their cups on the table as he returned to his seat. Sven turned to Rollo. 'You as well, Rollo. You reminded me of your father the way you fought.'

'Thank you, Sven.'

Sven smiled at him. 'I'll give you an arm ring later, but for now, go celebrate. We won a great victory today. The north of my lands is secure for now. Tomorrow we will decide how we deal with Gunvald to the east.'

Both Rollo and Oleg nodded and left Sven alone with Thora and Charles. Sven sat down in his chair and took a drink of his ale as he stared at Charles again. 'You didn't train for the last few days?' Charles took his attention away from the warriors and looked at him before he shook his head. Sven thought as much. The bruise on his eye was a few days old and he could see no new marks on the boy. He rubbed his temples as he felt the headache building behind his eyes. Sven was tired of this fight. It was worse than the one he had just fought because it was a never-ending circle, much like Jörmungandr, the giant serpent who bites his own tail to encircle Midgard. 'You need to train, Charles. Every day.'

'Why?' Charles asked, and Sven knew what he was going to say next. 'I don't want to be a warrior. I want to be a priest.'

Sven ground his teeth. 'Become a warrior first and then you can do whatever you want.'

'No.' Charles crossed his arms and lifted his chin, which irritated Sven even more. 'I will not be a killer. Not like you.'

Thora shook her head at Charles's words but said nothing as Sven slammed his fist against his armrest again. 'A wolf cannot become a sheep!'

The warriors sitting near them stopped what they were doing and stared at Sven before they got back to their celebration.

'I am no wolf,' Charles said, his face turning red.

Sven sighed as he saw the tears in his grandson's eyes. Again, it reminded him of the last time he had seen Torkel. 'And you are no sheep either. Charles, I will not be around to protect you forever and neither will Thora. You need to learn how to do that yourself.'

'But I don't want to.' Charles lowered his head.

'The gods make sure we rarely get what we want. That's why we have to fight for it.' Sven sighed again. 'If you want to be a priest in Denmark, then you'll have to learn how to fight, because most men will kill you because of the cross you wear around your neck.'

Charles nodded, but said nothing. Instead, he turned and walked away. Most likely to the tree he liked to hide in, Sven thought.

'You shouldn't be so hard on the boy,' Thora said. 'It's not easy for him here.'

'The boy just needs to make some friends.' Sven rubbed his temples.

Thora sighed. 'That will not be easy for Charles. He believed Gerold was his friend. We both know how that turned out.'

Sven thought of Gerold, the thrall his grandson had met and who had helped the boy reach Hedeby. Charles had trusted the snake, and even Sven had believed his grandson had been lucky to find someone who had been prepared to protect him. But the boy had been more than a thrall. He had also been a Frankish spy and had left a trail for the Franks to follow them. Sven had spent many days watching the thralls as they scurried around Ribe, wondering if any of them were spies for Horik. Sven emptied his cup as he forced Gerold from his mind. 'I only want him to be able to protect himself. You know that.'

Thora nodded. 'Aye, but he doesn't. He still thinks you want him to be like his father.'

'He already is like his father.' Sven swallowed back the knot in his throat. 'Why doesn't he train?'

Thora glanced at Charles as he left the hall. 'The boys don't accept him. They bully him on the training ground and old Randolf lets them.' Thora bit her lip before she added, 'And he doesn't sleep, Sven. He has nightmares about that night. You shouldn't have told him that he had killed that man. He's too young to deal with that.'

Sven rubbed his face and sighed. He had hoped that it would make Charles stronger if he believed he had killed the Frank who had been sent by the boy's mother to find him and take him to her. They had not known that at the time and had believed the Frankish spy worked for the same people who had ordered the death of Torkel. Sven had made Thora swear not to reveal the truth about the Frank to Charles. 'Aye, but it's too late to tell him that now.'

'Might help if you tell him his mother's still alive,' Thora said.

Sven shook his head. 'No. The gods know that he would want to go to her then.'

'Would that be such a bad thing? He doesn't belong here.'

Sven knew Thora was right. Charles didn't belong here, just like he didn't. Not really. But he said none of that. 'My son sent Charles to me. And until I know why, Charles stays where I can see him.'

Thora nodded, although Sven was sure she disagreed with him. 'Making him train with the other boys is not going to make it any easier for him.'

Sven looked at Thora and frowned as he thought about what she had said. 'Can you train him?'

Thora barely reacted to the question, which made Sven think she was expecting it. 'Sven, my fighting days are over.'

'I'm not asking you to fight, just to make sure the boy can. He trusts you.'

Thora sighed. 'Aye, Sven. I'll train Charles.'

5

'Charles, pay attention!' Thora snapped.

Charles shook his head and stared at Thora as she stood in front of him with a wooden staff in her hands, the same as the one he was holding. They were on the training ground near the river and Thora was wearing a tunic and trousers with her braided hair tied around her head to keep it out of her face. Charles did not like that she was dressed as a man again, but he knew she couldn't teach him how to fight in a dress. It surprised Charles when she had told him she would take over his training and he was even more surprised when he learnt that his grandfather had asked her to.

It had been a few days since his grandfather had returned from the battle and Charles had done his best to avoid him because he was still angry at him. It had been easy, as Sven was rarely seen outside of the hall these days. He claimed he was busy preparing to deal with Bjarni's other son-in-law, but Charles knew he was avoiding the people of Ribe. The only time his grandfather was outside was when he was training with Rollo, the giant warrior who had tried to help Charles against Gerold and the rest of the Franks. Charles had tried not to think of the young slave who had pretended to be his friend and had betrayed his trust. But Gerold wasn't a slave, not really. He was a spy and he and his master, an old spy who had pretended to be a trader and was now dead, were meant to take Charles somewhere, although Charles wasn't sure where and neither had Gerold been. Charles still struggled to understand any of that, but he often wondered where Gerold was. Was he back in Francia or had the sea claimed their ship that night? He remembered how the lightning had flashed, making his grandfather look like a demon, and how the rain had poured from the sky. Charles also remembered stabbing the Frankish man who had tried to kidnap him. He shuddered when he remembered how the knife had slid into the man's stomach and had become slick with his blood.

'Charles?' Thora asked, stepping closer to him and putting her hand on his shoulder. 'What's the matter?'

Charles's vision came back into focus and he realised he had dropped his wooden staff. His hands were trembling as he fought back the tears. 'Nothing. I...' Charles struggled to find the words.

'You're thinking of that night again?' Thora frowned at him. Charles nodded, not knowing what to say. 'You did what you had to to survive, Charles.'

Charles swallowed back the tears. 'But I didn't want to kill him. I...' He stopped again and stared at his hands, unable to say what scared him the most. That he was afraid of going to hell. The priests in Hügelburg had always said that you had to ask God for forgiveness for your sins, otherwise you could not enter heaven. Charles had tried to. He had tried really hard, but every time he closed his eyes, all he saw was the man's pale face and bulging eyes.

'I know you didn't want to kill him, Charles. You did what you had to.'

Charles looked at the staff on the ground. 'But now I am learning how to kill.'

Thora shook her head. 'No, you are learning to defend yourself.'

Charles looked at her as he bit his lip. 'But it's the same thing. My grandfather said so himself. To defend myself, I must kill them before they can kill me.'

Thora picked up the staff from the ground and handed it back to Charles. 'Your grandfather can talk a lot of nonsense, but he was right about one thing. Only the gods know our path ahead of us. The best we can do is to make sure we are prepared for whatever they throw at us. That is why you must learn to fight.'

Charles took the staff. He still didn't like that they kept talking of false gods, but he knew what Thora had said was true. Bishop Bernard had said the same to Charles once. *God chooses our path. He is our shepherd, and it is our duty to follow and not to question.* Charles wondered why God had chosen for the bishop to betray him and his father.

'Ready?' Thora asked him. Charles nodded as he forced the dead Frank from his mind. He would be prepared for the path God chose for him. 'Good. Now stand like I told you to.'

Charles gripped the staff in both hands and stood with his feet wide apart, his left foot forward, and the staff pointed in front of him. He felt silly standing like this and it didn't help that the staff was quite heavy. Thora walked around him, and with her staff, corrected his stance and his grip. She stepped back and smiled.

'Good. Now, thrust!'

Charles thrust the staff forward like Thora had shown him and pulled it back.

'Good. Again!'

The sun climbed and birds flew around the few clouds in the sky as Thora had Charles repeat the action. Charles's shoulders ached and his back was hurting as sweat poured down his face, but again Thora told him to thrust and again he obeyed. This time, the staff wavered and Thora knocked it to the side with hers. The move caught Charles by surprise, and he dropped the staff with a yelp.

Laughter erupted from near them, and both Charles and Thora turned to find a group of boys sitting near them and laughing.

'He can't even hold a spear!' one boy said, which only made the others laugh more.

'My little brother can do better and he is only three winters old!' the boy Charles recognised as Rollo's son hollered.

'Sigmund! Enough,' came a booming voice. All the boys jumped to their feet when they saw Rollo, still wearing his brynja as he had spent the morning training with the warriors, approaching them. 'What are you boys doing here?'

'We were bored, so we thought we'd watch the Christian try to fight with a spear.' The way Sigmund said *spear* made Charles feel even worse. It was as if they thought it was not a proper weapon.

'Do not mock the spear, boys,' Thora said. 'It's one of the most valuable weapons on the battlefield.'

'But it's a spear,' one boy said with a grimace.

'Thora is right,' Rollo said.

'I'll never fight with a spear,' Sigmund said. 'I'm going to have a giant Dane axe like you, Father, and slay all my enemies before they can get near me!' The other boys cheered as Thora shook her head. Charles felt his cheeks burn and wanted to slip away, but he couldn't. That would only make the boys tease him even more and the last thing he wanted was to have the boys of Ribe bully him like the ones in Hügelburg had done.

'First, you master the spear, and then you can think of the Dane axe.' Rollo smiled at his son. 'Now, go away and leave Charles and Thora to train.'

'But why is she training him?' Sigmund asked. The blond-haired boy was a year younger than Charles, but he was already taller.

'What's wrong with me training Charles?' Thora raised an eyebrow.

'You are a woman. Everyone knows men are better fighters,' Sigmund said, which caused his father to shake his head.

Before Thora could respond, a shrill voice screamed from behind them, 'Aunt Thora is the best warrior in Ribe and one day she'll be one of the Valkyries!' Charles did not know who the Valkyries were but decided now was not the time to ask. The boys would only laugh at him again. The ear-splitting voice came from Jorlaug, the daughter of Thora's cousin, who was waving her fist in the air.

'No, she's not. Everyone knows Father is the best warrior. That's why he's the new jarl's champion. And you can't join the Valkyries, can you?' Sigmund frowned at his father. Rollo shrugged with a smile, but said nothing.

'Aunt Thora can beat your father with both hands tied behind her back. She killed ten men with her eyes closed,' Jorlaug said as she stood next to Thora, her arms crossed and glaring at the boys. Charles wasn't sure what he made of her. She was always following him around and asking him about God and Christianity when she was free from her chores. Charles would have liked that if it wasn't for the fact that she then dismissed everything he told her.

'My father killed twenty men with his hands and feet tied up!' Sigmund retorted, and earned a slap on the back of the head from his father.

'Enough. Thora is a warrior of great renown. She fought many battles for Jarl Torgeir of Hedeby.'

'But you can still beat her, can't you, Father?' Sigmund asked, which caused Rollo to knit his brows. Even Charles understood that was a question the giant warrior could not answer without causing problems for himself.

Thora saw this as well. 'Well, Rollo. Can you defeat me?'

Rollo stared at her, his mouth open, and then he smiled. 'You heard the boy. I killed twenty men with my hands and feet tied up.'

Thora threw her staff at Rollo and took Charles's. 'Come on then, champion. Let's see what you can do.' Rollo caught the staff and rolled his shoulders to loosen them up.

'Go on, father!' Sigmund shouted, and his friends joined in with cheers of their own. The commotion was drawing the attention of nearby townspeople, and many stopped what they were doing to watch as Thora and Rollo prepared to fight each other.

'Are you sure this is a good idea?' Charles asked. He had seen Thora fight and knew she was a good warrior, even if she was a woman, but he had also seen Rollo fight. He remembered how fast the giant man moved when he had faced the Franks that night.

'You don't think Aunt Thora is going to lose, do you?' Jorlaug scowled at Charles, who could only shrug.

'Don't worry about me, Charles. Just pay attention.'

Both Thora and Rollo assumed their fighting position, their feet apart and staffs gripped firmly in both hands and pointed at each other.

'First one to hit the ground?' Rollo asked. More of the townspeople were walking towards them, joining those who had already formed a circle around them. The boys were cheering loudly for Rollo, while Jorlaug was doing her best to match their noise. Charles frowned as he took in Rollo's relaxed stance, as if he thought this would be easy for him.

Thora smiled. 'No, a fight to the death.'

Rollo widened his eyes, and before he could respond, Thora lunged at him. She jabbed at his chest and Rollo just had enough time to twist out of the way. The sudden attack caused the boys to howl at how Thora cheated, while some of the townspeople gasped. Rollo jabbed with his staff, but let the staff slide through his hands as if he was throwing it, before he gripped the end with his left hand. Charles struggled to understand what he was doing as Thora ducked under Rollo's attack. She then had to jump back as Rollo swung the staff around and swiped it at her feet. The boys cheered and Jorlaug booed as Rollo and Thora took a step back from their initial bout.

'Not bad,' Rollo said, smiling at Thora. 'Almost had me there.'

'Aye, you won't be that lucky next time,' Thora said and attacked again. This time she aimed her thrust higher, towards Rollo's face. Rollo deflected the blow with his staff and Thora stepped forward while bringing the back end of her staff around to strike at Rollo's exposed midriff. Charles marvelled at the move as Rollo barely reacted to the blow, although the boys cried out, which only made Jorlaug laugh. Rollo rushed forward and shoulder-barged Thora, his giant frame easily throwing her to the ground, but she quickly rolled to her feet in time to avoid Rollo's jab with his staff. The townspeople gasped at the speed Rollo moved, but Thora was still faster as she swung her staff at Rollo's head. To Charles, it looked like the fight would be over, as he saw no way for Rollo to bring his staff up in time to block the blow. But Rollo surprised him when he let go of his staff and ducked under Thora's attack, only to grab her in a bear hug from behind. Jorlaug screamed, and the boys cheered, but Thora only smiled as she kicked Rollo's shin with the heel of her boot. Rollo hollered and let go of her and as soon as Thora's feet hit the ground, she turned and swung the staff at Rollo's head again. This time, the giant warrior caught the staff with his left hand and used his right elbow to break it in half. Again, the boys cheered and chanted his name, and Jorlaug cried in dismay. Thora did not stop though, as she turned in the opposite way and jabbed the broken staff at Rollo's waist. Rollo jumped out of the way, weapon-less and his face turning red as he struggled to avoid Thora's onslaught. Thora jabbed and slashed as she used the broken staff like a sword, a weapon Charles saw she was more comfortable with, while Rollo twisted out of the way and used his thick forearms to block blows aimed at his head. Everyone watching the fight had gone quiet, even the boys and Jorlaug as they watched the two warriors battling each other. Rollo twisted out of the way of one attack and, with no weapon at hand, threw a punch at Thora. She brought her broken staff around and used it to deflect Rollo's enormous fist, but then Rollo stepped forward and tripped Thora. As soon as she hit the ground, he was on top of her, one hand on her throat and the other raised as if he was going to punch her. The crowd gasped at Rollo's red face and clenched jaw and even Charles thought he was going to punch her, but then he smiled.

'I win.'

Thora said nothing for a while as she breathed heavily under him, but then she, too, smiled. 'Aye, you win.'

'I told you.' Sigmund pointed a victorious finger at the red-faced Jorlaug as the boys cheered Rollo's victory. The townspeople applauded Thora and Rollo, many looking entertained as the giant warrior got to his feet and helped Thora up. Charles shook his head. He still struggled to understand the Danish people's lust for violence, but then he remembered how the people of Hügelburg had cheered Drogo and his friends when they were beating him up in the market square. It had been five boys against him, all of them bigger and stronger, and Charles had hoped the people of Hügelburg would help him. But they had only cheered as Pepin, a boy who had once been his friend, punched him in the face. Charles watched as the people of Ribe returned to their homes and chores, many talking about the fight they had just witnessed, and again marvelled at how similar the Christians of Francia were to the heathens of Denmark. Perhaps if the people of Denmark would give up their false idols and followed the path of Christ, then the two nations would have no need not to trust each other. Charles wondered if God wanted him to convert the Danes. Perhaps that was why he had to come here. But Charles did not know how he was supposed to do that. Or why his father had to die for God's plan.

Sigmund rushed up to Charles. 'See, Christian. She was no match for my father. Men are better warriors!'

Rollo smacked his son on the back of the head. 'Enough, Sigmund! Thora is a great warrior. Odin knows it's a pity you don't want to take up your sword again.' This was said to Thora, who shrugged.

'My time in the shield wall ended with my husband's life. I see no sense in taking the life of another.'

The boys and Jorlaug frowned at this, but Charles understood. Thora was an angel sent by God and angels were supposed to not want to kill others. The lives she had taken before were to protect him, and Charles knew God would forgive her for that.

'It's a pity, like I said.' Rollo turned to his son and his friends. 'Never underestimate your opponent, boys. Doesn't matter if it is a man or a woman or,' he glanced at Charles, 'how short they are. The giants are much bigger than Thor, but he still defeats them every time.'

'But that's because he is Thor!' Sigmund said.

'And he has Mjöllnir,' another boy added.

Thora had told Charles about the Norse god of thunder and his mighty hammer, but Charles still couldn't make any sense of it. Especially the hammer. The handle was too short and the story of how that happened only made his head spin. What bothered him even more, though, was that the Mjöllnir pendants the Danes wore almost looked like the cross he wore, just upside down. But before Charles could lose himself in that thought, Jorlaug shouted.

'Look, a ship!' She pointed towards the wharves along the river. The new ship did not look like the many trading ships that arrived every day, but more like the warships the Danes were so fond of. It was long and sleek, its sides so low that Charles wondered how the men on board did not fall over the sides. Rows of shields hung over the sides of the ship as oars moved as one to bring it closer to the wharf.

Rollo scowled as he stared at it. 'I don't recognise it.' That was another thing that had surprised Charles about the Danes. Their love for their ships and sailing. In the few weeks since he had arrived, the men would often take the ships out and would be gone for days. But every time they returned, those who stayed behind could recognise the ships even when they were still a distance from the shore. It was the same with the trading ships that came to Ribe regularly. Charles had asked Thora about it one night, and it was her aunt who had responded, telling Charles that ships were very important to the Danes. It was their gateway to the world and no other nation possessed the skill of the Danes when it came to building them. Not even the ugly bastards from Norway. Thora had told Charles not to ask about that, so he didn't. 'I better go see who that is,' Rollo said before he turned to Thora. 'Thank you for the fight, Thora.' She smiled at him, but said nothing as the giant warrior turned and made his way to the hall, his son and the other boys following in his wake.

Charles turned to Thora. 'You let him win.'

'What?' Jorlaug asked as Thora raised an eyebrow at Charles.

'What makes you think that?'

Charles thought back to the day in the forest when Thora fought the warriors from Hedeby. 'You moved slower and had about three chances to defeat him, which you didn't take. And even on the ground, you could have used your broken staff to defeat him. A knock to his head would have done it.'

'Aunt Thora, is that true?' Jorlaug asked, her green eyes wide.

Thora laughed, which confirmed what he had said was correct.

'You know, for someone who doesn't want to be a warrior, you sure see a lot.'

Charles had surprised himself. 'I've seen you fight before and, besides, my father was a warrior and I spent a lot of time watching the warriors of Hügelburg train.'

'Because you wanted to learn how to fight?' Jorlaug asked.

Because I was hiding from those who wanted to hurt me, Charles thought, but didn't say. He looked at Thora and saw the knowing smile on her face. Perhaps he was more like his father than he knew.

6

Sven raised an eyebrow when he heard the commotion outside the hall and Alvar came rushing into the hall, wearing his brynja and carrying his weapon belt in his hands. He glanced at Oleg, the old warrior sitting on a bench near him, but Oleg only shrugged. Sven was sitting in his chair at the back of the hall, trying to solve some of the many problems plaguing him. The raids were depleting the treasure chests left behind by Bjarni as Sven was forced to compensate the farmers for the crops and livestock they had lost. There was nothing he could do to replace their children who had been killed or taken, though. Their daughters would most likely become the wives of the warriors who had taken them while young men were either killed or sold as thralls. Not for the first time since he had killed Bjarni, Sven wondered if he really wanted to be the jarl of Ribe again.

The few other people in the hall, young warriors with nothing to do and grey beards avoiding their wives and the summer's sun, also looked perplexed as Alvar reached Sven where he was sitting in his chair while tightening his belts around his waist.

'We have visitors,' Alvar said to him. Sven glanced at Oleg and

wondered if these visitors were sent by Horik, the king of the
Danes. Like most in the hall, Oleg was staring at the entrance of the
hall where men were arguing.

'Make sure they leave their weapons at the door.' If they were
men sent by Horik, then Sven did not want them armed.

'Rollo's taking care of that.' Alvar smiled and Sven understood
what the commotion was about. Warriors did not like giving up
their weapons, but it was the custom in their land to leave your
weapons outside the hall when you were a guest.

Since they had returned from the battle against Asger, both
Rollo and Alvar had decided to be Sven's personal guards. Not that
he minded, though. Their presence on either side of his chair with
their constant scowls dampened the fire of the farmers when they
came to complain about the raids on their farms.

Sven glanced at Rollo's sweaty face as he led a group of men into
the hall and saw him puff out his reddened cheeks. He was about to
ask him about it when the gasp from Oleg made Sven turn to the
group behind the large warrior, and his breath caught in his throat
as the narrow-shouldered man he had not seen for more than
twenty winters strode towards him. Sven scowled as he took in the
grey hair with streaks of brown and the matching beard, the dark
eyes glancing uninterestingly around the hall. Just behind the thin
man was another who had a similar face, but his hair was still dark
and his face unlined.

'Guttrom,' Sven said as both Rollo and Alvar tensed beside him.

'Sven the Boar, as Odin is my witness.' Guttrom stopped a few
paces away and put his hands on his hips as he smiled broadly at
Sven. He wore a fine brynja which glimmered in the hearth's fire-
light and on both his thin arms he had three golden arm rings.

'Thought you were dead,' Sven said as he glanced at the group
of warriors who followed Guttrom into his hall. Most of them
looked old and a few of them he thought he recognised from battles

long in the past, but there were a few younger warriors as well. All of them were confident as they stood behind Guttrom and they were all dressed in their war gear.

'I could say the same about you.' Guttrom's voice was deeper than you would expect for a man as narrow as him. Sven decided the group behind his visitor wasn't here to attack, but merely to impress. He saw it was working from the wide-eyed stares his own young warriors were giving them. Sven glanced at Oleg and saw him frown.

Sven rubbed his scalp and felt the stubble. He wished he had known the bastard was going to show up, then he could have bathed and shaved his head, but then he guessed that was Guttrom's intention all along. To catch him off guard. Sven could only hope the rest of his men were as quick to prepare as Rollo and Alvar. 'What brings you to my hall?'

Guttrom pretended to look shocked. 'Is that how you greet an old friend?'

'Who is this man?' Rollo asked.

Guttrom looked at the young warrior and smiled. 'You don't know who I am?' He looked back at Sven again. 'By Odin, what do you teach your youth?'

Sven scowled as Oleg responded, 'This, Rollo, is Guttrom. The nephew of King Horik.'

'The nephew of King Horik.' Rollo whistled. 'How come we've never heard of him?'

Guttrom just stood there, looking bored as they spoke about him. But Sven was sure the bastard was enjoying the attention. He always had been a whore for it. 'Because he was exiled before you were born.' Sven scowled at Guttrom again, and at the man standing behind him who could have been his son. 'The bigger question is why you are here, Guttrom? If old Horik finds out you are in my hall, then he'll likely send his army here for both of us.'

Guttrom walked to the bench where Oleg was sitting. He picked up the jug of ale and filled one of the empty cups before he took a drink. 'Since when are you concerned about what my sour uncle wants?'

'I'm not.' Sven signalled for the thralls to give the rest of Guttrom's men drinks. There were about ten of them, but Sven was sure there would be more men outside. He glanced at Rollo and hoped he had told some of the warriors to keep an eye on them. Guttrom's warriors found some empty benches and sat down as the thralls brought them jugs of ale and cups. Sven saw one of them eye up Alfhild and clenched his fist at the glint in the man's eyes. Sven turned his attention back to Guttrom. 'But I want to fight the bastard when I'm ready. Not before.'

Guttrom smiled at Oleg, which made the old warrior look uncomfortable, and Sven wondered about that. 'Aye, I'm sure old King Horik was as surprised as I was to hear of the return of Sven the Boar. I'm surprised the old bastard didn't drop dead from the shock. Mind you, that would have made things easier for me.'

Sven raised an eyebrow. 'Make what easier?' Again, he sensed the two young warriors tense behind him. But Guttrom's men had stopped paying any attention to them as they talked amongst themselves and drank Sven's ale. He hoped the thralls had given them the nasty stuff and not the good ale he liked to keep for himself.

Guttrom took his time to respond as he took a sip from his cup and eyed the different weapons and shields which hung on the walls of the hall. His eyes lingered on the old boar head above Sven and he smiled. Sven was growing impatient but stayed quiet as he tapped his fingers on the armrest of his chair. Behind Guttrom, his men burst out laughing, and many of Sven's warriors in the hall frowned at them. Eventually, Guttrom answered, 'To take what should be mine.'

Sven sighed. 'And what, in Odin's name, is that, Guttrom?'

The smile on Guttrom's face disappeared for the first time since he had walked into the hall. 'The throne of Denmark.' Even the flames in the hearth fire fluttered as Guttrom said this. Oleg's eyes widened as both Rollo and Alvar gasped behind Sven. But he was not surprised. Ever since the nephew of the king had been exiled, he had been claiming that the throne belonged to him.

Sven signalled for Alfhild to bring him ale. He would need it for what was going to come next, and he also wanted to keep the young thrall away from the leering warriors. The men in Ribe believed she was Sven's favourite and so they left her alone. Perhaps that was why she clung to him. She rushed to do his bidding, a look of relief on her face to be called away from the young warriors trying to get her attention. 'Why now?' Sven asked, although he knew the answer to that already.

A large grin parted Guttrom's moustache from his beard. He took another sip of his ale and pointed a thin finger, with a large golden ring on it, at Sven. 'Because of you, my old friend.'

Sven was sure he could hear the gods laughing in the silence that filled the hall. One of the hounds that liked to sleep in the hall let out a small whine, and Sven glanced at the beast as it stood up, stretched and walked out of the hall. He resisted the urge to rub the large ivory Mjöllnir he wore around his neck. 'What does this have to do with me?'

'Everything.' Guttrom looked around the walls of the hall again. 'You came back from the dead, Sven. Killed one of his favourite jarls and took Ribe from under his nose. It makes Horik look weak.'

'Horik is weak,' Sven growled.

'Exactly.' Guttrom's eyes lit up. 'And that's why we must move now. There are many more who are tired of Horik's grovelling to the Franks. For his refusal to allow them to raid the bastards when they were weak.'

'Horik allowed men to raid. He even sent Ragnar with a large force. Made quite a name for himself, Ragnar did,' Oleg said. Sven had heard this as well while he had roamed Denmark as a drunk, but he could never believe it was true.

Guttrom waved a dismissive hand at Oleg. 'That was only because many of the jarls complained and he was forced to keep his crown on his empty head. And besides, he called Ragnar back as soon as the Frankish kings barked at him.' Guttrom looked at Sven. 'Your brother joined Ragnar, as well as old Oleg here. Made themselves very rich.'

Sven glanced at Oleg. That explained the many treasure chests filled with Frankish coins and jewellery in Bjarni's room. Sven still couldn't think of it as his room, and doubted he ever could. Every time he looked at the door, he had a flashback to that night and all he wanted to do was to burn the hall to the ground and build a new one. But he knew he couldn't. This hall was older than he was and to burn it down would anger the gods and his ancestors. And they had enough reason to be angry with him. 'To move against Horik now will not work. Especially with Ragnar by his side.' Sven had heard of Ragnar. The man was a great warrior and leader. Even when they were young men, Ragnar was a name on the lips of many.

'Ah, you don't know.' There was a glint in Guttrom's eyes again. 'Ragnar is dead, my old Sven. Died a few winters ago. Some say he was thrown into a pit filled with snakes in Britain, but most know that's not true. Horik had him killed. He became too popular amongst the jarls and that had made him a threat to the old bastard.'

Sven raised an eyebrow and glanced at Oleg, who nodded to show that it was true. He rubbed his beard and wondered if that really changed anything, but then decided it most likely did not. Horik was a shrewd bastard, just like Loki, and knew how to win battles. There was a reason that he was the last one standing of all the men who had claimed the throne of Denmark. Sven looked at the smiling Guttrom. He knew what the bastard wanted from him and he would have jumped at the chance to take on the army of Horik when he was a younger man. But he was an old man now. Sven trained daily with Rollo to regain his former strength, but still could not wield his Dane axe one-handed like he used to. All those training sessions did was prove to Sven that he was not the man he used to be. But perhaps that was a good thing. The gods knew that the man he had been when he first became the jarl of Ribe was a terrible father and husband, and now the gods had given him a second chance with his grandson. They might have a difficult relationship, but he had sworn an oath that he would protect Charles and storming off to fight a battle against the king of Denmark was not the way to do that. But would Charles really be safe while Horik was on the throne? The words came to him, and Sven shivered as he wondered where they came from. 'Makes no difference,' Sven said at last.

Guttrom put his cup down. 'Easy for you to say. You were lucky. Horik did not banish you or send you to Hel without your head.'

Sven gripped the armrests of his chair as he felt his face flush. Images of his son on the beach, surrounded by Frankish warriors, and Eydis, dying with his knife in her stomach, came to him. With a clenched jaw, he growled, 'Lucky?' Rollo and Alvar took a step forward and even Guttrom's warriors stopped their laughter as they turned their attention to Sven. 'Lucky?' Sven growled again as he struggled to stop himself from attacking a guest in his hall.

'Aye. I was banished from Denmark while you got to keep your lands and Ribe.'

Before Sven could stop himself, he launched himself from his chair and reached Guttrom before the man could react. Sven grabbed the bastard by his brynja and screamed into his face. 'I lost everything because of that worm-riddled bastard! Everything! My son, my wife, my life!' Rollo and Alvar reacted quickly as they rushed to his side, their weapons ready before Guttrom's men could do anything. The rest of Ribe's warriors in the hall also jumped to their feet as the flames from the hearth fire and the torches seemed to stutter in the sudden rise in tension in the hall. Even the remaining two hounds got to their feet and growled.

Guttrom ignored the spit that landed on his face from Sven and held a hand up to stop his men from doing anything. 'Then join me, brother. Together we can kill the dog that took everything from us to please the Frankish scum.'

Sven still gripped Guttrom by his brynja as he glared at the old warrior. Images of his son and wife flashed through his mind again, this time accompanied by Bjarni laughing at him when Sven had finally understood his treachery.

'Sven?' Oleg tried to calm him, but Sven paid no attention as he continued to glare at Guttrom. 'Sven,' Oleg tried again.

Sven took a deep breath and let go of Guttrom, who straightened himself on the bench he was still sitting on and adjusted his brynja. 'Your brynja is too big for you,' Sven said as he returned to his seat. Alfhild was there, holding a cup of ale in her hands and her face pale after witnessing his sudden outburst. Sven took the ale from her and sat on his chair, trying to calm himself as he drank. Rollo and Alvar eyed Guttrom's men for a few heartbeats before they returned to Sven's side. The young warriors of Ribe also sat down, but they were warier of Guttrom's men now. One of the two hounds yawned as both of them lay down again and closed their eyes.

'Aye,' Guttrom said. 'Old age takes much from us.'

Sven nodded. Guttrom had never had broad shoulders, but he still had a warrior's build with strong arms and fast reactions. His head used to be covered in long brown hair and he had a thick brown beard covered in gold and silver rings. Now, like Sven, the muscle was gone, making the brynja too big, and the colour had gone from his hair and beard, and so were the rings. But Guttrom had been a good friend to Sven when they were younger. Sven sighed. 'Thor knows that even if I wanted to, I can't. I'm jarl only in name. The people of Ribe still fight me and Bjarni had many friends. Barely a day goes by without one of those bastard jarls raiding my lands.'

Guttrom nodded. 'Aye, we heard of your victory against Asger and of the troubles you have in the east of your lands. Bjarni's sons-in-law want Ribe for themselves.' Sven wondered how Guttrom knew all this and glanced at Oleg, who avoided his gaze. 'That is why I come to you now, old friend. I will aid you in your battle against Bjarni's other son-in-law, Gunvald, and his father, Jarl Ebbe. In return, you fight with me against my uncle.' Guttrom emptied his cup. 'And when I am the king of Denmark, I will declare you jarl of Ribe again.'

Sven stared at the man he had not seen for many winters, seeing how wrinkles dominated his face. Guttrom was older than Sven, although not by many winters. The smile on the man's face showed he thought the offer was very generous, but Sven wasn't so sure. He wondered if the gods of Asgard felt the same uncertainty he was feeling now when Loki made promises to them. Even if Guttrom won the battle and declared Sven jarl, the people of Ribe still wouldn't accept him, especially if more of their husbands and sons had to die for him to achieve that. And then there was another thought that plagued his mind. Sven looked at his cup and was surprised that he did not feel like drinking the golden liquid inside. *Do I really want to be jarl?* He glanced at Rollo, standing just behind, and remembered how the young warrior commanded the men during the battle against Asger. Even the older warriors obeyed him when he had called for the shield wall. Rollo was a natural leader, whereas Sven had always ruled with the threat of violence. Sven sighed and put his cup down on the armrest of his chair. He stood up and said, 'Alvar will show you where you and your men can sleep. Tonight we will have a feast to welcome you to Ribe and perhaps then I will have an answer for you. But this is something I need to think about.' Guttrom nodded, but said nothing as Sven walked out of the hall, Rollo close behind him.

7

COURT OF KING CHARLES II, PARIS, WEST FRANCIA

Roul tried to ignore the empty feeling in the pit of his stomach as he walked towards the great hall, his footsteps echoing off the stone walls. His mouth was so dry that he wondered if he'd be able to get two words out in order to deliver his news. Perhaps that was a good thing because he was sure he'd be in the dungeons before the sun went down. He resisted the urge to turn around and walk the opposite way, knowing it would not save him. His arrival would already have been reported and the man he had come to see did not like to be disappointed or made a fool of. *Maybe I should have waited before coming back*, he thought to himself. *Make sure it was done, so that I had good news.* Roul shook his head at his own folly. No, he had to come to Paris. He had to deliver the news. Besides, he had done all he could. The rest was now in the hands of God. Roul crossed himself as he stopped in front of the large wooden doors which led to the hall of Charles II, the king of West Francia.

The two guards standing on either side of the door eyed the thin man standing in front of them, his dark cloak still covered in dirt. His features were unassuming, which was why the king of West Francia liked to use him for missions where one had to be unnoticeable. That most who laid eyes on Roul ended up dead also helped. Roul had been in King Charles's service for most of his life, but not as a simple warrior you sent into battle. He was a spy and an assassin and worked in the shadows, not in the daylight. In his many years as one of King Charles's spies, he had killed those who threatened his king and blackmailed those who could be useful.

Roul had been a homeless child, living on the streets of Paris, until he was caught stealing a purse from a man who had been the king's spymaster. The man had seen something he liked in Roul and had taken him under his wing. Roul's mentor was dead now, killed by the current spymaster to take his place, but the lessons he had taught Roul had kept him alive and, more importantly, made him very valuable to the king of West Francia.

'Weapons,' one guard said, and Roul sighed as he handed the knife from his belt to the man. 'I wasn't born yesterday,' the guard said as he pointed to Roul's leather boots. Roul noticed how the other guard tightened his grip on his spear. With a sigh, he pulled the smaller knife from the inside of his boot and handed it to the guard. The man eyed Roul for a few more heartbeats before he nodded to his companion.

As the door opened, Roul straightened his cloak and wished he had discarded it before he came into the palace of King Charles. But then the rest of his clothes were not in much better condition either. He adjusted his cloak to hide the dried bloodstain on his tunic and then, with a deep breath to calm his fluttering heart, he walked through the doors. The great hall was the largest room in the castle, but Roul had been there too many times to be impressed by the great stone columns which supported the high roof. Or the many braziers which lined the walls to bring as much light to the room as possible. Not that they were needed. There were many large windows, most of them decorated with stained glass showing images of Jesus and the Blessed Virgin Mary, which allowed ample light into the hall. The walls were painted with bright colours and depicted different scenes, like the king hunting deer and the king prostrating himself in front of Jesus. At the far end of the room, raised up on a dais, was the golden throne where King Charles would sit and be seen by everybody in the room. There were no other chairs apart from the throne and the chair beside it where the queen would sit. Everyone, including the old bishop, was forced to stand when they were in attendance of the king. Household warriors lined the walls of the hall and glared at you as you made your way to the dais, a ploy designed by Roul's former mentor to make a person feel more uncomfortable as they approached the king of West Francia. Roul tried not to pay attention to these warriors he despised so much. They thought little of him, often calling him a snake or a rat. A vile creature who did the work of the devil, even though he attended church more often than any of them. These warriors were nothing more than dogs used by the king when he needed to be seen doing something. Whereas men like Roul were the poison King Charles would use when he needed to remain invisible.

King Charles was in his early thirties and if it wasn't for the rich clothes he wore or the crown on his head, he could have been mistaken for a trader in the market. He was not a man known for his strength with a sword or shield, but he had a shrewd mind and a mean temper. His brown hair was neatly trimmed and his beard was kept short. He wore gold rings with large gems on his fingers and a golden cross around his neck.

The king looked up from his conversation with the bishop when he heard the door open and frowned as Roul entered the room. Roul kept his head high and did his best to ignore the eyes on him. The throne room was not busy. It never was this time of the day. Apart from King Charles and the bishop, there were other men Roul knew to be part of the king's inner circle, including Bero,

Roul's superior and the king's spymaster. Like Roul, Bero looked like your average man, apart from his sharp eyes and permanent scowl. Bero hated Roul as much as he hated Roul's former master and would happily kill him as well. The warriors were stationed in such a way that they were close enough to protect the king, but far enough not to hear the hushed conversations the king would have with these men as he discussed his kingdom's affairs.

'Roul?' King Charles raised an eyebrow. 'You've returned at last. We expected you back days ago.' The men around the king nodded as Roul bowed low.

'Forgive me, my lord king.' Roul straightened and risked a glance at his superior, but Bero seemed too interested in the hem of his tunic to notice it. Not a good sign. Roul was sure King Charles already knew much of what he had come to say, which was another reason Roul had rushed back to deliver his news.

'The boy? Is he with you? I don't see him. Perhaps you are keeping him safe somewhere?' King Charles stroked his short-trimmed beard, his eyebrow still raised.

Roul took a deep breath and wished he had something to wet his dry mouth. He had never been this nervous before when facing his king, but then Roul had never failed before. Although, what had happened in Hügelburg, the wretched town in East Francia, had not been his fault. Not that the king would see it that way. Roul just hoped he had done enough to keep his head on his neck. 'There was a problem, my king.'

King Charles leaned forward and locked his fingers together under his chin as his brown eyes scrutinised Roul. 'A problem?'

Roul took another deep breath and told King Charles how, after he had delivered his message to their man in Hügelburg to seize the boy and to find the cross, he had returned to Hamburg to wait for his men. But instead of arriving with the boy and the cross, they had come with bad news. The boy was gone and Lothar, the warrior who had been very important in their efforts to destabilise the border of East Francia, was dead.

'How did this happen?' King Charles asked, his face creased.

Roul's fingers fidgeted behind his back so the king, and Roul's superior, could not see it. 'No one knows for sure. All my men could find out was that there was a fight between the boy's father and some warriors of the town. The house the boy shared with his father also burnt down, which led to a lot of confusion and this may have helped the boy escape.'

The king's face turned red. 'I thought the man you had there, what was his name?'

'Lothar, my lord king,' Roul's superior answered while smiling at Roul. 'He is, or was, the chatelain of the town.'

King Charles shook his head. 'I thought he was a reliable man. We paid him enough to be reliable, did we not?'

'He was very reliable, my lord king,' Roul said, desperate for the king not to think otherwise. It was he who had recruited Lothar, and Lothar's failure reflected on him. 'He made sure that his men could never prevent incursions into East Francia from the heathen tribes to the east. That kept King Louis focused on the east instead of what we were doing in the west.'

'He still failed, though, didn't he?' King Charles leaned forward on his throne.

'If I may, my lord king,' Ignomer, one of the king's old generals, said. 'A cornered animal is very dangerous, especially if it is protecting its child.'

The king glanced at the old warrior and then nodded as if he accepted what the man had said, before he turned his attention back to Roul. 'There is nothing to tie this Lothar back to us?'

'No, my king. My men were quick to spread rumours that the boy's father had plotted to kill the duke of Saxony, who was in the town at the time, and that Lothar had foiled that plot.'

'And what of the payments?' Bero asked.

'I paid him with East Frankish coin,' Roul said. Bero glared at Roul, but Roul ignored him as the king spoke again.

'The cross?'

'Regretfully, no sign of it. One of my men searched the house after the fire had been put out. He found a hidden compartment in the floor, but it was empty.'

King Charles drummed his fingers on the armrest of his seat as he thought about what Roul had said. 'Do we know where the boy is? Or if he even has the cross with him?'

Roul took a deep breath as he tried to find the best way to explain the next part to the king. 'I'm afraid not, my king. There were sightings of the boy the next day and then there is...' He paused as he tried to find the right words.

King Charles was not known for his patience, though. 'There is what?'

'A trader was found dead about a day's ride north of the town, along with some bandits.'

'This is significant?'

Roul resisted the urge to shrug. 'It's hard to say. Most of the bandits had their throats cut and one died from a chest wound. It looked like there had been some fight, but I mention this because my men had found some tracks leading further north from where the trader and the bandits were found. One set belonged to a small child.'

'They could belong to any child,' Bero said, his arms crossed.

'Yes,' Roul agreed. 'But my men found a man in Hügelburg who saw the trader's slave hide a small boy in the trader's cart.'

King Charles stroked his beard as he thought about this and then said, 'So, assuming this is the boy we are after, where did he go? And where is this slave?'

'I believe both the boy and the slave went to Denmark, my lord king.'

'Denmark?' The king of East Francia raised an eyebrow. Why would they go to Denmark?'

Roul nodded, still furious with the woman who had told them about the boy in the first place. The woman had been the handmaid of King Louis's daughter and had been present at the child's secret birth. She had also been the one who had helped the young princess steal an important cross from her father, one that he had kept hidden from his brothers. King Louis had the handmaid and her husband banished from East Francia, most likely because he did not want anyone who knew about the child near his kingdom. Although Roul believed King Louis would have been better off executing the woman. The husband had some kin in Paris, so they had come here, hoping to start a new life. Things had been going well for them until the previous year when the husband died and the woman was left to fend for herself. That was when she had approached King Charles with her secret. She must have believed that the king would pay her for the information. Instead, she had been thrown into a prison cell where the guards got to have their way with her. They were under strict orders to keep her alive, though. Roul was glad that he had given that order because the woman had left out some important information about the father of the child, who she had claimed she did not know. 'The boy's father was a Dane and not just any Dane, but one my lord king might be familiar with.' The king frowned at Roul, so he explained. 'He was the son of Sven the Boar, my lord king.'

King Charles sat straight on his throne as he scowled at some distant memory. 'You mean that boy my brother took hostage many years ago?'

'It's possible, my lord king.'

'By God!' The king smacked his leg as the thought seemed to

amuse him. The old bishop frowned at the king but knew better than to say anything. 'But Sven the Boar is dead. It's been years since anyone has heard anything of him.'

Before Roul could respond, Bero jumped in. 'He was believed to be dead, but we have recently had some interesting news from Denmark.' Bero smiled at Roul as if he had the upper hand on him, but Roul wasn't concerned. He knew what Bero was about to tell the king.

'And?'

Bero cleared his throat by coughing into his hand. 'Sven the Boar returned to Ribe, a trading town in East Denmark, a few weeks ago, accompanied by a woman, a young man and a small boy.'

The mention of the small boy got everyone's attention. 'And why am I only being told of this now?' King Charles asked.

Bero lifted his hands. 'If I had known that Roul had failed in his task, I would have mentioned this earlier, but I had faith that Roul had the boy in his custody, my king.'

'How do we know this boy is the one we are after?' Ignomer asked. 'He could be the son of the woman.'

Bero nodded as if the old warrior's point could be true, but then smiled. 'Because Sven told his brother, Jarl Bjarni, that the boy was his grandson. And there is more, my king.'

'More?' King Charles raised an eyebrow.

The spymaster nodded again. 'Sven and his brother had a falling out, something to do with a group of Franks that had arrived the day before. My informant is not sure what happened exactly, only that a fight broke out and that Sven killed his brother.'

'And these other Franks?'

'Some of them died, but a few made it to their ship and they fled.'

King Charles rubbed his bearded chin. 'Do we know who these Franks are?'

'Most likely men sent by your brother, King Louis of East Francia, my lord king.'

'Louis knows about this as well then?'

Bero could only shrug. 'We are not sure. My informant in King Louis's court has heard nothing, but it's possible he is keeping this to himself and a few trusted people. It might also be that he knows nothing about this and that someone else is after the child.'

'My niece?'

'Could be, my lord king. We know she has powerful allies, including the duke of Saxony.'

King Charles stroked his beard again as he thought about this. 'How do we know this information is accurate?'

'The trader who told me has been a trusted informant for many years.' Bero smiled at Roul, who could only glare back.

King Charles turned his attention to Roul. 'So, you not only failed what was a simple task, but the boy is now in Denmark and out of our reach? Worse than that, we may assume that Sven the Boar has the blessed cross that once belonged to my grandfather. The cross that helped my grandfather build his empire. The same empire I want to rebuild and cannot without that cross!'

'God have mercy on us!' the old bishop said, but everyone ignored him.

Roul still didn't understand how the cross was going to do that. He had tried to find out about it, but none of his sources anywhere in the three kingdoms could tell him anything.

'Why would the man send his son to his father and not to his mother? She is an important woman, isn't she?' Ignomer asked before Roul could say anything. 'Isn't that why we want the boy? To blackmail Abbess Hildegard?'

King Charles scowled at the man who had been at his side the longest of the group surrounding him. 'That is a good question, but one that is not important right now.' The king glared at Roul.

Roul took a deep breath and ignored the smile on Bero's face. The man knew that Roul was after his position and if he had brought the boy back, he would have been one step closer. But all was not lost. Roul still had one move to make, and he prayed this one would not go wrong. Otherwise, he might join the old maid in the prison cell. 'My lord king, after I had learnt that the boy might be in Denmark, I immediately went to Hedeby, where I also heard the news Bero has spoken of. I also believe that the boy Sven had with him was the one we are after and so I came up with a plan.' Roul explained his plan to the king, as he tried to pretend the sweat rolling down his face was because of the heat. King Charles listened and, as Roul spoke, a smile appeared on his face. Bero, though, could only glare at him.

King Charles leaned back in his seat and locked his fingers together under his chin when Roul had finished. 'Yes, I like that plan. That could work very well for us. See that it is done.'

Roul bowed, pleased with the king's reaction and more so by the deep red colour on the spymaster's face. 'If my king will forgive me for my insolence, but I did not want to waste any time, so I have already set the plan in motion.'

King Charles raised an eyebrow. 'You have? And when can we expect our man to be there?'

'Any day now, my lord king, if he is not there already.'

'Good.' The king glanced at Bero beside him. 'If your plan works, Roul, then I might have a new spymaster.'

Roul bowed again, more to hide the smile on his face than anything else. All he had to do now was make sure he didn't fail again, then he could finally avenge his mentor.

8

Sven stormed out of his hall, his fists clenched by his side as he tried to calm the rage that was threatening to erupt. 'Thor's hairy fucking balls! Who does that bastard think he is? Showing up here! Now of all times!'

The people in the market rushed to get out of his way as Rollo scrambled to keep up. He apologised to the people on Sven's behalf, which only made Sven glare at him.

'Don't do that!'

Rollo flinched away from Sven's red face. 'Forgive me, Sven. But I don't want the people to think that you are angry at them.'

Sven glared at the people in the market as they all turned away, eager to get back to what they had been doing before. 'I don't care what these people think! I want to know what that bastard is really doing here!' Sven jabbed his finger towards the hall. But that was not the only thing he wanted to know. He also wanted to know what Oleg's relationship was with Guttrom because he was sure that Oleg was the one who had given Guttrom all the news about what had happened here. He was about to turn and storm off again when he heard Thora's voice behind him.

'Sven?'

Sven sighed. Thora was the last person he wanted to see now because he knew she would only make him angrier. Sometimes he wished she feared him like most people, but then he remembered he needed her honesty and sharp tongue. 'What?' He turned and was surprised to see Charles half hiding behind Thora. What surprised him even more was how Thora was dressed. 'You've been training?' he asked before she could say anything.

Thora looked at Charles and smiled. 'Aye, we've been practising how to fight with a spear. Haven't we, Charles?'

Charles nodded, still not wanting to speak to Sven. Sven wanted to shake his head, but didn't. He knew it was his fault for the strained relationship between him and his grandson. He had tried to understand the boy, who looked more like Torkel every day, but Charles's Christianity was a difficult thing for him to accept, and the boy refused to recognise Sven's need for him to learn how to fight.

'Charles did well?' Sven asked, smiling at his grandson and feeling his anger swept away by the gentle breeze.

'He did.' Thora ruffled Charles's hair, but the boy refused to look at Sven. Instead, his focus was on Guttrom's ship on the wharf. Thora followed his gaze and frowned. 'Who is our visitor?'

Sven ran his hand down his face and pulled on his bushy beard. 'Guttrom.'

Thora looked at Rollo, who shrugged, and then asked, 'Who's Guttrom?'

'The fucking nephew of Horik.' Sven clenched his fist again as he thought of the slim bastard sitting in his hall and drinking his ale, no doubt listening to all the news Oleg had to share with him.

Thora looked towards the hall. 'The king sent him?'

'No.' Sven shook his head. 'He was exiled by Horik a long time ago. Before Bjarni...' Sven didn't finish the sentence, but then he didn't have to, as Thora nodded. Charles looked at him and frowned, no doubt also thinking about what Bjarni had done.

'I still don't understand why he angers you so much.' Rollo scratched his head.

Sven sighed. 'It's not Guttrom who angers me. Odin knows we were good friends once.'

'Then what is it?' Thora asked.

Sven glanced at the hall and then at the market they were standing in the centre of. It was not as busy as it had been when Sven first arrived a few weeks back. Many of the Frankish traders had left, fearing retribution from Sven. The people of Ribe and surrounding areas stayed away from the market, many of them not pleased with Sven as jarl or too afraid to travel here with the constant raids. Sven had to resist the urge to increase the taxes the traders had to pay to trade here. It would only scare the rest away, he had been told. He looked at Thora again and saw she was waiting for his response. 'It's why he is here.'

'And why is he here?' Charles asked, surprising everyone. The boy had a curious mind, something Sven recognised from Torkel.

Rollo explained what Guttrom had offered as Sven watched the people of Ribe trying to listen to their conversation. He wondered which one of them would run to Jelling to tell Horik what they had heard. When Rollo finished, Thora turned to Sven.

'What are you going to do?'

Sven shrugged. 'For now, nothing. We give the bastard a feast, make him feel comfortable and then I'll decide.'

'Should he really be king?' Charles asked, scratching his red hair.

Sven looked at him and shrugged again. Smarter men than him were needed to answer that question. 'His father was king once, with Horik, a long time ago when my father was still jarl and I wasn't much older than you.'

'Then what happened?' Charles tilted his head as he looked at Sven.

Sven responded, not because he wanted to tell the story, but because he was glad that his grandson was talking to him. 'Before Horik was king, there were two brothers who claimed the throne of Denmark. Harald Klak and Reginfred.' Sven scowled as he dragged the names from the depths of his memory. 'They weren't popular kings because many believed that the Franks were using them to gain control of Denmark.' Sven thought about the cross and the man it had belonged to. 'When the two brothers had to travel to the north to deal with a revolt, Horik and his brothers declared themselves the new kings of Denmark. There was a battle, my father fought for Horik then, and Horik and his brothers won. Reginfred was killed and Harald fled to the Franks.'

'And what does this have to do with Guttrom?' Thora asked.

Sven glanced at her and then continued. 'Because Loki was having too much fun for it to end there. Harald had somehow convinced the Frankish emperor, Louis,' he almost growled the name, 'to help him get his crown back. Louis agreed and invaded Denmark.'

'Your father fought with Horik again?' Rollo asked.

Sven nodded and continued his story. 'Horik and his brothers beat the Franks back. Horik had hoped that this would encourage the Franks to take them seriously and negotiate a peace agreement. But Louis was stubborn and had rejected any peace talks unless Harald Klak was given his crown back. A few of Horik's brothers refused, but Horik has always been a coward. The brothers fought each other, and Horik won. He exiled two of them and agreed for Harald to be joint king alongside him.'

'And how does Guttrom come into this?' Thora asked.

Sven rubbed his neck as he remembered the days of his youth.

'He was exiled with his father, but was later allowed to return if he swore an oath to Horik.'

'And what happened to Harald?' Charles asked.

'Aye, I've not heard of him,' Rollo added.

'He and Horik had a falling out and Harald was sent back to the Franks with his tail between his legs. Last I heard of him, he was leading a large fleet and raiding Friesland, even attacked Dorestad. Although there were rumours that one of Emperor Louis's sons was paying him to do it.'

'Why?' Charles asked, scratching his head. 'Why would they pay a Dane to attack their own empire?'

Sven looked at his grandson. 'Most likely to give their father something else to think about so he wouldn't have time to punish them for rebelling against him.'

Charles frowned and Sven knew what he was going to say next. He almost shook his head at the boy's naivety, but then remembered he was still only a child. 'But they are Christians and Christians would not use heathens to attack other Christians.'

'They are men, Charles. And it doesn't matter which god you believe in. At the end of the day, we are all the same.'

'Your grandfather is right, Charles,' Thora said before the redheaded boy could argue. 'Just think of what has happened to you recently.'

The short boy's brow furrowed, and he nodded as Rollo asked, 'But if Guttrom was allowed to come back, then why was he exiled again?'

'Because like me and other jarls, he refused to listen to Horik when the bastard told us to stop raiding Francia. We all saw how Harald was getting rich from the raids and wanted some of that wealth ourselves. But Horik wanted peace, so he forbade us from raiding them.'

'By Odin, I imagine that did not go down well with some.' Rollo whistled.

'No, it didn't.' Sven scowled as he remembered those days. He saw no point in wondering if he had made the right choices then. What was done was done, and all he could do was focus on what was in front of him. But that still didn't stop the question from coming to him. *What if I had listened to the bastard?* Sven shook his head to chase the question away. 'We often joined Guttrom but sometimes went by ourselves. Horik had to show that he had nothing to do with the raids, so those he could, he punished. Guttrom was stripped of his lands and exiled for the second time, and me, well, we all know what happened.' Sven looked at his grandson, seeing Torkel in the boy's round face and blue eyes.

'Where has he been all this time then?' Thora asked.

Sven shrugged. 'I don't really know. I heard he went to Norway, but I haven't heard his name mentioned for many winters.'

'And Harald? How come we haven't heard of him?' Rollo asked. 'It seems like we should have done.'

'Harald Klak?' an old voice asked from behind them. They all turned and saw a bent-over grey beard standing there, leaning on his walking stick. The man must have been listening to their conversation because he answered Rollo's question. 'Harald was made lord of some land in Francia and got greedy. He invited men from Vestfold to his new lands and used them to raid the kingdoms of the other brothers. But then the bastard lost control of his men and the Christians suffered for it.' The old man smiled a big toothless smile. 'Died a few winters ago, I think.' He cackled and walked off, muttering something to himself.

Rollo and Thora looked at Sven, who shrugged. 'Could be true. I lost track of everything after I left here. I didn't care about any of it any more.'

'I still don't understand why Guttrom has returned to Denmark now and is claiming the throne,' Thora said.

Sven sighed. 'Because me killing Bjarni and taking Ribe back makes Horik look weak. And Guttrom wants to use that against him. He has always been angry with Horik for what he did to his father and I think he has always planned on taking the crown from the old bastard. That was why he came back in the first place. He was hoping to gain the trust of most of the jarls and then make a move against Horik.'

'But he didn't get enough support?' Rollo asked.

'No, he did. The gods know there were many of us who were unhappy with Horik's grovelling to Louis and his sons, but Horik is a clever bastard and he had Ragnar by his side. Many of us hated Horik, but we respected Ragnar.'

'But Ragnar is dead now,' Rollo said.

'Aye. Ragnar is dead, and I have returned. So Guttrom thinks now is the perfect time to attack Horik.'

'He believes the other jarls will join his cause,' Rollo said, looking back at the hall.

'Will they?' Thora asked.

Sven could only shrug. 'Only Odin knows that, but Guttrom seems confident.'

'Many of the jarls are unhappy with Horik.' Rollo rubbed his neck.

Before Sven could say anything, Charles turned and pointed at a man walking on the main road towards the market.

'Look!'

Sven looked at the man wearing a brown robe and a large wooden cross around his neck and growled. Two unexpected arrivals in one day was never a good thing and Sven wondered which one would cause him more problems. *Loki must be enjoying this*, he thought as he glared at the priest. The top of the man's head was shaved, leaving only a ring of hair around his scalp, and he carried a large sack in his hands. This was the last thing he needed.

'A Christian priest?' Rollo asked with a raised eyebrow. 'Is the man that eager to join his god?'

Charles glared at Rollo, but the giant warrior did not notice as the priest made his way towards them. Many of the people in the market also stopped what they were doing as they stared and whispered to each other. Sven was grinding his teeth, preparing himself to chase the Christian priest away, while just in front of him, his grandson watched the man with wide eyes.

'What do you want?' Sven asked, not caring if the man spoke the Danish tongue or not when the priest stopped in front of them. The man looked like he had not even seen twenty-five winters as he returned Sven's stare with bright eyes and his head raised. His scalp had been shaved recently, Sven could tell by the small bleeding cuts he saw, and it looked like the young priest was trying to grow a beard, but was failing at that. *Bloody Christians, can't even grow proper beards*, Sven thought as he waited for a response from the priest.

'God bless you, old man. My name is Father Leofdag and I am seeking the new jarl of this town,' the priest said, his voice soft. His dark eyes scanned the group and fell on Charles, who was still staring at the priest with wide eyes. The priest frowned when he spotted the small wooden cross that Charles wore.

Sven bristled at being called old, even as Rollo tried to hide the smile on his face. 'I am the new jarl of this town,' Sven said, and was about to say more when someone shouted.

'No, you're not!' This caused a small cheer from the crowd, but it quickly died out when Sven glared around the market, trying to find the bastard who had shouted that. Accepting he wouldn't, Sven glared at the priest instead.

'What do you want?' he asked again.

The priest bowed slightly and said, 'Forgive me, jarl. I meant no offence.'

Sven tried to find some mockery in the young man's tone, but the priest sounded sincere.

'Father Ansgar has sent me from Hedeby. He heard there was a new jarl in Ribe and bid me to come and spread the word of God the Almighty. He also wanted me to ensure that you honour the deal he had made with your king.'

'Horik is not my king,' Sven growled. 'What deal?'

Father Leofdag seemed taken aback by Sven's hostility, but he managed to continue. 'The king has given Father Ansgar some land across the river where we could build a church.'

'A church?' Charles's eyes lit up as another growl escaped from Sven's throat.

'There will be no Christian church in my town.'

'Who is this Ansgar?' Rollo asked before the priest could respond to Sven.

'I've heard of him!' Charles piped up, his voice almost shrill with excitement.

'You have?' Father Leofdag looked at Charles, surprised by what he had said.

Charles nodded. 'Bishop Bernard told me about him. Said that he had been sent to Denmark to help the Danes become Christians.'

Again, the young priest raised his eyebrows. 'You know Bishop Bernard? He is a good man, may God bless him,' the priest said, but then frowned when he saw Charles lower his head and grip the small cross around his neck. 'Forgive me. Did I say something wrong?'

'You said everything wrong,' Sven growled, determined not to like the man just because he was a priest. Of all the Christians, he hated the priests the most. They all believed they spoke for their god and that made them more arrogant than the other Christians, but they all died the same in the end. Squealing for their god to save them. 'Who is this Ansgar?'

'He is a Christian priest in Hedeby,' Thora said, eyeing up the priest as if she was trying to recognise him. 'I'm sure you would have seen him in front of their church in Hedeby, Sven. A short, thin man with a birdlike face. Likes the sound of his own voice. Also, a close friend of Horik, if the stories are true.'

The young priest smiled. 'Yes. Father Ansgar and King Horik share a close friendship. The king has been kind enough to allow us to build the church in Hedeby, from where we can spread the word of God.' More of the townspeople had come to the market to stare at the priest. Sven saw a few of them pointing at the man while whispering to each other as young children hid behind their mother's skirt. He saw a small red-headed girl with freckles on her nose staring at the priest, in much the same way as Charles was, and remembered that she was from Thora's family. 'I don't remember the man,' Sven said at last.

'Well, you were barely sober enough to notice anything,' Thora said.

'I remember the church,' Charles said, but he did not sound as enthusiastic about it as Sven imagined he would be. The priest smiled, but then his smile faltered when he saw the glare on Sven's face.

'Why would I want a friend of that bastard Horik to build a Christian church in my town?'

The priest frowned and responded, 'Do you not want to save your people from the sin of following false idols?'

Sven shot forward and grabbed the priest by his habit, and pulled the man down so their eyes were level. Leofdag paled as Sven spoke. 'Call my gods false idols one more time, boy, and I'll cut your tongue out before I sacrifice you to the All-Father.' Some of the townspeople cheered, as well as some warriors who had come to see what all the commotion was about.

'Sven,' Thora said, and when he looked at her, he saw her pointing at Charles, who was biting his lower lip.

Sven knew what Thora wanted from him and he growled, which only frightened the priest even more. He did not want to, but he knew his grandson was struggling to adapt to life in Ribe and perhaps the priest could help him. Sven let go of the priest and prayed to Odin that this would at least improve his relationship with Charles. 'Fine, you can stay. But if you cause any problems, I'll feed you to the dogs.'

9

Charles sat up and wiped the sleep from his eyes. As he sat there, rubbing his sore arms, he looked around the house he had been living in since they had arrived in Ribe and saw that everyone was still asleep. It was like a smaller version of the hall, and smaller than most of the houses in Ribe. It had a hearth fire, which had gone out during the night, but it was still summer, so apart from providing them with light inside the dark house and cooking their meals, it wasn't really needed. There were no windows, only a hole in the roof to let the smoke from the hearth fire out, which meant it was always smoky and stuffy inside the house. Apart from the hearth fire, there were two small beds on the far side of the house. One for Thora's cousin, Audhild, and her husband, Haldor, the other for their daughter, Jorlaug, and Thora's aunt, Ingvild. There was a table with benches to one side, where the family would eat their meals or where Haldor would spend most of his days drinking ale. A loom sat in one corner of the house where Audhild would spend her days making cloth, which she would then sell at the market because Haldor did little work other than the occasional fishing trip. A large barrel was near the door, which had to be filled daily with trips to the river. This was the water the family used for cooking, cleaning and drinking. Also, to make the ale that Haldor liked to drink so much. The family had some old furs which they slept under and two chests where they kept their clothes and other possessions. At first, Charles had felt uncomfortable living in the small house with strangers. They all slept, ate and lived in the one room, and Charles was glad that at least the privy was outside. Something which had surprised him as he had expected the Danes just to use a corner of the house for that. In Francia, the Danes were thought of as dirty barbarians who lived in their own shit. But Charles had learnt that was not true. They bathed almost daily, apart from Haldor, and even the warriors spent a lot of time on their appearance. Some even whitened their hair, although Charles did not know how they did that. Their appearance was very important to the Danes, and Charles found they were cleaner than most of the people he had known in Hügelburg.

For the first few nights, Charles had slept with Thora under the furs his grandfather had given her, but as he started feeling more comfortable with her family, he started sleeping by the hearth fire. Jorlaug would sometimes sleep near him, and Charles struggled to understand the red-headed girl. She constantly made fun of him, but not in the mean way that the other children would. She also seemed curious about what he was doing. Most of Thora's family had accepted him, apart from Haldor. He would complain about having extra mouths to feed, although Charles knew his grandfather was paying them for allowing him to stay there. Something Ingvild would always bring up. Charles sensed the old lady did not like her son-in-law.

Charles got up quietly so he wouldn't wake everyone else. He stretched and wiped his long hair from his face and was about to sneak out when he heard Jorlaug behind him.

'Where are you going?'

Charles turned and saw her sitting on the bed she shared with her grandmother, her eyes still filled with sleep and her hair all over the place. 'Nowhere,' he whispered, not wanting to wake her parents. Haldor would only complain.

'You're going to see that priest, aren't you?' Jorlaug said.

Charles was about to deny it but knew there was no point. Jorlaug wouldn't believe him. It was the day after Father Leofdag had arrived and Charles was eager to talk to him. Thora wouldn't allow him to do it yesterday, saying the priest needed time to settle into the empty house his grandfather had provided him. Some of the townspeople had complained about that, but those who had lived in it had left, like many others, and the house just sat empty. Better that than let the bastard build one of their churches, his grandfather had said. Although Charles would have preferred a church, like the one they had in Hügelburg, with large windows and beautiful paintings on the walls. He missed that church. It was the only place he had ever really felt like he belonged, and even the memory of hearing Bishop Bernard and Duke Liudolf's conversation about planning the death of his father could not diminish his love for it. 'Why do you care?' Charles asked.

'Can I come with you?' Jorlaug jumped out of the bed.

'No, you cannot,' her father snarled from under his furs.

Jorlaug pouted as she looked behind her. 'But, Father. Please.'

'No! Odin knows no daughter of mine will go near that man. He'll bewitch you with his Christian magic.'

Charles frowned. There was no such thing as Christian magic, but then he remembered the people in Hügelburg being afraid of the heathen magic they had said his father possessed.

'But why can Charles go?'

'Because the boy is not my child. He can do what he wants. It's bad enough having one Christian under my roof already.'

Charles clenched his fist, surprising himself with the sudden rush of anger he felt, but before he could say anything, Thora sat up and rubbed her face. 'Well, I can always tell Sven you don't want his grandson to stay here.'

'Go tell the old bastard that. I don't care. I'm not afraid of him. Ouch!' Haldor shouted as his wife slapped him.

'What? And then the boy goes somewhere else and we lose the money Sven is giving us for letting him stay? You fool!'

Charles shook his head and turned to leave. He was about to collect his shoes when Thora said, 'Just don't be late for training.' Charles scowled. His arms were aching from his training session with Thora the day before and he was not looking forward to repeating that again, but he knew he could not avoid it. Thora knew of all his hiding places in Ribe.

'And be back for breakfast!' Thora's aunt shouted after him, which made him shake his head again as he left the house.

It was still early morning and the sun was barely above the horizon, so the town was still quiet. It was Charles's favourite time of the day. There were no people to stare at him as he walked around and no boys to make fun of him. At least they didn't beat him like Drogo and his friends had done, not outside the training sessions, anyway. The market was empty; the traders were not around yet to set up their stalls and most of the people he saw were women emptying buckets or collecting water from the river. Charles smiled as he breathed in the fresh morning air, feeling optimistic for the first time in a long time. He was sure it was because of the priest. Father Leofdag's arrival was a message from God not to give up on his faith, not that there was a chance of that happening. Charles might have been struggling to pray, but he still believed.

The door was open when he reached Father Leofdag's house and as he approached it, his heart started racing in his chest. Charles wasn't sure why, but something about it made him feel uncomfortable. 'Father Leofdag?'

There was no response at first, and Charles wondered if he should run back to the house and fetch Thora. But then he heard a groaning noise inside and rushed in.

'Father!' he gasped when he saw Father Leofdag lying on the ground, his face bloody and his robe ripped. The priest's few possessions were scattered across the house, and the tables and benches were upturned. Charles was about to fetch Thora when the priest sat up and rubbed his head.

'Who's there?' he asked with a groan. It was dark inside and Charles guessed the priest could not see him.

'It's me,' he responded, and then realised Father Leofdag did not know who he was. 'Charles.'

'Charles?' the priest responded. 'You must be the grandson of the jarl.' Charles's eyes widened, trying to understand how the priest knew that. None of them had said anything to the man about that the day before. He thought of Gerold and how the slave had pretended to be his friend and wanted to run out of the house when the priest said, 'I saw the resemblance yesterday, and the jarl looked too old to be your father.'

Charles guessed that made sense. A few people had told him he looked like his grandfather since they had arrived. 'Because we're both short?' he said, more to calm himself. He started looking at the priest's possessions on the floor and then saw the Bible lying near him.

'That, and that you have the same eyes.' Charles heard the smile on the priest's voice as he stared at the Bible. He had not seen one since he had left Hügelburg and missed the comforting words written inside. Father Leofdag groaned as he got to his feet and moved towards Charles. 'It's a Bible. The word of God that guides us through this life and ensures we make it to heaven.' He bent to pick it up.

'I know. I just haven't seen one for a while.' He saw the priest raise an eyebrow when he noticed the cross around Charles's neck.

'You are a Christian?'

Charles nodded. 'I am. I've even read some of the Bible.' He puffed out his chest.

The priest frowned. 'Charles? Not a very Danish name.'

'No.' Charles shook his head. 'I was born in Francia. My father named me after Charlemagne, but everyone calls me Charles.'

'In Francia?' The priest stroked his face and winced. Charles looked around for a bucket so he could fetch some water for the priest to clean himself up with.

'Yes, but my father was a Dane,' Charles said before he left the house to fill the bucket with water. Outside, the people of Ribe were starting their day, but Charles noticed how they kept glancing at the house. A few even rubbed the Mjöllnir pendants they wore around their necks. Charles wondered who had attacked the priest and if he should go to his grandfather about it, but then decided against that. His grandfather despised Christians and, right now, the old man had other things to concern himself with. He remembered the feast Sven had thrown the previous night for the king of Denmark's nephew. Charles didn't understand why the man wanted to fight his own uncle and why he wanted Sven to help. What surprised him most, though, was his grandfather's reaction to the man. Sven had told them he and Guttrom used to be good friends, but at the feast, his grandfather barely said a word as the few people of Ribe who attended the feast drank and ate. The warriors had enjoyed themselves and, by the end of the night, Charles's ears hurt from all of their laughing and terrible singing. Rollo, especially, had a horrible singing voice. Charles was glad when Thora decided they had stayed long enough. He asked her if she thought his grandfather would fight with Guttrom, but all she said was that that was for the gods to decide. Charles did not like that response. Not only because their gods were not real but also because he knew adults only said that when they themselves did not know the answers. But then, Christians would often say the same thing. *That is for God to decide.*

Charles made it to the river and saw Sigmund and his friends standing there, doing nothing but scratching their heads and yawning. He had to fight the apprehension he felt as they reminded him of another group of boys who had tormented him for many years. Charles wondered what had become of those boys, especially Drogo, now that his father was dead. He did not know if Drogo had any other family and wondered what would happen to him and his mother without Lothar there to provide for them. Had they left Hügelburg to stay with family they had elsewhere? Did they even have family who could help them? He wondered if the duke would look after them, but then was distracted from his thoughts by Sigmund shouting at him.

'Christian! You better be at training today. We need to practise killing Christians.' The boys around Sigmund laughed as Charles shook his head. He was glad he did not have to train with them any more. His arms might have been sore from training with Thora, but at least he had no new bruises.

'Sigmund! You be nice to that boy or I'll thrash the skin of your backside,' Oda, Sigmund's grandmother, threatened as she stood near the river. Charles knew she was one of the few who was glad to see his grandfather back, but he rarely saw her. He also remembered that night, when he had run from the room at the back of the hall. She and Thora were outside, and he remembered how she had tried to smack one of the Franks as they rushed after him.

Sigmund's cheeks turned red at being berated by his grandmother in front of his friends, and Charles had to hide his smile. He did not want to give the boys here a reason to bully him. So he kept his head down and filled the bucket before he made his way back to the priest's house.

Back at Leofdag's house, he saw the priest had cleaned the mess left by those who had attacked him and was just sitting by the table with the Bible in front of him. He looked up when Charles walked into the house and smiled at him.

'Thank you.' Father Leofdag took the bucket from Charles and dipped a cloth in the water before he wiped the blood from his face. 'I guess I should thank God they didn't kill me.'

Charles looked at the priest. 'They don't like Christians here. That's why I have to hide my cross.'

'You should not have to hide your faith, my son. You should bring light to these people, not hide yours.'

Charles frowned. 'I tried. Especially with my grandfather, but he refuses and only gets mad at me.'

Father Leofdag nodded. 'God challenges us in many ways. Perhaps one of your challenges is saving your grandfather's soul.'

Charles's eyes widened. That was how he felt. He wondered if Father Leofdag had been sent here to help him. Charles couldn't help but smile at the thought, but then frowned when he saw the priest staring at him. 'What?'

'I'm just wondering how the grandson of a heathen jarl can be a Christian and be born in Francia?'

'My father...' Charles started, and then stopped himself. His grandfather had told him not to tell anybody about his father or the cross. 'I'm not allowed to say,' he said, not wanting to lie to a priest.

Father Leofdag nodded. 'I understand.' They sat in silence for a while as Charles stared at the Bible. Father Leofdag must have noticed because he picked up and handed it to Charles. 'You can look at it.'

Charles smiled as he took the Bible, taking comfort from its weight. It was not as big as the Bibles in the church in Hügelburg or as richly decorated. There were no gold-plated covers with colourful gems or depictions of Jesus on the cross. Charles was glad for that, otherwise whoever had attacked the priest would have taken it. He opened the Bible, his eyes wide as he stared at the words inside. Charles could read, the priests in Hügelburg had taught him and they had used a Bible similar to this one to do so. He flicked through the pages, reading the names of the Gospels, as he remembered sitting in the small room at the back of the church with Father Gebhard. Father Gebhard had been a patient teacher, and Charles missed the lessons he had with the old priest.

'You are also from Francia?' he asked Father Leofdag.

'Yes,' Father Leofdag said. 'From West Francia.'

'And why did you come to Denmark?'

Father Leofdag smiled. 'To do God's work, of course.'

'Of course,' Charles said, feeling his cheeks go red at asking a dumb question.

Father Leofdag smiled again. 'I heard of the work Father Ansgar was doing and felt compelled to come here and aid him.'

Charles returned the priest's smile. 'And he sent you to Ribe.'

'Yes. He would have come himself, but he is in Sweden at the moment, visiting the court of King Olof. So he asked me to come to Ribe to see that the church is built.'

'Like the one in Hedeby?'

'You've seen it?' Father Leofdag's eyes lit up.

Charles remembered the small church. 'I saw it when I was in Hedeby. I didn't like it. It's not like the church in Hügelburg.'

'Hügelburg?'

Charles's heart skipped a beat when he thought he had said too much and didn't know how to respond.

'That is where you are from?'

Not wanting to lie, Charles nodded. 'I wasn't born there. I don't know where I was born, but that was the last place we lived.'

'With your grandfather?' Father Leofdag asked with his head tilted.

Charles shook his head, not knowing what to say. He knew his grandfather would be angry if he found out that Charles had told the priest where he was from. He looked outside the door when he heard a noise and saw some people standing by the door, waiting to come in. Charles guessed they were some of the Christians who lived in Ribe. 'Forgive me, I have to go.' He put the Bible on the table and stood up, not wanting to make the other people feel uncomfortable.

Father Leofdag looked shocked at Charles's reaction, but then composed himself and nodded. 'Very well. But you are always welcome to my...' – he stared around the house as he tried to find the right word – '*church* if you ever want to read the Bible or pray.'

Charles smiled and, as he left, he wondered if Father Leofdag would help him convert his grandfather, but he knew that was for God to decide.

10

Charles was on his way back to Thora's house when Jorlaug jumped out from behind a house. He screamed and almost collapsed in fright as Jorlaug stood there, bent over with laughter. Taking deep breaths to calm his racing heart, Charles glanced around to make sure that no one had seen this, especially not Sigmund and his friends. But all he saw were a few thralls trying hard not to smile as they carried out their tasks. Charles scowled at the red-headed girl.

'That's not funny.'

Jorlaug straightened herself up and wiped a tear from her eye. 'For you, maybe not. But for me it was.'

'Why are you following me?' Charles asked, still scowling at her. 'I'm not.'

'Then why are you here?'

Jorlaug opened her mouth to respond but then closed it quickly and stuck out her tongue at him. 'I'm not,' she repeated.

With a sigh, Charles turned and walked towards the small girl's house where Thora would be waiting. After what had happened the day before, Thora decided that it was better for them to train behind her cousin's house. That way, the other boys could not distract Charles. He sped up, not wanting to be late for training, not because he enjoyed it, but because he didn't want to upset Thora. He knew she did not want to fight and although training him was not fighting, it must still have reminded her of that part of her life. A life that Charles still struggled to understand. He had seen many women warriors in Ribe and had thought the men would be against it. Charles certainly could not imagine any Frankish warrior being happy about having to fight alongside a woman. The men here, though, seemed fine with it. They often trained with the women and would drink ale with them. He wondered what Father Leofdag would make of it. And then he thought about the attack on the priest. Charles wanted to go to his grandfather about it, to ask him if he knew anything about it, or perhaps even to find the men who did it and punish them. Maybe after his training with Thora, he would do that. He remembered, though, how unhappy his grandfather had been when the priest had arrived and told them that King Horik had given land to the Christians to build a church. The idea had excited Charles, and he wondered how the other Christians in Ribe felt about it.

'What happened to the Christian priest?' Jorlaug asked.

Charles glanced at her with a raised eyebrow. He had not realised she was walking with him. 'He was attacked.'

'Did they take all his gold?' Jorlaug said, her eyes wide.

Charles rolled his eyes. Even from a young age, the Danes seemed to be obsessed with Christian gold. 'He had no gold. Only a few things and a Bible.'

'All Christians have gold. Lots of it. That's what Sigmund always says.'

'And how does Sigmund know? Has he ever left Ribe or seen a Christian church?' Charles shook his head. Sigmund reminded him a lot of Drogo and he remembered how his former bully would often boast about how many heathens he was going to kill when he was old enough. Just like he had heard Sigmund say the same about Christians.

Jorlaug shrugged beside him. 'I don't know.' Charles felt her staring at him and tried not to return the look. 'What's it like being a Christian?'

Surprised by the question, Charles stopped and looked at Jorlaug. He almost expected her to be mocking him, but she looked earnest. His heart fluttered as he thought she could be his first convert. Granted, she was only six years old, but he had to start somewhere if he wanted to help Father Leofdag convert Ribe's heathens. He was about to respond, but then couldn't find the words. Instead, he asked, 'What do you mean?'

Jorlaug scratched her head. 'Well, you Christians are weak. So you must always be afraid and I don't get why you'd want to live like that.'

Jorlaug's response surprised him, and Charles rubbed the back of his head as he tried to think of the answer. It didn't help that he spent most of his time being afraid, but for most of his life, he had been afraid of other Christians. Charles thought of his father. He had never been afraid, or not that Charles could ever see. 'Not all Christians are weak. My father was very brave.' Charles remembered the last time he saw his father by the gate of Hügelburg, covered in blood, mostly his own, and about to give his life so that Charles could flee. He felt the knot in his throat and coughed to push it back down again.

'Your father was a Dane. That doesn't count.'

Charles frowned. 'Why not? He was still a Christian and there are many Christian Danes in Hedeby. There is even a church.'

'No, there isn't!' Jorlaug scowled at him. Charles surprised himself by smiling.

'Yes, there is. And I know many Christians in Francia who are not always scared.' He thought of Lothar and tried not to shiver as the image of the large warrior stabbing his father in the back came to him.

Jorlaug frowned as she thought about it. 'So it's only you that is always afraid?'

Charles did not want to answer that question. Instead, he turned and carried on walking. 'I need to hurry. Thora will be angry if I'm late.'

Jorlaug ran after him and when she caught up, she asked, 'So, why did they attack the priest if he has no gold?'

'I don't know.' Charles saw Jorlaug's house and sighed when he spotted Thora waiting for him. She was wearing men's clothing again and was doing some stretches to warm her muscles up. Charles sighed when he also saw the staff on the ground. His arms still ached from the day before, and he doubted he could repeat all of that again.

'When I'm old enough, I'm going to train so I can be a great warrior like Aunt Thora. Then I will earn my place in Freya's Hall.' Jorlaug puffed her chest out and stared at Thora.

'Freya's Hall?' Charles asked. He had heard of Valhalla, where warriors who died in battle would go. There, they trained all day and drank all night as they waited for Ragnarök. The day the heathens believed their gods would die and a new world would be born. That was another thing he struggled to understand about the heathens. Their gods did not live forever. For as long as Charles could remember, the priests had told him that God was eternal and that men were made in His image. God would be around forever and, if they were faithful, they would join Him in heaven for eternity. But the heathens believed otherwise about their gods and the afterlife. Their gods were not perfect and listening to the stories that his grandfather and Thora had told him about the Norse gods, they sounded very human. Which made no sense to him. Gods were not supposed to be an image of a person. It should be the other way around. And that their gods died confused him even more. He had asked Thora about that, wondering why they weren't afraid of Ragnarök.

'Everything has to die eventually, but death is never the end. When our gods die during Ragnarök, others will replace them and the world will start anew,' Thora had said.

Charles struggled to make sense of that. Still lost in his thought, he realised Jorlaug was talking.

'... so Freya's Hall is like Odin's, and she also chooses warriors who will fight for her during Ragnarök. I would rather fight for Freya than Odin. He is ugly and has only one eye, whereas Freya is the most beautiful of all the gods. Are you listening to me?'

Charles looked at Jorlaug and was about to respond when Thora called to him.

'Charles, you're late. Now, run to the river and back. And be quick about it.'

Charles sighed and hoped that Sigmund and his friends had left the river. He did not want to run into them again.

'Can I go as well?' Jorlaug asked.

'Not today, Jorlaug.'

'But why? Boys my age get to start their training. Why can't I?'

Charles heard the frustration in Thora's voice as he set off on his jog. 'That's not for me to say and you know it.'

Charles kept his head down and jogged to the river. He had to do the same the previous day and barely made it while Thora didn't even break a sweat. And he knew it was only going to get worse after that. Then he had to stretch to warm his muscles up before Thora made him do strength training. It was the same when he had to train with the other boys, and a few girls, and even when he had trained in Hügelburg. The strength training was the worst part for Charles, because everyone was always stronger than him, even the boys who were younger.

As Charles jogged, he heard a training sword striking a shield. He looked up, expecting to see the other boys training with old Randolf, but then stopped in his tracks when he realised it was his grandfather and Rollo. Both men wore only trousers and boots as they faced each other with their shields and training swords, which were made of wood and were heavier than normal swords. Charles could barely lift them, but then the children trained with smaller ones which weren't as heavy. Not that that had made any difference to Charles. Sven looked like a child compared to the giant Rollo, a fat and hairy child. Rollo was bigger, stronger and faster than his grandfather, that Charles could see, but his grandfather refused to back down as he ducked under Rollo's sword swing and shoulder-barged the large warrior. Rollo had to duck low to meet Sven's shield with his own but was soon pushing the older man back a few steps. Charles wondered why his grandfather was fighting a man he could never defeat, but then gasped when his grandfather twisted out of the shoving match. The move caught Rollo by surprise, and he stumbled forward, allowing Sven to get behind him. Sven had a chance to land a killing blow then, and if this had been a real fight, he would have done it. Instead, he smacked Rollo's side with the flat of the training sword and the two of them faced each other again.

'Experience is a weapon more dangerous than any sword or axe.' Oda's voice came from behind him.

Charles nodded as Rollo beat down on his grandfather's shield. He wondered about his grandfather's shoulder. The wound had healed, but he often saw his grandfather rolling that shoulder and grimacing as if it still bothered him. Soon Sven's arm dropped, unable to hold the shield again. Rollo lunged for his exposed chest, and Sven just got his sword up in time to deflect the blow.

'But then, old age doesn't help much in a fight,' Oda said, a smile obvious in her voice.

Charles's brow furrowed as his grandfather rolled out of the way of Rollo's attack, but he could see that the giant warrior was holding back. He was sure his grandfather saw the same as well. 'Then why does he keep on fighting?' Charles felt the knot in his throat at the thought of losing his grandfather. He might not have been close to the old man, or disagreed about most things about him, but Sven was the only family he had left. He heard old Oda sigh.

'Thor knows it's not out of choice. I imagine there's nothing that old bastard wants to do more than just to sit by the fire and drink his ale.'

'Then why doesn't he? There's always a choice.' He remembered saying the same thing to his grandfather not so long ago when Sven explained why he had given Charles's father to the Franks. It did not surprise him when Oda gave the same response his grandfather had done.

'Not always, young Charles. We like to think we have a choice in our actions, but the Norns have already decided our fate.'

Charles scratched his head. He didn't understand how the Danes could just accept that their fate was not in their hands, but then many Christians believed the same about God. Even he did. He carried on watching as his grandfather fought against Rollo. Other warriors had arrived and were also watching as their new jarl trained. 'You think he will accept Guttrom's offer?'

Oda was silent for a few heartbeats: so quiet, Charles had to turn to see if she was still there. She stared at him, her old eyes searching deep into his soul as if the answer to his question was inside him. 'Like I said, young Charles. He has no choice. He has to. And he knows it. That's why he's there trying to chop my son in two.'

'But why?' Charles still didn't understand.

'Because if he chooses not to fight and Horik wins, then there is nothing to stop the old bastard from marching here with his army and killing your grandfather. If Guttrom wins, then the bastard will remember that your grandfather did not fight for him and the outcome will be the same.'

'You really think Guttrom will do that? I thought the two of them were friends.'

Oda barked a laugh. 'Guttrom has no friends. There are people who are useful to him and people who aren't. Right now, your grandfather is very useful to him.'

Charles nodded as if he understood, but he still didn't. Not really. 'So Guttrom isn't a good man?'

'Very few are.' Oda's face was grim as she watched the fight.

'Do you think my grandfather is a good man?'

The question seemed to catch Oda off guard, and she rubbed her chin as she thought about it. 'He is not a bad man. Not really.'

Charles thought about her response. 'He killed my grandmother.'

Oda sighed. 'Aye, he did. But he did not mean to, and he has spent a long time punishing himself for it.'

Charles remembered that night in the hall when Sven's brother told him what had happened to his grandmother. He remembered the pain he saw in his grandfather's eyes, but he still could not overlook the sin Sven had committed. Perhaps that was why he struggled to talk to his grandfather. 'He still killed her.'

Oda sighed again, and when Charles looked at her, he saw her shake her head. 'I pray to the gods that you never make the mistakes that your grandfather made, and that if you do, you have someone more supportive by your side.' Oda's response made Charles's cheeks burn and he looked at his feet as she continued. 'Only Sven really knows what happened that night, and he says he did not know it was Eydis behind him. And I believe him. The man that returned to Ribe a few weeks ago is not the same man that disappeared so long ago.' Oda sighed again. 'You shouldn't be so hard on him, Charles. Everything that old bastard is doing, he is doing to keep you safe. Unfortunately, he is not a very smart man, so he is doing that by doing what he does best.'

'By fighting?' Charles asked. He remembered how Sven had ripped through the men in the forest that had tried to kill him. The image of his grandfather standing there, covered in their blood, his eyes wild as he panted, sent a shiver down his spine.

'Aye. Fighting is what he does best, but only because he never had a choice.'

Before Charles could respond, he heard Thora behind, and his heart skipped a beat. He had not realised how long he had been standing there.

'Should have known you'd find a reason to avoid training.'

Charles turned to apologise, but the words died on his lips when he saw the smile on Thora's face.

'Don't blame the boy. I kept him here.' Oda defended him.

'Aye, a bad influence you are.' Thora looked at where Sven and Rollo were training. Both men had stopped to catch their breaths as the other warriors who had been watching started training as well. They paired up, each warrior with a training weapon and a shield, and when both men were ready, their bout would start.

'We were only talking about Sven.'

'So is everyone else.' Thora looked at Charles. 'Now, come. You still need to train.'

Charles sighed and bid farewell to Oda before he followed Thora back to her house. 'Father Leofdag was attacked last night,' Charles said.

'I know,' Thora responded. 'Jorlaug told me,' she explained when Charles raised his eyebrows. 'She said his face is all beaten up.'

'She thinks it was to steal his gold.'

Thora nodded. 'But you think otherwise?'

Now it was Charles's turn to nod. 'They did it because he is a

Christian and they don't want him here.' That was something Charles knew all about. His entire life, people had bullied him because they didn't want him around. Because of who he was and who his father had been. He wondered if he would ever be accepted anywhere. Charles's brow furrowed as he thought about what Father Leofdag had told him and of his conversation with Oda. He stopped and looked at Thora. 'Can you teach me how to fight without a weapon?'

Thora stopped mid-stride and stared at him. 'I thought you didn't want to learn to fight?'

Charles looked at his feet and then at Thora. 'I don't want to be a warrior. But I...' He hesitated as he thought about how he had found Father Leofdag all beaten up. 'I don't want to be picked on any more.'

Thora smiled at Charles and put her arm around his shoulders. 'I understand. We can start as soon as you finish your warm-up.'

11

Sven wiped the sweat from his brow and watched as Charles walked away with Thora. He shook his arms as he wondered what Oda had told the boy and whether he should be concerned about it. Oda had never liked him much. She had disapproved of her husband's friendship with Sven, which was why he had been so surprised that she had come to him that night and helped him.

'Another round?' Rollo asked. Sven glanced at the younger warrior, his huge muscular frame drenched in sweat, just like Sven. He flexed his arms to see if they still had any strength left in them, but then decided they didn't. He had already pushed himself too far. The warriors who had watched them before had started training themselves and the training ground was filled with men grunting and screaming, and wooden weapons striking shields.

'No, we'll call it a day.' Sven turned and saw Guttrom standing there with Oleg, the two of them gossiping like two young maidens. It had been the same the previous night during the feast. Guttrom had been given the seat of honour at Sven's table, but he had barely spoken a word to Sven all night. Instead, he and his son, Ivor, were constantly talking to Oleg. Sven growled when he remembered how empty the hall had been last night. Not like the night when he had returned. Most of the warriors had been there, but very few of the townspeople came. Sven knew it was because of how they felt about him, but it did not look good. The food had been plentiful though, and the ale was flowing all night long. Not that Sven had drunk much. He did not trust Guttrom's arrival and did not want his mind fogged up with ale. Which meant it had been a sour night for him, especially when one of Guttrom's warriors grabbed hold of Alfhild. Sven remembered the fury that spread through him, and it took all of his strength not to launch himself at the arrogant young bastard. But Rollo must have seen what was happening because he soon rescued the thrall from the warrior and took her away. That was one of the reasons why Sven had pushed himself so hard this morning. He needed to burn the anger out of him. The other reason was because Charles was watching and he didn't want to seem weak. Which was difficult while fighting a man almost twice your height and half your age.

'You used to be stronger,' Guttrom said as Sven walked past him.

'Used to be younger, too.' Sven hawked and spat on the ground. He wiped the sweat from his face again and handed the training sword to one of the younger warriors.

'You should row. You'll get your strength back faster than Fenrir grew to his full size.' Guttrom's men around him nodded as if that was sage advice. Sven knew that rowing built strength, but since he had arrived, he had not had the time to set foot on any of the three ships left behind by Bjarni. He had stood on the wharves and admired them, taking in their long, slender shapes and picturing them full of men. But with the constant raids from Bjarni's sons-in-law and that the people of Ribe did not want him back, Sven had not found the time to take any of the ships out. And he had to admit it, he missed being on the whale road. He missed the feeling of the powerful ship under his feet as she sliced through the waves and feeling the saltwater spray over him. Sven could almost taste the salt on his lips from his memory. The wind blowing over him as he fought to control the sea beast and the thrill of taking on Ran and her daughters. Sven had been on small fishing boats over the many winters since he left Ribe, but it had been a long time since he felt an oar or rudder in his hands. He wondered if he still had it in him to handle one of the warships on the wharf, and then remembered his last attempt to get his son back from the bastard Franks. He had left with four ships, all of them bristling with men he had given most of his treasure to, as no one in Ribe or the surrounding towns would sail with him. They had claimed he was cursed and no one wanted to sail with a cursed man. That had been his last battle with Ran, and she had been victorious. Three of the ships had been sunk, only his had survived. Sven had been sad to see his old ship was not there on the wharves, but one of the grey beards had told him that Bjarni had sold the ship a long time ago. He guessed his brother had not wanted anything that could remind himself or the people of Sven and his failures.

Sven sighed. 'Aye.'

'I go out every day with my men,' Guttrom continued with a big smile. 'We row until our arms fall off and then we row some more. You should join us one day.'

Sven looked at the old warrior and saw the strength in his thin arms. 'One day.' He was about to go to the bathhouse to clean himself up and shave his scalp when a boy ran towards them.

'Oleg! Oleg! There's been a raid!' A crowd was forming behind the boy as other children and dogs ran with him.

Sven bristled at the fact that the boy was calling for Oleg and not him, but he told himself to stay calm and to ignore the glances from Guttrom and his son, as they, too, noticed this. 'Where?' he responded before Oleg could say anything, eager to show he was in charge.

The boy stopped in front of him, his eyes wide and chin trembling. His clothes were dirty and torn, and his cheeks were stained with dried tears. He almost reminded Sven of the day he had first seen Charles in Hedeby.

'Where was the raid, boy?' Sven asked again, this time with a softer voice.

'Halstein's farm,' the boy managed. 'They attacked us before the sun came up. They burnt everything. My father... my father sent me. Told me to tell Oleg. To fetch help.' Fresh tears erupted from the boy's eyes as the warriors who had been training stopped and made their way towards them. Even the women who were by the river stopped their tasks as they stared.

Sven looked at Oleg. He did not know where Halstein's farm was.

'To the east, half a day's walk. A big farm.' Oleg sucked air in through his teeth. 'It'll be a huge loss if that was true.'

Sven growled and turned to one of the warriors. 'You, get the boy fed and something to drink. Oleg, get forty men and horses ready. We leave now!' He did not wait to see if Oleg was doing what he asked as he made his way to the hall. Rollo was soon by his side, the younger warrior using his long legs to catch up with him, but stayed silent.

Word had already spread through Ribe and as Sven walked past the market, he heard the people talking about the raid and what it meant for them. Sven growled at the grey beard, who spat at his feet as Sven continued, but the old man only glared at him and walked away. Sven knew the people of Ribe would blame him for this raid, just like they had blamed him for all the others. He reached the hall and was surprised to see Alfhild waiting by his war chest with a bucket of water and a clean tunic. Sven nodded his thanks as he cleaned his face and used a cloth to wipe the sweat from his body. He had been looking forward to sitting in a tub with warm water to let his muscles relax, but he had no time for that now. He needed to get to this farm quickly, and if Odin was with him, he might even find the bastards that had raided it. The bath would have to wait until he got back. Once he was as clean as he could get himself, Sven slipped on the clean tunic and pulled Arnbjorg's old brynja out of his chest. He had tried to give it back to Oda the day after he had killed Bjarni, but she had refused. He needed it more and Arnbjorg, her deceased husband, was not wearing it anyway, she had told him. Rollo didn't need it either as he already had one of his father's old brynjas. Arnbjorg had loved collecting war trophies and had many brynjas, helmets and weapons from the warriors he had slain. Rollo rushed to his house to get his own war gear as Alvar arrived wearing his brynja and with his shield strapped to his back and his Dane axe in his hand.

'The horses are ready, jarl.'

Alfhild offered Sven his helmet as he slipped the leather cap he wore under it over his scalp. He left his Dane axe, doubting he could lift it after his training fight with Rollo earlier on, but made sure he had his sword and a sax-knife.

'May Thor protect you,' Alfhild said just as Sven was about to leave. He stopped and glanced at her, struggling to find the right response, so instead, he just nodded and left the hall.

Outside, his men were already mounted, all of them dressed in their war gear and with their weapons ready. Townspeople gathered around the warriors, while the traders stood by their stalls and stared. Guttrom and about fifteen of his men were mounted as well on horses that Oleg must have provided them, and Sven knew he shouldn't have been surprised that they were coming. He was surprised, though, to see that Guttrom's son, Ivor, was not amongst the mounted men.

'Sven, what is happening?' Thora came rushing towards him, with Charles right behind her, as Alvar helped him mount his horse. The animal complained under him, and Sven had to grip his reins to make sure he didn't fall off as the beast took a sudden step to the side.

'Aye, well, I don't like you either,' Sven muttered under his breath. He was not good at riding them because his father had decided that Sven didn't need to learn that skill. 'Another raid. Halstein's farm.'

'Do you know who?' Thora asked.

Sven shrugged. 'Jarl Ebbe or his son Gunvald, most likely'.

Thora nodded as Charles stared at the warriors on their horses. 'And you are taking so many men with you?'

Sven shrugged. 'The raiders might still be around. It's better to be prepared.' He leaned forward so the others could not overhear. 'Keep an eye on things while I'm gone. If the gods are good to us, then we should be back by nightfall.' Thora nodded and said nothing, but Sven frowned at the look Charles was giving him. It was not the usual look of uncertainty, but one of understanding. Sven nodded at the boy, who nodded back before he looked around to see if his men were ready. The priest Horik had sent was standing outside the house Sven had given him, and Sven raised an eyebrow at the man's bruised face. Sven wondered who had attacked the bastard as Rollo returned from his house and mounted his own horse. Satisfied that everyone was ready, Sven turned his horse. 'We ride!'

The people of Ribe watched as Sven, flanked on either side by Rollo and Alvar, led his men along the main road and out of the town. He kept his eyes fixed on the horizon, not wanting to see how the people reacted to him riding out with so many men. He gripped the reins of his horse tightly. This was not what he had wanted when he came back to Ribe. He had only wanted to protect his grandson from a danger he had not understood. A danger he still did not understand. All he knew was that the king of West Francia wanted his grandson and that cross. King Charles believed the cross would protect his kingdom from his brother, King Louis of East Francia, although Sven did not understand how. He had not seen the cross since the night he had killed Bjarni, Charles had it hidden in his chest, but its image was burnt into his mind. What was so special about that cross? That was the question that kept him awake most nights. The cross was magnificent, the giant red ruby breathtaking, but it was still just a cross. Or was it? Sven wished he had a way to find the answers he needed. The only way he could think of finding them was to go to Francia and find this bishop that Charles had told him about. The man might have betrayed his son, but he might also know why the cross was so important. But Sven could not leave Ribe and sail to Francia. Not with the threat of Horik looming over him like the storm clouds that had followed them from Hedeby to Ribe. He knew that as soon as he left the town that Horik would send an army and capture it. And Sven was sure the people would just open the gates and let Horik's men through. They loved Bjarni, and so they loved Horik. They had prospered under his brother, and since Sven had returned, there had been nothing but misery for them. Sven's head started hurting as these thoughts raged in his mind and, not for the first time, he longed for the days when his only concern was where he could get more ale from. Sven never thought he would miss those days. He had always believed that Odin was punishing him for what he had done, but perhaps the All-Father had been protecting him from himself. But Sven could not abandon Ribe, not after he had killed her jarl. As much as the people here hated him, Ribe was still his town, the place where he was born and raised and, more than anything, he still believed that the only way to protect Charles was to stay here. Without realising it, his hand went to his head, and he pretended to adjust his helmet as he thought of the raven tattoo on his scalp. Something in the distance caught his eye and, when he looked, he saw a crooked figure wearing a dark cloak standing on a nearby hill.

'Odinson.' Alvar saw what Sven was staring at. 'Can only be trouble if that ancient bastard was dragged out of his cave.' Alvar rubbed the Mjöllnir around his neck and took his eyes away from the stooped figure that watched them from the hill.

Sven resisted the urge to do the same. He remembered the old godi who lived somewhere in the forest near Ribe, although no one was sure where exactly. Neither did anyone know his true name. Everyone called him Odinson because they believed he could speak to the one-eyed god. Sven felt the flutter in his heart and wondered if the old bastard could tell him about the cross. Perhaps he would visit the godi when he returned from this hunt.

Rollo led the way as they raced to the farmstead in silence, the men too tense to speak or to joke as they normally would. Sven had to resist the urge to glance over his shoulder at where Oleg was riding beside Guttrom, instead of at the head of the small force with Sven. He tried to ignore the strange feeling in his gut as he kept his eyes peeled for any signs of the raiders. But all he saw was the plume of smoke they were riding towards growing larger with every heartbeat. Sven prayed they caught the bastards who had attacked the farmstead. The training session this morning had done nothing to quell his anger and Sven clenched his fist around the reins as he felt the bloodlust inside awakening.

'By Odin,' Rollo said when they finally reached the farm. The farmhouse and surrounding buildings were still aflame, and so were the fields nearby. Thick black smoke rose to the sky as the flames roared like the rage inside of Sven. The people that lived here just stared at the flames as they consumed their homes and food, as if they were worshipping Surtr, the fire giant. Young children and old men wept, while one man was walking around in a daze as blood leaked from a head wound. Sven frowned when he realised there were no young women or men. Sven looked at Rollo and saw the tears in his eyes. The large warrior jumped off his horse and rushed towards the survivors. Many of the other warriors did the same as Oleg drew his horse level with Sven.

'They've never done that before,' he said, his voice strangely calm. Sven nodded and eyed the land around the burning houses.

'No livestock.' Sven scanned the fields where cows, sheep or even goats should be grazing. But they were empty, apart from a few dead dogs, which meant the raiders had taken them, along with the young women and boys. Sven ground his teeth. 'Find out which direction the raiders went. They'll be moving slowly so, if the gods are with us, then we can retrieve what they have taken.'

Oleg nodded. 'They'll not thank you for that, even if you bring their children and livestock back.'

Sven glared at the old warrior. 'They don't need to.' Sven was aware of Guttrom and his men waiting behind him. He rubbed the Mjöllnir around his neck and searched the sky for a sign from the gods, anything to guide him. He spotted some small birds, sparrows most likely, flying around, but saw no pattern in their flight which he could take for a sign. Ravens also flocked nearby, but he knew they were only looking for food near the flames. The death-eating birds had learnt a long time ago that large fires usually meant that a meal was on offer, so he didn't think their presence was a sign from Odin. Movement not far from them caught his eye and Sven turned in time to see a fox slink away. That was a sign, but one he did not need. He was already sure there was a sly fox near him, waiting to betray him when the moment was right. Sven glanced at Oleg as the man relayed his orders to the warriors. He was about to turn around when someone shouted at him.

'You! What are you doing here?' It was the hunter that had saved them from the Franks in the forest not far from here. Sven tried to remember the man's name but then realised he had never known it. The hunter stormed towards him, his red face creased and wet with tears. Rollo rushed after the man, his eyes wide as Alvar moved his horse to block the man, but Sven shook his head. The hunter was right to be angry at him. 'I should have let them kill you that day! I never should have wasted my arrows to save your worthless skin!' He stopped a few paces away and shook his fist at Sven. 'She would still be here if I'd let you die!' The man hawked and spat at Sven, who did not react as the spit landed on his brynja.

Alvar jumped off his horse and grabbed the hunter by his tunic, almost lifting the man off his feet. 'Do not talk to your jarl that way!'

The hunter's anger made him brave, and he never took his eyes off Sven. 'The fat bastard is not my jarl.'

Alvar lifted his hand to strike the man when Sven stopped him. 'No, Alvar. The man has a right to be angry. Let him go.' Alvar let go of the hunter, who almost dropped to the ground. 'We'll do what we can to bring her back.' Sven tried to placate the hunter, but the man only shook his head, and before he walked away, he said,

'You can't bring her back from the dead.'

Sven sighed and again missed the days when he was wandering around Denmark with no burdens. No warriors to feed or people to protect. When his decisions affected no one but himself. A raven cried above his head and this time Sven resisted the urge to rub his Mjöllnir pendant again.

'You never used to let your people talk to you like that,' Guttrom said from behind him. Sven turned and saw the smirks on the faces of Guttrom's men. He clenched his fists around the reins as he glared at them. What did they know of his life for them to smile like that?

'My people never spoke to me like that,' Sven said, still glaring at the men around Guttrom.

'Aye, they used to fear you back then.' Guttrom's thin face was serious as he stroked his beard.

'I was a different man back then.' Sven searched the sky again, but again there was nothing from the gods. He sighed as he looked at Guttrom and saw the triumph in the man's eyes. 'You will help me fight Ebbe and his son?' Sven knew they were responsible for this attack and others they had not heard of yet. He wondered if they acted on their own, or if Horik had told them to because of Guttrom. But that was a problem that had to be solved another time. Right now, Sven had to find the bastards who had done this and kill every one of them.

Guttrom nodded, his eyes bright.

Sven heard the ravens again and knew that Odin was laughing at him. But he had no choice. He never really had. 'Then I'll fight Horik with you.'

12

Abbess Hildegard fingered the small golden cross she wore as her carriage drew to a stop outside of the house of Duke Liudolf. She was twenty-six years old and had spent the last ten years of her life in service to the church. Like her father, King Louis of East Francia, she had dark eyes and dark hair, although no one saw her hair because of the hood she wore as part of her attire. Hildegard was slim because of the strict diet she followed and made her sisters in the nunnery follow as well, but she had a keen mind which had helped her become one of the most powerful people in her father's kingdom. But since her last visit to Ehresburg, Hildegard had been unable to concentrate on her duties, her mind constantly wandering as she worried over the fate of her son.

She remembered the day when she had heard the news of what had happened to Torkel. Hildegard had been praying in the church when she was interrupted by a nun who told her that there was an important message. She had almost collapsed when the man delivered the news from Bishop Bernard. The father of her child had been killed and her son was missing. Even thinking about it now made her legs feel weak. The nuns had been concerned by her state, the weeping and the anger, but none of them knew of her past sin. That's what the Bible called it, but Hildegard was never so sure. She pictured the young Danish warrior who had been part of her father's, King Louis of East Francia, court for as long as she could remember. He had been shorter than most men, but no less confident. He had also been a great warrior, and people often talked about how unrelenting he was in combat. Too stubborn to die, someone had once said. Her father, perhaps. But she had not known that side of Torkel, the son of a Danish jarl who had terrorised the Frankish coast, but then vanished as if God had plucked him away. The Torkel she had known was intelligent, observant and always quick to laugh. He was also a very devout Christian, something that had surprised her and most who knew of his father. They had spent a lot of time together, often in the church, discussing many things from religion to their dreams of the future. She had fallen in love with his mind, which was as sharp as she was sure his sword was. Bishop Bernard had warned her about spending too much time with the young Dane and told her as well that her father had noticed and was not pleased. Torkel had been one of his best warriors and he did not want him or her to be corrupted. But she had been young and taken by Torkel's confidence, so she had ignored the bishop, believing she was in control of the situation. Hildegard smiled at her youthful arrogance, but then the smile faltered as she remembered the day she had lost control of herself. That had been the only time she had been with a man, and if she had to be honest, she couldn't even remember if she had enjoyed it or not. Things soon got worse when she found out she was with child.

King Louis had been furious and demanded to know who the father was, even though she was sure he already knew. Hildegard had tried to convince Torkel that the two of them should run away, perhaps to one of her uncles or even to Denmark, to Torkel's father. But Torkel had refused. He had wanted to do the right thing and so he had gone to her father and knelt before him. Torkel had even requested her hand in marriage but her father had refused. King Louis was visibly pained from learning that one of his favourite warriors had defiled his eldest daughter, but at first had done nothing about it. Not until after the child had been born. Hildegard had been sent to a nunnery so that no one could see she was with child. She had known then that her father would never let her keep the child. It was bad enough for the king that he could not marry her off for a political alliance, but to have her parade around with a child out of wedlock would ruin his reputation. It was the only time in her life that Hildegard had given in to her anger. She had ordered her maid, one of the few people she could trust, to take something important from her father, just like he was taking something important from her. A cross that had once belonged to her great-grandfather, Charlemagne. Hildegard never knew why this cross was so important, but it was one of the reasons that the sons of her grandfather rarely spoke to each other.

After the birth, she was not allowed to say her farewells to the man she loved or to the son she would never get to know. It still pained her that she didn't even know what he looked like. Did he have her hair colour or her eyes? Or did he look like a smaller version of Torkel? Not that she really remembered what the Dane looked like, only that he was short and that the other warriors always mocked him for it. But Torkel had been strong and never let the taunts get to him. She wondered if Charles got that from his father. She hoped so because he would need that strength to survive amongst the Danes. Hildegard had told her maid to give the cross to Torkel, after she had heard that her father was banishing him from the court, with a letter she had written for him. She still remembered what that letter said, as if she had written it that very morning.

> *Protect our son and keep the cross safe. When he is old enough, give him the cross and send him to me. That way, I will know he is my son. I pray God will keep both of you safe and that one day we can be reunited.*

When Hildegard had recovered, her father had made her the abbess of Münsterschwarzach, an abbey on the river Main, in the middle of her father's kingdom. Everyone had been told it was because of her devout nature and because she had wanted to be closer to God. Hildegard was never sure if her father had done that because he was ashamed or angry with her. He would visit often, but she never asked him. She didn't really want to know. So she had thrown all her energy into the role and now she was one of the most powerful women in East Francia. Hildegard had learnt to use her role as an abbess to tilt the scales in her favour and the fact that she was the king's daughter also helped. She had formed a powerful alliance with Duke Liudolf over the years. Their love for Torkel had formed the base of that friendship, but their desire to protect East Francia had strengthened it. Bishop Bernard had also been a good friend over the years and the two of them had kept her informed about everything that happened, not only in East Francia but also in the kingdoms of her uncles. Liudolf often lent her his spies when she needed something delicately done. There was little in East Francia that she did not know about and she had used this to grow her influence not just over the dukes of East Francia, but her father as well. And she feared that that was the reason King Charles wanted her son. She might not have raised the boy, but she would still do anything to keep him safe and she was sure her uncle wanted to use that against her and her father.

Through the years, Bishop Bernard had kept her informed of Torkel and her son. She had smiled when she had found out that Torkel had named the boy after her great-grandfather. His real name and not the one most knew him by. Torkel had always been an admirer of Charlemagne and she had wondered if it had anything to do with the cross she had given him. The bishop would never tell her where Torkel or Charles were, only how they were doing. She always believed that it was to stop her from going to them, but the old bishop had nothing to fear. As the years passed and Hildegard grew into her role as abbess, she understood she could never be a mother to Charles. As much as she yearned to see him, she understood the danger she would place him in if anyone ever discovered who the boy was. But that was what had happened in the end, and it infuriated Hildegard that no one could tell her how King Charles of West Francia, her uncle, had found out about her son. She had known for a long time that her uncle had been searching for the cross, but she never believed that Torkel or Charles were in any danger. No one knew they had the cross, not even her father. But King Charles had found out somehow and must have used Lothar to retrieve it. That was the only reason she could think of for Lothar attacking Torkel.

Hildegard stepped out of the carriage in front of Duke Liudolf's house and smiled as the servants scurried around to prepare for her unexpected visit. She knew it was wrong, but she enjoyed watching men panic and squirm. Hildegard glanced at the church beside the duke's house and crossed herself. It was the only stone building in the small town on top of a large hill, apart from the keep on the far side of the town. Hildegard knew it was built on the ground which had once been a heathen holy site. She also knew it had a strong connection with the cross she had given to Torkel. She walked into the duke's house, ignoring his servants as they ran around and the man who was greeting her and telling her where Duke Liudolf was as she wondered about that cross. It was certainly beautiful. She remembered staring at it when she was a child, but her father would never let her near it and she never understood why he had kept it hidden. Hildegard thanked the guard who had opened the door for her and made her way to the library where she knew Liudolf would be. She also knew of the secret door behind one bookshelf where his spies would enter unnoticed.

Hildegard paused just before she reached the library, her eyes locked on the dark-haired young man brooding on the floor, the one who had escaped from Denmark. The one who had travelled with her son. The bruises on his face had healed well, but she still saw the anger in his eyes as he glared at her. Gerold, she remembered his name.

'You are well?' she asked him.

Gerold cleared his throat as if he had not spoken for a long time. 'Yes, my lady.'

'There's no need to call me that.' Hildegard smiled. 'Abbess will do.' Gerold nodded, but said nothing. 'They have treated you well?'

'They feed me, give me somewhere to sleep. But I'm still a prisoner in this house. The duke wants me nearby so he can watch me.'

Hildegard nodded. She understood the young man's anger. He had done everything he could to complete a task he knew very little about, and now he was being punished for it. 'Patience, young Gerold. Our Lord has more need for your services.' She left him confused as she turned and walked into the library without being announced.

Duke Liudolf sat behind his desk, his large shoulders hunched over as he read a document. He lifted his head and frowned at Hildegard, but did not look too surprised to see her. 'Hildegard.' He stretched his back and leaned back against his chair. Hildegard was sure that most women found the duke attractive, and she had heard rumours of his late-night visitors, but that had nothing to do with her. Apart from the grey which invaded his black hair and his beard, he still looked much the same as the first time she had met him. He had tried hard to get her attention in those days, but Hildegard had never been interested in him. Liudolf was a smart man, but he missed that one quality Torkel had. Eyes that saw everything.

'Any news?' Hildegard asked, not wanting to waste time.

Liudolf sighed and then stood up. She knew it was not to intimidate her, but the man still towered over her. He walked to a beaker and offered her a cup of wine before pouring one for himself. Hildegard was not here to drink. She wanted to know why her son was not on his way back to her yet. 'Nothing good,' Liudolf said after drinking from his cup. 'Torkel's father has made himself the jarl of Ribe again and King Horik is not pleased about this.'

'Torkel always said the man was stubborn.'

Duke Liudolf glanced at Hildegard as he filled his cup again. 'I still don't understand why Torkel would send his son to Denmark and not to me or the bishop?'

Hildegard fingered the cross around her neck. 'That question is simple to answer.' Liudolf raised his eyebrows at her. 'Lothar.'

'Lothar?'

Hildegard nodded. 'You said Lothar had been one of your men for a long time. You made him the chatelain of Hügelburg. Torkel must have believed that you had sent the man.'

'Me?' Liudolf almost dropped his cup before he walked back to his desk and collapsed in his chair. 'I thought Torkel trusted me more than that.' He slammed his fist against his table. 'By God! I thought we were friends!'

Hildegard wanted to pity the man, but she was still angry at his failings. Even if she considered him a close friend. She would forgive him one day, but not until her son was safe. 'Torkel would have known that one day someone might come for the boy, perhaps sent by my father, or one of my brothers if they found out about the cross.' She knew her brothers knew nothing about Torkel having the cross. Rumours had been spread that it was stolen and was hidden in one of the other kingdoms. 'So when Lothar tried to kill him, he must have decided that Charles was not safe in Francia any more.'

Liudolf scowled, his fingers linked under his chin as he thought about what she had said. 'But why send the boy to his father? Torkel can't have heard anything from him since he was a boy. How could he have known the heathen bastard was still alive? We didn't even know that.'

Hildegard could only shrug. It was a question she struggled with as well. 'Did you know that Torkel's father was not jarl any more?'

'There were rumours long ago that his brother became the new jarl, but the Danish traders refused to tell us anything and since we had no problems from Ribe, we stopped trying to find out.'

Hildegard rubbed her cross again as she thought about it. 'Torkel told Charles to find his grandfather and that his grandfather was the jarl of Ribe. That's what Gerold told us. So he must have believed his father was still jarl.' She looked at Liudolf again. 'Did Torkel know of these rumours?'

'I don't know. But I doubt he would have believed them, anyway. Torkel was a stubborn bastard and believed his father was unbeatable.'

Hildegard nodded. She remembered how Torkel would talk of the man who had given him up to the enemy. Torkel had always wanted to be a great warrior, just like his father. But then she scowled as she thought of the other question that had been plaguing her mind. 'That is not important for now. The bigger question is, how did my uncle find out about my son and the cross?'

Liudolf sighed and slumped even more into his chair. 'I don't know. I knew nothing about the cross until Gerold told us about it.'

Hildegard scowled. 'Only two people knew Torkel had the cross and about Charles. Me and my maid.'

'What happened to the maid?' Liudolf asked.

'I don't know. My father ordered her and her husband to leave East Francia. He did not want her around to remind him of my sin. Her husband was a blacksmith for my father and had family in Paris. They might have gone there.'

'But you think she might have told your uncle?'

'That's want I want to find out. Liudolf, I want you to send men to West Francia. See if they can find anything.'

Liudolf sucked in air through his teeth. 'West Francia is a large kingdom. Could take many years before my spies find her and that's if she's still alive.'

'Your men only need to search in Paris, not the entire kingdom. If she was my uncle's source of information, then that's where she'll be.'

'If she was your uncle's source of information, then she's surely dead by now.'

Hildegard nodded. She had thought that as well. 'I still want to be sure.'

'Why not ask your father? He has men in your uncle's court. Maybe they can find out.'

Hildegard shook her head. 'My father cannot find out that I'm trying to find the boy or that I gave him the cross. I dread to think of the consequences.'

'What's he going to do? Lock you away in a nunnery?' Liudolf smiled, before his face grew serious again. 'You really think he doesn't know already?'

Again, Hildegard shook her head. 'He thinks he has people in Fraumünster to keep an eye on me, but they've been in my pockets for a long time. They feed my father what I tell them to.' Fraumünster was a new nunnery her father had built the previous year and had made her the abbess of. It was smaller than Münsterschwarzach and it did not have the same sense of history, but Hildegard had managed to bring along those most loyal to her, so, unlike in Münsterschwarzach, she had complete control of the ongoings and the lands around Fraumünster. But it was also further away from where Torkel and her son had been. Hildegard went to the table where the duke kept his wine. She would need a drink for what she was going to say. 'Now, what are you doing to bring Charles to me?'

Duke Liudolf sat up straight as the sudden change caught him by surprise. He stammered for a few heartbeats before he finally responded. 'Hildegard, the situation there is now very difficult. The return of Torkel's father has caused chaos, and it's hard to know what's really happening.

'But chaos can be good for us, no?'

Liudolf scowled. 'It can also be dangerous. There are reports of constant raids on the different jarldoms.'

'So, it's even more important that we find him then.'

A pained expression flashed across Liudolf's face again, which only annoyed Hildegard. 'I'm sorry, Hildegard, but my hands are tied at the moment. Your father fears more raids from the Danes, and so do I. I need to protect my lands.'

Hildegard took a sip of her wine as she tried to calm her nerves. 'So you will do nothing to bring the boy back?'

'There's nothing I can do until the situation calms in Denmark.'

'My son could be dead by then!' Hildegard threw the cup at Liudolf, who barely reacted. She had been careful not to refer to Charles as her son, just in case someone not so loyal to Liudolf was listening, and berated herself for her lapse.

'Perhaps you can write to Ansgar. He is still in Denmark, in

Hedeby, I believe. I'm sure he would be happy to help the abbess of Fraumünster in her need.'

'Father Ansgar is my father's man, and he is in Sweden now. No, there is only one thing for it.' Hildegard steeled her nerves as she stared at Duke Liudolf. 'I will go to Ribe myself. If you cannot bring Charles to me, then I'll go get him myself.'

13

Sven ground his teeth as they raced after the men who had burnt down the farm, the words of the hunter still ringing in his ears. *I should have let them kill you that day.* Even if the hunter had not arrived, Sven was sure he would have survived the ambush near Ribe. Odin would not have let him die, for the same reason he had kept him alive even during the cold winter nights when he had been forced to sleep outside, blanketed by the snow. Charles and Thora might have been killed, but Sven would have lived.

They had found the raiders' tracks soon after arriving at the farmstead and, after sending a few men back to Ribe with the farmers and with a message to Thora, Sven had given chase. It had not taken them long to find the raiding party, which did not surprise Sven. They had captives and livestock with them, so they wouldn't have been able to travel at a quick pace. What did surprise Sven, though, was the size of the force. His heart raced as he eyed his prey ahead of him. There were about sixty men that he could see, all of them on horseback. They were all dressed for battle, as you did when you went raiding, even if you didn't expect to do any real fighting. Everyone knew the gods were bastards and liked to play tricks. You might have thought it would be a simple raid, just to end up facing a small army. So you dressed for war when going on a raid. Most wore leather jerkins and some brynjas, but all of them had helmets on and shields strapped to their backs. The raiders were travelling in a large circle, the women and children kept in the middle and a few men trailed behind with the cows and goats. They stopped as they spotted Sven and his men cresting the small hill, and a boy took his chance and ran for it. Sven's men cheered the boy on as he dodged through the horses' legs and ran towards them. One of the raiders was about to rush after the boy when he was called back. Sven could not see or hear who had shouted the order, but the raider suddenly pulled his horse back and returned to the group. As Sven and his men raced towards them, most of the raiders dismounted and a handful rushed their captives and live-stock on, perhaps hoping to reach the safety of Jarl Ebbe's lands before the men of Ribe could catch them. Sven urged his horse on, not sure how close they were to Ebbe's domain, and he did not want these bastards to escape. The fatigue from his training session with Rollo was forgotten and the sound of the horses thrummed in his ears as his forty men kept pace with him. Danes did not fight on horseback. They never had and Sven was sure they never would, but he imagined the fear the raiders must have felt when they turned and saw the warriors on horseback chase after them. A warrior stepped towards Sven and his men and shouted orders. They were still too far and Sven could not hear the man, but he knew what he was saying because it was the same thing Sven would have said. The raiders formed a shield wall, about thirty men wide and two men deep, between Sven's men and their plunder. It reminded Sven of that day in Francia, so long ago when he had been outnumbered and far from home. The memory only angered him more and he pulled his sword from its scabbard and shouted, 'Kill the bastards! Leave no man alive!' Sven was not sure if his men could hear him. Nor was he aware of Guttrom and his men pulling away from them. The boy who had freed himself saw that Sven and his men weren't stopping, so he turned and ran to the side before he could be crushed.

Sven was close enough to see the faces of the raiders, to see the dirt and dried blood from their attack on the farm, and he kicked the side of his horse, willing the beast to crash through the enemy shield wall and trample the men. Just like the Franks had done to his own men so long ago. But unlike those horses, Sven's wasn't trained to fight battles and the bastard animal turned at the last moment, frightened by the shields and weapons of Ebbe's men. Sven was not prepared for the sudden turn and was thrown from the horse towards the shield wall. He just had enough time to register the wide eyes of the raiders before he crashed into them. The rest of his men had not been so caught up in their rage and had jumped from their horses a few paces away.

'Charge! Attack!' Rollo screamed, his Dane axe in his hands as he and Alvar charged at Gunvald's stunned men.

The warrior Sven had landed on softened his fall and the anger coursing through him numbed the pain. Sven jumped to his feet and stabbed another warrior who was gaping at him. Blood sprayed over him as Rollo swung his Dane axe in an arc and cleaved a man's chest open. Alvar rushed to Sven's side and blocked a blow aimed at Sven's exposed back. Sven turned and sliced the man who had tried to stab him in the leg, and as the man dropped to his knees, Sven rammed his sword through the bastard's throat. Sven roared as he pulled his sword free, ignoring the blood drenching him and the fact he had no shield. All the anger and frustration of the last few weeks drove him on, and his eyes darted around as he tried to find another of the raiders to kill. Alvar caved a man's skull in with the head of his axe while Rollo danced past another attack and buried his axe in the man's back.

'Shield wall! On me!' one raider shouted as he waved his sword in the air. Sven did not know the man but guessed he was important because of the gold-rimmed helmet he wore and the many arm rings on his arms. The raiders fell back from the fight and started forming a shield wall as Sven growled. Rollo and Alvar fell in at his sides as the rest of Ribe's men formed their own shield wall without being told to do so. Sven spotted Guttrom leading his fifteen men around the enemy shield wall and attacking the few men left to guard the captives and the livestock, hacking at them with their swords and axes from on top of their horses. The leader of Ebbe's warriors turned his head to see what was happening behind him, and so did most of his men, a mistake that would cost them their lives. Sven wasted no time.

'Kill the bastards!' He charged at the enemy, armed only with his sword. His helmet and shield were lost when he flew off his horse, but that wasn't going to stop Sven the Boar. The leader of the enemy turned back in time to see Sven charging at him, and he stabbed at Sven with his sword. Sven ducked under the blade and hurtled into the man's shield, forcing him back and causing their shield wall to collapse. Alvar jumped through the gap and killed two warriors with a swing of his axe and the rest of Ribe's warriors crashed through the enemy shield wall just as Guttrom and his men attacked them from behind. The man Sven had barged into had disappeared in the melee as another raider swung his axe at Sven's head. Sven was forced to jump back as he had no shield to block the blow. He then rushed forward and stabbed at the man, who blocked his sword with his shield. The warrior chopped his axe down on Sven's helmet-less head, and this time Sven jumped to the side and kicked the bastard's leg. As the man dropped to his knee, Sven stepped in and opened his throat. He sensed another attack behind him and twisted out of the way and one of Guttrom's men stabbed his attacker in the back from atop his horse. Sven looked around, wild-eyed, at the battle that was unfolding around him. It was chaos and he could hear the gods laughing as men fought for their lives. The only way to tell your enemy from your friend was by looking at their shields. Ebbe's shields were all painted blue and had a white raven on them, while Sven's men had shields still painted in his brother's colours. Green and red. Rollo and Alvar made sure they stayed near Sven as they killed any who came too close to their Dane axes, while Guttrom and his men rode their horses through the battle, trampling those who could not get out of the way, and killing men with glee. Sven deflected the sword aimed at his head and kicked at the shield of the bastard who attacked him.

'You're dead, old man!' the young warrior screamed at him as he took the blow on his shield and attacked again.

Sven turned, grimacing at the pain in his left leg, and wished he had a shield so he could at least stand his ground. The warrior attacked again by cutting at Sven's stomach. Sven was forced to block the strike with his sword, and felt the strength of the warrior's attack rattle up his arm and numb it. He gritted his teeth as he struggled to keep hold of his sword. Rollo and Alvar were too busy fighting men of their own to come to his aid, and Sven was forced to duck under the warrior's blade as he stabbed at his head. The young warrior kept screaming at Sven, although he struggled to understand what the bastard was saying with all the noise raging around him and blood pumping in his ears. The young warrior was strong and he was fast, and Sven struggled to find any space to launch his own attack. To make things worse, his sword arm was numb, and his left leg struggled under him. Sven knew he needed to do something, or he would never see his grandson again. He could not rely on his strength. The young warrior was stronger, but Sven had age on his side. He took a step back, feigning injury and exhaustion. Filled with arrogance, the young warrior took the bait and rushed forward, his sword ready to skewer Sven.

'This is for Bjarni, you stinking swine,' the young warrior roared, his eyes wide and teeth bared.

The mention of Sven's brother sent his heart racing, and Sven deflected the bastard's sword and grabbed the rim of his shield with his free hand. The warrior paled under his helmet as Sven pulled his shield down and struck him on his head with the pommel of his sword. His legs buckled under him as the blow rattled his head and he dropped to his knees. Sven kicked the warrior's sword from his hand and lifted his own sword.

'Send my regards to my treacherous brother, whoever you are.' He was about to stab the young warrior when Oleg grabbed hold of his arm.

'Sven, stop!'

Sven turned on his former hirdman, his face red with anger. 'By Odin! Don't you tell me what to do!'

Oleg, his brynja bloody and his sword dirty, took a step back. 'Sven, that is Gunvald.'

Sven did not hear Oleg and turned to finish the job when Rollo intervened.

'Sven, Oleg is right. That's Gunvald, Ebbe's son!'

Sven stopped and frowned at the young warrior, still on his knees and glaring at him. 'Gunvald?'

'Aye, Bjarni's son-in-law,' Oleg said.

'Doesn't matter.' Sven tightened the grip on his sword. 'The bastard raided my lands.'

Gunvald spat at Sven's feet. 'These lands are not yours. They belong to Bjarni.'

Sven placed the tip of his sword against Gunvald's neck. 'Bjarni is dead, and soon you will join him.' Gunvald showed no fear as he glared at Sven, who was about to force the blade through the young bastard's neck.

'I'd keep him alive if I were you, Sven,' Guttrom said as he brought his horse closer. 'He could be useful to us.'

'The shit dies,' Sven growled, getting more annoyed by the moment.

'Think about it, Sven. His father is a powerful ally of Horik. If we control his son, then we might control Ebbe. You of all people should know how powerful a weapon an only son can be.'

Sven growled again as the memory of Torkel being left on the beach in Francia came to him. He pressed the sword into Gunvald's neck and a thin line of blood leaked out of the wound.

'Guttrom is right, Sven. Do what he says.' Oleg stepped forward and put a hand on Sven's shoulder.

Sven glared at the old warrior. 'Whose man are you, Oleg?'

Oleg's eyes widened at the question. 'What do you mean?'

His sword point still pressed against Gunvald's neck, Sven turned and grabbed Oleg by his brynja. 'Who has your loyalty? Me or Guttrom? Because you've been spending a lot of time talking to him.'

'Sven, now is not the time for this,' Rollo, who had approached Sven, whispered to him. 'But Guttrom has a point. We need to march through Ebbe's lands to get to Jelling. If we kill Gunvald, then we never make it to that battle.'

Sven glanced at the young warrior, still on his knees and glaring at him, as he considered what Rollo had just said. He twisted the blade, making Gunvald grimace and the men around him tense, before he stepped away. 'Fine, we do this your way, Guttrom. But, Odin knows, you better not be wrong about this.' Rollo grabbed Gunvald and stripped him of all his weapons while the rest of Gunvald's men were rounded up.

'What do we do with the rest of them?' Rollo asked.

Sven looked at the battleground. About half of Gunvald's men were dead and quite a few were injured. He then glanced at Guttrom, who only shrugged. 'Kill them, but keep one alive.'

'You bastard!' Gunvald tried to free himself from Rollo's grip. Rollo punched him in the stomach and the young warrior dropped to his knees again. Tears streamed down his face as Sven's men killed his. He then turned to Sven and cursed him, but Sven was no longer paying attention. He was exhausted and his left leg ached, along with his shoulder, which he guessed was from him falling off his horse. Sven looked for the beast, wondering if he should kill the bastard animal as well. But then he thought against it. The horse was not trained to charge at a shield wall and it was dumb of Sven to think the animal would do so.

'That was an interesting approach to breaking a shield wall. You should teach it to my men,' Guttrom said, as Sven walked away from them.

Sven growled in the back of his throat and stared at the man he had landed on. The man looked like he had seen enough winters to almost be called old. He was one of the few who wore a brynja and his arms had three arm rings each, the mark of an experienced warrior. His hand axe lay near him, his fingers stretching towards the weapon. Someone had stabbed the warrior through the chest, and Sven wondered if he had done it. He looked at his sword as if it could answer him before he turned and took in the surrounding carnage. His blood still beat in his ears, but he could just make out the women and girls crying and the ravens arriving for their feast. Sven glanced up at the death eaters and felt a tickling sensation on his head. He reached for his scalp and felt the small cut.

'They're all dead, apart from one man,' Oleg said, and Sven glanced at him, still wondering who the old warrior was more loyal to. Three of Guttrom's men were returning with the captives and the livestock, as well as four horses in tow. The small boy who had freed himself sped past Sven towards the freed captives as one woman broke away from the group and rushed towards the boy. The two met in a strong embrace and Sven was forced to push the memory of Eydis hugging Torkel like that just before they had departed on that raid.

'The captives?' Sven asked, his throat dry and his hands trembling.

'Shaken, most likely, but Odin knows they'll be fine.' Oleg cleaned his sword on his trousers before putting it in its scabbard. Sven did the same with his sword as his men looted the dead raiders, taking anything of value, while Guttrom's men talked amongst themselves. Guttrom stared at Sven, his eyes scrutinising him, and Sven wished the man would stop. He scanned the land-scape as Rollo sent a few men to collect the horses of the raiders and Sven glared at his horse as the animal stood to one side, staring back at him and pawing the ground as if showing its own frus-tration.

'Where are we exactly?' Sven asked to distract himself. The land looked familiar and in the distance he saw some farmsteads, but he could not remember if they were still on his territory or Ebbe's.

'Still in your lands,' Oleg said. 'What do you want to do with the warrior you spared?'

Sven glanced at where the man was being watched by Alvar and another warrior. 'Bring him to me.' He waited while Oleg called the order and the two warriors brought the remaining raider to him. They dropped the man on his knees in front of Sven and Sven was pleased to see that they had taken his weapons and armour from him. The warrior couldn't have been more than twenty winters old and as much as he tried to be brave, he could not hide the quiver of his chin. Sven grabbed the man by his hair and forced the warrior to look at him. 'I want you to send a message to your jarl. Can you do that for me?' The warrior nodded and Sven smiled. 'Tell the bastard that I have his son. That if he raids my lands again, then I'll gut his boy and feed him to the fish. But I won't finish there. For every woman he takes, I'll take two. For every man he kills, I'll kill two. For every farm he burns, I'll burn two. The gods themselves won't be able to stop me as I burn his lands around him.' The warrior paled so much that Sven worried the man might faint, but he carried on. 'If that shit of a jarl tries to stop me, then I'll make him wish he never even thought of marrying his son to Bjarni's little bitch. You get that?'

The warrior nodded and Sven turned to Alvar, who hauled the warrior to his feet and sent him running towards Ebbe's town. The man looked over his shoulder once and then fled.

'You always had a way with words,' Guttrom said with a smile and his men around him laughed, but Sven ignored them.

Sven looked at the sky instead as the daylight faded, but saw no sign from the gods as Rollo brought him his horse. He stroked the animal's nose before mounting her, grimacing as he tried to ignore the pain. Sven hoped that Loki wasn't paying attention to him because he was sure the god of mischief would find a way to ruin Guttrom's plan. 'Let's go home.'

14

Charles dropped to the ground, the sweat pouring down his face, but his trembling arms were too tired to wipe it away.

'I think we'll call it a day.' Thora smiled as she wiped her forehead with the back of her hand. 'You did well today, Charles. Just remember to keep your arms up and always watch your opponent. They will always show what they are about to do.'

Charles sucked the air in so he could respond. 'You didn't though.'

Thora laughed and offered him a hand to his feet. 'I did. You just didn't see it.'

As soon as Sven had left with the warriors, he and Thora went back to her family's house and she showed him how to defend himself with no weapons. Not long after, a few warriors had returned, bringing with them the survivors of the attack on the farm. One of the warriors sought out Thora and told her that Sven was going after the raiders and might not be back until the following day. Training had to be stopped after that as Thora and the other women from Ribe helped the farmers who had survived the attack on their farmstead. Wounds were cleaned and food was provided to those who wanted to eat, but most of them didn't. They were still grieving those who had died or were taken and the loss of their homes. Charles had prayed. That was the only thing he could think of doing. He had prayed for his grandfather, so that he would return, and he had asked God to help those affected by the raid.

The training the following day had been harder than training with a staff. Thora had shown him how to stand and how to hold his arms. She even showed him some counter-attacks, but Charles had struggled to understand it all. He was not meant to be a warrior, that he had learnt a long time ago. It didn't matter who his grandfather was or who his father had been. Charles would never be like them. Despite that, he had tried to pay attention and learn from Thora. The attack on Father Leofdag had shown him they would never accept his faith in Denmark. And Charles realised that if he was going to live amongst the heathens and spread the word of God, then he needed to be able to protect himself. 'You make it look so easy,' Charles said, remembering how Thora had fought those warriors in Hedeby.

'I've been training my entire life. You, Charles, are just starting.' She put her arm around his shoulder, and Charles grimaced at the smell of her sweat. She did not stink, not like the men did, but it still smelt unpleasant. Unwomanlike. 'Besides, you're a natural fighter. I can see it in the way you move.'

Charles pouted. 'No, I'm not. I can't fight. And never will be able to.'

Thora scrutinised him, and Charles wondered what she saw. A small, frail boy who couldn't fight and who was frightened of everything? 'No, Charles. The gods know there is much more to you than you realise. You have your grandfather's and your father's natural talent. You just need to stop fighting yourself. Once you do that, then you'll understand.'

Charles scratched his head. He did not understand, and neither did he agree with Thora. Was God testing him through her? Was he supposed to deny her words? 'No, I'm not. God does not want me to fight with sword and spear. He wants me to use his words to show people the righteous path.' Charles smiled, feeling like he had passed the test, but what Thora said next confused him again.

'You are too young to really think that, Charles. Your father never believed he would be a great warrior like his father. Just remember that. Now get yourself cleaned up and go visit your priest. I know you want to,' she said before Charles could respond, and walked away.

Charles stood where he was, still scratching his head. He did believe that he was meant to be a priest. He had always felt more at home in the church in Hügelburg, where he could read the Bible while the priests corrected his pronunciations, than he did in his own house. But he also remembered how good it had felt when he had punched Drogo, Lothar's son, that day. And that feeling had left him confused. God's punishment had been swift, though, and now Charles was forced to live amongst the Danes. It was a test of his faith, that he was sure of, no matter what Thora said. A raven cried behind Charles, and his heart skipped a beat as he jumped in fright. As he turned and saw the large bird sitting on the roof of the house and staring at him, he remembered Sigge's voice from not too long ago. *Odin is watching you.* A shiver ran down his spine and Charles rushed to the house his grandfather had given Father Leofdag, eager to get away from the raven and its beady eyes.

Father Leofdag was standing by the door of his house, his face bruised from his beating and with his Bible in his hands as he encouraged people to pray with him.

'Come, people of Ribe! Come and hear the words of the one true God! Be no longer led astray by your false idols. Your salvation is here in this book. The word of God!'

'Shut up, you bastard!' Someone threw a stone at Father

Leofdag. The priest ducked behind the Bible, which the stone struck and caused the people to laugh.

'See how his god protects him!'

Charles shook his head as Father Leofdag looked at his Bible to see if there was any damage to the book's leather cover. Satisfied, he turned to Charles. 'He's not wrong. God's book protected me from that stone.'

Charles smiled, but it didn't last long when he saw the glares directed at him and the priest. He wondered who the people of Ribe despised the most. The grandson of the jarl they hated, or the Christian priest? 'Was it like this in Hedeby as well?'

Father Leofdag glanced at the townspeople as they walked past on their way to the market or back home carrying things they had bought. 'It wasn't very different. But there we are under the protection of Jarl Torgeir, so the people tended to just ignore us.' He smiled at Charles. 'You came to read the Bible?'

Charles nodded, unable to stop himself from smiling. 'If that's fine with you?'

'Of course. Jesus would not want me to turn one of his flock away.' Father Leofdag grimaced when he saw the dirt on Charles's hands and the sweat stains on his face. 'First, though, clean yourself and then join me inside.'

Charles looked at his hands and nodded. Thora had told him to clean himself, but that raven had frightened him so much that he had forgotten to do that. He looked around and spotted the bucket of water outside Father Leofdag's house. The water looked clean, so he dipped his hands in the bucket and rubbed the dirt from them before he rinsed the sweat from his face.

'Why are you here again?' Jorlaug's voice from behind him made Charles jump for the second time that day. Jorlaug realised she had scared him and smiled victoriously at Charles as he took deep breaths to calm his racing heart.

'Why are you here?' He scowled, which only made Jorlaug smile even more.

The small girl shrugged. 'I followed you.'

'You should stop doing that.'

'Doing what?' Jorlaug asked with an innocent expression on her face.

'Following me.' Charles wiped the water from his face. He had no cloth or a clean tunic, so he just used his hands.

'But scaring you is so much fun.' She laughed as Charles scowled at her again.

'Well, you can go now.'

Jorlaug stopped laughing and peered into the priest's house. 'What are you going to do in there? Make a sacrifice to your god? Are you going to kill a dog or a thrall?'

'What?' Charles frowned. 'We do not make sacrifices to our God. That's something you heathens do. We're going to read the Bible and pray.'

'What's the Bible?' Jorlaug wrinkled her nose and tilted her head.

'The Bible is the word of God. It tells us how we should live if we want to go to heaven.' Charles puffed out his chest.

'Your god speaks to you through this Bible?' Jorlaug's eyes widened. 'What does he sound like? I bet he sounds really old.'

Charles stammered, not sure how to respond to that, but was saved by Father Leofdag. 'God does not speak to us directly through the Bible, but indirectly. The Bible tells us the stories of those who had lost their way so we might learn from their mistakes to be better Christians.' The young priest smiled.

'It also tells us of the life of God's son, Jesus, so we can follow his example and be better people,' Charles added, remembering the words of the priest in Hügelburg.

Father Leofdag smiled at Charles before he turned his attention back to Jorlaug. 'Would you like to join us? I could show you how we pray to God.'

Jorlaug frowned and looked around her, although Charles wasn't sure why she was so hesitant. She was always asking him about being a Christian and now she had a chance to learn about it from a priest. He would have jumped at the chance if he were her. 'I don't know. Everybody says you shouldn't trust Christians.'

'Why not?' Father Leofdag raised an eyebrow. 'We do not eat children, despite what some might believe.' He held out his hand for Jorlaug to take. 'Come in and see for yourself.'

Jorlaug was about to reach out and take the priest's hand when her father's voice reached them. 'Don't touch my daughter, you Christian scum!'

They all turned and saw Haldor standing, or rather swaying, on the path in front of Father Leofdag's house. 'Father,' Jorlaug gasped and pulled her hand away from the priest.

Father Leofdag raised his hands, the Bible still in his left hand, and said, 'Forgive me, I did not mean to upset you. Your daughter is perfectly safe. Perhaps you would also like to join us. God's words can save you from the devil that I can see is tormenting you.'

'The only thing that is tormenting me is you in my town!' Haldor stomped towards the priest. 'Now get away from my daughter and never go near her again!'

'But your daughter is curious about the Bible.' Father Leofdag held the Bible out for Haldor to see, but the drunk man had no interest in it as he smacked the book out of Father Leofdag's hand. There was a stunned silence from the onlookers as the Bible hit the ground, its pages fluttering in the dirt. Someone gasped as if they were expecting something to leap from the pages, but finally, the Bible settled and everyone turned their attention back to the confrontation between Haldor and the priest.

'You bewitched her! Used your Christian magic on her to

confuse her mind. She's only a child!' Haldor's face turned red and spit was flying from his mouth. He then turned his fury on Charles. 'And you, you little worm!' He jabbed a finger at Charles. 'I should never have let you into my house! Don't think I haven't heard how you whisper spells into her ears, turning her away from the gods!'

Charles took a step back as if he'd been slapped. He had done no such thing. He only ever answered the questions Jorlaug had asked him. Charles looked at the red-headed girl, but she stayed silent as she stared at her feet.

'Don't blame the boy for carrying out the duty given to him by the one true God. To save you all from the clutches of the devil and his false idols,' Father Leofdag said, and Charles knew the priest had made a mistake even before Jorlaug's father punched him in the face. The blow sent the priest flying into the wall of his house, yet somehow he stayed on his feet as blood started leaking from the cut on his lip.

'Kill the Christian!' someone shouted from the crowd that had gathered around them.

'Aye, send him back to his god! Odin knows we don't want him here!' The crowd cheered at this and Father Leofdag's face paled. Charles looked around, trying to find anyone that could help the priest in the crowd, but saw no one. Not even the few Christians who lived in Ribe were prepared to help Father Leofdag. Thora was not here, either, and any of the warriors who might have helped had left with his grandfather. The remaining warriors were content to watch the confrontation, and some were even cheering Haldor on.

'Please, there is no need for violence. God says we must love our neighbours,' Father Leofdag pleaded, his hands held up in front of him. But that only angered Haldor even more.

He grabbed Father Leofdag by his robe and shoved him hard against the wall of his house again. 'You should have said that to the

Christian warriors who slaughtered our Saxon cousins,' he growled before he punched the priest again. The blow caught Father Leofdag in the middle of his face and the priest's legs wobbled under him before he dropped to the ground.

Charles could not stand there and do nothing as the crowd cheered Haldor on and he was tired of people attacking those weaker than them. Haldor was no warrior. He was a lazy drunk who sat around all day and complained about his life, about all the wrongs that had been done to him by an imaginary enemy, but he was still bigger than the priest. 'Leave him alone!' Charles shouted, his fists clenched as an unfamiliar heat spread through his limbs and caused him to tremble. 'Leave him alone, you dumb pig!'

The crowd fell silent as Haldor turned towards him. Charles felt his anger vanishing as he saw the angry glare in Haldor's creased eyes. 'I've had enough of you!' He backhanded Charles and sent him spiralling to the ground. Charles landed hard next to the Bible and rubbed his burning cheek as Haldor stormed towards him.

'Touch my grandson again and I'll cut your hand off!' There was a gasp from the crowd and even Haldor wavered as the voice of Charles's grandfather echoed over them. The crowd parted and Charles saw his grandfather jump off his horse, grimacing as he landed because of his bad leg. Rollo and the rest of the warriors stayed mounted, all of them eager to see what was about to happen. Sven made his way to Haldor, his brynja covered in blood and dust, his crinkled face red and his jaw muscles working hard under his bushy beard. Charles remembered what Thora had said about watching your opponent for signs of what he was about to do. Even in his dazed state, Charles knew what was about to happen. He prayed, asking God to intervene, to stop his grandfather from killing Haldor, but knew it was too late for that when he saw the violence in his grandfather's eyes.

'Run, Haldor, you dumb bastard,' someone shouted from the crowd.

'Fight the boar!' another shouted. 'Avenge our jarl!'

Sven took in the surrounding sight, his gaze stopping on the priest knocked out on the ground. 'What is the meaning of this, Haldor?' he asked, his voice strained.

Charles sat up and looked around, trying to find Thora. He spotted her in the crowd, her face flushed as if she had just run here, and his eyes pleaded with her to do something, but she only shook her head. There was no stopping his grandfather now.

'This is your fault, Sven!' Haldor shouted, finding courage in his drunken state. 'You came back here and brought the curse of Christianity with you!'

Charles could feel his grandfather's anger coming off of him and looked up to see the whitened knuckles of his clenched fists. 'This is my fault?'

'Aye,' Haldor responded, slightly swaying. 'You brought these Christians here! You cursed us with their presence!'

Charles's grandfather glanced at him and Charles could not stop the shiver that ran down his spine. *Please, God. Stop my grandfather from killing the man. He is tormented by the devil. He does not know what he is saying.*

'It's my fault the Christians are here?' Sven asked again, a vein pulsating on his forehead. 'It's my fault they are here and so you attack my grandson?'

As Charles's grandfather said those words, Haldor suddenly realised what he had done. His eyes widened as he pleaded, 'Sven, no—'

But the words stopped as Sven launched himself at Jorlaug's father with a roar. A woman from the crowd screamed as Sven punched Haldor in the stomach, the blow hard enough to lift the larger man off his feet. As Haldor bent over, Sven grabbed him by his hair and drove his face into his knee. Haldor's head snapped up, his nose nothing but a bloody mess, and before he could hit the ground, Sven grabbed him by his tunic, his face red with fury. 'This is all my fault?' he screamed at the crowd, who watched on in silence. 'This is my fault?' He turned to Haldor and punched him in the face. A sickening crunch echoed over the people of Ribe and Haldor collapsed in a heap. Charles's grandfather kicked him in the chest before he turned to the people watching. 'You think I wanted any of this? You think I wanted my brother to betray me? To give my son to the bastard Franks!' Spit flew from his mouth as he screamed the words and even Charles was stunned. 'I did not want any of this! I did not want to be jarl of this cursed town again. It took everything I wanted!' Charles's grandfather paced in front of the people as he screamed at them. Behind him, Father Leofdag was coming to and looked confused at the sight in front of him. He looked at Charles, who shook his head. The last thing that the priest should do was to try to calm his grandfather.

'Then why did you come back?' someone shouted from the crowd.

Sven glared at the people, trying to find who it was before he sighed and looked at Charles. 'I only wanted to protect my grandson, to keep him safe from those who took my son away from me,' he said in a quiet voice. Charles felt the knot in his throat when he saw the pain in his grandfather's eyes. But it did not last long as Sven faced the crowd again. 'But I did not bring the Christians here!'

'Then who did?' another voice shouted, and the people jeered.

'Who did?' Sven growled the question. He turned and stared at the priest, whose face paled. 'Your king Horik brought the Christians here!'

'That's a lie,' the same voice as before responded.

Charles's grandfather faced the crowd again with curled lips.

'Who do you think gave the Christians the land across the river to build their church? Who do you think allowed them to build a church in Hedeby and in Jelling?' Sven jabbed a finger in the direction that Charles guessed those places were. 'Who do you think has a Christian priest sit at his table during feasts?' his grandfather continued, silencing the people of Ribe with questions they knew were true. 'Horik whored himself out to the Christians a long time ago, just as your beloved Bjarni whored all of you out to the Franks!' Sven clenched his fists as he waited for someone from the crowd to respond, but no one did. 'Those old enough to remember me know I am no lover of the Franks or their god, so don't tell me this is my fault. Do not tell me I brought the Christians here!'

'But your grandson is a Christian!' a woman shouted.

Charles struggled to read his grandfather's eyes as he stared at him. But then his grandfather looked at the people of Ribe and his words sent a chill down Charles's spine. 'Aye, he is. But he is my grandson and if any of you touch him again, then I'll burn this whole town down with all of you in it.'

Fists clenched, Sven glared at the people of Ribe. He wanted them
to attack him, wanted them to retaliate against his words. But none
of them did. Not even the brave voice hiding amongst the crowd
that had challenged him before. They all just stared at him in
silence, their mouths agape and eyes wide as he heard the flap of
wings of the birds that filled the sky above their heads. But Sven did
not look at the birds. He was no longer interested in any signs from
the gods.

'Sven?' Thora's voice came and Sven glared at her. She glanced
at Haldor on the ground. The man wasn't moving, but Sven could
see his chest rising and falling. A jarl should not kill one of his
people. It turned the rest against him, made them resent him. He
was supposed to protect those who lived on his lands. But these
people did not see him as their jarl. They did not want him as their
jarl either. He knew what they said about him, and saw the way
they looked at him. For weeks he'd been trying to ignore it. But the
words of the hunter still plagued him and the image of the burning
farmstead tormented his mind. He looked at Haldor again, glad the
man still lived. That was not who Sven wanted to be any more. That

life had cost him everything, but no matter how hard he tried to be different, the gods kept pulling him back to that life. Perhaps that was the sign he'd been looking for, but he just didn't want to see it.

None of the townspeople moved. Not the women or their children. The grey beards, the warriors and the traders, for once silent, all stared at him. All the while, ravens flew above them, their cries mixing in with the seabirds that flew up the river to look for food. Sven unclenched his fists. He was aware of Guttrom, still on his horse, looking at him with a smug smile on his face. Sven wished the man had never come here. But he had, and Sven's fate was now tied in with his. He cursed Odin for not letting him die while he had wandered the lands of Denmark, before he turned his attention back to the townspeople.

'I know you don't want me as jarl. I hear the words you whisper and see the way you look at me. The gods know that I never wanted to be jarl again. Not after what happened last time.' Sven looked at his grandson and took a deep breath. The boy still reminded him so much of Torkel. 'It was never my plan to kill Bjarni. If I had known that he was the one who had betrayed me all those winters ago, then I never would have come here. But I didn't know. I didn't see it even though many had tried to tell me. All I wanted was to keep my grandson safe, and I hoped Bjarni could do that because I knew I couldn't.' The people glanced at each other as he spoke, many of them taken aback by Sven's honesty. But they remained quiet and let him speak. Even Guttrom and his men listened intently. Gunvald, their captive, scowled as he sat on his horse with his hands tied in front of him. 'The gods are bastards. We all know that. They are mischievous and like to cause chaos just to amuse themselves. And it seems that was what they intended when they brought my grandson to me. Chaos.' Sven sighed and looked at Rollo. The young warrior stood tall, his shoulders broad and face stern. He was a good leader, better than Sven ever was. 'War is coming to Denmark, whether we like it or not. And it's not coming from the Franks to the south or the Norse to the north,' Sven said, and the townspeople started whispering to each other. 'Horik is old, and he is weak. He has been king for a long time and there have always been jarls opposed to his rule. It's no secret that I was one of them. But now, there are those who feel the time is right for a change and we must choose a side.' Sven paused as the whispers grew louder, the people shocked by what he had said. Sven glanced at Charles and saw the fear in the boy's eyes. 'Ribe will stand with Guttrom against Horik, and when the battle dust settles, I will leave Ribe and you can choose a new jarl.' Sven turned as the noise exploded from the townspeople, some of them screaming questions at him, others just screaming. But Sven ignored them as he saw Thora's cousin rushing out of the crowd to Haldor. Ingvild, Thora's aunt, stood next to her, her old eyes scrutinising him as Audhild dropped to the ground and cradled her husband's head. 'I'll pay weregild for his injuries. Come to the hall tomorrow and it will be ready for you.'

Ingvild looked at Sven and shrugged. 'I'd say don't bother. Frigg knows the bastard is a waste of space and he most likely will only drink it away. But my daughter still loves him and she needs to support both him and their child.'

Sven nodded and looked at Thora's cousin, almost expecting to see her glaring at him, but she wasn't. Audhild just sat there, her eyes blank. Perhaps she knew the truth about her husband or she was just accepting the shame the dumb bastard had brought to them. Sven sighed and turned to the priest, who was on his feet again. His face was a bloody mess and his eyes were dazed as he tried to understand what had happened. 'Priest, I suggest you pack your things and go to the land Horik has given you across the river. I can't promise you'll be safe if you stay here.'

The priest nodded, but Sven doubted the man understood. Not

that Sven cared. The only reason he didn't kill the priest himself was because of Charles. Sven looked at the boy and saw him staring at the open Bible by his feet. He never understood why the Christians cared so much about those books, but then, the Danes liked to tell stories of the gods over the hearth fires. His mother had told him the tales of Thor's battles against the giants and of Loki tricking the other gods and being punished for it when they caught him. Eydis had told the same stories to Torkel, but their son had still chosen to follow the Christian god over the gods of the Danes. When Charles looked up, Sven saw his cheek swelling and knew the boy would have another bruise in a few days. The people of Ribe would be speaking about this for a long time and he knew that many would use that to argue that he shouldn't be jarl. That was why Sven had made the decision to leave. He had not thought about it for long, but he didn't have to. Sven did not have the strength a jarl needed to protect his lands and people. Not any more. After the battle, if he survived, and he knew that was for the Norns to decide, he would take Charles and the two of them would leave Ribe. He was not sure where they could go. He needed to survive the coming battle before he could think about that.

'Thora, get your belongings. You are no longer staying with your cousin.'

Thora looked at him. 'And where will we stay?'

'You can stay in the hall, in the sleeping quarters. I'm not using them.'

'No,' Charles said, his lips trembling. 'I can't. Not after I...' Charles trailed off.

Sven sighed again. He did not need to look at Thora to see the glare she was giving him. He had thought that if Charles believed he had killed the Frank, then the boy would toughen up. But Sven did not know his grandson well enough to realise it would do the opposite. It was too late now, though, to tell his grandson the truth.

Just like it was too late to tell Charles that his mother still lived and who she really was. It was better he didn't know that. 'I'm sorry, Charles. But there is nowhere else for you to stay. The room has been cleaned, the blood washed away.'

Charles's eyes darted between him and Thora, his lips still trembling. Thora put an arm around the boy and led him away. 'Don't worry, I'll be there with you,' Sven heard her say before he turned to the people who were still standing there, watching him.

'Get back to what you were doing. The entertainment is done,' he said, and made his way to the hall.

'You heard the jarl,' Rollo said, and the people finally went back to their business. But the air had been sucked out of the town and Sven felt the glances from the townspeople on his back.

'That was quite the speech,' Guttrom said as Sven walked past him. Sven grunted his response, not wanting to talk to the bastard, but Guttrom wasn't done yet. 'You don't really plan on giving up Ribe, do you? By Odin, you only just got your town back.'

Sven stopped at the door to the hall and glared at Guttrom. The smug smile on Guttrom's face and on the faces of his men irritated Sven even more. He wished he had never come back to this wretched town. He wanted to blame Thora for that. It was her idea to come to Ribe in the first place. But he knew they had had no other choice. No, he only had himself to blame. If he hadn't been so blinded by his arrogance, then he might have spotted Bjarni's treachery sooner. 'Ribe was never my town. I was a fool to ever think it was.' He turned and walked into the hall and didn't see the scowl on Guttrom's face.

Sven ignored the people inside the hall as he made his way to his chair. The warriors that had stayed behind were relaxing after their training session and were offering greetings and drinks to those who had returned with Sven. Thralls were cleaning the hall and preparing food for the evening meal. Alfhild stopped what she was doing and fetched him some ale as soon as she spotted him. He reached his chair and collapsed into it, his dirty brynja making it difficult to sit comfortably, but Sven did not care. Neither did he care about the rumble in his stomach. He wondered what would have happened if they had arrived later than they did. Would Haldor have killed Charles? Sven shook his head. No, he was sure Thora would have stopped him if Sven hadn't.

'It's good to see you have returned, Jarl,' Alfhild said in her soft voice as she handed Sven a cup of ale. Sven took the cup and stared at Alfhild, again wondering what she was hoping to gain from this. She had not once tried to sleep with him, although neither had he tried to sleep with her. So what did she want from him? He almost asked when Oleg walked into the hall.

'That was not a smart thing to do, Sven. The people already don't like you.' Oleg signalled for Alfhild to get him some ale, and she turned to do his bidding as Oleg sat down on the bench near Sven.

Sven growled and took a drink from his cup as he tried to calm himself down. Oleg was another person he struggled to understand. He had helped Sven against his fight with Bjarni, but Sven did not feel like he had the warrior's full support. He wondered if that was how the gods felt about Loki. And then there was the close relationship he seemed to have with Guttrom. Sven did not trust that and decided he needed to keep the two bastards separated.

'Are you really going to do what you said?' Oleg asked when Sven did not respond. Alfhild returned with Oleg's ale and, after giving it to the old warrior, she glanced at Sven and left them to talk. 'Thor knows, I don't understand why you haven't bedded her yet.'

Sven looked at the man, not sure which question he was supposed to answer, so he decided on the easier one. 'The people will never accept me as jarl, so it's better for everyone if I leave.'

'But when Guttrom defeats Horik and becomes king, then he will declare you jarl and the people will have to accept you.' Oleg drank from his cup but kept his eyes on Sven.

Sven felt like laughing at the comment. If he hadn't been so angry, then he might have done. He glanced at all the old shields and weapons that hung on the wall of the old hall and tried to remember which ones were from his victories. 'If Guttrom wins and does that, the people will still not accept me.' Sven looked at Oleg, seeing the dirt trapped in the lines on his face. Sven guessed he looked the same. 'Danes don't just bow down to anyone, Oleg. You know that. By the gods, if we did, then Horik would have us all be Christian by now just to please the Franks.'

Oleg raised an eyebrow before he glanced over his back towards the door of the hall. 'You don't believe Guttrom will win?'

Sven smiled, not surprised that was what Oleg had picked up on from what he had said. He wondered what Guttrom had promised Oleg. 'I believe the gods are cruel and who wins will depend on what mood Odin is in on the day of the battle.'

Oleg scowled, but did not respond as Rollo approached. 'Haldor lives, although he won't want to show his face for a while.' The large warrior shook his head. 'By Týr, what was the fool thinking?'

'Haldor doesn't do much thinking, that is the problem,' Oleg said, and drank his ale.

'Rollo, find that hunter and bring him to me and find a place where we can keep Gunvald,' Sven said, not wanting to talk about Haldor. He knew he should not have attacked the man, but when he had seen his grandson on the ground, his cheek red and eyes wet, he had lost it. Sven glanced at Oleg and then spoke in a softer voice so Oleg couldn't hear him. 'Make sure he is guarded by men you trust, not Guttrom's.' Rollo nodded and left while Oleg frowned at him.

'What do you want the hunter for?'

Sven finished his ale and looked around for Alfhild, but could not see her in the hall. He frowned at that and then turned his attention back to Oleg. 'The man lost everything because of me. It's only right that I give him what he is owed.'

'You really think that's going to make a difference?'

Sven sighed. 'No, I don't.' He signalled to another thrall to get him more ale. He had got used to Alfhild always hovering around him and wondered where she was.

'Who do you think the people will choose as their jarl?' Oleg scratched his neck, trying to look as if his question was not important, but Sven could see the shine in his eyes.

He shrugged. Sven knew who he thought would make a good jarl, but he wasn't going to tell Oleg that. 'Only the Norns know that.'

'Aye,' Oleg answered, and turned as Rollo returned with the hunter. Alvar was also with them, his eyes fixed on the hunter. Sven wondered what the man thought the hunter would do. The hunter kept his eyes down, preferring to look at the floor of the hall instead of Sven. The man was not so sure of himself any more, not now that his anger had left him.

'The hunter,' Rollo said as they stopped in front of him. Some of the townspeople had entered the hall, eager to see what Sven had planned for the man who had insulted him. He was sure they all knew about that already. Nothing stayed quiet in this town. Perhaps they expected him to attack the hunter as well.

He took the refilled cup from the thrall and drank from it before he spoke. 'What's your name, hunter?'

The hunter looked up, his eyebrows raised. 'Geir Halsteinson. Jarl Sven, please forgive my outburst from yesterday. I was angry and wasn't thinking clearly.' The man wrung his hands together as he bowed his head again.

Sven took another sip of his ale. He saw one of Guttrom's men at the back of the hall, most likely to report to Guttrom what Sven was going to do. Sven wondered why Guttrom wasn't here himself. 'No,' Sven said, surprising everyone. 'It's me who should apologise.' The hunter's eyes bulged, and Sven thought the man might collapse. 'You saved our lives a few weeks ago and I've repaid you with nothing but misery and death. We took several horses from the men who attacked your father's farm.' Sven remembered from before that Geir had said the farm belonged to his father. 'I give them to you, with some weapons we have taken from their corpses as recompense for the damage the raiders have caused. They will not be able to bring those who died back from Hel, but I pray to Odin, it will help you rebuild your father's farm.'

There was a gasp from one woman in the hall before whispers erupted from everyone. The hunter paled and looked like he was about to pass out, and even Oleg could not hide his shock. Horses were valuable and for Sven to gift them to the hunter was something no one ever expected from him. Jarls were supposed to be generous, but not that generous. But Sven understood the man's pain. He felt it himself every day, and just like with his own, the hunter's pain was because of his actions.

'Th... thank y... you, jarl.' The hunter struggled to get the words out. A woman started wailing, and Sven guessed it was one of the people they had rescued from the raiders.

'Rollo, see that it is done,' Sven said, trusting no one else but Rollo to do it.

'Yes, Sven.' Rollo turned and walked out of the hall. The hunter stayed where he was, uncertain of what to do now. He glanced at a group of people behind him, where a woman was on her knees, her cries filling the hall.

Sven looked at the man. 'Go to your family. Eat and drink and remember those who died, Geir Halsteinson.'

The hunter nodded and went towards his family as Oleg leaned closer. 'That is a mighty gift. The warriors might not be pleased.'

Sven glanced at his former hirdman. 'The warriors don't have to give anything up. I'm only giving my share of the plunder. And besides, the warriors will have plenty of opportunities to get more plunder if they survive the storm that is coming.' And Sven knew a storm was coming. He could feel it in the ache in his joints. A storm was coming, and they were all going to drown in it.

16

Charles rushed to help the dazed Father Leofdag after his grandfather had gone into the hall, ignoring his own stinging cheek. The priest was bleeding from his nose and Charles knew from experience that soon his eyes would be blue and swollen. The crowd that had gathered still stood there, too shocked to get back to their lives as they discussed what Sven had said. Charles's forehead wrinkled as he tried to make sense of what had just happened and what it meant for him. If his grandfather left Ribe, would Charles have to stay here in Ribe with Thora? Would she stay or leave as well? He turned to where Thora was helping her cousin pick Haldor up off the ground. The man's face was covered in blood and his eyes struggled to focus as he stared around him. Charles knew Haldor was lucky to be alive. He had learnt that his grandfather did not care about killing people. He did not care about giving in to the devil inside him.

'Let go of him! This is your fault! By Frigg, we should never have let you into our home!' Thora's cousin shouted at her. Thora took a step back and raised her hands. 'You and that boy have been nothing but bad luck!'

'Audhild?'

'No.' Thora's cousin stopped her from saying anything. 'I should have listened to my husband. He was right about that boy!'

'Your husband has always been a fool and always will be!' Ingvild glared at her daughter. 'What happened here has nothing to do with Thora or the boy.' The old lady spat on the ground. 'By the gods, only Haldor would think it's a good idea to strike the grandson of Sven.'

Audhild shook her head. 'Haldor is a good man. He just wasn't thinking. He is drunk!'

'Aye, that is the problem.' The old lady jabbed a finger at the dazed Haldor, who was leaning on his smaller wife. 'The bastard never thinks and is always drunk. And now Sven is going to stop providing us with extra food and money. By Frigg, Audhild. I told you not to marry this oaf!' Ingvild turned to Thora and shook her head. 'Forgive my daughter. She's as dumb as my husband was and for some reason only the gods can understand, she loves this man. I'll prepare your belongings for you to collect when you are ready.' She then looked at Charles and smiled at him. 'You better make sure you eat, boy. You're too thin for this world.'

Charles could only nod as the old lady turned and walked away, leaving her daughter struggling to support her drunk husband. Jorlaug appeared with red eyes and a snotty nose, and almost gave him a fright when she spoke. But unlike before, she didn't seem to take pleasure from it.

'I'm sorry.'

'It's not your fault.' He rubbed his cheek where it was burning. The blow had been hard, and he knew he would have a large bruise by the time he next woke up. But then, Charles was used to having a bruised face.

'Where will you stay now?' she asked him, her eyes fixed on her parents.

Charles looked at the hall and had to suppress the shiver which ran down his spine. The memory of him stabbing the Frank came to his mind and Charles rubbed the small cross around his neck. 'In the hall.' He was about to look at Jorlaug when he noticed Guttrom was still sitting on his horse, staring at him with his eyebrows drawn together. Charles wondered about that as the old warrior turned his horse and walked away. He also wondered who the other man was, the one with his hands tied together.

'You must be happy about that,' Jorlaug said. 'You get to be with the warriors.'

Charles shook his head, his eyes still on the new warrior. He did not tell her that the hall was the last place he wanted to be or why. And it was not just because of the memory of what had happened that night. Instead, he looked at the Bible, still on the ground, open on the page where the line had caught his attention.

Be alert and of sober mind. Your enemy the devil prowls around like a roaring lion looking for someone to devour.

Charles frowned as he wondered if it was a message from God and what it meant. He glanced at Father Leofdag, thinking to ask him, when he saw the priest was also staring at him, his face dark.

'Jorlaug, why don't you run home? Your mother has enough to worry about,' Thora said and then looked at Charles as Jorlaug nodded and ran after her parents. 'Come, let's get your priest friend inside.'

Father Leofdag was leaning against the wall, his head in his hands now as if he was in pain. Charles guessed Father Leofdag must have been, but frowned as he thought of how the priest was looking at him only moments ago. He decided he must have been imagining things. 'Do we have to stay in the hall?'

Thora sighed. 'The gods know I know you don't want to, but we have nowhere else to stay.'

Charles looked at the hall and saw Rollo walk out of the building, his face turning as if he was looking for someone. Rollo was as dirty as his grandfather was. His brynja was stained with dried blood and his face covered with dirt. It looked like they had no time to clean themselves after whatever battle they had fought. Rollo grabbed hold of a few men and said something and Charles frowned as these men rushed to where Guttrom had taken the captive. 'Can't we stay here, with Father Leofdag?'

Thora shook her head, the stray hair blowing in the breeze. 'No, Charles. That would not be a good idea.'

'Why not?' Charles frowned.

Thora shrugged. 'Go get a bucket of water so we can get him cleaned up.'

Charles grabbed the bucket he had used to clean his face before and went down to the river. The people of Ribe stared at him as he walked past them and Charles kept his eyes on the ground, not wanting to see the look in their eyes. He was sure they were blaming him for everything that had happened in their town. Charles shook his head and wondered if the Danish Christians who lived in Ribe had to deal with the same things he had to. Or did the hatred he had to face have more to do with his grandfather than his religion?

Lost in his thoughts, Charles did not notice the group of boys blocking his path to the river and almost bumped into Sigmund.

'If it isn't the Christian?' Sigmund said, and the other boys laughed, although Charles wasn't sure why.

'Let me pass,' Charles said, scowling. He was not in the mood to deal with their taunting.

'Someone's brave now that his grandfather killed Haldor and threatened to kill everyone else,' one boy said. Charles raised his eyebrow at the brown-haired boy, who was almost a head taller than him. He didn't know the boy's name but knew he was the son of one of the warriors. As all the boys around Sigmund were. Charles thought about what Sigmund's grandmother had told him. How Sigmund had to be the way he was because of the other boys and because his father was close to Charles's grandfather.

'My grandfather did not kill Haldor,' Charles said, with a pinched expression on his face.

'And how do you know that?' Sigmund crossed his arms across his chest.

Charles shook his head. 'Because I was there. I saw him get to his feet and walk away.'

The boys glanced at each other as they tried to find a response, but then Sigmund asked, 'What happened to your face? Is that where Haldor hit you?'

Charles rubbed his cheek and felt it was swelling. 'Yes.'

Sigmund smiled an unfriendly smile. 'Well, Thor knows that when I hit you, you won't be so lucky, Christian.'

The boys behind Sigmund laughed. 'Hit him, Sigmund!'

Charles tensed and tried to remember what Thora had taught him as he saw Sigmund clench his fists.

'Oi! Leave the boy alone! Sigmund, I'll tell your father you're up to no good again!'

They all turned and stared at the blacksmith at the riverbank, waving a fist at them.

'Run!' one boy shouted, and they all fled.

'I'll get you one day, Christian,' Sigmund said before he ran after his friends. Charles shook his head and wondered why other boys always wanted to pick on him. In Hügelburg it had been because he was shorter than everyone and because his father was a Dane. Here it was because of his religion. He wondered if he would ever find a place where he would not be judged or beaten up

because of who he was or who his family was. He shook his head
and made his way to the river, unaware that the blacksmith was
walking towards him. Charles jumped when he saw the large
shadow looming over him and turned to see the man standing
there. His black hair was tied up and his beard was kept short. The
man wore trousers and a thick leather apron and was covered in
black soot from his work. He glowered at Charles as his muscles
shone with sweat. Charles's eyes darted around as he tried to find
someone who might help him, when the blacksmith smiled.

'Relax, boy. I'm not going to hurt you.' The blacksmith glanced
around and then pulled something from a small pocket at the back
of his apron. Charles frowned at the small metal cross in the man's
large hands.

'You are a Christian?' The man nodded and quickly put the
cross away. 'But why hide it?' Charles asked, and then remembered
that he had been told not to draw attention to his religion.

The blacksmith shrugged. 'All you have to worry about are the
other boys. For me and my family, things will be a lot worse if
people find out we are Christians.'

Charles nodded. He understood the man's fear. He had felt it
himself. 'But my grandfather can protect you.'

The blacksmith laughed. 'Sven the Boar? A man famed for
torturing Christians to amuse himself. I don't think so. No, we keep
our heads down. Attend the festivals and at night we pray to God,
asking him to forgive us for our weakness.'

Charles tried to think of what a priest would say in a situation
like this, but the only thing he could think of was the line he had
seen in the Bible. He had tried to not think about it, because he
wasn't sure what it meant, but he felt that whatever it was, it would
not be good. 'How...' Charles started asking, but wasn't sure what
the correct sentence would be.

The blacksmith smiled and responded, 'My wife and I are from the south, near Hedeby. We converted there and gave up the false gods. The blessed Father Ansgar baptised us himself.'

'So why are you in Ribe?'

'People in our village found out and chased us away. There might be a church in Hedeby, but the people still hate Christians.'

Charles nodded and then looked at the blacksmith with a raised eyebrow, wondering what the man wanted.

The blacksmith must have seen his confusion and then asked, 'Father Leofdag, how is he? We heard he was attacked again.'

'He's fine. Haldor hit him pretty hard, but God willing, he will recover.'

'God willing,' the blacksmith said and then looked over his shoulder. 'I need to get back to the smithy. It was good to meet you, Charles.'

'And you,' Charles said as the blacksmith walked away. He realised he had never asked the man for his name or about the other Christians in Ribe. Perhaps later he would visit the man in his smithy, Charles thought as he filled the bucket with water, before rushing back to Thora. She would wonder where he was. Charles only hoped that he didn't run into Sigmund and his friends again.

As he walked past the hall, he saw a large group leaving the building, some of them shaking their heads and others crying. He recognised the hunter who had saved them in the forest and was about to greet the man when he saw the tears in his eyes. When he reached Father Leofdag's house, he asked Thora if she knew what had happened.

'I don't know,' Thora said as she wet a cloth in the bucket Charles had brought from the river and cleaned the blood from the priest's face. Father Leofdag winced as she pressed the cloth against his broken nose.

Charles wondered if he should say anything about the black-smith. He had seen the man many times working in the smithy, his face always stern as he hammered the metal into weapons which would most likely be used to kill Christians.

'I saw the hunter who helped us in the forest,' Charles said as he watched the group walk away.

'It was his father's farm that had been attacked. They say his wife was killed trying to protect their child.'

Charles gripped the cross around his neck. 'I will pray for him,' he said without thinking. 'Where do heathens go when they die?' He remembered what Gerold had told him before, about how the souls of the heathens just roamed the forest because they didn't know about heaven, so didn't know how to get there. But he also knew that the Danish warriors believed that if they fought well and died in battle, they went to a place called Valhalla where they fought battles all day long and feasted all night long. Charles didn't understand why they would want to do that, but then he still didn't really understand the Danish people.

Thora stopped what she was doing and stared at Charles for a few heartbeats before she cleared her throat and responded, 'Those who die of old age and sickness go to Hel—'

'Where they burn in the devil's fires for all eternity,' Father Leofdag interrupted her. Charles frowned at the priest. The blood had been cleaned away, but his eyes were swelling and had red rings around them.

'No.' Thora shook her head and stepped away from the priest. 'There are no fires in Hel. Unlike your hell, people don't go there as a punishment.' Thora glanced at the warriors who were lounging outside the hall. 'Although, if you ask the warriors, they think it is.'

'So what happens in your Hel?' Charles scratched his head and tried to ignore the look Father Leofdag was giving him.

'Why are you so curious about the ways of the heathens?' Father Leofdag asked, not noticing the glare from Thora.

Charles shrugged. 'I'm just curious. Maybe it will be easier to convert them if we try to understand their ways.' This was not something Charles had ever felt before, but since he had been in Ribe, he had been struck by how similar the people of Denmark were to the people of Francia.

'We do not need to understand them. They need to give up their false gods and follow the light of the one true God!' Leofdag intoned, puffing his chest out.

Thora sighed and shook her head. 'That is the reason the Danes hate you Christians. You always think you are better than us. Perhaps you should remember why you are still alive.'

'I'm alive because God protected me.'

'No, you are alive because a boy of nine winters tried to defend you while you were cowering behind your book.' Leofdag recoiled from the words as if Thora had struck him and he gaped at her as he struggled to find a response. Thora dropped the cloth she had been using to clean the priest's face and said, 'I've done enough. I need to get our things and move them to the hall. Charles, you stay with your priest friend. Keep him safe from the townspeople.'

Father Leofdag's cheeks turned red as he watched Thora storm off. 'I think I might have upset her.'

'You did,' Charles agreed. 'You should apologise.'

The priest nodded. 'Yes, you are right, I should.'

Charles thought about what Thora had said and what had happened before. 'Why didn't you defend yourself?'

'I am a priest, young man, not a warrior.'

'But you must have realised that when you came to Denmark, they might try to kill you.' Charles scratched his head.

Father Leofdag smiled. 'No, I believe that God will keep me safe. Your friend was right. It was you who stopped that man from killing me, but then who sent you to do it? And how did your grandfather know when to arrive to protect you?'

Charles thought about what Leofdag had said and found he

agreed with the priest. He had felt the same in the past, after all. His grandfather would say that it was because of the Norns that he had arrived when he did, but the Norns weren't real, so it had to be because of God. But then Charles frowned as he thought of something else his grandfather had said. 'But what happens when there is nobody to protect you?'

Father Leofdag smiled. 'Then I will gladly martyr myself in the name of God. Priests do not fight, Charles. We spread the word of God, not death.' The priest stood up and had to reach out for Charles as he was unbalanced. 'Come, let's read the Bible and pray. We should thank the Almighty for coming to our aid.'

Charles thought of the hunter whose wife had been killed. There was no one to protect them when their farm had been attacked. He then looked at Father Leofdag as the priest wiped the dust from the Bible. Charles wanted to be a priest more than anything, but was he really prepared to turn the other cheek as God commanded him to?

17

Sven drank his ale as he watched the warriors in the hall celebrating their victory. After compensating Geir, the hunter, for his loss, Sven had ordered a feast be prepared for the warriors who had fought the day before and then gone to the bathhouse and cleaned himself of all the dirt and dried blood. He had shaved his head and braided his beard, but that had still not improved his mood. It was still early in the evening and the warriors had finished their evening meal of pottage, beef and pork roasted over the hearth fire and fish from the river, as well as vegetables, like carrots, parsnips and cabbage, berries and freshly baked bread, and were now sitting in groups and talking to each other. Occasionally, one warrior would laugh and others would join in. Sven remembered the conversations he had in the past with Arnbjorg and Thora's father. How they would sit together, like these warriors, and tell stories of battles and the gods. Bjarni had sat with them as well, as had other men whose faces haunted Sven's dreams. He had never thought that he would outlive any of them, yet here he was, sitting by himself and watching as the younger warriors enjoyed themselves. Although he wasn't really alone. Alfhild hovered nearby, her eyes constantly flicking towards him to see if he needed anything. Sven still struggled to understand what she wanted, but he had more important things to worry about. Guttrom.

The nephew of Horik was with his men in the house that Sven had provided to them, one of the larger ones in Ribe, but even though he was out of sight, he was not out of mind. But it wasn't Guttrom that concerned him, although Sven was curious about where his son had gone. He would have thought that Guttrom would want his son with him during the battle, but before they had set off, Guttrom had sent his son and a few men away. Guttrom had told him it was to deliver a message to another jarl who had sided with Guttrom, but Sven wasn't sure if he believed him. He knew the man was up to something, even if he didn't know what that something was. And he knew Oleg was part of that something. He took another swig of his ale and wondered if Oleg would make a move to become jarl if Guttrom won this battle. He had seen the glint in the man's eyes when they spoke of it earlier. But Sven did not think his former hirdman would make a good jarl. Oleg could only ever follow, never lead. Sven believed Rollo would make a good jarl, though. He had his father's strength and his mother's shrewdness. Not only that, Rollo understood the people of Ribe and was liked by them. Sven had also seen how he led in battle and how others, even the more experienced warriors, paid attention when he spoke. Sven took another swig of his ale and then realised his cup was empty. Alfhild noticed as well as she appeared by his side to take the cup. But Sven did not let go of the cup. Instead, he gripped it and stared at the young thrall. Her dark eyes showed no fear, which only intrigued Sven even more.

'Where are you from, Alfhild?'

Alfhild's eyes widened, and she let go of the cup. 'From... from Norway, a small town in the east.'

Sven nodded. 'And how did you get here?'

'Your brother raided my town and took me and my sisters when we were still young.' Alfhild wrapped her arm around herself and looked away.

'Where are your sisters now?'

Alfhild shrugged. 'One of them died. A warrior killed her after he had his fun with her. The other, I don't know. She was sold at the market.' It did not surprise Sven to hear that. Ribe had a small thrall market, although the thrall traders had stayed away since he had returned. Sven didn't understand why. He had made many of them rich men in the past.

'But my brother kept you?'

Again, the young thrall shrugged. 'He...'

Sven sighed and gave her the cup. 'Would you like to go home?'

Alfhild looked up, her eyes wide. 'I... I... don't know.' She glanced around the hall at the warriors laughing at the tables and the hounds lounging by the hearth fire. 'This is the only home I really know.' Sven nodded and let Alfhild go.

The men in the hall went quiet as Thora and Charles walked in and stared at the two for a moment before they went back to their conversations. Sven glanced at the door behind him where they would be sleeping. He had asked the thralls to prepare the room for them and had left Alfhild in charge of that. Sven had also bought new furs from some traders so that there was nothing to remind his grandson of what had happened that night. That had been Thora's advice, and Sven guessed it made sense. The less there was to remind Charles of what had happened, the easier it might be for him to stay there. Although Sven knew the same did not work for him. He had not been in the room to see if the thralls had done a good job, but Rollo had, and the large warrior had been satisfied by what he saw.

'Sven,' Thora said as they approached. They carried nothing with them as their belongings had already been sent to the hall by

Thora earlier on while Charles was with the priest. There wasn't much, just two small chests with their clothing and the little jewellery Thora had. Unlike many of the women in Ribe, Thora wore little of it. Only the necklace that had belonged to her mother and some brooches. She was still a warrior, even if she tried not to be. 'The room is ready?'

Sven nodded and wished Alfhild would return with his ale. He needed the strength it provided for what he had to do. Taking a deep breath, Sven got up from his chair and walked towards the room at the back of the hall. He felt the eyes of the warriors on him, even though they were pretending not to be watching. He knew that none of them understood why he did not use the sleeping quarters like he was supposed to, but none of them was brave enough to ask him. Sven put his hand on the door, feeling the rough wood on his palm, and hesitated for a heartbeat before he pushed it open. He forced a smile on to his face. 'Welcome to your new home.'

Thora walked in, but Charles hesitated. Sven understood how the boy felt and felt like a hypocrite for making the boy sleep in the room when he himself avoided it. He could sleep with the warriors in the hall, though. Thora and Charles couldn't. After taking a deep breath, just like Sven had done a few moments ago, Charles walked into the room. Sven forced himself to enter, only because he wanted to see his grandson's reaction to the surprise he had left for him.

Thora scowled as she scrutinised the room, but she seemed satisfied. And so was Sven. Fresh rushes had been laid on the ground, so the room smelt fresh and all the weapons and armour had been removed from the walls. The mattress on the bed looked comfortable and the furs Sven had bought had been laid out on the bed.

'What's that?' Charles pointed to the corner of the room where

Bjarni had kept his brynja and helmet before. In their place was a small table with a large wooden cross and some candles.

'Is that a shrine?' Thora raised an eyebrow at Sven.

Sven grunted, not sure how to respond. He was holding his breath as he waited to see how Charles would react. The boy looked at him, his eyebrow raised as well.

'Why?' Charles asked him.

Sven let go of his breath so he could answer. 'Well, I don't know if Christians have shrines in their homes like the Danes have, but I thought it would make you feel more comfortable.'

Thora smiled as Charles frowned. 'We don't. That's what the church is for.' He looked at the shrine again and then smiled at Sven. 'Thank you, grandfather.'

Sven felt his heart race in his chest and glanced at Thora as she placed her hand on his shoulder. 'Perhaps you could put your mother's cross on the shrine when you want to pray.'

Charles looked at Thora. 'Would it be safe?'

'I wouldn't leave it there during the day, but when you are in the room, it should be,' Sven responded. Charles scratched his neck and then nodded before he went to his chest and pulled the large golden cross out from under his few tunics. Again, Sven marvelled at its beauty and felt his cheeks burn when he remembered he had almost traded the cross for a jug of ale. Sven then remembered the godi and looked at Thora. 'Why don't we let the boy settle?'

Thora looked at him and must have sensed that he wanted to talk. She turned to Charles. 'Will you be all right, Charles?'

Charles looked at the spot where he had stabbed the Frank. There was no sign that that had ever happened. Sven had made sure of that. But he knew how powerful memories were. Charles nodded as he gripped the cross in his hand, as the light from the few candles danced in the large ruby.

'Good, I'll be in the hall if you need me.' Thora turned and followed Sven out of the room.

Sven saw Alfhild had returned with his ale. He took the cup from her and drank from it as he sat down on his chair.

Thora sat on the bench near him and took the cup Alfhild offered her. 'What is it?' she asked him.

Sven rubbed his forehead and glanced at the room, and wondered if his grandson was praying. He had tried to find a Bible in the market, but none of the traders claimed to sell any. Although Sven was sure they were too afraid to tell him if they did. 'I need the boy's cross tomorrow.'

Thora frowned at him. 'Why?'

Sven drank from his cup. 'I want to take it to Odinson.'

'Odinson!' Thora's eyes widened. Some warriors near them glanced their way and Sven wished Thora had not said the godi's name out so loud. 'Why in Frigg's name do you want to do that?' she hissed at him.

'Because I want to know why that cross is so important.'

Thora shook her head. 'Sven, it is just a cross. A pretty cross, but still a cross. It's nothing but gold and gems.'

Sven looked at his cup and then at Thora. 'Then why did a king of Francia kill my son for it and why are they after Charles if it is nothing but a cross?'

Thora glanced at the door behind Sven. 'They want Charles because of who his mother is, you know that.'

Sven shook his head. 'No, that is only part of it. I'm sure the sons of Louis have plenty of bastards of their own, so why is Charles so special?' Sven left the question hanging, knowing that Thora couldn't answer it. 'They want him because he has that cross.'

'The cross belonged to their grandfather. Of course they'd want it back.' Thora drank her ale, but Sven shook his head.

'They have plenty of other pretty jewels that belonged to that bastard. There is something more to that cross. I can feel it.'

Thora looked at Sven. 'You feel your age and it's messing with your head. Either that or you are letting Loki's whispers get to you.'

Sven stared at Thora. It had nothing to do with his age, and he knew she understood that. He was also sure she felt there was more to that cross; he saw it in the way she had looked at it when Charles took it from the chest. But Thora, he knew, wanted to protect Charles, and perhaps she felt the best way to do that was to forget about where that cross came from. After a while of staring at each other, Thora sighed.

'You stubborn bastard,' she muttered. 'Do you really think that old godi can tell you about that cross? By Odin, is he still even alive? The man must be as old as the gods themselves.'

Sven nodded. 'The bastard is still alive. I saw him the other day.'

Thora nodded at him. 'And you really think he can tell you anything about the cross? Most likely, he will slit your throat and take it from you.'

'No, he wouldn't. That I know. But whether he can tell me about why the cross is so special,' Sven shrugged, 'I don't know. But I need to try.'

'That cross really bothers you?' Thora tilted her head to the side.

'I see it every time I close my eyes. I know there is something more to that thing.'

Thora moved the stray hair from her face and then finished her ale. 'I'll talk to Charles, but you know he might not agree. He thinks our gods are not real, so he won't understand how a crazy old man in the forest can help you.'

'Thank you.'

Thora nodded and went to the room that she now shared with Sven's grandson. Sven looked around the hall and saw that most of the warriors were sleeping, but a few were still awake, sitting in a small group and talking to each other while glancing his way. The hearth fire was still going strong as the thralls made sure it wouldn't burn out during the night. Sven sighed and decided that he might as well try to get some sleep, although he was sure he wouldn't get much. He had too many burdens that kept him awake at night. Once again, Sven missed the days when he had been a drunk wandering around Denmark and looking for ale.

The following morning Sven sat on his chair, his fingers drumming on the armrest. Some warriors still lay where they had passed out the night before from drinking too much and there was a faint whiff of vomit in the air. But Sven ignored that as he kept glancing over his shoulder at the door behind him, finding it hard to resist the urge to storm into the room to find out if Charles would allow him to take the cross to the godi. He could just take the cross, but his relationship with Charles was already strained, and he did not want to do anything that would only turn the boy against him.

It was still dark in the hall. The hearth fire had died out during the night, but the thralls were lighting torches and getting the fire going again, and the warriors in the hall were stirring. That meant the sun was rising. The warriors would go to the training field and train before they cleaned themselves by the river and ate the breakfast that the thralls would prepare soon. Rollo would walk through the door soon so that he and Sven could train, although the large warrior would have to find someone else to train with if Charles agreed to let Sven take the cross.

The door to the sleeping quarters opened and Sven jumped to his feet, wincing at the pain the sudden movement caused in his back. Thora and Charles walked out of the room and Sven raised an eyebrow at the bundle Charles carried in his hands. His heart raced in his chest and already his mind was scrambling with all the things he needed to prepare to see the godi.

'Did you sleep well?' Sven asked when they stopped in front of him. Behind Sven, the warriors were waking up, some groaning as they stretched. They greeted each other and talked about their dreams while they got dressed. One man called for some ale and others quickly added their voices.

Charles nodded at Sven, but his eyes were on the warriors behind him. In the dim light, Sven saw the dark rings under his grandson's eyes and guessed the boy struggled to sleep as much as he did. 'Thora said you know a man who might tell us about the cross?'

Sven glanced at Thora. 'Aye. He's one of our priests. An old man wise in the ways of our gods.'

'But how will your priests know anything about this cross?' Charles lifted the bundle.

Sven shrugged. 'He might not, but I still want to ask him.'

Charles frowned. 'Why can't we just ask Father Leofdag? He's a real priest.'

Sven clenched his fists and saw the warning look Thora gave him. He still hated it when Charles rejected the existence of the gods of Asgard, especially when Sven was trying hard to accept his grandson's religion. 'Leofdag is too young to know anything about that cross. And besides, I don't know if we can trust him.'

'Why not?' Charles asked. The warriors were slowly leaving the hall as the thralls started preparing the hearth fire for the morning meal. Alfhild brought Sven a cup of ale, which he gladly took and drank from before he responded to Charles.

'Because he just appeared out of nowhere, claiming he was sent by some priest in Hedeby.' Sven shook his head. 'I don't like it.'

Charles scowled as he thought about it, and then he said, 'I want to come with you. I want to see this priest.'

'That is not a good idea, Charles. I don't know how long this will take. The man is very unpredictable,' Sven said.

'And dangerous,' Thora added.

But Charles jutted his chin out and set his jaw. 'It's my cross. And besides, God will keep me safe.'

Sven shook his head and looked to Thora for some support, but she only shrugged. 'It's his cross, Sven. I tried to get him to change his mind last night, but he's as stubborn as you.'

Sven sighed and looked at his grandson, seeing the resolution in his eyes. He realised he could not get the boy to change his mind, or at least not in a way that would not ruin their already fragile relationship. Rollo walked into the hall and greeted the few warriors that were still there before he turned his attention to Sven.

'Are you ready, Sven?' He stopped when he saw Thora and Charles. 'Good day.'

Thora nodded a greeting to the large warrior, but Charles kept staring at Sven. Sven turned to Rollo. 'No training today. There's something I need to do.'

'You want me to come with you?' Rollo asked.

'No.' Sven shook his head. 'Alvar will come. I want you to prepare the men. As soon as we get back, we leave to fight Horik.' Rollo frowned but said nothing. 'How's our guest?'

'Gunvald is fine. Still sleeping when I checked on him before coming here. I made sure he got fed last night and gave him some ale.'

Sven nodded. 'Did Guttrom talk to him?'

'The men guarding him said that no one went near the house we're keeping him in. Are you sure you don't want me to come?'

Sven looked at Charles again and sighed. 'I need you here.' He prayed to Odin that he would not regret this because he knew the old godi might decide to sacrifice his grandson to the gods. But he needed to ask him about that cross. Sven looked at Alfhild, who was hovering nearby. 'Alfhild, prepare some food for me and my grandson. We might be gone all day.'

18

Charles smiled when his grandfather agreed he could go with him. He had been unsure when Thora had told him about his grandfather's plan the previous night and had spent most of the night lying awake in the large bed staring at the cross. But that was not the only reason he could not sleep. The memory of what had happened that night kept coming to him every time he closed his eyes. And not just the image of him stabbing the Frank, but also of Gerold, the slave he had thought of as a friend, laughing at him when he revealed his treachery. He had tried to pray while Thora was speaking to his grandfather, but that hadn't helped. Even Thora's presence wasn't able to keep the memories away and so he had just lain there, staring at the cross until he eventually fell asleep. Charles was curious about the cross. He had spent many days staring at the large ruby and the symbol under it, wondering why his father had kept it hidden from him and why it was so important. That was why he wanted to go when his grandfather took the cross to the heathen priest. Charles did not believe the man was a real priest, but his curiosity had got the better of him.

He watched as the thrall left the hall and wondered how long they would be away for and where they would find this priest. He had seen no churches or temples when they had walked towards Ribe. That was another reason he wanted to go. Charles wanted to see one of their priests. Despite what Father Leofdag had said before, Charles still felt that he had to understand the heathens better if he wanted to convert them to Christianity.

'Ah, the fire is ready. That's good. Get that pot warmed up and, you, go fetch me some water!' a familiar voice said and they all turned to see Thora's aunt walking into the hall and carrying a basket in her hands.

'Aunt Ingvild, what are you doing here?' Thora asked, her eyebrows raised.

The old lady walked to the hearth fire and put the basket down. Charles saw it contained the ingredients for porridge, along with some berries. 'I came to make sure that the boy gets a good breakfast. He's too skinny.'

Rollo laughed while Sven stared at the old lady before he shook his head. 'I have enough thralls here to make sure the boy gets fed.'

The old lady looked at Charles's grandfather, her eyes fixed on his large stomach. 'By the looks of you, you'll most likely steal the boy's food. No, Frigg knows, that boy needs to fatten up.'

'Aunt Ingvild—'

'Don't Aunt Ingvild me. Are you going to help, or just stand there? Girl, where is that bucket of water I asked for?' Ingvild berated the thrall, who was standing there, stunned.

Charles's grandfather shook his head. 'Fine, I need to prepare some things for our journey. Charles, make sure you bring your knife with you.' Sven turned and left, with Rollo behind him. Charles's heart thudded hard in his chest as he thought of the knife his grandfather had given him after the warriors from Hedeby attacked them. He never liked the thing and only carried it because he was scared of his grandfather, but since he had stabbed the Frank, Charles had been unable to touch the blade.

Charles went back to the room and cleaned his face with water from the bucket left by a thrall. He glanced at the chest where his belongings were kept. He did not want to take the knife, but he knew his grandfather would be angry if he didn't. Putting the cross, still wrapped up in the cloth, in his tunic, Charles went to the chest and opened it. He dug around the few tunics and a pair of trousers he had until he found the knife at the bottom. With trembling hands, he tucked it into his belt, praying that he would not need to use it.

'Is the boy ready?' Charles heard his grandfather's voice in the hall and closed his chest.

'Ready for what?' Thora's aunt asked as Charles went to the door.

'We're going on a trip.'

'But the boy hasn't eaten yet!' Ingvild protested. Charles walked into the hall in time to see her waving her wooden spoon at his grandfather. A few young warriors were sitting in one corner of the hall, laughing as they watched.

'We'll eat along the way. We need to leave now.'

'Where are you going?' Jorlaug asked as she ran into the hall. 'And why is there a calf outside?'

Charles raised an eyebrow and wondered how Jorlaug managed to appear everywhere.

'You don't need to worry about that,' Thora said and then saw Charles. 'Take a cloak with you, Charles. You might be gone all day.'

'Where are you going?' Jorlaug asked again and then turned to Sven. 'Can I go with you?'

Sven shook his head. 'No, you can't.'

'Where are you going?' Ingvild asked as she scrutinised Charles's grandfather. 'And what's this about a calf?'

'There is a calf outside. Alvar has it tied to his horse. It's very pretty.' Jorlaug turned back to Sven. 'What's its name?'

Charles's grandfather rubbed his temples and Charles could see the old man was losing his temper. 'I'm ready, grandfather. We can go.' It surprised Charles that Jorlaug wanted to go with them, especially after what had happened. He would have thought that she wouldn't be allowed to go anywhere near him. Charles briefly wondered how her father was, but then he dismissed the thought when he remembered his swollen and blue cheek.

'But the boy needs to eat,' Ingvild tried again.

'That's what the calf is for,' Sven growled, his patience running out before he turned and left the hall.

Thora grabbed hold of Charles and handed him his cloak, her face stern. 'Listen to your grandfather and do whatever he says.' Charles wondered if he was doing the right thing. He saw Ingvild raise an eyebrow. 'And whatever you do, do not question what the godi says. He is a man even your grandfather fears.'

'Odinson,' Ingvild hissed, and Thora held a hand up to silence the old woman. She looked Charles in the eyes and Charles almost shivered at the hardness of Thora's blue eyes.

He nodded. 'Yes, Thora.'

'Good,' she said, her brow furrowing. 'Now go.'

Charles ran out of the hall and saw his grandfather and Alvar waiting for him on their horses. Unlike his grandfather, Alvar was wearing his brynja and was holding his Dane axe in his hand with his shield strapped to his back. His grandfather only wore his tunic, but had his sword and a sax-knife on him. There was another horse for him. It was smaller than the ones his grandfather and Alvar were on, but Charles still hesitated. He was not good with horses. And then there was the calf, a small brown creature with a rope tied around its neck.

'Come on, Charles. We don't have all day,' his grandfather said.

'I'm not good with horses,' Charles said as he approached the beast.

'Aye, neither am I, but walking would take too long.'

'Don't worry,' Alvar said. 'He's gentle. He won't throw you.'

Charles glanced at Alvar. He didn't really know the large warrior very well, but his grandfather trusted the man. Gripping the saddle, Charles held his breath and mounted the horse, just like his father had taught him many years before. The horse stepped forward, but other than that, did not react to Charles and he let go of the breath he had been holding, before he smiled, pleased he had not made a fool of himself. He was aware of the townspeople watching him, including Father Leofdag, who was standing outside his house, his eyes and nose swollen and blue.

'Let's go.' His grandfather turned his horse towards the main gate. Alvar winked at Charles and followed. Charles glanced at the hall and saw Thora standing there with Ingvild and Jorlaug by her side. Neither woman smiled at him, and Charles wondered why they were so concerned about a priest as he tapped the horse with his heels, gripping the reins tightly when the animal trotted after his grandfather and Alvar. They rode out of the gate in silence and Charles spotted Sigmund and his friends glaring at him while whispering stuff to each other. The boys were probably hoping he would fall off the horse.

Once away from the town, Charles finally asked, 'What is the calf for?' He looked at the animal that Alvar was pulling along and was sure it was not for them to eat.

'You'll see,' Alvar said, and Charles frowned at the smile he heard in the man's voice. They rode past the grave mounts outside the walls of Ribe and Charles kept his eyes peeled as he searched for a church where this godi lived, all the while trying to ignore the cries of the calf as it called for its mother. His grandfather took them off the road and towards the forest which was near the town.

The same forest they had walked through on their way to Ribe and where the Franks had attacked them. Charles pushed those memories out of his head as he wondered where his grandfather was taking them. He didn't remember any buildings that could have been churches in the forest, and apart from the farmsteads they had seen in the distance, he had seen no other buildings. Charles wanted to ask his grandfather, but then saw how tense the old man's shoulders were. He glanced at Alvar and saw that he too had turned serious, with his hand – which held on to the rope the calf was tied to – hovering near his sword. The calf's cries got louder as the trees grew larger and, to Charles, it seemed that he was the only one who didn't understand what was going on.

'Are you sure about this?' Alvar asked his grandfather and the uncertainty in the large warrior's voice made Charles grip the small wooden cross around his neck. He felt the weight of the large cross in his tunic, especially when Sven glanced at him.

Sven rubbed the Mjöllnir around his neck before he answered. 'Not really, but there are some questions only the gods can answer.'

Alvar scowled at Charles, no doubt trying to understand what all this was about. He did not know about the cross or who Charles's mother was, so Charles guessed that this must have been very confusing for him. He wondered then why his grandfather had not chosen Rollo to come with them.

'Let's go,' Charles's grandfather said as he nudged his horse forward. Charles's horse followed without him needing to do anything. Unlike the calf, who refused to move so Alvar had to yank hard on the rope to get the animal going. Charles did not blame it. He, too, was wondering why he had insisted on coming, especially when a raven cried out from the branches above. Charles shivered as he reminded himself that he had been through this forest before and that nothing bad had happened. Well, nothing bad if he ignored the Frankish assassins who had ambushed them.

They travelled through the forest in silence, his grandfather stopping now and then as he tried to work out which way to go. Charles tried to spot the clues Sven was using. He struggled to understand how people navigated when every tree looked the same to him. He also wanted to distract his mind from all the memories that were fighting for his attention. The air in the forest smelt the same as before, earthy and fresh, while different birds sang from the branches and flew overhead. Charles kept his eyes peeled, hoping to see some deer or perhaps a fox, but he doubted he would, not with the noise the calf was making as it kept on bleating. After a while, Charles's grandfather held a hand in the air and stopped. Charles's horse stopped behind his grandfather's, and he wondered if that was why Alvar had chosen it for him. The animal had been very calm and seemed to follow the lead of the horses in front of him without Charles having to do anything.

'We're close,' Sven said, his voice strained. He turned to Alvar, who was scanning the trees, most likely searching for the same signs Charles was. 'Alvar, you stay here. Guard the horses.' The large warrior nodded, his face grim as Sven dismounted. Charles stayed on his horse, suddenly too afraid to move. His eyes darted between the trees, but he saw nothing that showed a church was nearby. As far as he could tell, they were deep in the forest and the trees were too thick for any building to be built there.

'How do you know?' he asked his grandfather.

The old man looked at him and then glanced around the trees. 'Are you sure you want to do this? You can stay here with Alvar,' he asked instead.

Charles looked at Alvar, who smiled at him, but Charles noticed how his knuckles were white as he gripped his reins. Warriors were all the same. It didn't matter if they were Christian or heathen. They were all superstitious and believed in the supernatural more than most people, despite the fact they spent most of their time trying to show how brave they were. 'No, I want to come.' Charles tried to sound strong, but he doubted he managed to hide the tremble in his voice. His grandfather nodded and helped him off his horse.

'Come on then. Alvar, any trouble, blow your horn.' Charles only now spotted the horn Alvar had on his belt as the warrior nodded.

'How long do I wait for?'

Sven looked at the sky. The trees made it hard to see the sun, but Charles guessed it wasn't long after the morning meal. His stomach rumbled when he remembered he had missed the first meal of the day. Old Ingvild wouldn't be happy if she found out. 'If we're not back by nightfall, ride back to Ribe. Return in the morning with more men. If we are not here, then we are most likely dead.'

Charles's heart skipped, and he wanted to grip the golden cross hidden in his tunic, but remembered in time that he shouldn't. He saw his grandfather staring at him and Charles took a deep breath to calm himself before nodding at Sven to show that he was ready. Sven nodded back.

'Remember, do exactly what I say and keep your questions to yourself. Especially if you want to see tomorrow.' He took the calf from Alvar and walked through the trees.

'May Thor keep you safe, young Charles,' Alvar said. 'Because your God has no power where you are going.' Charles glanced at the warrior, expecting him to be smiling as if he was mocking him, but saw the warrior's wrinkled brow. Charles swallowed down his fear and followed his grandfather.

'Why is everyone so afraid of this godi?' Charles asked when he caught up with his grandfather. The calf had gone quiet now, which made the birds sound even louder. Especially the ravens. Charles wasn't sure if he was just imagining it, but it sounded like there were more of the large black birds. 'He's like a priest, is he not?'

'Aye, but our priests aren't like yours. The only thing they have in common is their love of shiny things.'

Charles frowned. 'What do you mean?'

His grandfather kept his eyes fixed on the path ahead of them. 'Your priests claim to protect you from evil and to guide you to your heaven.' The old man spat on the ground as he said that. 'Our priests don't care about our souls or where we go after we die. They only care about what the gods want. They'll even go out of their way to ensure that the gods get what they want.'

'Which is what?' Charles watched where he was walking, so he didn't trip over a root or a stone. He also had to resist the urge to reach out and stroke the calf his grandfather was dragging behind him. He still wasn't sure what they needed the animal for.

'Trouble. All the gods ever want is chaos, and that usually means trouble for us. That is why we are wary of our priests. Their motives aren't always clear.'

'So they never help you?' Charles almost had to shout as the noise from the ravens was getting so loud it was hard for him to hear himself. He wondered where all the birds were coming from.

'They do sometimes, but only if it's what the gods want.' Charles's grandfather stopped. 'We're here.'

Charles's breath caught in his throat as he peered around his grandfather's large midriff. There was no church or even a building. Instead, all he saw was a large ash tree in the middle of a clearing. Around the clearing was a circle of stones, each marked with a different rune, much like the ones around the sacred site outside of Hedeby. He gaped at the large ash tree which seemed to be moving as if it was alive and couldn't stop the shiver down his spine as he expected the tree to reach out and grab him. It took him a few heartbeats, though, to realise it wasn't the tree moving, and he finally understood why the ravens were so deafening. The tree was covered with the large birds, flapping their wings and screaming at each other. With wide eyes, Charles stared at the different bones which hung from the branches, all of them different sizes and a few with some meat still stuck to the bones. Charles glanced at his grandfather, feeling his stomach turn as the stench of death reached his nose. He was surprised to see his grandfather gripping the Mjöllnir around his neck and the old man's creased forehead. Charles wanted to grab hold of his cross, but then remembered what Alvar had said. Charles refused to believe that God had no power here, so he crossed himself. For a moment, he wondered if this was the gateway to hell. But there were no flames and Charles was sure the entrance to hell would have fires burning nearby.

'Stay here,' Sven said as he led the calf to the large tree. Charles felt his skin crawl and glanced around the clearing. It felt like someone or something was watching him, but he saw nothing but the trees and more ravens than he could count. He knew ravens were important to Odin, but surely Odin did not need so many of the frightening birds.

His grandfather stopped by the large ash tree and all the ravens went quiet as if they were waiting to see what Sven was going to do. The calf, which had been silent before, started bleating as if it knew what was about to happen, and the ravens went wild with anticipation. Charles trembled at the sight and gasped as his grandfather took the sax-knife from his belt and, without a word, slit the calf's throat open. The old man held on to the calf as its lifeblood sprayed the bark of the ash tree. The ravens' cries were deafening, and Charles had to cover his ears. He wanted to turn and run and it was only his grandfather's eyes on his that stopped him from doing that. He now realised that Alvar had been right. God had no power in this clearing. Even all of His angels could not disperse the ravens from this place.

After what felt like a lifetime, his grandfather finally let go of the animal and its lifeless body just collapsed on the ground. Charles expected the ravens to flock to the corpse and devour it, but to his surprise, they stayed in the tree and called to each other as they all stared at the dead calf.

'Come here, Charles.'

Charles widened his eyes at his grandfather as the old man beckoned to him. He looked at the stones which surrounded the clearing and hesitated as he realised he did not want to step past them. On this side of the stone ring, he felt safe. God could still protect him, he was sure of that. Inside the clearing, he wasn't so sure.

'You need to be strong now, boy. We need to wait by the tree or he won't come.'

Charles looked at the large ash tree, its trunk red with the fresh blood of the calf, its branches filled with bones of dead animals, or so he hoped, and ravens. His legs felt weak, and his bladder suddenly full. Charles was afraid of pissing himself again, and then he looked at his grandfather. But instead of seeing anger in the old man's eyes at his fear, he saw his grandfather waiting for him with his hand stretched out.

'Come, Charles. There's nothing to fear. Just do what I say. Come to me.' There was no urgency in Sven's voice, only understanding.

Charles swallowed and closed his eyes as he took the first step into the clearing. He was not sure what he had expected to happen as he stood there for a few heartbeats, but when he opened his eyes, he saw his grandfather smiling at him. Finding some courage, Charles walked towards Sven and resisted the urge to look at the dead calf or the ravens in the tree.

'Good lad,' Sven said as Charles reached him. He put a hand on Charles's shoulder, which Charles found strangely comforting. He knew his grandfather was not a good man, a heathen feared by many Christians. But Charles also knew that his grandfather would not allow anyone to harm him.

'Now what?' Charles asked as his hand went to the golden cross hidden in his tunic.

His grandfather glanced around the clearing, his eyes briefly pausing on one spot before he looked at Charles. 'Now we wait.'

Sven crinkled his nose at the stench of death that surrounded the clearing as his eyes wandered over the branches of the large tree. He wondered why the old godi insisted on tying the bones to the branches and decided it must have been to keep the ravens here. There were more birds than Sven could count, and that only added to the sense of trepidation about the area. And that was what the godi wanted. He wanted people to be afraid when they came here looking for him. That way, they wouldn't notice that he was nothing but an old man. An old man Sven himself had chased out of Ribe when he first became jarl many winters ago.

'What is so special about this tree?' Charles asked.

Sven looked at his grandson. The swelling had increased and half of Charles's face was blue. Sven ground his teeth and tried to ignore the voice that was telling him he should have killed Haldor for striking Charles. He glanced at the tree behind him, seeing the trunk darkened by many offerings, like the one he had just made. 'Some say it is Yggdrasil, the great tree that holds the nine realms together.' Sven could almost smile at the frown on Charles's face and knew what the boy was thinking. *That the great tree wasn't real.*

'Is it really?' Charles asked instead, surprising Sven, who could only shrug.

'I don't know, but I know of at least three other such trees in Denmark and one in Norway. So probably not, but that's what people like to think.'

'Where is Norway?'

Sven scratched his head. 'To the north. The people there are much like us. We follow the same gods and live the same way. Vicious bastards, the Norse. Their land is mostly mountains, so they have to fight for every scrap of land there is. Even their farmers are deadly warriors.'

'More deadly than you?' His grandson tried to smile, but Sven saw it was forced. He knew the boy didn't like that side of him. Sven didn't either, not any more.

'Aye. I wouldn't want to fight a Norseman. Better to fight with them.'

'Have you fought with them?' Charles kept his eyes on Sven, and Sven wondered if it was to avoid looking at the dead calf behind them or the bones and ravens in the tree above them.

'A few times, aye. We would join forces with the Norse and go raiding together. We Danes are better sailors, though.' Sven winked at Charles, but he was sure the boy didn't understand why that was so important to them.

Charles nodded and they fell into silence again. Sven wondered why the old bastard was making them wait so long. He glanced at the sky and guessed it was past midday as he rolled his shoulder to loosen the joint. He was too old to sit like this. His back was on fire, his legs stiff, and he couldn't feel his backside any more. Sven knew he was going to struggle to stand and cursed the godi. The bastard knew they were here. He saw the movement in the trees after he had killed the calf. But Sven knew this was part of the test. The godi would make them wait. That was his way of judging how important the issues they were bringing to him were. Sven's stomach rumbled, and he wished they had eaten before they left, or at least brought the bag of food Alfhild had prepared with them to the clearing. But Sven had been so distracted with trying to remember his way to the clearing that he had forgotten to take the bag. He glanced at his grandson and realised the boy was hungry as well from the way he was holding his stomach.

'Why do people think this tree is Yggdrasil?' Charles asked after a while.

Sven shrugged. 'Most likely because it is old and because the godi told them it was.'

'The tree is not Yggdrasil,' an old voice shouted from behind the trees, startling both Sven and his grandson. Sven scanned the trees around the clearing and heard Charles gasp as an old, stooped figure dressed in nothing but a tattered deer hide walked out of the shadows of the trees. The man had no hair on his head apart from the long grey beard that came to his knees, but only because he was bent over from age. Just like the tree branches above them, the old godi's beard was filled with small bones, and Sven was almost surprised not to see ravens on the bastard's shoulders. 'I said the tree is one branch of the great tree, just like the others you mentioned. It's far too small to be Yggdrasil, you dumb pig.'

'So you were there all along, listening to us?' Sven clenched his fist. If his body would let him, he would have launched himself at the godi for making them wait so long.

The godi smiled, revealing blackened gums and no teeth. Sven felt his grandson tense beside him and glanced at his pale face. The boy might not have believed in the Aesir and Vanir, but the godi was something he could not dismiss. 'You bring me a Christian.' The godi's smile broadened. 'It's been a long time since I got to sacrifice a Christian.' The man hobbled towards Charles, but Sven did not move. He sensed there was someone else in the trees, most likely aiming an arrow at Sven.

'How... how do y... you know I'm a Christian?' Charles asked, his voice trembling with fear.

The old godi stopped close to the boy, who recoiled at his stench, and sniffed the air. Even Sven had to breathe through his mouth as the godi reeked more than the tree behind them. 'I could smell you long before you came to my clearing. The gods are not pleased that you are here. That's why the ravens make so much noise.' The godi pointed a bony finger at the ravens in the trees as they started crowing again.

Charles stiffened at this, and Sven thought the boy was about to faint. He shook his head and said, 'He can see the cross you've been gripping since he walked into the clearing.' Charles glanced at the small cross in his hand, seeing the marks it had left in his palm, and then at the godi, but the fear was still on his face. 'And you can tell whoever is hiding in the trees, they can come out now. If I wanted you dead, then I would have killed you a long time ago.'

The godi straightened as much as he could and waved his staff in the air while smiling at Sven. 'Very observant you are, Sven the Boar.' Sven grunted but said nothing as a young man walked out of the trees with a bow in his hands. Like the godi, the young man had no hair on his head and he had a beard, although his was not nearly as long as the godi's. His face and head were also covered in tattoos of different animals and patterns.

'Who is he?' Sven asked.

The godi sat down and readjusted his cloak as he made himself comfortable. 'A stray I picked up.'

'You didn't send him to the gods?' Sven watched as the man put his bow down and broke some branches from the trees. Ravens took to the sky, screaming at him, but the young man ignored them as he prepared to make a fire. Sven glanced at Charles, who was staring at the godi, his hand still gripping the wooden cross.

'No, he is special. Perhaps he will take my place one day.' The godi stroked his beard and returned Charles's stare. 'Now you tell me, Sven the Boar. Why do you bring your grandson to me?'

Sven arched his eyebrows and heard Charles gasp beside him. 'How do you know he is my grandson?'

'The same way I know where you were while you wandered drunk around the lands of the Aesir and the Vanir. The same way I know you killed your brother after your eyes were finally opened to his betrayal. And the same way I know that Horik almost dropped dead when he heard of your return and your new alliance with his nephew.' Sven glared at the man, but the godi kept his eyes on Charles. Near them, the young man had started a small fire and was busy gutting the calf. The smell of the beast's insides made Charles go pale, and Sven hoped the boy wouldn't empty his guts. But Charles swallowed and did his best not to stare at the young man.

'You are well informed for an old man who spends his time amongst the trees of this forest,' Sven said, his voice almost a growl. He did not like the fact that the godi knew so much, even if that was the very reason he had come to the man.

The godi smiled at him. 'I have many ears everywhere who listen and many mouths that whisper things to me. You know that better than most, Sven the Boar.'

Sven grunted. He looked at his grandson and was glad that the boy was holding himself together. 'Perhaps then you can tell me why the king of West Francia wants my grandson?'

The godi sighed. 'That information I do not have.'

'I thought you knew everything.'

The godi looked at Sven, the smile from his mouth faltering. 'Small wings can only fly so far, Sven the Boar.'

Sven glanced at the ravens in the tree. The birds had gone silent as they watched the young man skinning the calf. 'These have large wings.'

The godi also looked at the ravens and smiled. 'Aye, but you can't trust ravens.'

'Odin does.' Sven smiled at the twitch he saw in the corner of the godi's mouth.

'The frenzied one is just like them, that's why. Besides, he chose the wisest two of all the ravens. These,' the godi waved a hand in the air, 'are as smart as you and as likely to miss the obvious right in front of them.' This time it was Sven's mouth that twitched, and the two men sat there and glared at each other. 'Now, tell me, Sven the Boar. Why do you seek me out again?'

'Again?' Charles asked, and Sven winced, wishing the boy had stayed silent as the godi looked at him.

'Who do you think gave him that tattoo on his head, little piglet?'

Sven saw how Charles tensed out of the corner of his eye before he said, 'You claimed it would allow Odin to see me and to protect me. That it marked me as one of his warriors.' He resisted the urge to rub the raven tattoo on his head and wondered if the birds in the tree recognised themselves in it.

The godi laughed: a short, cruel bark. 'I said nothing about protection. You made a deal with the All-Father, Sven the Boar, and you know better than most that nothing comes for free, especially not when the gods are involved.'

Sven felt the growl in the back of his throat as he clenched his fist. The young man stopped what he was doing and watched Sven as if he knew what Sven was thinking. He also sensed his grandson's eyes on his as his heart thudded in his chest.

'What deal?' Charles asked. Sven wished he hadn't.

'After your grandfather became jarl, he came to me. He wanted to be a mighty jarl and wanted Odin's help.' The godi glared at Sven. 'But he was not prepared to pay the price.'

'Enough, uncle!' Sven said, and regretted it.

'Uncle?' Charles asked, and the godi's smile grew even more.

'Aye, there is much to learn, young piglet. Many things your grandfather has not told you about.'

Sven's heart skipped a beat, and he wondered if the old bastard knew the truth about Charles's mother. But that was impossible. Only he and Thora knew that Charles's mother was still alive.

'What does he mean, grandfather?' Charles frowned at him.

Sven cursed the godi and wished he had killed the bastard a long time ago. But he had been told not to, been warned that the gods would punish him by making him wander around Midgard as a *draugr*, unable to go to Valhalla or Hel. But Sven had spent many winters doing that, anyway. He gritted his teeth and then remembered why he had come to the godi. He held his hand out to Charles. 'Give me the cross.'

Charles hesitated and, when he realised Sven was not going to answer his question, he took the bundle out from where he hid it in his tunic. As he unwrapped it, Sven saw the godi's old eyes light up at the sight of the beautiful cross with the gems around its edge and the large ruby in the centre.

'So that is why you come to me.' The godi licked his lips as Sven handed him the cross. Even the ravens seemed to stare at it as the godi held it up so the dimming light in the clearing could catch the ruby, making it burn like the flames the young man was cooking the calf on.

'That is why my son was killed and why the kings of Francia are after my grandson. I want to know what is so special about it.'

The godi studied the cross, turning it around and watching as the light caught the different coloured gems. 'It belonged to Charlemagne,' the godi said.

'How do you know?' Charles asked, almost leaning forward.

The godi glanced at him. 'I recognise his symbol, but there is something else.'

'What?' Sven and Charles asked at the same time.

The godi did not respond. He turned the cross around and stared at the back of it. Sven wondered what the man saw as the godi sniffed the back of the cross. His eyes darted towards the large tree behind Sven, but Sven struggled to read them. He frowned as the godi licked the spot he had sniffed moments ago, his eyes still fixed on the old ash tree. The godi turned the cross around and hummed before he placed the cross on the ground in front of him. The old man locked his bony fingers together and closed his eyes as Sven and Charles waited.

Charles was about to say something, but Sven held his hand up to silence the boy. He wasn't sure what the godi was doing, but knew it was better not to interrupt the bastard. They did not have to wait long though as the godi opened his eyes and stared at Sven. Sven felt the shiver run down his spine at the hardness in the godi's eyes. 'What?'

'If I were you, Sven the Boar, then I would take this cross to the edge of Midgard and throw it into the seas where Jörmungandr can swallow it.'

Sven frowned and saw his grandson do the same. 'Why?'

The godi glanced at the cross as the smell of the calf being cooked reached Sven's nostrils, overpowering all the other scents and making his stomach rumble. 'I sense something old about this cross, something dark.'

'But it's just a cross,' Charles said and looked at Sven.

The godi stroked his long beard. 'It was just a cross once, but something was added to it. Something older than our gods, but...' The godi frowned. 'There's something about it that makes me think of Týr.'

'Týr?' Sven raised an eyebrow. 'Why Týr?'

'Long ago, Týr was the king of the gods, the ruler of these lands. And then Odin replaced him.'

Sven scratched his head. 'But Odin is Týr's father?'

The godi shrugged. 'The gods are strange, Sven the Boar. You know this.'

Sven nodded and looked at the cross. 'What was added to it?'

The godi followed his gaze. 'That, I cannot tell. Not without throwing it in the fire and melting the gold away.'

'No!' Charles said, and the godi smiled.

'I didn't think so. But I tell you this, Sven, even if you never heeded my warnings before, pay attention to what I tell you now. No good will come from this cross.'

Sven scowled at the godi, whose words only added to the concerns that already kept him awake at night. He picked up the cross from the ground and frowned when he saw what the godi had seen. On the back of the cross, there was a patch that differed from the rest of the cross. As if a hole had been made and sealed up again. He wondered what had been put in there that had made the godi nervous. And who put it there? Could it have been Charlemagne? Sven sensed Charles staring at the cross and so he handed it back to the boy. Charles also studied the back of the cross.

'We should go,' Sven said.

The godi raised his brows. 'You'll not share a meal with me? The calf should be ready soon.'

Sven glanced at where the young man was cooking chunks of meat he had cut from the calf over the flames, which sizzled as the fat dripped into them. He resisted the urge to lick his lips and heard Charles's stomach beside him. But then Sven looked at the tree filled with ravens and death. Odin's tree. He shook his head. 'No, we need to get back. I have a battle to prepare for.'

'Ah, the fight against the king of Denmark.'

Sven frowned, again wondering how the old man knew so much. He thought of Gerold then, the thrall who had worked with the Franks. Charles had told him that Gerold had actually been a spy and Sven wondered if the old godi got all his information from the thralls in Ribe. 'Aye.' Sven stood up and grimaced at the pain in his joints and back, and cursed his age. 'Come, Charles.'

Before he left the clearing, the godi said, 'You know the cuckoo mother will lay her eggs in the nest of other birds so they can be raised.'

Sven stopped and stared at the old man, his brow furrowed. 'What are you saying?'

The godi stared at him for a short while and then said, 'You have a cuckoo in your nest, nephew. And just like the cuckoo chick kicks the hatchlings of its host out of the nest, this cuckoo will kick you out of yours.'

'And who is this cuckoo?'

'Open your eyes, Sven the Boar. See the obvious.'

Sven grunted and wondered why he had thought the godi would actually answer the question. He turned and led his grandson away from the clearing as the ravens screamed at them.

Charles was still staring at his cross, but then he looked up. 'You called him uncle, and he called you nephew?'

Sven sighed. He knew the boy would have picked up on that. 'Aye. He is my uncle, although few know that. Perhaps only a few of the grey beards and I want to keep it that way.'

'Then why is he called Odinson?'

Sven shrugged. 'Because the bastard thinks he is the son of Odin.'

'But he's not.'

'No. He's the first son of my grandfather, but he was born to a thrall long before my father was born. They say he could speak to the gods as soon as he came out of his mother. The people of Ribe worshipped him. They thought that if they kept him happy, then the gods would reward them.'

'Then why does he live in the forest?'

'Because I chased him out of Ribe.'

'Why?'

Sven sighed as he remembered the past. 'You heard what he said about giving me my tattoo?' Charles nodded, and Sven continued. 'After your father was taken, I was angry with him and the gods. I'd believed Odin was with me. I was wrong, and I blamed the godi for it. He was very close to my father and never agreed with what I had done. So I banished him from Ribe and sent him to the forest.'

'Why?'

Sven looked at his grandson. 'Because I couldn't kill him and I hoped the forest would.'

Charles nodded. 'Thora said you were scared of him.'

Sven glanced at his grandson. 'I don't fear him. I fear what he knows.'

Charles frowned. 'What does he know?'

Sven sighed. 'Everything.'

20

Charles's stomach growled as they entered Ribe. The sun was setting which meant most people would be going to sleep now and Charles was starving. His grandfather glanced at him, but there was nothing Charles could do about it. He had been glad when his grandfather had decided to leave the clearing, but Charles had to admit, it would have been nice to eat some of the meat the heathen priest had been preparing. Although, he wasn't sure if he would have been able to eat it, not with the stench of death and the ravens frightening him. The godi had frightened him as well, especially with his black gums and face covered in tattoos. The young man who had been with the godi had been strange as well. He had said nothing and never looked their way. Charles wondered why anyone would want to live with the godi.

'You didn't feed the boy, did you? By Frigg, he looks even thinner now!' Ingvild berated Sven as they reached the hall and dismounted. Oda, Rollo's mother, was also there, which surprised Charles, but he was glad to see the smile on Thora's face. He wished she had been there when they spoke to the godi. He might have been less frightened.

Charles's grandfather ignored Ingvild as he walked past her into the hall, demanding ale, which Alfhild rushed to fetch for him.

'How was it?' Thora asked him.

Charles scratched his head and thought of the old tree filled with ravens. He could still hear their cries, even here. 'Strange.'

'The boy needs to eat,' Ingvild said.

'Leave the boy alone! He'll eat when he is hungry,' Oda scolded Ingvild and the two old women scowled at each other. Charles wanted to eat. He was starving, but he said nothing as he followed Thora into the hall.

'You want to talk about it?' Thora asked, but Charles shook his head. He wanted to, but he didn't know what to say. He couldn't believe what the godi had said, because to believe he would have to admit that the Norse gods were real. And they weren't, which meant that nothing the godi had said was true. Yet the knot in his stomach told Charles it was. Like there was more to the cross than the gems and the ruby. He knew his grandfather and Thora believed his father had been killed because of the cross. That the kings of Francia wanted the cross more than him, although Charles still didn't understand why they wanted either. Again, he wondered who his mother really was. His grandfather had told him she had been a maid who had stolen the cross from King Louis, but Charles wasn't so sure any more. Charles yawned, exhausted by the thoughts he struggled to understand.

Thora must have noticed because she said, 'You go sleep. I need to talk to your grandfather. There is a bucket of water in the room. Clean your face before getting into bed. And there's some bread if you are hungry.'

Charles nodded and went to the room. As he opened the door, the candle fluttered and Charles screamed. In the blink of an eye, Thora was behind him with a sax-knife in her hand.

'What is it?' Sven shouted as the rest of the warriors in the hall jumped to their feet, their hands going for their weapons.

Charles stared wide-eyed at the corner of the room where he thought he had seen the godi, with his black face markings and white eyes. 'I...' He turned and saw Thora frowning at him.

'What is it, Charles?'

'The boy's jumping at shadows,' one warrior said, and the others laughed. But the laughter quickly died and Charles guessed it was because his grandfather was glaring at the men.

'Charles?' Thora asked again, her hand on his shoulder.

His heart still racing, he looked at the corner and shook his head. 'Nothing, the man is right. The shadow frightened me.' His cheeks burnt but he was sure the godi was there when the candle-light fluttered. Thora walked into the room and checked the corner. Satisfied there was nothing there, she walked back to the door where Charles stood.

'You want to sit with me and your grandfather?'

Charles shook his head and forced himself into the room. He wondered how he was going to sleep now. The room was already filled with nightmares and now he saw the heathen priest in the shadows. Behind him, the hall hummed as the warriors continued their conversations and Charles tried to take comfort in their presence. He went to the bucket and wet the cloth lying next to it before wiping the dirt from his face. When that was done, Charles went to the corner where his grandfather had made him a small shrine. He knew Christians didn't have shrines, they went to churches, but he still appreciated what his grandfather had done for him. It also gave Charles the confidence that he could convert his grandfather.

Charles took the golden cross out of his tunic and unwrapped the cloth around it. He turned it around and looked at the back of the cross. He was surprised he had never noticed the spot that was different from the rest of the cross, but then he had only ever looked at the front of it. Again, he wondered if what the godi had said could be true. Charles shook his head and berated himself for his foolishness. It couldn't be true. There must have been another reason for the patch on the back of the cross. He took the small wooden cross off the podium and replaced it with his mother's cross before he sat on his knees in front of it. Clasping his hands in front of him, Charles closed his eyes and was about to pray when the image of the tree in the clearing flashed in his mind. Charles almost jumped back and stared around the room as his heart raced in his chest again.

'This is a test. The devil will not lure me away from the light of God.' Charles closed his eyes again and whispered the lines of the compline, the night prayer which was said before going to sleep, but he struggled to keep the image of the tree out of his mind. When the last lines of the prayer were said, Charles added a few personal lines, asking God to keep him and Thora safe and to help his grandfather see the light and forsake his false gods. Satisfied, Charles changed out of his dirty clothes and put his sleeping clothes on before he ate the day-old bread and got under the furs that kept him warm at night. He lay there, staring at the spot where he had stabbed the Frank, the memory of that as clear as if it had happened that day. But that frightened him less than the corner of the room, the one where he thought he had seen the godi. Charles lay in bed, not sure for how long, but at one point Thora came into the room and got in the bed. The bed was large enough for the two of them to sleep in it together, but still feel like they had their own beds. But it was only when he knew she was there that Charles felt safe enough to close his eyes and fall asleep. But his dreams were filled with dying men and a giant tree, its branches moving like arms, covered with thousands of ravens. A small figure sat under the tree, its thin shoulders shaking as it laughed at the surrounding death.

The next day, Charles sat in the hall, yawning while he ate the porridge that Ingvild had made for him. She had arrived early again, but this time would not let Charles leave the hall until he had eaten something. Thora had not been happy, and neither had his grandfather. They wanted Charles to train, but he was glad to miss the training session. Not that he had got off lightly though, as his grandfather had decided that seeing as he could not train, then he could help Alfhild clean and prepare his armour. So the entire morning, Charles and Alfhild had sat in the corner of the hall, cleaning his grandfather's brynja and helmet. It had not been easy. There was a lot of dried blood between the links of his brynja and Charles's fingers hurt from trying to scrub the chain mail vest clean. His arms felt heavier than when he trained with Thora, and Charles struggled to grip his spoon, which only made Rollo laugh.

'It'll give you big, powerful arms,' the large warrior said, as he sat on a bench next to Sven. Rollo and Alvar took turns guarding his grandfather unless they had a visitor. Then both men would stand on either side of Sven's chair, dressed in their war gear and weapons ready. But today Rollo was there to help prepare for the battle.

But that task was done and both Sven's brynja and helmet shone brightly. His axe had been cleaned and sharpened as well and Charles had marvelled at the blade as he cleaned it, even as he struggled to lift it. The blade of his grandfather's Dane axe was adorned with an engraving of a boar's head, with its large tusks, and surrounded by swirls that to him looked like the waves in the sea. He had left the sword for Alfhild to clean as the weapon made him think of how the warrior from Hedeby had almost killed him with it. Charles had a small scar on his neck where the man had pressed the sharp point of the sword before his grandfather had chased him away. Although, that warrior was dead now, killed by Sven a few days later. Charles pushed the thoughts from his mind as he swal-

lowed the last of the porridge. He was about to get up when Ingvild
stopped him.

'Not so fast!' She leaned over his shoulder. 'Have you eaten
everything?'

Charles nodded, wondering why the woman fussed so much
over him. Thora had said it was because she had no grandson, only
a granddaughter, but Charles didn't understand that.

'Let the boy go, Ingvild.' His grandfather scowled at Ingvild. His
grandfather had barely left the hall that morning as he issued
commands and sent men and thralls running around. Charles had
never known that so much needed to be done before warriors left
for war. His father had been in charge of that in Hügelburg and
would often spend the night in the fort when the duke's men
prepared for a raid against the heathens to the east. Charles had
never minded though, because he would then stay at the church,
but he had never seen what his father actually had to do. But now
he was amazed as Sven, Rollo and Oleg sat together and planned
what was needed. Enough food to last the men a week, something
Charles could not imagine. Food for the horses and many other
supplies. The warriors who lived in the hall had spent the morning
cleaning their weapons and armour, many of them joking about the
upcoming battle and making fun of each other.

'Fine.' Ingvild stood back so that Charles could leave. Charles
jumped to his feet and ran out of the hall, almost bumping into
Guttrom and his son, Ivor, as they walked through the door.

'By Odin, careful, young lad.' Guttrom smiled at him. 'Like a
young boar storming towards freedom.'

'Aye, perhaps eager to get away from all us heathens.' Ivor
laughed.

'I...' Charles glanced over his shoulder and saw his grandfather
glaring at them. 'Forgive me,' Charles said and left the hall, wanting
to get away from the two men. Outside, he blinked a few times as

his eyes adjusted to the morning sun. Charles noticed the shadow over him and when he turned, he saw the raven sitting on the roof of the hall. He shuddered as he remembered the clearing and made his way to Father Leofdag's house. He needed to talk to the priest. All around him, the town was busy as the people of Ribe prepared for the battle. In the market, the traders shouted over each other as they tried to sell their weapons and armour to young warriors preparing for their first battle, while others watched on, their faces glum about their lost income. Women and thralls were as busy outside the hall as those were inside. Wives and mothers made sure that their men had enough supplies, while young children ran around with sticks or wooden weapons as they fought their own mock battles. Charles caught sight of Sigmund and his friends doing the same, and it didn't surprise him that Sigmund was the one calling the orders in their mock charges. What did surprise him, though, was Jorlaug running after the boys with a stick in her hands as she tried to play with them, but none of them paid her any attention. Charles shook his head. Girls shouldn't want to be warriors. They should dream of being good wives and mothers, or perhaps nuns, so they could help the poor and the ill, but he knew the Danes saw it differently. They had no problems with their women fighting in battles and wearing leather jerkins instead of dresses. And Charles had to admit that he was conflicted with the idea. He was still against it, but he knew Thora was a great warrior and she had saved his life many times. Charles wondered then why Jorlaug's parents didn't allow her to train with other children her age.

Charles made his way to Father Leofdag before Sigmund and his friends could spot him. He ran to the priest's house and was surprised to find him packing up his belongings.

'Are you leaving?' Charles asked as he stood in the doorway. Father Leofdag looked up from what he was doing and Charles winced at the sight of the priest's face. His eyes and nose were still swollen, and the colour ranged from a deep purple to light blue. To Charles, it looked like the priest's nose wasn't straight any more and he guessed it never would be. If it wasn't for the man's slight frame and churchly robe, he would almost look like a warrior, as most of them had skewed noses. Charles had even seen one warrior with almost no nose at all.

Father Leofdag smiled at him. 'Morning, Charles. Your face is looking better.' Charles thought of his own face and knew the priest was lying. 'If only we had some holy water with us. It would have helped our faces heal much quicker.'

Charles nodded. 'Where are you going?' He wondered if Father Leofdag was moving to the land across the river, but then dismissed the idea. There were no houses there and nowhere for the priest to sleep.

'I'm going back to Hedeby for a few days.' Father Leofdag searched the house for something as he spoke. 'I need men and materials to build the church and I don't think that your grandfather will be forthcoming with either and there aren't enough Christians here to help me. I also need to see a friend and inform him of what has happened here.' Charles thought of the blacksmith and wondered if Father Leofdag knew about the man. 'And besides, with the upcoming battle, I don't feel like I would be very safe in Ribe,' Father Leofdag continued.

Charles frowned and wondered what had happened to Father Leofdag's idea of martyrdom. 'Oleg is staying behind to look after the town while my grandfather is away. He might help you.' It had surprised Charles when his grandfather had told Oleg to stay behind. The old warrior didn't seem to mind, though, but Charles had thought that the man had been one of his grandfather's allies. Maybe that was why he had asked Oleg to stay so that he had someone he trusted to keep an eye on the town while he was gone.

'I don't think Oleg is that fond of me or our faith, either.' Father Leofdag looked at him and Charles frowned at the spark he saw in the man's eyes. 'Why don't you join me? I'm sure it would thrill Father Ansgar to meet a young, devout man like you when he returns from Sweden.'

Charles smiled at the idea. He would like to meet the priest that the kings of Francia had sent to convert Denmark to Christianity. He had heard a lot about the man from the priests in Hügelburg, and even Bishop Bernard had spoken of him. But then Charles looked out of the door towards the hall. 'My grandfather won't allow me to go with you.'

'Really? I would have thought he'd be glad to get you away from here. Who knows what might happen with the battle ahead?'

Charles shook his head. 'Thora will protect me.'

'But she is a woman,' Father Leofdag protested.

'Yes, but she is also a great warrior and...'

'And?' Father Leofdag asked when Charles trailed off. He wasn't sure if he should tell the priest that he believed Thora was an angel sent by God to protect him and that she only pretended to be a heathen. He knew it sounded silly, but that was the only way he could make sense of how she was such a good fighter.

'Have you ever met any of the heathen priests?' Charles asked instead.

Father Leofdag frowned as he rubbed his chin. 'The godis? Yes, a few in Hedeby.'

'What do you think of them?'

'I think they are ill people that need our help more than most. But they are so deluded that they really think they speak to their gods. Why do you ask?'

Charles opened his mouth but then remembered his grandfather had told him not to tell anyone about their visit to the godi in the forest. Although many people knew about it already. He remembered the strange glances they had got when they returned the previous day. 'I heard someone talk about them the other day,' Charles lied and felt guilty for it. 'You don't think they could be minions of the devil?'

Father Leofdag rubbed the back of his neck. 'There are some who believe that. I know that Father Ansgar does, but I believe they are people whose minds just don't work properly. Perhaps because of all the nasty stuff they eat and drink.'

'So you wouldn't believe anything they say?'

Father Leofdag stopped what he was doing and again frowned at Charles. 'No, I wouldn't believe anything they say and neither should you. God warns us about false prophets and how they can lead us astray.'

Charles nodded, wanting to believe Father Leofdag. But he still couldn't get the image of the old ash tree out of his mind and neither could he forget the words spoken by the godi as they left. But only because they reminded him of the words he had seen in the Bible the day before that. Charles thought of the golden cross hidden in his chest. The chest was locked and Thora had the key so his cross could be kept safe, but Charles wondered if he or his grandfather were as safe. His grandfather would march for war soon and both the Bible and the godi warned them of betrayal. Outside, the raven on the roof of the hall crowed again, and Charles couldn't stop the shiver that ran down his spine. He gripped the small cross around his neck.

God Almighty, protect me, Thora and my grandfather. Keep us safe from the dangers we face.

21

A few days later, Sven gripped the hilt of his sword, trying to ignore the tingling sensation in his chest as he watched the warriors of Ribe saying their farewells to their families. Sons and daughters hugged their parents. Husbands hugged their wives and gave words of encouragement to their children. Few tears were shed as the warriors forced smiles on their faces to comfort those they'd be leaving behind. The Danes knew their tears would not protect their loved ones during battle. As Sven ran his eyes over his warriors, he wondered how many of them would return. It was something Sven had never really thought about when he had been jarl before. As far as he had been concerned, his men had sworn oaths to him and it was their duty to die for that oath. But none of these men had sworn any oaths to him. Sven could not get the image of the battle-field on the beach in Francia out of his mind, even though it was so long ago that it felt like it had happened to a different person. He had always prided himself on returning from a raid with most of his men, if not all. But that day Odin had not been with him and he left that beach with most of his men still on it, including his old friend Arnbjorg. Sven glanced at Rollo as the large warrior ruffled his son's hair, smiling while his wife scowled at him. He remembered the wailing of the wives and mothers when he had returned to Ribe with only one ship and half a crew. So many lives had been wasted just so that the Franks could get hold of his son. So many sent to Valhalla because Horik had been weak, and still was. Sven looked at the grim faces of the townspeople. None of them understood why their children and husbands had to go to war with their king. Horik had been good to them. He knew that. The town had prospered while Bjarni had been jarl and the people knew only peace. Sven sighed, resisting the urge to rub his chest. The Franks had given them that peace and prosperity, though. Denmark's fate was not in her own hands any more. Her gods were not so secure. The Frankish kingdoms to the south were forcing their religion on to the Danes, and Horik was doing nothing to stop it. Sven glanced at the house he had given to the priest. The house was empty now. The priest had left at first light to return to Hedeby, although Charles had told him the bastard would be back with more Christians to build their bloody church.

Behind Sven stood Charles and Thora, both silent as they waited. Charles had not spoken to Sven all morning, and he wasn't sure if it was because he was leaving for war or because of their visit to the godi a few days ago. They had not really spoken since they had returned to Ribe, but Thora had told Sven that Charles was sleeping even less than before. Sven glanced at the sun as it drifted through the sky. It was after their morning meal. Sven had decided the men should eat first before they left. Guttrom had wanted to leave at first light, but they had a few days to reach the place where they were to meet the rest of Guttrom's coalition, and Sven did not want to rush his men. Especially because they weren't really his men. They were the men of Ribe and he had promised them more than he could deliver to get them to fight against their king. Sven turned to face his grandson and Thora. Oleg stood to one side, the only warrior not wearing any armour or preparing to leave. Sven had asked him to stay and keep an eye on Ribe. Oleg had thought it was a mark of honour, but Sven just wanted to separate him from Guttrom. He still did not trust the close relationship they shared and the words of the godi rang in his ear every time he looked at his former hirdman.

'Do you have to go?' Charles asked him, his left arm holding his right as if he was hugging himself.

Sven knelt down, grimacing at the pain in his knees, and put a hand on Charles's shoulder. 'It's the only way I can keep you safe.'

'By fighting a battle you don't need to fight?' Charles scowled at him.

Sven sighed. 'We will not be safe here while Horik is still king. And neither will the people while we stay here.'

'Then why don't we just leave? I don't like it here and you already said that you will leave.'

Sven stared at his grandson, seeing how he was fighting back the tears. 'I have to fight this battle. I—'

'You have no choice?' Charles's face creased. 'Everybody keeps telling me that. But you have a choice. You can just leave. We both can. We can go somewhere else.'

'Where will we go, Charles? You can't go back to Francia and neither can I. We can't stay in Denmark if Horik is still king. He knows I'm alive. I need to do this to keep us both safe.'

'No.' Charles shook his head and Sven saw the anger in his eyes. 'You're doing this because you want to. Because he was the king that made the deal with the Franks to have my father taken. This is about revenge, not protecting me!' Sven winced as Charles turned and stormed off. He was aware of others looking at them and cursed the gods for the boy being so smart. Because Charles was right. Partly anyway. Sven did believe the only way to protect Charles was to make Guttrom king, but he could not deny that there was a part of him that wanted Horik dead for his part in Bjarni's betrayal. Horik had been the one who had struck the deal with the Franks, just so he could keep his peace treaty with them. He had executed other jarls or banished them, like Guttrom. But Sven had been too powerful, Ribe too rich, and so Horik had sought a way to control Sven. He had convinced Bjarni to lure Sven into the trap which saw him lose Torkel. Sven had lost everything while Bjarni and Horik had got rich with Frankish gold. He grimaced again as he stood up and looked at Thora.

'Charles is upset. He's afraid you might not come back,' Thora explained, and Sven nodded. He had the same fears. Sven was too old to fight in shield walls. He should be sitting on his chair and enjoying his old years while his son fought his battles for him. But the Norns had other ideas and so Sven must still fight.

'Keep him safe for me,' Sven said. 'And if the Norns decide it's my time...'

'I'll raise him as if he is my son. But you'll come back, Sven. Odin is not ready for you in Valhalla yet.' Thora smiled, but Sven did not feel her confidence.

'There are other places for the dead to go.'

'Aye, but they don't want you either.'

This time Sven did smile. 'One more thing,' he said, as his face grew serious. 'Keep an eye on Oleg.'

'You don't trust him?'

Sven glanced at his former hirdman. 'I don't know.'

Thora nodded, and Sven glanced over his shoulder to see that his men were ready. Thora saw the same as well. 'May Thor protect you.'

'And you,' Sven said, turning to face his men as Rollo brought him his horse. Sven grunted as he mounted the beast and tried to find a comfortable position, as those with horses of their own did the same. Sven glanced at Guttrom and his warriors: the men who had arrived with Guttrom, as well as another crew's worth who had arrived in the last few days. More than eighty men who had been a drain on Ribe's food and ale stores. Gunvald, his brother's son-in-law, was on a horse behind Guttrom, his hands untied this time, with two of Ribe's men on either side of him. He glared at Sven and spat on the ground when he saw Sven looking at him. Sven had avoided the bastard over the last few days, afraid he might beat him to death, but Rollo had kept an eye on him. Once they reached Guttrom's camp, Gunvald would be kept in Guttrom's tent as a guest and not a prisoner. Sven would rather have slit his throat, but Gunvald was the son of a jarl and had to be treated as such. He just hoped that Guttrom was right and that Gunvald's father would not join the fight against them and let them pass his lands. Guttrom had sent his son, Ivor, with a group of men to deliver the message to Jarl Ebbe, and even though two of the men that Ivor had travelled with had returned, Ivor and most of his group had not. Guttrom had told Sven that he had sent his son onwards to meet up with the rest of Guttrom's army to make sure that everything was ready. Sven did not want to concern himself with that, because it was in the hands of the gods. Guttrom nodded at Sven, who nodded back before he cast his stern eye over the hundred men he was taking to war.

'Men of Ribe, women of Ribe! We ride to war!' Sven roared and led his horse up the main road as the warriors cheered and called out to the gods before they followed him. Rollo and Alvar fell in beside him, but Sven ignored them as he stared at the tree Charles would often hide in. He could not see if his grandson was in the tree now, but he wished he had hugged the boy before he left. Sven felt the knot in his throat at the thought that he might never see his grandson again. Something that surprised him more than it should have done. He had not realised how attached he had become to the boy.

They left Ribe and rode past the cemetery as an eagle soared above their heads, its cries ringing in their ears.

'Odin is with us!' Rollo shouted and the men cheered. Sven hoped that was true, because they would need the god of chaos to be with them to win this fight. He glanced towards the forest as the old godi's words rang in his ears. *Thor, let me come back to my grandson. Don't let me die on that battlefield.*

The warriors of Ribe were in good spirits as they marched towards Jelling, where Horik had his hall. They were not marching to Jelling, though. Guttrom had arranged for his forces to meet up about half a day's march from Jelling and there they would battle Horik and his forces. Sven did not know who would fight for the king, and he knew most of the jarls who had sided with Guttrom by name only. Most of them were the sons of men he knew, but some of them he had seen when he passed through their towns during his drunken wanderings. Most of the jarls had joined forces with Guttrom, which didn't surprise him, because many of them felt constrained by Horik's peace treaty with Francia. The jarls needed to raid and fight battles to keep their warriors happy and loyal, and Francia was a land with enough treasures to make all the jarls of Denmark richer than Fafnir. But Horik would not allow them to raid and punished those who disobeyed him. So now they joined Guttrom in his attempt to become king of Denmark. Sven wondered if the kings of Francia were aware of what was happening in Denmark. Did they even care, or were they too busy dealing with their own problems?

Many farmers stopped what they were doing and Sven's and Guttrom's men marched past their farms. Some wished them well, but most just stared. The men called out to the women they saw and were usually cheered on by their friends as they made promises to the young daughters of the farmers that they would never keep. Young boys ran along the line of warriors, cheering the men on and asking how many men they were going to kill. Sven shook his head and wondered about the fascination of battles and killing that young boys had. He blamed the bards for the sagas they told, which encouraged men to want to die on the battlefield.

'Are you sure you want to give all of this up, Sven?' Guttrom's voice distracted Sven from his thoughts. He had not realised the man had ridden towards him and had forced Alvar to the side so he could ride next to Sven. Sven scrutinised the fertile farmlands around him. He saw herds of cows, sheep and goats grazing on the last of the summer grass. Fields of barley and cereal crops were browning and soon the farmers would harvest them. Some of that harvest would be sent to Ribe as part of their landgilde, and Sven would sell what he didn't need to the traders. Nearby forests were filled with deer, foxes and other animals that could be hunted for their meat and pelts. These lands had made him wealthy once.

'I'm too old to keep control of these lands. You'll need a younger jarl,' Sven said, his eyes still on the horizon.

Guttrom shrugged. 'What I need is a man that can instil fear like you. Your reputation is enough to keep these people in their place.'

'Wasn't enough to stop others from raiding my lands and killing those who were supposed to be under my protection.' Sven hawked and spat. 'My reputation means nothing to these young jarls who replaced their fathers. Not while they are trying to build their own reputations.' He thought of Gunvald, riding in the back somewhere. From what Sven had been told, the young man was a great warrior and, indeed, he had fought well in their battle. But now he was their prisoner and Sven knew that if his father went back on his word, then Guttrom would kill Bjarni's son-in-law. Not that Sven cared. He had wanted to kill the bastard on the battlefield. He had wanted to send a message, but Guttrom had convinced him otherwise and now the bastard was talking about his reputation. 'What happens to Gunvald after the battle?'

Guttrom glanced over his shoulder and then shrugged. 'I'm a fair man. When I am king I'll give him the chance to swear an oath to me.'

'And if he doesn't?'

Again, Guttrom shrugged. 'Then he dies.'

'Should have just let me kill the bastard on the battlefield,' Sven muttered.

Guttrom stayed silent for a short while as if he had not heard what Sven had said and then asked, 'Then who should I make jarl?'

Sven glanced at Rollo, but said, 'Let's win this battle first, and then you ask me that question.'

This made Guttrom laugh. 'By Odin, Sven the Boar doesn't think we can win.'

Sven glanced at the thin man. 'No, I've learnt not to look too far into the future. Norns willing, we win and I get to kill that bastard Horik. Then I will tell you who I think should be jarl.'

'And if you die in the battle?'

The question sent a shiver down Sven's spine, which he tried to hide. 'Then I die and you can choose whoever you want.'

'Then tell me now, then I will know.'

Sven shook his head. 'I need to make sure he survives first.'

Guttrom laughed at this, although Sven wasn't sure why. 'By the gods, Sven. You have changed.' He turned his horse and went back to his men.

Sven rubbed the Mjöllnir around his neck. He searched the clear sky above them for any signs from the gods, or perhaps he just didn't want to look at Rollo as the warrior brought his horse closer to Sven.

'So, who do you want to be jarl in your place?'

Sven was sure Rollo already knew the answer, but just wanted him to say it. 'Your mother.'

Rollo laughed and let his horse fall back. Sven wasn't sure if it was to give him some space, or so the younger warrior could talk to others behind him. He was pleased, though, that the men were in good spirits. Sven led them on a path that avoided where they had fought Gunvald's men a few days ago. He did not want to remind them of what their fate could be. Let them joke about the upcoming battle and dream of glory. The Norns already knew who would not return to their families and Odin's Valkyries were already choosing those who would join his Einherjar.

They marched on for another two days at a slow pace, as there had been no need to rush the men. Although Sven had waited until they were through the lands of Ebbe, Gunvald's father, not trusting that the old bastard would not attack them while they slept. Sven's shoulders and neck had ached from the tension as they marched through the lands of a man allied to Horik. Sven wasn't sure if it was his imagination, but the rest of the men were quieter as if all of them had the same concerns he had. But Gunvald's father had kept to his word, and no one had attacked them. Sven still avoided the large town where the man kept his hall. There was no need to upset the bastard any more than he already was. And Sven knew the man would be furious. Just like he had been when they had taken his son from him.

'By the gods!' Alvar exclaimed as they reached the place where they were supposed to join the rest of Guttrom's forces.

Sven felt the fluttering in his chest when he saw the sight in front of him.

'Still think we might lose?' Guttrom said as he approached Sven.

Sven gripped the reins of his horse as his eyes took in the dark sea of warriors in front of them. Hundreds of tents were dotted amongst the sea of men, like stones jutting out of the ocean, and a dark cloud hovered over the camp from the many campfires. It reminded Sven of a brooding sea storm waiting to break over unsuspecting sailors. Banners of all colours fluttered in the wind. Some he recognised, others he had seen before. Many of the banners had animals on them: wolves, bears, boars and eagles. A few had deer and Sven spotted one with what looked like a rooster with teeth. Other banners had weapons, swords, and axes or spears with shields. Sven guessed there were more than a thousand men as the camp stretched over the horizon. It was the largest force he had ever seen, and Sven wondered if there would ever be a larger one. He could not see how, though. It seemed like all the fighting men in Denmark were in the field in front of them, but then Sven remembered that Horik would have men fighting for him as well. He wondered if the king could call on so many men as well. The smell of all the men camping so close to each other reached him on the breeze and Sven crinkled his nose as the noise they were making drowned out the birds that flew overhead. Large black birds as well as white seabirds, which had come for food. Guttrom laughed when Sven did not respond and made his way down to the army that he believed would give him the crown of Denmark. Sven stayed behind, gritting his teeth and again wondering how many of Ribe's warriors would return home.

'Never seen so many warriors in one place,' Rollo said, and Sven heard the trepidation in his voice. Sven looked back at the mass army and rubbed the Mjöllnir around his neck.

'Aye. And we will merely be a drop in the ocean amongst them.'

'Do you think Horik will have as many men?' Rollo asked him. Behind them, the warriors of Ribe waited for Sven's command, but they too were all talking to each other as they took in the size of Guttrom's army.

Sven looked at the birds flying above the vast camp. 'Odin will make sure he does, of that I'm sure.'

'Then this will be a battle that will be spoken about for many generations.'

Sven glanced at Rollo. 'Then let's make sure that we are on the right side of that saga.' Sven gave the signal, and the warriors of Ribe made their way to Guttrom's army. Sven kept his eyes on the ravens and seabirds and knew that Odin was watching them. And that's what bothered him. Nothing good ever happened when the All-Father had his eye on you.

22

Charles walked through the streets of Ribe, surprised at how empty the town was since the warriors had left. The market was almost empty as well, as most traders had left soon after. Thora had told him it was because of the battle. The traders didn't want to be in Denmark as they feared they might be attacked by those seeking to take advantage of situations like this and so they returned to their homes and waited for the battle to pass and things to calm down. But it was not just that. There seemed to be fewer women and children around as well. Normally, these streets would be filled with women talking to each other and children running around playing games. Slaves would be busy with their duties, and old men would sit outside and enjoy the weather. That was why Charles never really came this way. He didn't like the way people stared at him. But even those outside were subdued. The women barely spoke to each other, many of them lost in their own thoughts, and the grey beards just sat there and scowled at everyone. Charles yawned as he strolled past the houses and the townspeople. His concern for his grandfather and the nightmares had made it impossible for him to sleep again. Charles had tried to pray, but that hadn't helped. To make things worse, he couldn't even go to Father Leofdag and ask him for guidance or just to read the Bible. Charles wondered if he would see the priest again. He hoped he would. He liked Father Leofdag, even if he didn't understand why the young priest didn't defend himself when Haldor had attacked him. Father Leofdag listened to Charles, something which not many people did, especially his grandfather.

Charles turned down a street and paused when he saw the black dog lying by one house. He hesitated, his fear not allowing him to continue, but Charles did not want to turn back. The dog lifted its head and licked its lips as it stared at Charles before it got up and stretched. It gave Charles one more look and walked away. Charles sighed, relieved that he did not have to face the dog. It looked friendly enough, but he was still frightened of them. It was then that Charles realised he was holding the small cross around his neck and wondered if God had told the dog to leave. A smile came to his lips as he carried on walking, but the smile quickly faded when he thought of his grandfather. Charles wondered where he was and if he had fought his battle yet. Thora had explained to him where his grandfather was leading his men, but Charles knew nothing of Denmark and gave up trying to understand. He was still angry at his grandfather for leaving to fight this battle, but he had nevertheless prayed for the old man the previous night and this morning. He did not know why, but Charles had a strange feeling in the pit of his stomach and he didn't know what to do about it. That was why he wished Father Leofdag was still here. Thora had told him he had nothing to worry about. That Odin was not ready for Sven yet, but Charles did not find those words comforting. And the line from the Bible only made him feel more uncomfortable. *Your enemy the devil prowls around like a roaring lion looking for someone to devour.* Charles remembered the words as he struggled to make sense of what he was feeling, but he knew that something bad was coming. That had been the reason he had got so angry with his grandfather the day before. Instead of giving Sven words of encouragement, Charles had shouted at him and run away, not wanting to see his grandfather leave. He had run to the tree near Thora's family's house and climbed as high as he could. From there, he had watched as the warriors of Ribe left the town, and Charles had prayed that it would not be the last time he saw his grandfather.

Charles carried on walking, his head hung low and lost in his thoughts, and did not realise that he was not alone. The first he knew of the presence behind him was when he heard their snickering. Charles sighed and turned around. Sigmund and his friends were the last people he wanted to see, and he hoped they would leave him alone if he asked them to.

'Who do we have here?' one boy asked.

'The Christian and he's all alone.' Sigmund glared at Charles, who wondered for the first time why Rollo's son did not like him. He had done nothing to Sigmund or the other boys, and yet they still felt the need to pick on him. To call him names and make fun of him whenever they could. Charles clenched his fists as he felt his anger grow.

'Just leave me alone,' he said. Charles glanced around and realised he did not know where he was. He must have wandered into a part of Ribe he had never come to before. The houses all looked the same as the rest of the houses in the town, but they were still unfamiliar to him. As were the faces he saw in the doorways.

'Why should we?' Sigmund asked, taking a quick step forward to frighten Charles. But Charles was too busy trying to work out where he was to notice, and Sigmund's face creased when he didn't get the desired response. 'There's no one to protect you now. Your grandfather is not here and you're too far from the hall, so Thora can't help you either.'

'Aye, your grandfather is not here,' another said, and the others laughed. Charles didn't understand why that was funny as he stared at Sigmund.

'Your grandfather is going to die in the battle and then we get to sacrifice you to the gods,' the first boy who had spoken said. Charles glared at him and felt his face go red as his nails dug into the palm of his hands. The boy was about the same age as Charles and taller, although he was shorter than Sigmund. He reminded Charles of one of the warriors who had left with his grandfather, and Charles wondered if he would want that. Did he not realise that his father would also die if Sven fell in battle? Charles glanced at Sigmund and saw the taller boy smile.

'I don't know why you think it's funny,' Charles said through clenched teeth. 'Your father is close to my grandfather. What do you think will happen to him if my grandfather dies?' Sigmund's eyes creased and Charles saw the boy hadn't thought of that.

'Get him, Sigmund!'

'Aye, punch the Christian.' The boys shouted behind Rollo's son. Sigmund clenched his fists and Charles was surprised when a part of him wanted Sigmund to attack him.

'Nothing is going to happen to my father! He is a great warrior!' Sigmund shouted, his face turning red. 'Unlike your grandfather, who is old, fat and ugly. It'll be easy for them to kill him because he is too slow!'

Charles took deep breaths to calm himself as his heart thudded in his chest. He shook his head and decided that he needed to get away from the boys. 'Just leave me alone,' he said again and turned to walk away.

Sigmund grabbed Charles by his shoulders and spun him around. Charles just reacted and before he knew what he was doing, he swung his fist and punched Sigmund in the face.

Sigmund's head snapped to the side as the boys behind him were stunned into silence.

Charles glared at Sigmund, his fist hurting from the punch. He had not wanted to hit Sigmund. He had tried to get away from them, but they would not let him. *This is not my fault*, Charles thought as Sigmund wiped the blood from his mouth. But Charles could not ignore the flames in the pit of his stomach.

'Now you're going to get it, Christian.' Sigmund launched himself at Charles. He threw a punch, which Charles blocked, something that surprised both boys. Charles guessed his training sessions with Thora were paying off. Sigmund attacked again with another wild punch. The blood pumping through Charles made Sigmund seem too slow, and Charles reacted without thinking. He did not copy a move that Thora had taught him, but did something he had seen his grandfather do. Like him, his grandfather was shorter than anyone else, but he had learnt to use his lack of height. Sigmund was about a year younger than Charles, but he was still taller, and Charles used this to his advantage. He ducked under Sigmund's swinging arm and threw his own punch. It was an ugly punch. Charles was not used to fighting and didn't aim his attack, but the blow caught Sigmund in the stomach.

Sigmund gasped as the air was knocked out of him, and before he could even bend over, Charles pushed him to the ground. Charles did not hear the other boys cheering Sigmund on. All he heard was his grandfather's voice, telling him to fight harder than his opponent. To make him wish he had never wanted this fight. Charles was angry. He was tired of always being the one who was picked on. He was tired of no one liking him because of who he was. In Hügelburg, it had been because his father was a Dane and he had no mother. Here it was because of his grandfather and because of his God. Charles was fed up with not belonging anywhere, of not being welcome anywhere.

And he was angry at his grandfather for leaving him to fight a stupid battle. All these thoughts raged through his mind as Charles jumped on top of Sigmund and threw punch after punch, his eyes screwed shut and tears streaming from them. He screamed as his punches struck Sigmund on the head, neck and chest. The younger boy was unable to defend himself against the ferocity of Charles's outburst.

Hands grabbed Charles and pulled him off Sigmund, but Charles carried on, screaming and kicking out at whoever had pulled him off Rollo's son.

'Charles, enough!' Thora's voice broke through the fog and, as the mist cleared, he saw Sigmund on the ground, curled up in a ball and crying. The boy's face was covered in blood and Charles suddenly felt ashamed of what he had done.

'I... I...' he started, but then stopped when Thora shook her head, her lips pressed together. Charles looked around and saw others were there as well. Oda, Sigmund's grandmother, stood over her grandson, tutting as she helped the boy up. Jorlaug's pale face and wide eyes stared at him. Sigmund's friends were all glaring at Charles. 'I didn't mean to. I'm sorry.'

'Quiet now, Charles.' Thora looked him over and Charles was aware of his back and shoulders aching as his heart calmed down.

'I'll get you, Christian. You wait!' Sigmund pulled himself free from his grandmother and pointed a finger at him.

'No, you won't!' Oda's sharp voice made the boy jump. 'You've been hounding that boy since he arrived and now you are angry that he had had enough.'

'But, Grandmother—'

'No, Sigmund. Charles beat you. He won the fight and you have to live with that. If any of you boys touch that child, then I'll drag you into the forest and leave you for the spirits to feast on!' The boys' faces all paled, even Sigmund's, but Oda was not done yet. Charles had not realised that the old lady could be so fierce. 'Now, go home, Sigmund, so your mother can clean your face and I don't want to see you near Charles again!'

Sigmund lowered his head and stomped away, with the other boys following him.

'I'm sorry,' Charles said again as Oda turned to face him.

Oda shook her head. 'Don't be. That boy has been getting a bit too cocky since he became popular. He's already forgotten that those same boys were making fun of him not so long ago.'

Charles frowned. 'What do you mean?'

Oda sighed. 'His father is one of the biggest men in the town and his grandfather was a great warrior that people still talk about. Yet Rollo never went on any raids or took part in battles. Bjarni did not like him and so kept him away from places where he could make a name for himself. The other boys saw this and made fun of Sigmund.'

'Why did Bjarni not like him?' Charles's body ached, and he wondered why as he rubbed his shoulder.

'Because of me. I knew Bjarni had done no good, and he knew I knew. But he could do nothing against me, so he punished my son. Not that I minded, though.'

'You didn't mind that your son was rejected like that?' Charles frowned.

Oda looked at Charles. 'I had already lost my husband and I did not want to lose my son either. I've seen too many of my friends having to go through that. But now your grandfather has taken my son under his wing, and I fear for him. Just like you fear for your grandfather and my grandson fears for his father. Unfortunately, he decided to take it out on you.'

Charles lowered his head, feeling ashamed of not seeing it, but also could not stop his anger. 'I'm tired of always being picked on.'

'I know, Charles,' Thora said as she rubbed his head. 'Come, let's get you cleaned as well. Thank you, Oda.'

'Don't thank me. I just hope Charles has knocked some sense into my grandson. He's a lot like you, Charles. Frigg knows it's a pity that neither of you can see it. You might make good friends then.'

Charles did not believe Oda, but he smiled anyway as she made her way back to her house. 'How did you know where to find me?' Charles asked Thora as they walked back to the hall.

'Jorlaug was following the boys and saw the fight,' Thora explained and Charles looked at Jorlaug, who was still staring at him.

'The other boys tried to get you off Sigmund. They kicked you and punched you, but they couldn't get you off him. So I ran to tell Thora.'

Charles nodded and guessed that was why his back and shoulders ached. But he did not remember the other boys attacking him, so focused had he been on venting his frustrations on Sigmund, and that scared him even more.

* * *

Roul, King Charles's spy, smiled as he walked through the market in Hedeby. He had been there for a few days already, having set off as soon as his meeting with King Charles had finished. Roul had not wanted to stay in Paris longer than necessary. Bero had been furious after the meeting and Roul knew he would be safer if he left the capital. He did not want to share the same fate as his former master had done at Bero's hands. Hedeby was quieter than usual. Most of her warriors had gone, with only a few left to keep the peace in the large trading town. Roul had heard the jarl of Hedeby had taken his warriors north for a battle which many believed would decide the fate of Denmark. The people were concerned and everywhere Roul looked, he saw creased brows and pursed lips. People huddled in groups as they whispered to each other, while others walked around in a daze, their minds elsewhere. Many of the traders had left as well, not wanting to be in Denmark until the dust had settled and either King Horik remained or his nephew, Guttrom, was the new king. Roul had been in Hedeby for a few days, waiting to hear from his man in Ribe and all the time he had been here, he had heard the rumours of Guttrom, the nephew Horik had exiled for attacking the Franks against his wishes. Roul knew the small Christian community in the Danish town was afraid of Guttrom. They believed the man hated their religion and that he would burn the small church that Horik had allowed to be built in Hedeby. They also worried that their neighbours who had tolerated them because their king accepted the Christians might now turn against them. So, just like the traders, many of them had left. But Roul knew that even though Guttrom hated Christians, he was more than happy to take money from them to attack their enemies. It didn't matter if those enemies were other Christians or heathens, as long as he got paid for it. In fact, both King Lothar of Middle Francia and Roul's king, Charles of West Francia, had paid Guttrom for his services. And now the man had decided that he should be king of the Danes. Roul wondered, if he succeeded, whether he would still take money from the Frankish kings to do their bidding, or would just raid the Frankish kingdoms.

Roul paused by a jeweller's stall and picked up a beautiful brooch made of ivory and gold. It had delicate carvings on the ivory that looked like intertwined branches, while the gold rim almost looked like a large flower.

'From the north,' the trader said as he smiled at Roul. 'I can give you a good price for it.'

'No, thank you.' Roul put the brooch down again and moved on. He had heard the ivory came from an animal larger than a horse and with teeth longer than his arm. He would have liked to see this animal if only to make sure it was real, but he hated the cold. Just like he hated having to come to Denmark. It was too far from his home, which he rarely saw, but he had to stay here until the boy and the cross were delivered to him. Roul could not return to Paris empty-handed again. But that was why he was smiling, while everyone else looked as glum as a winter storm. He had just heard from the man he had sent to Ribe and the news was even better than he could have hoped for.

Sven the Boar had left Ribe to fight the king of the Danes and had left the boy behind. Roul had sent the man back with instructions to grab the boy as soon as possible and to keep him somewhere safe. God willing, Sven the Boar would not survive the battle, which would make it easier for Roul to find the cross, because he was sure the boy would not be carrying it on him. He could have told the man about the cross and let him find it, but Roul did not trust him. Even the most loyal hound would turn on its master if it was offered more food by someone else. Roul's smile grew even more as he looked at the brooch still in his hand. The trader never noticed that he had not really put it back on his table. Roul thought of the whore back in Paris he liked to visit. She would like this gift. The girl wasn't very smart and liked shiny things, but she was good at listening and Roul knew the information she gave him about the men that spent time with her would be very useful to him. Especially when he returned to his king with the boy and the cross. Roul crossed himself, hoping that God would make sure that happened because he knew he could not return to Paris empty-handed again.

Sven sat outside his tent and ate his porridge as he eyed Guttrom's tent, near where he and his men had their camp. It was larger than everyone else's and Guttrom's banner, a black raven's head on a red background, was on display on a long pole by the entrance. There was no wind, so the banner hung limp. After they had arrived, Sven had left Rollo in charge of getting their camp set up while he went to Guttrom's tent to meet the other jarls who had tied their fate with the would-be king. Guttrom had allocated the men from Ribe a space near his camp, a sign of honour which made his warriors walk around with puffed-out chests and their heads high as if they were cockerels showing off to hens. But Sven had to admit that surprised him. He had not brought the biggest army to Guttrom's forces and even though they had been close friends once, Sven still had not expected this. The greetings he had received from the other jarls were less than welcome, whether it was because they didn't like him or the other jarls were upset that he had been honoured by Guttrom. Sven didn't know, but he didn't really care.

'Sven the Boar. We all thought you were dead,' a one-eyed jarl had said. The man was old enough for Sven to have known him, but he could not remember the name. Neither could he remember a jarl with only one eye.

Guttrom had thrown a large outdoor feast for his jarls and their men that night, although Sven was not sure where he had found enough food and ale for everyone, especially as he had been in Ribe with Sven for the last few weeks. But then, Ivor and some of Guttrom's more senior men had constantly been coming and going, so perhaps it was one of them who had prepared everything for this gathering. The tables were filled with wild boar, venison, as well as fish from the nearby rivers. Vegetables and bread had been taken or bought from the farmers in the surrounding lands, and Sven knew there was a heavily guarded tent filled with barrels of ale and mead. Even Gunvald had been given a seat at the feast and Sven guessed it was an attempt by Guttrom to win him over. Sven had said little during the feast and didn't drink much, either. He wasn't sure why, but he could not get himself to relax near Guttrom and so he preferred not to drink too much when the man was around. Sven was glad, though, that he had left Oleg in Ribe. Watching him and Guttrom constantly whispering to each other would just have annoyed him even more. But his men and the other jarls did not take the same precaution.

Sven chewed on his porridge as he watched his men sitting around their fire, all of them grey-faced as they ate or tended to their weapons. Sven was not sure when the battle would take place, but he hoped it was soon. No fights had broken out yet amongst the men of Guttrom's mass force, but Sven knew it was only a matter of time. Many of these warriors had fought against each other at some point, and you could taste the animosity in the air. The jarls might have mixed at Guttrom's feast, but their warriors stuck to their own camps and few had mingled with men from other regions.

'Sven?' A voice distracted Sven, and he looked up to see one of Guttrom's men standing over him.

'What?'

'Guttrom wants you in his tent.' The man was much younger than Sven, his broad shoulders and scarred arms showing he had fought in many battles, but it still annoyed Sven that he was so disrespectful.

Rollo must have felt the same as he stood up and towered over the warrior. 'Show my jarl some respect,' he growled at the unfazed warrior. The man had not been part of the group that had been in Ribe and he didn't seem to care who Sven was.

'Please,' the man said after he shrugged.

Sven swallowed the porridge in his mouth and put his bowl down. 'It's fine, Rollo.' He stood up and grimaced at the pain in his back. Sven would have thought his many winters of sleeping rough would have made his body used to it, but he still woke with a sore back and neck each morning, no matter where he slept. Perhaps it was just his age. Apart from Guttrom, Sven was one of the oldest of the jarls here. Some jarls looked like they hadn't even been born yet that night he had fled his town after the death of his wife. Sven stretched his back and followed the man to Guttrom's tent.

Inside, he saw that some of the other jarls were already there, many of them looking as rough as his men. They all looked up from their discussion when he entered as Guttrom greeted him. Gunvald was sitting in one corner of the large tent, a cup of ale in his hand and a bored expression on his face. Sven clenched his fists at seeing his brother's son-in-law being treated so well, but knew there was nothing he could do about this. Gunvald was Guttrom's prisoner now.

'Odin has blessed us with a fine day for a battle, don't you think?' Guttrom grinned as the others nodded, but Sven only scowled.

'Horik is here?' Sven took a cup from the table in Guttrom's tent and filled it with ale.

'Aye. My scouts spotted his force last night. He is camped not far from here. I imagine he's marching his men towards us as we speak.'

'Or he's waiting for us to go to him.' Sven drank his ale, savouring the flavour as it washed the taste of the porridge out of his mouth.

'Why would the bastard do that?' one of the younger jarls asked. Sven looked at the man who was the same age Torkel would have been. Sven caught himself wondering what kind of jarl his son would have made. The thought caught him off guard, and Sven almost choked on his ale.

'No, Sven is right,' Guttrom said as he raised an eyebrow at Sven, who was wiping his mouth from the ale he spat out. 'Horik is coming, but not all the way here. We march soon to meet him where the battle will take place.'

'And where is that?' Sven asked. Even though Guttrom had done much of the planning for the battle while he had been in Ribe, Sven knew few of the details. Guttrom had kept most of the information close, as he had been concerned that Horik would find out. Sven would have argued with that, but he was sure that Horik had people in Ribe who kept him informed of what Sven was up to. He only wished he had the same in Horik's hall, but Sven had been away for too long to know anyone in Jelling he could trust.

'There's a valley. Not too far from here. The land is flat and there are no forests nearby where Horik can hide some of his men.'

'But neither can we.' One jarl scowled.

'Aye, neither can we. But it shouldn't matter. My scouts tell me we have more men than my uncle.'

Sven took another sip of his ale and wondered if that was true. Guttrom had said that his scout saw their camp last evening. It would have been impossible for the man to work out how many men

Horik had. Sven kept those thoughts to himself, though. He was sure the other jarls had the same thoughts, but they needed their men to be assured of victory, just like he had to do with the men of Ribe.

'So what is the plan for the battle?' the one-eyed jarl asked. The man seemed to be one of the leaders of the gathered jarls, and Sven wondered who he was and why he didn't know the man. He had travelled all over Denmark, but he had made it a habit to stay clear of the jarls' halls in the towns he had visited in case they recognised him. Because of this, he had lost track of whom most of the jarls in Denmark were. The few he knew, he knew because they were close to Horik.

Guttrom explained the battle plan to the jarls while Sven studied the men in the tent. Most of the jarls looked battle-hardened, their arms and faces covered in scars, but there were a few young ones who seemed nervous as they listened to Guttrom's plans. They all nodded when Guttrom had finished and Sven had to admit that it was a good strategy, although he noticed the glares aimed at him when Guttrom had said that Sven would fight in the centre alongside Guttrom and his men. Sven stayed behind as the other jarls left the tent.

'You've spent a long time thinking about this battle,' Sven said as he put his cup down and stroked his beard.

Guttrom smiled. 'You still not sure that we can win this?'

Sven shrugged. 'That's up to the gods to decide. Not me.' He glanced at Gunvald and saw how the young man was listening to their conversation. Sven hoped that Guttrom knew what he was doing with the bastard.

'Aye. That's why we will make a sacrifice before we leave. Just to make sure that the gods are on our side.'

Sven raised an eyebrow at Guttrom. He should have thought to do the same in Ribe before he had left. Although, he doubted it would have made any difference. He had made many sacrifices to Odin, begging to die. 'Horik will do the same.'

This time Guttrom laughed. 'Then we better hope the gods prefer our sacrifice.' He clapped Sven on the shoulder and left his tent. Sven stood there for a while, looking around the tent, and wondered why Guttrom's son wasn't there. He would have expected to see Ivor in the tent with the other jarls, and when he thought of it, he couldn't remember seeing him at the feast the night before. Sven shook his head. He was getting paranoid. He was sure Ivor would be here somewhere. It was a large camp, and the man was probably busy somewhere else.

Not long after, Sven rode beside Guttrom as the army marched towards the place of battle. He glanced behind him and his heart raced in his chest as he saw what he could only think of as a giant snake following them as he rode at the front next to Guttrom.

'It's impressive, isn't it?' Guttrom smiled at Sven. The man was very confident, and Sven guessed he had a right to be. He had most of the jarls on his side and more than a thousand men to fight for him. But Sven could not share Guttrom's confidence. Guttrom might have had many jarls with him, those who were disgruntled by Horik not allowing them to raid the Frankish kingdoms, but Horik would have the most powerful jarls, the ones that benefited the most during his reign and had become wealthy. Men like Jarl Torgeir of Hedeby. And those jarls would have armies larger than those who sided with Guttrom. Sven said none of this, though. Guttrom was aware of his apprehensions and Sven didn't want the other jarls to think he was weak. He knew they were already whispering about him behind his back. Stories of him wandering through their lands as a dirty drunk were everywhere, and Sven guessed they must have been wondering why Guttrom had asked him to bring his men. Sven ground his teeth as he glanced at the other jarls, some of them still unable to grow full beards. Cocky young bastards who were yet to understand how harsh the gods really were. They had all stood proud when Guttrom made his sacrifice to the gods. Thirty oxen and ten thralls were killed to convince Odin that they were worthy of his attention. Sven did not know where they had got those oxen and thralls from, but he imagined there were a few unhappy farmers around. He was glad he had left Alfhild in Ribe. A beautiful girl like that would have been the first one they sacrificed to the All-Father, and Sven did not want to see such a young life wasted. One jarl – a man of about thirty winters, Sven guessed – had wiped his face with the blood of the thrall that had belonged to him, and now he rode near the front, his face still red. Rollo had told Sven he had heard of the man. Hallr Red-Face, they called him, and he was said to be a great warrior. Judging by his brynja and sword, as well as the many arm rings and scars he wore, Sven guessed it was true, but he still didn't get why the man needed to do that. But then, he had a raven tattooed on his scalp.

'It is,' Sven responded when he realised Guttrom was staring at him.

'The gods know Horik can't win this battle,' one of the other jarls boasted, his blond beard filled with golden finger rings. 'He won't have an army big enough to stop us and by the time the sun goes down, the ravens will be too fat to fly after they have feasted on Horik's dead army!' He pumped his fist into the air and the men who heard him cheered. But Loki must have been annoyed by Guttrom's confidence and those cheers quickly died when they crested a small hill and saw Horik's army waiting for them.

Sven shook his head as Guttrom swore under his breath. 'Odin's arse.'

The jarl, who had boasted only moments ago, gaped as he stared at the horde that Horik had gathered. It was hard to say, but Sven guessed it easily matched Guttrom's and he could almost hear Odin laughing in the whispers of the men behind him.

He glanced at Guttrom. 'Should have sacrificed more oxen.'

Guttrom glared at him before he turned and forced a smile on his face. 'Men! Look at all those bastards Horik has brought for you to kill!'

The men who could hear the would-be king cheered, but to Sven the cheers weren't as loud as before. And he understood why. He gripped his reins tight to stop his hands from trembling. Even if Guttrom still had more men, and Sven wasn't so sure now that he saw Horik's army, this would still not be the easy fight that Guttrom had promised them. The thin man had underestimated the support Horik still had, and Sven prayed to Odin that he would not regret joining forces with Guttrom.

A group of men broke from Horik's army and came towards them.

'Looks like Horik wants to talk,' Hallr Red-Face said. 'I think he wants to surrender.' Forced laughter greeted Hallr's words, but Guttrom only scowled as he stared at his uncle and the four men accompanying him.

'Sven, come with me,' Guttrom said and selected three others, including the one-eyed jarl. 'Hallr, get the men ready.' He turned to the jarls who had answered his calls. Men who depended on him winning this battle. 'Men. Jarls of Denmark. This is our moment. As Odin is my witness, today we take back our kingdom and lands from the control of the Christian Franks and their puppet king. Go to your men, you know what to do.' The other jarls nodded their agreement but said nothing as they went to join their men. Guttrom turned to Sven and the other three jarls. 'Let's go see what the old fool wants.'

They rode in silence towards where Horik was waiting for them, all of them with grim faces, as Sven glanced at the cloudless sky. He wondered if the gods were watching. They must have been. No one could ignore the two vast armies about to face each other. Sven imagined Odin sitting on his chair in Asgard and rubbing his hands together with glee.

Sven did not recognise three of the jarls with Horik, but he recognised Jarl Torgeir of Hedeby. The tall, dark-haired and barrel-chested man was glaring at him. One of the other jarls looked like an older version of Gunvald, whom Guttrom had left guarded in his tent. Sven guessed the man was Jarl Ebbe.

'Jarl Ebbe.' Guttrom greeted the man, confirming Sven's thoughts. 'Your presence disappoints me. You don't value the life of your son.'

'Go fuck a pig, Guttrom,' Jarl Ebbe said, his face dark with fury. 'I brought no men with me, but I came to make sure you kept your word. Where is my son?'

Guttrom smiled. 'Gunvald is fine and being treated well. He is back at my tent, but don't think about sending men to rescue him. He is being guarded by men who have orders to kill him if you try anything dumb.' Jarl Ebbe glared at Guttrom as Sven frowned at Jarl Torgeir, who was smiling at him.

'Sven the Boar,' Torgeir said. 'The last time I heard, you were a filthy drunk littering my roads and upsetting my traders with your smell.'

The other jarls glanced at him, and Sven noticed the smiles on their faces. But he said nothing because he didn't know what to say. He could not defend himself because what Torgeir had said was true, and he was sure the man would have told everyone about it when they had heard that Sven was fighting alongside Guttrom. Sven glanced at Horik's army and wondered if Ketil was there. Ketil was an old warrior, although not as old as Sven, and one of Torgeir's most trusted friends. Sven and Ketil had fought against each other before, and Sven had let Ketil live after he had defeated his men.

Ketil had repaid the favour after some of Torgeir's men chased Sven and Charles out of Hedeby and tried to kill them. Those men were dead now, along with Ketil's nephew, a friend of Thora's who had been killed when he had tried to help.

'I look forward to killing more of your men, Torgeir. Even as a drunken fool, they were no match for an old man like me.'

Torgeir bristled at the insult to his army. 'Ketil was a fool for letting you live. I lost some good men because of you.'

'You lost good men because they were fools.'

'Enough!' Horik said. 'We did not come here so the two of you can bicker.' Horik's old eyes fixed on Sven. 'Although Odin knows I agree with Torgeir. His man should have killed you.'

'Many have tried,' Sven said as he bared his teeth. His muscles quivered and his heart pounded in his chest as he glared at Horik, the man who had taken everything from him. The man who had always felt threatened by Sven's power. Horik was older than Sven by at least fifteen winters, and Sven liked to believe that Odin had kept the fool alive only so that Sven could kill him. Horik sat straight-backed on his horse, his heavily lined face stern as he glared at the men who had come to take his crown. His long hair and beard were grey and thin and his old shoulders narrow. Horik had been a large-shouldered man once, but age had taken much from him and Sven was determined to take the rest. The old king wore a brynja, which had gold around its edges and which was too big for him, and a sword with a large jewel-encrusted pommel. Although Sven doubted the sword would taste any blood in the upcoming battle.

Horik glared at his nephew. 'You are another runt I should have killed a long time ago.'

Guttrom grinned. 'Uncle. It's good to see you are well and still strong for a man your age. The gods have blessed you.'

'What do you want, Guttrom?'

'To kill you and take what is mine!' Guttrom forced his horse to take a step forward. The jarls surrounding Horik reacted by bringing their horses forward as well.

'My crown is not yours and never was.' Horik's wrinkled face creased even more.

'You shared it with my father once. It belongs to me!'

Horik barked a laugh. 'Well, the gods know that if your father had been a smarter man, then he would still have shared the crown with me, or perhaps you would be now. Your fight should be with him. Not me.'

Sven had to admit that Horik was right, but he knew Guttrom would not see it that way. Horik, and Guttrom's father, along with their other brothers, had all shared the crown of Denmark. But they had fallen out and Guttrom's father and another of the brothers had been exiled.

'Odin is with me, old man. And so is Denmark. Your reign has been too long and you too weak. The people demand change and before the sun sets today, you will be dead and your crown will be on my head.'

Horik glanced over his shoulder at the enormous army he had assembled. 'Not all of Denmark is with you, Guttrom. The gods will decide who wears my crown at the end of today.' Deciding the conversation was over, Horik turned his horse and rode back to his army, his jarls following him apart from Torgeir.

'Thought you'd like to know that Jarl Asger is dead. Wound rot crept up his arm and took his life. He refused to let the healers amputate his arm and it killed him. You are the wound rot of Denmark, Sven, and we should have killed you a long time ago.' Torgeir turned his horse and followed Horik before Sven could respond.

Not that Sven could. He had barely heard the words as he glared at Horik's back, his jaw clenched and body trembling as he remembered the day he had been forced to give his son to the Franks because of the deal Horik had made with them. Sven had to resist the urge to charge after Horik and slay the old bastard before he could reach the safety of his men. Even his horse sensed his anger as it pawed the ground and shook its head.

'Sven, let's go. You can kill the old fool on the battleground,' Guttrom said, and turned his horse around. Sven did not follow him, not straight away. He stood there and watched as Horik was swallowed up by his army and then he ran his eyes over the men that Horik had assembled. *Odin, I swear to you that not a single one of them will stop me from killing the old bastard who took my son away from me.*

Sven turned his horse and followed Guttrom and the other jarls back to their army. He heard the eagle cry above him and couldn't stop the shiver that ran down his spine. The gods were watching.

24

The two armies faced each other. Two armies with more men than Sven could count. Banners of all sizes and colours fluttered on the breeze while the air stank of stale ale, vomit and piss. Some warriors shouted insults to their enemy, while others prayed to the gods, either asking for glory or begging not to die. Somewhere a man was weeping, and Sven was sure he was not the only one. The noise drowned out the ravens and eagles which soared above their heads: spectators come to watch as the warriors of Denmark killed each other so they could feast on the remains. This was a battle which would decide the future of Denmark and Sven knew that, no matter who walked away victorious, Denmark would not be the same again. Sven struggled to breathe as he tried to ignore the pain in his chest. His heart throbbed in his ears and his mouth was as dry as it had ever been. His old legs felt weak, his left leg hurting more than it had ever done, as his hands trembled so much that Sven worried he might not be able to hold his sword. Sven wasn't just afraid as he stared at the dark sea of men in front of him. He was terrified. Terrified that he would never see Charles grow into a man, just like he never got to with his son. Every time he closed his eyes, he saw his grandson, his eyes filled with tears and reminding him of Torkel. Every time he opened them, he saw the man who had taken everything from him. Sven cursed the gods and the Norns for bringing him here. He cursed them for everything that had gone wrong in his life, even though he knew it was all his fault. He had been arrogant, just like Guttrom was now, and he had lost everything. And now, when he had seen more than fifty winters, he was standing in the largest shield wall Denmark had ever seen and all he wanted to do was to turn and run away. To go back to his life of wandering around Denmark with a jug of ale in his hands and his mind too numb to remember. But Sven knew he could not. He had to fight and survive for the sake of his grandson.

Guttrom's army stood ten men deep, with a river to their right. The warriors in the first rank were the elite fighters, the jarls, their champions, and the best of their warriors, all of them wearing brynjas and helmets. They carried swords or axes and their shields were all painted with their emblems and matched the banners which stood behind each jarl. Those in the second row were the experienced warriors. The ones that had been around for a while, but never had the ambition to get the attention of the gods. They also had swords and axes, as well as shields they would use to protect the heads of the men in the front rank. Most wore brynjas, but many only had leather jerkins. Their helmets were not as richly decorated as those in the first row, and they had fewer arm rings around their wrists. The warriors that filled the rest of the shield wall were the ones with less skill, or those still too young to have made a name for themselves. Warriors who wore leather jerkins or no armour other than thick woollen tunics and were armed with spears which they would use to skewer those in the first rank of the enemy's shield wall. Not all of them had shields, so they had to pray the gods were with them when the archers at the back of the shield wall fired their arrows. Sven glanced at his banner behind him, held by one of his men. Rollo's mother had it made, and it sported a black boar's head, its mouth open and tusks sharp on a red background. It was the same banner he had made for himself when he had first become jarl. He was the boar standing on a field made red with the blood of his enemies.

A deafening cheer erupted when a large warrior with light-coloured hair sticking out from under his helmet stepped out of the shield wall, striking the back of his shield with his axe as he challenged Horik's men to single combat. The man had three arm rings on his right arm and his brynja glimmered in the sun's light. Sven shook his head at these young warriors, so eager to die, as one of Horik's men accepted the challenge. He had done the same, though, when he had been young and eager to make a name for himself. Horik's warrior, a red-headed man, also wore a brynja and a helmet but had a sword instead of an axe. The two men faced each other, calling out insults as they crouched behind their shields. Guttrom's man launched at his opponent, who was smaller than him, and put his shoulder behind his shield as he tried to run the man over. Horik's man stepped out of the way and struck the back of the light-haired man with his sword. Horik's men cheered, but Guttrom's warrior was unharmed as his brynja took the blow. Before he could turn though, Horik's warrior attacked. He stabbed high with his sword, forcing the other man to lift his shield. As soon as his sword struck the man's shield, he kicked out at his opponent's front leg. Guttrom's man must have sensed the attack because he jumped back. Horik's man rushed at the larger warrior, eager to keep him on the back foot, and the two came together, their shields between them. The larger warrior forced the smaller one back a step and before Horik's man could do anything, he hooked the man's shield with his axe and pulled it down. Guttrom's warrior punched the red-haired man in the face with the rim of his shield and the man's legs crumbled under him. Guttrom's army roared and

Sven felt the noise rattling through him as Horik's warriors fell silent. They watched as the large warrior buried his axe in the man's skull before he turned and, with his arms wide, taunted Horik's army. Another man stepped out of Horik's shield wall, but he fared little better, although he managed to cut the arm of Guttrom's warrior before he lost his head. Guttrom called the man back as others stepped forward to challenge Horik's men.

Sven glanced at the warriors of Ribe. 'If any of you even think of doing that, then I'll kill you myself.'

'I'm surprised you aren't challenging Horik.' Rollo smiled.

Sven tried to look over the heads of Horik's men, but he could not see the old king. 'The old bastard will not fight. If we want to kill him, then we have to defeat his army first.'

The light-haired warrior stopped before he reached the shield wall and turned around. He pulled his pants down and he shook his bare arse at Horik's army. The cheer from Guttrom's army drowned out the sounds of the birds circling above them and Sven was sure that even the gods would be startled by that cheer if they weren't watching already. He took a deep breath to calm his trembling nerves when Guttrom stepped forward. The old warrior lifted his sword into the air.

'The gods are with us! The gods are tired of Horik's weakness. His inability to stop the Christians from taking over our lands. They are angry that Horik allows them to build their churches in our towns and decry their existence.' The men roared their anger at Guttrom's words, and Sven felt the noise vibrating through his old body. 'We fight for our gods! Our gods that have made us strong! Our gods that have given us victory over the Christians! Our gods that my weak uncle wants to give up!' Again the men roared, but this time they banged their weapons against their shields. Sven felt the headache growing from all the noise and wished Guttrom would stop talking so the fighting could begin.

Across the battleground he saw Horik on his horse riding along the front rank of his men, most likely saying the same nonsense to get his men ready for the battle. 'The gods came to me last night,' Guttrom continued. 'They came to me in my dreams and told me we will win today! That they will grant us victory because we fight for them! Warriors of Denmark! Warriors of the gods! Odin watches us today. His Valkyries wait to take the bravest of you to Valhalla should you fall. Ready your spears, your axes and swords. Keep your shields high and your arms strong. For today, we will drench this ground in the blood of the Christian-lovers. We will give the ravens and the wolves a feast they will never forget!' The men roared as they thrust their weapons in the air, and Guttrom winked at Sven. He had to admit, the man knew how to speak. These bastards really thought they'd be fighting for their gods, when really they were fighting because Guttrom wanted a shiny crown on his head and his uncle dead. Sven hawked and spat as he tightened his grip on his sword. He did not want to fight. Not in this battle. All he wanted was to keep his grandson safe and, standing here now as most of the warriors in Denmark prepared to kill each other, he realised Charles had been correct. He did not need to fight. Just like they had never needed to return to Ribe. All they had to do was find a small town far away where nobody knew who they were and where they could have lived in peace. But Sven could not let go of the past. He had lost his son because of Horik. That was the real reason he was here. Killing Bjarni had not got rid of the pain and he knew that Horik's death wouldn't either. But he still wanted to make the old bastard pay. If helping Guttrom take the crown from his old skull was going to do that, then Sven would fight like a god to make sure it happened. Sven took a deep breath. *Gods, I need ale.* Once the cheering had died down, Guttrom stepped back into the front rank. 'For the gods!'

'For the gods!' more than a thousand men echoed, and the
ground trembled as they marched towards their enemy.

Sven gripped his shield and lifted it in front of him as he walked
in line with the rest of the men in the front rank. He grimaced at the
pain in his left leg, but pushed the pain out of his mind as he forced
himself to keep up with the younger warriors. Rollo had wanted
him to fight in the second rank, but Sven had refused. This was
where he belonged. In his right hand, he gripped the sword he had
taken from the bastard who had tried to kill him and his grandson
not so long ago. His head was sweating already under the leather
felt cap beneath his helmet while his brynja weighed down on his
shoulders. Rollo and Alvar stood on either side of him, Rollo with
his short one-handed axe and Alvar with his sword in his hand.
Both men looked worthy of the gods' attention in their brynjas and
helmets with eye guards and their arms covered in arm rings to
show that they were warriors of acclaim. But they would be targets
for anyone who wanted to make a name for themselves, just like
Sven's banner behind him. They showed the enemy where he
stood, the jarl of the men they faced. He did not envy any warrior
who tried to claim his scalp, though, because they had to get past
Rollo and Alvar first, and both younger warriors had shown Sven
that they deserved their places. They had kept him alive in the
battles against Asger and Gunvald, and Sven felt certain they would
do the same today. That had not stopped him from making an
offering to Odin, Thor and Týr before the battle, though. Thor to
protect them and Týr to make them fight better than the enemy.
And Odin for the chaos of battle. Odin was known as the frenzied
one because the All-Father loved chaos and Sven needed there to
be chaos in this battle. Because that was where he thrived. Sven
never enjoyed fighting in shield walls, even less now that he had
Charles to think about. But in the chaos of open battle, that was

where he fought best. That was where he could use the Dane axe he carried on his back to sever limbs and end lives.

'They're coming,' Rollo said, dragging Sven back to the battle-ground. The surrounding land was flat. There were no hills to take advantage of or nearby forests where Horik could hide a reserve force. Guttrom had chosen the ground well. Ravens and eagles circled above the two armies as they marched towards each other, but Sven could not hear their calls. Not over the din of the men who were shouting insults at each other again. Sven and his two cham-pions were silent though, as were most of the men of Ribe. He glanced to the side to where Guttrom stood and wondered why Ivor was not there. Surely, Guttrom would have wanted his son to fight by his side. Sven knew he did.

'Archers, ready!' Sven heard the call as a bead of sweat ran down his face. Sven hated wearing helmets, and unlike most of the warriors around him, his did not have an eye guard. It did have a nose guard, though, which was rubbing against his large nose.

Sven had brought about twenty archers with him, mainly hunters and a few warriors who were good with bows. They were standing at the back of the shield wall with the archers brought by the other jarls. Sven didn't know how many archers there were, but guessed more than a few hundred. He wondered how many archers Horik had brought with him. Sven gritted his teeth. There was no point in worrying about that now or his grandson back in Ribe. His fate was in the hands of the Norns. But Sven made an oath that if he died in this fight and went to Valhalla then he would punch Odin in the face as soon as he saw the one-eyed bastard.

'Archers, shoot!' Guttrom roared when his men were close enough for him to see the grim faces of Horik's men. Men blew on horns, and Sven flinched at the noise of hundreds of arrows being sent into the sky. From behind Horik's shield wall, he watched as the black cloud rose up, like a swarm of evil spirits wanting nothing else but to pluck your life away.

'Shields!' Rollo shouted, along with others in the front rank of the shield wall, and Sven lifted his above his head. His left shoulder protested, old age and his scar making the shield heavier than what it was and his arm shuddered as arrows struck his shield. Sven roared as he fought to keep his shield above his head. Somewhere near him, he heard a warrior cry out, and then another, and knew he had lost some men already.

Both shield walls waited with bated breath as the last of the arrows struck wood and flesh, and then for a few heartbeats more, just to make sure that the archers had really run out of arrows. Sven blew the air out of flared nostrils as he let go of the breath he had been holding. When they felt sure there would be no more arrows, the warriors on both sides lowered their shields and glared at each other. Sven saw Torgeir facing him and to his right stood Ketil, the black-haired warrior who had spared his life earlier that summer, just like he had many winters ago. Sven wondered which one of them would regret those decisions.

'Today, you die, Sven!' Torgeir shouted and his men cheered, but Ketil remained silent. 'Today, I will kill Sven the Boar. And when the day is done, I will find your corpse and hack it into tiny pieces! I will pull your eyes out and piss in your eyes' sockets. I will rip your tongue out and feed it to my pigs.' Torgeir's men roared behind him and the men of Ribe shouted their own insults back at Torgeir. But Sven paid attention to neither. He knew what Torgeir was doing. He knew the jarl of Hedeby was expecting him to return the insults. Many of Ribe's warriors expected the same. It was all part of the battle, the boasting and threatening beforehand to show your warriors that you were not afraid. It filled them with confidence and made them fight better. But Sven was too old to play that game, just like he was too old to be fighting in a battle like this. Sven tightened his grip on his sword as Torgeir continued making threats and struck the back of his shield with the pommel of his sword. Beside him, Alvar and Rollo started doing the same and soon all of Guttrom's men joined in. The thunderous noise drowned out the insults being shouted by Torgeir and the rest of Horik's men as Sven felt his heart beat in rhythm with the prelude to the battle song. His limbs trembled as his battle rage coursed through his veins and made him feel as young as the men around him. The pains of his age and old injuries disappeared and his senses sharpened. Sven closed his eyes and sent one last prayer to the All-Father, the god that made him what he was. *Odin, let me survive this battle and get back to my grandson. Do not let me fail him as I failed my son. Frigg, watch over Charles if the Norns decide that today is my day.*

Guttrom, standing in the third rank, lifted his sword in the air and the sound of more than a thousand men beating their shields was replaced by a silence that took Sven's breath away. Even the ravens and the eagles fell silent as they soared above. Sven opened his eyes and saw Torgeir tense. They all knew the time for words had ended. 'Odin! Charge!'

Horik's men stood firm as Guttrom's army surged forward. The sound of the two shield walls colliding was loud enough to tumble into mountains as men grunted and roared. But Horik's men held their ground and, over the din, Torgeir shouted one more time.

'Today, you die, Sven!'

'Shut up, you fucking idiot,' Sven growled as he stabbed his sword through a small gap in the shield wall. But his hopes of injuring Torgeir early were dashed as his blade struck the jarl's shield. Out of the corner of his eyes, Sven spotted the Dane axe coming for his head and had to resist the urge to lift his shield to block it. That would only allow Torgeir to stick his sword in Sven's gut. He had to trust the man behind would stop the axe, which he did. He brought his shield up and Sven had to fight hard not to flinch as the axe struck the shield above his head. Torgeir screamed, his eyes wild as he shoved his shield forward and drove Sven back a step.

'Sven, hold on, you old bastard!' Rollo screamed as he dug his shoulder into his shield to stop the shield wall from collapsing. The men behind Sven got their shoulders behind him, and Sven roared as he tried to reclaim the step he had lost.

'You're too old for this, Sven!' Torgeir shouted as he tried to push Sven back another step.

Head low, Sven did his best to resist, but he did not have the same strength of his youth. Rollo had been right. He should not have been fighting in the front rank of the shield wall. He felt the pressure from Torgeir at the front and his men behind him and thought he was going to burst when he looked down and saw that Torgeir's leading foot was under his shield. 'And you're too dumb!' Sven stabbed down with his sword. Torgeir screamed and, as he pulled his bloody foot back, Sven pushed forward. The sudden change had caught everyone off guard and Sven almost found himself in the middle of Torgeir's men before Rollo and Alvar came up on either side of him with the rest of the men of Ribe. Ketil grabbed his jarl and pulled him back before Sven could kill him, and this left a gap in their wall. Sven's heart skipped a beat, and he was about to rush into that gap before he checked himself. It was still too early in the fight and he would only die if he did that. Instead, Sven turned and stabbed the man who was fighting Alvar in the side. As his blade broke through the warrior's brynja, Sven twisted it and stabbed up into the man's chest. The warrior grunted and his eyes widened before Alvar pushed him back and buried his axe in the man's neck. But in a few heartbeats, more of Torgeir's men stepped forward and closed the gap. Sven swore under his breath that he had not got the chance to kill the jarl of Hedeby, but at least the bastard was out of the fight. All around Sven, men fought for their lives and for their jarls and kings. They screamed to the gods as they killed their enemies and cried for their mothers as they died. Blood sprayed through the air, drenching all those in reach as the ground beneath became slick with it. A small axe hooked over the rim of Sven's shield, but instead of resisting, Sven let the shield be pulled forward, trusting that Rollo and Alvar would keep him alive. As soon as Sven saw the face of the man pulling his shield away, he stabbed forward, his sword slicing through the bastard's neck. The warrior stared at Sven, his eyes wide as his mouth fell open and he choked on the sword. He pulled his blade to the side, almost decapitating the bastard and spraying all those around with blood. Sven realised he was laughing as his blood boiled. He had given in to his bloodlust, his battle rage.

'Fight me!' he roared as another warrior stepped forward to take the place of the man he had just killed. Torgeir's warrior hesitated when he saw Sven's blood-covered face and bared teeth, and this gave the man behind Sven time to bring his axe down and split the warrior's skull in two. 'Fight me!' Sven brought his shield up to block an axe aimed for his head, while Rollo killed the man holding it. The fighting went on, with Sven and his two champion warriors killing all who came before them. The men behind them blocked the axes coming from those in Horik's second row, while spears streaked past Sven's head and into the faces of the men he was fighting. One spear took a warrior's eye and, as the man screamed, Sven buried his sword in the bastard's stomach. As the warrior collapsed, Sven saw Horik on horseback behind his shield wall. 'Horik! You bastard! Come and fight me! Horik!' Sven roared as he hacked and stabbed. His rage drove him on as he killed any who dared to stand before him. Because Sven saw that the man who had agreed to let the Franks take his son was within reach. And today, Sven the Boar was finally going to ram his sword down the old bastard's throat. 'Horik! Fight me!'

25

Abbess Hildegard stood on the riverbank in Bremen and watched as men prepared Duke Liudolf's personal ship. The sun was out and the weather warm, so most of the men were shirtless as they carried barrels with provisions on board while others scrubbed the deck clean and checked the sail. Hildegard fingered the cross around her neck as she stared at the men, their sweat-covered muscles straining with the effort. But then she turned her attention away from them and studied the ship. It was like most of the other ships docked on the wharf, with its single mast and steep sides. But this ship had two fort-like structures, one on the front end of the ship and the other on the rear end, which made it look like a battle fortress on water. The men on board were all loyal to the duke, sailors and warriors that he entrusted to keep her safe. The warriors were more respectful, but the sailors seemed to believe that she was eager for their attention as they called out to her and made crude comments. Hildegard had no interest in the men other than making sure they performed their duties. She had been an abbess for almost as long as she had been a princess and, since her time with Torkel, she had not wanted another man. God and His son were enough for her as she strove to forget the sins of her youth. But now she was standing on the wharf in Bremen, waiting impatiently for the men to complete their tasks, so that she could board the duke's ship and find her son. The son she had tried so hard to forget, but one that God was refusing to let her let go of. She wasn't sure if she should be mad at Torkel for not being able to protect their son, or for sending him to the devil.

Hildegard bit the inside of her mouth as she thought of the gossip that she had been hearing amongst the traders in Bremen. War had broken out in Denmark. King Horik's nephew had returned from exile and wanted to be king. The abbess shook her head at how easy it was for greed to taint the souls of men. Nephews should not be fighting uncles. Brothers should not be fighting brothers either, she thought as her mind turned to the turmoil that was closer to home. Her father, the king of East Francia, had sent her brother, also named Louis, to battle their uncle, the king of West Francia. Her brother had set off for Aquitaine not so long ago, after being delayed for more than a year. Although, Hildegard had a good idea of what had delayed her younger brother. The sin of the flesh, most likely. She knew her brother had not wanted to go because it meant he could not spend any more time with the many women he enjoyed. But word had reached her father that King Charles of West Francia was searching for the missing cross and was close to getting his hands on it. Hildegard had prayed that it was not true, but it had spurred her father on and he had told her brother to get on his horse and lead his army west. Her father had also demanded that she attend his court, most likely to make sure she did nothing rash like board a ship and sail to Denmark, but Hildegard had ignored his summons. She hoped that her sisters in Fraumünster would not be in trouble for helping her deceive her father and king, but she had to do this.

Hildegard was tired of waiting on the men she had entrusted to protect her son, to find Charles and to bring him to safety. Now she was going to get on a ship and sail to the man her father's warriors had told her horror stories about. Liudolf had done his best to convince her not to go. He had even offered to go himself instead, but she had been too determined and in the end all Liudolf could do was offer his ship and some men to protect her. Hildegard ignored the butterflies in her stomach. God would keep her safe and protect her from the devil's bastard. Hildegard also wanted to be angry at Duke Liudolf and Bishop Bernard, but she knew that she only had herself to blame. Her rash actions as a child had now put her son at risk and had got the man she had loved killed. Hildegard closed her eyes, wondering why she had taken that cross. There had been so many other pieces of jewellery she could have taken. But that cross had been important to her father. And that was why she had taken it. She had wanted to hurt him, just like he had hurt her.

'Are we going to be here long?' Gerold asked as he stood behind her.

Hildegard turned and glared at the young man, irritated that he had disrupted her thoughts. She took a deep breath and calmed herself. He had most likely done her a favour because she had been struggling with those thoughts ever since she had heard the news. Gerold's bruises were gone and he had put some flesh on his bones with the meals she had provided him since she had taken him from Liudolf's court. He was a handsome man and she recognised the intelligence in his eyes. It was a pity things had gone wrong for him. He would have made an excellent servant to her and the duke. She had seen how he walked unnoticed through busy streets and markets, how his eyes and ears caught everything. It was Gerold who had told her of the news from Denmark after Liudolf and the bishop had done their best to keep it from her. She knew that if she confronted them about it, then they would only say that it was so that she wouldn't do anything rash. Hildegard smiled. It was far too late for that. 'You don't have to stand here. You can go back to your room, or to the tavern, get something to eat perhaps.' She knew little about the young man, other than that he was from the south of her father's kingdom. His darker skin and dark hair told her that, so did his accent, but she had been unable to find out anything else about him. Still, she felt like she could trust Gerold, despite what Duke Liudolf believed.

Gerold shook his head as his dark eyes focused on the men on the wharf. 'I'm only leaving when you do.'

Hildegard smiled and turned to the wharf where some men were watching her. That was another thing that surprised her about Gerold. He had become her guard without her asking him to. She wondered if the duke had ordered him to protect her, but she had not seen the two of them speak before she had left Ehresburg. 'When will the ship be ready?'

Gerold scowled. 'Tomorrow. The weather is not good today, or so the captain says.'

Hildegard nodded. She glanced at the river and saw nothing in the sky which warned her of a storm. Perhaps there were darker clouds over the seas, but she could not see them from here. She had to trust the captain knew what he was doing. The duke was paying the man a lot of money, and Hildegard had given him some extra coins to ensure his loyalty.

'I still don't understand why you want me to come with you. They'll kill me as soon as I step off the ship.'

Hildegard kept her eyes on the ship. 'Because you know the town and Charles. I don't know what my son looks like and I need you to identify him.'

'I doubt Charles would trust me now. God knows we didn't exactly end on good terms last time. He believes the duke and the bishop were behind his father's death and he knows I worked for them.'

Hildegard ignored the fact that Gerold had used God's name in vain. 'Yes, that will be a problem we'll have to overcome, but I'm sure that God will provide us with a solution to that before we reach Ribe.'

'You sound just like him,' Gerold said, and Hildegard felt the thud in her chest as her heart skipped a beat. She turned and faced Gerold.

'What do you mean?' She scowled at the dark-haired young man.

Gerold shrugged. 'I told you, he wanted to be a priest and constantly believed that God would come to his rescue. He even believed that one of the heathen women was an angel sent by God to keep him safe.'

'And did she?'

Gerold frowned at Hildegard.

'Did this angel keep him safe?' Gerold had mentioned this woman before and Hildegard had to admit that she wanted to meet this woman warrior who had killed men to protect her son.

'You know she did. I told you all this before.'

'Yes, you did.' Hildegard turned and watched the ship again. Her hand went back to the cross around her neck as she thought of her conversation with Bishop Bernard after she had been to Ehresburg. She had tried to find out more about the cross that had belonged to her grandfather. Bishop Bernard claimed not to know much about it. He had suggested she ask her father about the cross, but Hildegard knew that if she went to her father's court, then he would be furious to learn that she had been the one who had it taken and would not let her leave until he had the cross back. She wondered if he would send one of her other brothers to hunt for it. Hildegard had sent word to those she trusted to search through her father's libraries, but no one had found out why the cross was so special. All Hildegard had was a fragmented memory of her grandmother telling her about her great-grandfather's victory over the Saxons at Ehresburg. But a part of that memory eluded Hildegard. That had been another reason she had gone to visit the duke. Hildegard had hoped that if she went to Ehresburg, then the missing part of the memory would reveal itself. But it had not and no matter how hard she tried or prayed, God had decided that she should not know the truth of the cross that threatened the life of her son. Hildegard was convinced it had something to do with her great-grandfather's victory at Ehresburg. Hildegard took a deep breath and said, 'Come, let's go find the bishop. It's almost time for the evening prayers.' She heard Gerold sigh, but ignored him as she made her way to the church of Bremen. That was where she would find the old bishop. He had insisted on coming with them on this journey and Hildegard wasn't sure if it was because he wanted to help, or because he didn't trust Gerold. In the end, Hildegard had agreed, more to keep an eye on the old man because she was convinced that he was the one keeping her father informed of her movements, just like he had kept her informed of Torkel's. She thought of Torkel again, something she had tried hard not to do, as she blinked away the tears.

Why, Torkel? Why did you not send our son to me?

26

'Lift your shield higher,' Thora said as she appraised Charles's stance. It was the day after his fight with Sigmund and Thora had decided that she needed to keep him busy. So they had started the day with a run around the wall of Ribe and were now training on the training ground with a small shield and a staff, which was meant to be a spear. The shield was smaller than the one the warriors used and was made especially for the children so that they could get used to fighting with it. Charles had seen how easily the warriors moved while holding the shields and even used them as weapons, but he doubted he could ever do the same. He tried to lift the shield higher, but his shoulders and back were sore from his fight, and this made the shield feel heavier than it was. It also didn't help that his hands were bruised, which made holding the shield difficult. But Thora had insisted they moved on to training with weapons. Charles, though, felt like she was punishing him for his fight. 'Good, now hold it there.' Thora walked around and prodded the shield with her staff. 'Charles.' She shook her head as he dropped the shield.

Charles creased his face. 'It's heavy and my shoulders hurt.'

'It'll get lighter. Now lift it again.'

'Why? I don't understand why I need to learn with a shield.' Charles pouted as he sat down. His legs were tired from the run and, as always, he had barely slept the night before. The usual nightmares of the Frank and the raven tree were now joined by a small monster devouring a child. Charles had been confused by that when he got up in the morning and guessed the monster must have been him and the child Sigmund.

'A shield is as important to a warrior as his armour. That is why you must master it. Blades can break through even the strongest brynja, but a shield, if used properly, is impenetrable.' Thora picked up the small shield and handed it to Charles, who glared at it.

'But it's uncomfortable to use.'

Thora smiled. 'Yes, for now, but that's why we train with it. So that by the time you stand in your first shield wall, it'll feel like it's a part of your arm.'

Charles scowled at Thora. 'But I'm not going to stand in a shield wall!'

A sigh replaced Thora's smile. 'We will see, Charles. We will see.'

Charles looked away from Thora towards the hall. That was where he had spent the rest of the previous day after his fight. Jorlaug had been there for most of the day as well, while her grandmother, Ingvild, had made sure the thralls gave him a good meal. She had tutted at the state of him and had said that he was just like his grandfather. Perhaps that was what that dream was. Alfhild had wiped his face and hands clean with a wet cloth before bringing him a clean tunic to wear while Jorlaug kept on telling him about the fight. Charles had wanted to scream at her to stop, but he had kept his mouth shut, afraid that Thora would scold him. She had said little to him, and he guessed it was because she was disappointed. 'Do you think my grandfather will return?'

Thora also looked at the hall across from the empty market. Most of the traders had gone, but there were still a few who came to sell their wares. The rest of the townspeople carried on with their daily lives, making or mending clothes, preparing meals and keeping their houses clean, something Charles struggled with. Every time someone had walked into the hall the day before, Charles had expected bad news when it wasn't his grandfather. 'He will. No one fights better than your grandfather.'

'But he is an old man.'

'Aye, he is.' Thora gave him a comforting smile. 'Don't worry. Rollo and Alvar will keep him safe.'

Charles glanced at Thora. She had said that as if they were children running around in the fields, not fighting an enormous battle. And they knew it was large. A man had arrived before sunset and told them the battle had started and that there were more men than he had ever seen in one place. The old grey beards, men who had been warriors in their youth, had whistled at that and some even commented that they wished they were younger so they could fight in the battle, while others were sceptical. But the messenger had said that the battle was still raging when he had been sent to give them the news. Oleg had taken the man to one side and had given him ale as they spoke. Charles had decided that he did not like Oleg. The man had sat in the hall, either eyeing Sven's seat or him, and Charles did not like the dark look in the old man's eyes.

'Come on, that's enough rest. Let's train.' Thora toed his boot. Charles groaned and stood up, but before he could assume the position that Thora had taught him, she said, 'What, in Odin's name, are they doing here?'

Charles followed Thora's gaze and saw a group of men dismounting in front of the hall. He frowned when he recognised Ivor, Guttrom's son. That surprised him as much as he guessed it had surprised Thora. 'Should he not be fighting with his father?'

Thora glanced at him but did not respond. She didn't need to, though. Her creased brow showed she thought the same. 'Stay here.' Without waiting for a response, Thora dropped her staff and walked towards the hall.

Charles dropped his shield and looked around. He did not want to be left here on his own. He did not know where Sigmund and his friends were and was sure they were just waiting for the right opportunity to attack him again. So he followed Thora. Besides, he also wanted to know why Ivor was here. Maybe the man had some news about the battle and his grandfather. Charles ran to the back door, the one that went into the bedroom he and Thora were using because he knew Thora would be upset that he had disobeyed her. As he neared the door, two warriors stepped around the corner and smiled at him.

'Well. What do we have here?' one of the warriors said with a leer.

'Just who we've been looking for.' The other grinned like a hunter who had finally got his prey. Charles frowned as he recognised the men. They were Guttrom's warriors. He had seen them in the hall with the rest of Guttrom's men.

'Why were you looking for me?' Charles took a step back so that he was out of reach of the two men. 'Do you have news of my grandfather?'

The two warriors looked at each other and shrugged before one of them said, 'Aye. News from your grandfather. He sent us to keep an eye on you.'

Charles did not believe that. Not just because of the leers on the faces of the two men, but also because he knew his grandfather trusted no one more than Thora to protect him. Charles took another step backwards and glanced around, trying to find someone who could help him, but saw no one. All the warriors he knew were with his grandfather, and even if Father Leofdag had been there, Charles doubted the man could have done anything. He couldn't even protect himself.

'So, be a good lad and come with us now. Ivor wants you in the hall.' The man took a step forward and reached out for Charles. 'Come now, boy.'

Charles took another step back as his heart raced. Just then, there was a loud noise from the hall, as if a table had been thrown over. The back door to the hall swung open and Alfhild appeared. She stopped, her eyes wide, when she spotted Charles with the two warriors. 'Charles! Run!'

Everything happened at once, like a storm that came out of nowhere. One of the warriors snarled as he launched himself at Charles, while Alfhild jumped on the back of the other warrior and bit the man's ear. The warrior screamed and grabbed the thrall by her hair and yanked her off of him. As she landed on the ground, he kicked her hard in the stomach, his ear missing and blood pouring from the wound. Charles ducked under the arms of the warrior trying to grab him, for once glad he was so short, and ran as if the devil was chasing him. And, to Charles, the devil was.

'Get the little shit!' the warrior with the missing ear roared at his companion as he held his hand to the side of his head, the blood leaking out between his fingers. He kicked Alfhild one more time before both men chased after Charles.

Charles ran to the front of the hall, to where Thora was. He did not know where else to go and, as he rounded the corner, he ran into one of Ivor's men.

'What the—' the man started, and then grinned when he saw Charles. As fast as a viper, his hand shot out and grabbed Charles by his tunic.

'Let go of me!' Charles kicked out, striking the man in his leg. The warrior screamed and hopped on one leg, but he kept hold of Charles as his two companions arrived. But God was with Charles, or so he thought when Thora came rushing out of the hall. She saw what was happening and kicked the warrior holding Charles in the groin before the man realised she was behind him. The warrior let go of Charles as his eyes bulged out of his head and he collapsed with his hands between his legs. Charles had enough time to see the red mark on Thora's face before he remembered the other two warriors behind him.

'Run, Charles!'

This time, Charles obeyed Thora and ran towards the market, hoping that he could hide between the stalls, but quickly dismissed the idea. He looked over his shoulder and saw Thora twist out of the way of a punch before kicking the side of the man's leg. He was sure he heard the leg crack, but then he put his head down and ran as fast as he could. Charles did not know where to run, so he ran towards Oda's house.

'Catch the runt!' he heard behind him and knew that the other warriors were after him.

Charles rounded one house, not knowing if he was going the right way. He didn't know how to get to Oda's house. Every time he had been in that area before, he had wandered there by mistake. But all Charles knew was that he had to keep going. He was about to turn down another road when a hand grabbed him from behind and plucked him off his feet. Charles screamed and lashed out, trying to get the man to let go of him, but the warrior only laughed as he held Charles in the air as if he weighed nothing.

'Let go of me! Thora! Help!' Charles tried to kick the tall warrior holding him in the chest, but the man twisted out of the way and, with his free hand, smacked Charles on the side of the head.

'Stop that, you little bastard. You're coming with us.'

'No!' Charles kicked out again and missed, which only made the three warriors laugh.

'Do that again and I'll have to knock you out,' the tall warrior holding him warned. But then they all turned in surprise when there was a shriek from behind as Sigmund and his friends stormed the three warriors. Oda stepped out of one of the side streets while the warriors were distracted and struck the one holding Charles on the side of the head with her stick. The man's head snapped to the side, but he kept hold of Charles and snarled. 'You stupid old bitch.' He smacked the old woman with the back of his hand and she collapsed. Charles screamed, which made Sigmund look their way.

'Grandmother!' the boy shouted and charged at the tall warrior. Before the man could do anything, Rollo's son grabbed hold of his leg and bit him. The warrior screamed again, and this time let go of Charles. As soon as Charles's feet touched the ground, he attacked the man. His anger at what had happened to Oda blinded him to what he needed to do, and he punched the tall warrior in the groin. The man grunted and, as he bent over, Charles punched him in the face. He wasn't sure what he expected to happen, but the warrior only reacted with a snarl. He grabbed Charles by the throat and, with his free hand, punched Sigmund in the head. Sigmund let go of the man's leg and fell to the ground, his hands on his head.

'Will you two stop fucking around and deal with these shits!'

The other two warriors smacked the boys holding on to them, one of them deciding to kick a very stubborn boy before chasing them away.

'Come on, Ivor will be waiting,' the tall warrior said, and walked back to the hall, still gripping Charles by the neck. Charles's vision was blurring as he struggled to breathe. He tried to pry the man's fingers loose, but he was not strong enough.

As they walked through the empty market, the three warriors were greeted by a roar as the smith came out of nowhere and struck the man holding Charles in the skull with his smith's hammer. Charles heard a loud crack as the man let go of him and both

Charles and the now dead warrior dropped to the ground at the same time.

'Run, boy!' the smith shouted as he faced the two remaining warriors. He held his hammer in one hand while the other was clenched in a fist. The two warriors circled him while others joined them, and soon they had Charles and the smith surrounded.

'You're going to die for that!' one warrior threatened the smith as he pulled his sword out of its scabbard.

'What's going on here?' a woman said as she came back from the river and saw the commotion. She dropped the bucket she had just filled and her hand went to her mouth when she saw the dead warrior and Charles and the smith surrounded by men she did not recognise. By the hall, Thora stood covered in the blood of the two warriors she had killed, snarling at the rest of Ivor's men as they forced her back. In her hand, she had an axe that Charles guessed she had taken from one of Ivor's men. He willed her to save him, but he knew she couldn't. There were just too many men for her to fight. He glanced at the warriors from Ribe, the ones his grandfather had left behind with Oleg, and wondered why they weren't doing anything. Beside him, the smith roared again as he charged at the men surrounding him. He swung his hammer at one warrior, who jumped back to avoid the blow, while another rushed in and stabbed the smith in the side. The smith grunted as the warrior twisted his sword and Charles stood frozen to the spot as two more warriors joined in and hacked the smith to death. They seemed unaware of the women and grey beards of Ribe crowding around the market, all of them screaming their discontent at the men Ivor had brought with him.

This finally encouraged Ribe's few remaining warriors to do something. They charged at the warriors who had killed the smith and drove the men back. Thora used this distraction to bury her axe in the chest of the warrior facing her, and before the man dropped to the ground, she pulled the sax-knife from his belt and stabbed another through the neck. One warrior stabbed at Thora, but she twisted out of the way and punched him in the face before she ran to where Charles stood.

'Charles, are you all right?' Thora grabbed his shoulders and all he could do was stare at her. 'Bastards!' Thora roared and picked up the sword which had belonged to the tall warrior. She glanced at Ivor's men before glaring at the warriors of Ribe. 'These bastards attacked our people, killed one of our own, and you just stand there and watch!' Thora pointed her sword at the dead smith. 'He fixed your armour, sharpened your blades, and you do nothing while these scum slaughter him!'

'Thora, enough!' Oleg stepped out of the hall, with Ivor by his side. Guttrom's son saw his dead men and bared his teeth at Thora.

'Oleg, you treacherous worm. What have you done?'

Oleg ran his eyes over the bodies and shook his head. 'What I had to do to protect this town from Sven and the bastard Christians.'

'So you betray Sven for the second time?' Thora hawked and spat towards Oleg, even though he wasn't close to her. 'You allow these men to kill the people of Ribe?' The townspeople roared at this, but none of them made a move. They were mainly old folk and women with families to protect while their men were away fighting the king of Denmark. Charles's throat ached as he fell to his knees and stared at the dead smith. The man had died trying to protect him, and Charles hoped he would find his way to heaven.

'I did what I needed to. And as for the smith, the bastard was a Christian.'

'He was still a man of Ribe,' Thora growled. She took a step forward and Ivor's warriors smiled at her, as if they wanted her to attack them. Charles prayed she wouldn't. He knew she could not defeat all of them, even if the warriors of Ribe helped her.

Charles looked at Oleg and with a sore throat said, 'Oda wasn't a Christian.'

'What?' Oleg raised an eyebrow as if he had not heard him.

Thora turned to Charles. 'What do you mean?'

Charles looked at Thora and felt the tears running down his cheeks. 'Oda wasn't a Christian, and they killed her. Alfhild as well.' Charles did not know if any of this was true, but he doubted that Oda or Alfhild had survived the attacks on them. 'They died trying to help me.' He lowered his head as the tears flowed.

'They killed Oda?' one of the townspeople asked.

'Who killed Oda?' Thora asked Charles, and he pointed at the dead warrior with the caved-in skull.

'Well then, Oda has been avenged.' Oleg crossed his arms.

Ivor glared at the old warrior. 'That was one of my best men. I've had enough of this. Men, kill the bitch and grab the boy.'

Ivor's warriors surged forward and Thora tensed as she prepared to fight them. One of Ribe's warriors rushed forwards and Charles thought the man was going to help Thora, but then he grabbed her from behind and dragged her back.

Thora screamed at the man. 'You bastard! Let go or I swear by Odin, I will kill you and all your sons!' She tried to strike the man with the back of her head, but the warrior kept his head out of reach.

'Forgive me, Thora. I'm only doing this to keep you alive. You should not have to die for a Christian bastard.'

Charles just sat there, too stunned to move, as Ivor's warriors grabbed him and lifted him off the ground. Ivor and Oleg walked towards them as the rest of Ribe's warriors turned and faced the people of Ribe to make sure they did nothing else as well.

'People of Ribe, go back to your homes. Attend to your duties. None of you wanted Sven or his grandson here. Guttrom has made sure that neither of them will ever curse our town again.' Oleg stopped and looked at Charles as one of Ivor's men held on to him. 'Christians are not welcome in our town.'

Charles found some spark of anger in him and he glared at the man who had betrayed his grandfather. 'My grandfather will kill you for this. God will make sure of it.'

Oleg only smiled. 'Your grandfather is already dead. Guttrom made sure of it.'

Before Charles could respond, Thora freed herself from the grip of the man holding her. She still had the sax-knife in her hand and before Oleg could even look away from Charles, she stabbed him in the neck with the blade.

'And I made sure you die for your treachery, you worm,' she growled into his ear as Oleg's eyes bulged. Charles just stared at the man, unable to react to all the violence around him, as blood started leaking out of his mouth. Two of Ivor's men grabbed Thora and pulled her back as Oleg dropped to his knees and grabbed the knife still in his throat, his mouth gaping as he struggled to breathe. Blood soaked into his tunic and, with his free hand, he reached out to Charles, who just stared at the man his grandfather had never really trusted. He felt the anger coursing through him and Charles found he was glad when Oleg's life finally left him and the old warrior fell to the ground. A stunned silence filled the town, even the birds and other animals seemed stunned into silence.

Ivor shook his head as he glanced at Oleg's corpse, his blood reddening the ground around him and mixing with the blood of the smith and the other warrior. The smell of death filled Charles's nostrils. The metallic scent of blood with the stench of emptied bowels and bladders would have made him feel sick in the past, but now Charles found that he had got used to it. Death and violence had followed him from the quiet town in East Francia where he had lived with his father, through Denmark and to Ribe. Everywhere he went, people died because of him. Charles had always believed he had been destined to be a priest. But perhaps he had been wrong. Perhaps he had never been a child of God, but a child of the devil. He glared at Ivor as the tall warrior stood in front of Thora.

'You are more deadly than the Valkyries,' he said, smiling at her. 'Perhaps I could convince you to join my men. When my father becomes king, then I will need someone like you by my side.'

Thora spat in Ivor's face. 'Your father will never be king. As soon as Sven finds out what has happened, he will slaughter all of you.'

Ivor laughed. 'The old fool is dead, like Oleg said. There's no way he could survive a battle like that.'

'Only the gods can kill Sven and even they fear his wrath. Nowhere in the nine realms will be safe for you. Sven will tear them all apart until you are dead.' Thora glared at Ivor and his men.

'Fine, have it your way.' Ivor stabbed Thora in the stomach.

'Thora!' Charles screamed, fresh tears streaming from his eyes. He struggled to breathe as if he had been struck in the chest as Thora dropped to her knees, her hand on the wound in her stomach. She looked at Charles and smiled.

'Don't be afraid, Charles. Sven will find you.' She looked up at Ivor. 'He will find you and kill you all. Not even the gods can protect you from him.' Some of the men took a step back from the venom in her voice, while others grabbed the Mjöllnirs around their necks.

'I've had enough of this.' Ivor turned to his men as he put his sax-knife back in its scabbard without cleaning it. 'Let's go.'

'Didn't the Frank say we had to stay here?' one of the warriors asked, frowning. Charles stared at Thora as the tears ran down his cheeks, but she only smiled at him, her skin turning pale as her blood leaked out of her wound.

'Fuck the Frank. No spy for the West king will tell me what to do.'

'And the people?' the warrior asked.

Ivor glanced at the townspeople who had gathered around

them. Their voices were getting louder as they were slowly understanding what was happening. 'My father will be their king soon
and they wouldn't want to anger him.' The townspeople backed off
as if agreeing with Ivor, but continued to glare at him while some of
his men brought their horses. Charles's hands were tied up, and he
was thrown over the back of Ivor's horse. 'Let's go! We ride for my
father!' Ivor kicked his horse and his men followed him out of the
gates. They left their dead where they lay as the people of Ribe did
nothing to stop them, but Charles saw that some women rushed to
help Thora. Charles thought of the golden cross hidden in the chest
and prayed Thora would survive. He did not want her to die
because of him and the cross, just like he had not wanted Alfhild or
Oda to die. He thought of the threat Thora had made before Ivor
stabbed her. Charles felt the strength in her words and realised that
he believed her. He believed his grandfather would kill these men.
God had sent the devil to keep him safe and the devil would send
these bastards to hell for what they had done.

27

Sven stared at his porridge, but could not get himself to eat it. He knew he had to. He needed his strength for what surely would be another long day of fighting. Sven sighed as he looked around the camp which had been moved closer to the battleground. The men looked like he felt. Pale faces, blue-rimmed eyes and barely a man with not some kind of injury. This was the third day of the battle, and there seemed to be no end to it. On the first day, the men had fought like gods. Sven had felt like a younger man after he had given in to his bloodlust and he had hacked and stabbed at the men of Horik. That was until his body reminded him he was not young any more.

Sven had stepped forward to stab the warrior facing him when the man lifted his shield to block the axe aimed at his head. But then Sven's left leg, weakened by an old injury, gave way, and Sven collapsed. He cried out as the sharp pain shot up his hip and thought that someone had stabbed him. This gave the man facing Sven an opportunity to do what no one else had been able to. Kill Sven the Boar. But the gods weren't ready for him yet, and Alvar blocked the warrior's sword while Rollo opened his throat.

'Sven,' Rollo shouted over the battle din. 'Get back, Sven. Recover your strength!'

'No! I can still fight!' Sven struggled to his feet, but could not put any weight on his left leg. Rollo was right, but Sven did not want to leave the fight. He needed to be there. He needed to be the one who killed Horik. But as soon as the next warrior stepped forward and hacked at Sven with his axe, he knew he could not carry on fighting. Sven lifted his battered shield to block the blow and was driven to his knees again. Once more, Alvar and Rollo had to ignore the men they were fighting to protect him. Alvar's opponent took advantage and cut a deep gash into Alvar's arm. From his position on his knees, Sven stabbed the bastard in the groin while he tried to go for the killing blow. Sven twisted his sword before pulling it out and knew he had struck a major artery with the amount of blood that came gushing out of the wound. But Sven realised he had to get back. His age was putting his men at risk, and he did not want to be responsible for their deaths. Rollo glanced at Sven, who nodded to show that he was going to step back.

'Get the jarl back!' Rollo shouted, and Sven felt himself being dragged through the ranks of the shield wall until he was spat out the back of it.

Sven's body trembled as he stumbled back to his tent. His body ached and his legs would barely obey him, so Sven just collapsed where he was. He stared at the back of the shield wall and shook his head. They had started with at least ten ranks, but now there were only eight or seven. So many men dead. A young warrior rushed to his side and Sven recognised him as one of the men from Ribe.

'Jarl, are you injured?' The warrior checked Sven over. Although, Sven doubted the young man could do anything, even if he was.

'No, just get me something to drink.' Sven saw the many minor cuts on his arms. He looked at the edge of his sword and saw the many nicks on the blade's edge. The sword would need to go to the smith to have its edge repaired. But first Sven had to survive the battle. The young warrior gave Sven a water skin and Sven drank deep from it before taking his helmet and the leather felt cap off and pouring the rest over his head. He glanced at the young warrior and saw he carried no injuries and showed no signs of fighting. 'Why aren't you fighting?'

'I... I...' The young warrior looked away from Sven.

Sven sighed. He needed something stronger than water. 'The first battle is always hard, and the gods weren't kind to you to make this your first. Just keep your shield up and eyes open.' The young warrior nodded as he glanced back at the shield wall. Sven guessed he was in the rear rank, where all the inexperienced warriors were. The boy didn't even have a leather jerkin, only a thick woollen tunic and an old bowl helmet. His only weapon seemed to be a spear. 'Go get me some ale.'

The young warrior nodded and ran back to their camp while Sven rubbed the raven tattoo on his scalp. He sat like that, resting, until the young warrior brought him some ale and, after emptying the flask, Sven struggled to his feet and sheathed his sword. He put his helmet and the leather felt cap he wore under it and took the spear from the young warrior. 'Loot the dead, find yourself a good weapon and shield. And then get back in the shield wall. You won't go to Valhalla by hiding from the fight.' The younger warrior nodded and Sven limped back to the shield wall. He forced his way through to the third rank, behind Rollo and Alvar, and used the spear to stab at any exposed head he could see.

They fought like that until the sun started its descent and only stopped when horns started blowing on both sides. The men stopped fighting and cautiously moved back without lowering their shields or taking their eyes off their enemy. The ground between the shield wall was littered with the dead and Sven knew not many would sleep that night, not with the noise the ravens and other carrion birds would make as they feasted under the moonlight. Guttrom stepped out of the shield wall, covered in blood and limping while Horik led his horse forward. Sven growled at how clean the king was. With the rest of the men from Ribe, he watched as the two leaders spoke, and then they both turned and went back to their camps.

Sven slept like the dead that night, but felt no fresher when they formed the shield wall for the second day, which went much like the first. A few warriors stepped forward to challenge others to single combat, but there weren't as many as on the first day. This time the result of the few fights was more even. The horns blew and the two shield walls came together again. Sven fought until he could not manage any more before stepping back and resting. They had agreed the night before that they would only fight for as long as they could and then rest for a short while before joining the fight.

Now, Sven put his porridge down and winced as he got to his feet and rubbed his left leg, but that was not the only part of his body that was struggling. His knees ached and Sven feared they could give way at any moment. His shoulders refused to obey him, and it was harder to lift his shield than it had been on the first day. Even his sword felt heavier. And then there was the constant headache which had made him more irritable. Sven was too old for this. He knew that. But he could not refuse to join the shield wall. The warriors of Ribe had sworn no oath to him, but he was still their leader and they needed to see him fight in the front rank. Sven looked at his two champions. Both warriors were still on the ground. Alvar was stretched out on his back and Rollo was sitting next to him, sharpening the edge of his hand axe. Sven was envious of the bastard's energy, but he knew it was because of that, that he was still alive. Alvar's right arm was bandaged where he had been cut on the first day and he had another cut on his cheek. While

Rollo had a long cut along his neck from a spear the day before. It wasn't deep, and it didn't seem to bother the man, and neither did the cut on his leg. Sven shook his head as he missed his youth. So many winters wasted wandering drunk around Denmark. He rubbed the tattoo on his head when he saw the sun had climbed high enough for the battle to start.

A warrior limped out of Guttrom's tent and took a deep breath before he lifted the horn to his lips and blew on it. The men groaned and got to their feet while putting on helmets and checking their armour and weapons. Sven scowled as he scrutinised Guttrom's men and still saw no sign of Ivor. He wasn't sure why, but that bothered him more than it should have done.

'Come, men.' Sven's voice was raw from all the fighting. They had run out of ale as no one had expected the battle to last this long and Sven did not want to drink water. Water did not give a man the courage to stand in the shield wall, especially not for the third day in a row. Sven pulled the leather cap over his head, doing his best to ignore its stink before putting his dented helmet on. 'Time to do what we do best.' He picked up his shield and grimaced at the pain in his shoulder. He spotted the young warrior he had spoken to on the first day. The man had an axe and a shield now, and his tunic was covered in dried blood. The man's face was drawn, his eyes red from not sleeping, and Sven knew he would never be the same again. None of the young warriors would be if they survived this battle.

Rollo jumped to his feet. 'Today is the day.' He collected his shield and flexed his shoulders while Alvar got to his feet. 'Today, we kill Horik.'

'You said that yesterday,' one man said.

'Aye, Odin knows he'll probably say the same tomorrow as well,' another said, and a few of the men laughed.

We need to survive to find out, Sven thought but did not say. He did not need to. All the men here knew that already. They made their way to the battleground and formed their shield wall. Sven glanced over his shoulder and saw it was only five men deep in the centre where he fought near Guttrom's men, and knew it would be even less on the flanks.

'What, in Odin's name, is the old bastard doing?' Alvar frowned at the centre of Horik's shield wall. Sven looked at where the tall warrior was pointing and raised an eyebrow when he saw Horik standing amongst his men. He wore a silver helmet with a golden eye guard, his silver hair hanging loose under it. Horik lifted his shield which bore his mark while two giant men flanked him.

'It seems Horik has finally decided to join the fun.' Rollo shook his head before he spat on the ground.

'He needs to,' Sven said. 'His men will be exhausted, and he needs to motivate them. That's why he fights today.'

'And we're not exhausted?' a warrior asked from behind Sven.

'Aye, but say what you might about our loving leader, Guttrom, he has fought every day.' The men around Sven grunted their agreement as Sven glanced at Guttrom while the man took his place opposite his uncle. Rollo might be right, Sven thought. Today might be the day.

This time, there were no brash warriors stepping forward to challenge men to single combat. They were too exhausted for that. Instead, the two shield walls faced each other in grim silence, the warriors of Denmark just waiting for the signal to be given so the slaughtering could begin again. Even the scavenger birds seemed to have had enough of this battle, Sven thought as he glanced at the sky. He was sure there were fewer birds than there had been the previous two days.

Guttrom lifted his sword, and the man beside him blew on his horn. Across the battleground, Horik's man did the same. The two shield walls took a collective breath and inched towards each other.

Ketil stood in front of Sven. Sven had not seen Torgeir since he had stabbed the bastard in the foot, and unlike Torgeir, Ketil remained silent. There was no taunting on this day, not like the previous two days. No cries to the gods, and Sven wondered if they were still watching. Surely, even they must have lost interest in this long battle. The two lines paused about two feet from each other, and Ketil nodded to Sven. Sven returned the nod as he took in the large blue bags under Ketil's eyes and his pale skin. Sven guessed he looked the same before he pushed the thought from his mind. As if some unspoken signal had been given, the two shield walls came together, the noise loud, but not as loud as on the first day. No mountains trembled, no distant snow peaks shaken from the tops of the mountains. Sven grunted as he pushed against Ketil's shield and tightened the grip on his sword. Ketil used his height to bring his sword over Sven's shield, but Sven lifted his shield enough to deflect the blow, and Ketil pulled his arm back before Sven could cut it. An axe chopped down from behind Sven, and Ketil was forced to block it with his shield. Sven used this to his advantage and shoved his shield forward. The move caught Ketil by surprise, although it shouldn't have done, and Sven forced a small gap in the shield wall. His sword snaked through the gap and he stabbed the man fighting Rollo in the leg. As the warrior screamed, Rollo stabbed him through the mouth, breaking teeth and severing his tongue. Sven felt his battle lust taking control, but it was not as strong as before as a new warrior took the dead man's place, and Ketil closed the gap in the shield wall. They fought like this while the sun moved across the sky, both Sven and Ketil unable to land a killing blow on each other. Along both shield walls, men fought almost methodically as they went through the motions. They stabbed and hacked with swords and axes. Spears tried to find exposed flesh, but there were no cries to the gods this day. The only noise was metal striking metal or wood and the grunting of fatigued men as they tried to get the better of their opponents. Even the ravens were silent, the birds of Odin too fat to bother flying overhead and cheer for their next meal.

Sven had lost track of how long he had been fighting for, and as his sword struck Ketil's shield, he noticed Ketil wasn't lifting it as high as he had before. Ketil was tiring, but so was he. It was only a matter of time before one of them made a mistake. Sven lifted his sword and brought it down with as much strength as he could muster. The blow was enough for Ketil to drop his shield when he tried to block the blow, and Sven followed up by punching out with his shield. This forced Ketil back into the man behind him, and before the two warriors on either side of Ketil could react, Alvar jumped into the gap and killed one of them by chopping his axe into the back of the man's neck. Rollo followed and blocked the sword aimed at Alvar's back while Sven just stood there and stared at Ketil, who grimaced.

'See you in Valhalla,' Ketil said, and rushed at Sven.

Sven lifted his shield, ignoring the pain in his shoulder, and blocked the blow before he stabbed his sword at Ketil's stomach. He did not have enough strength to drive his blade through the brynja, but Ketil's momentum helped the tip of the sword break the metal links and slice into his stomach. Ketil's eyes bulged and he grunted when Sven pulled his sword free and pushed him back with his shield so that he fell amongst his own men. 'Get back!' he roared at Alvar and Rollo, both warriors obeying and locking their shields with Sven's before the warriors of Hedeby could kill them. Hedeby's warriors dragged Ketil's body out of the shield wall. 'Keep a seat warm for me, old friend.'

Sven had no more time to reflect on the death of Ketil as the enemy rushed forward to avenge the death of one of their leaders. He gritted his teeth as the warrior in front of him hacked at his shield with his axe, each blow shooting pain into his already weakened left shoulder, but Sven held firm and kept his shield lifted until the warrior wore himself out. As soon as the blows stopped, Sven lowered his shield and sliced the bastard's neck open while he was gasping for breath. The warrior's eyes widened as his blood reddened his blond beard and he collapsed only for another to take his place, but this man moved slowly and Sven sensed the momentum of the battle turning in their favour. He twisted his head, trying to see how the battle fared along the rest of the shield wall, and noticed that Guttrom was not there any more.

'Where's Guttrom?' he shouted.

Rollo glanced to his left and shrugged before he drove his sword into the shield of the man facing him. The blow was powerful and forced the warrior back which allowed the man on Rollo's right to stab him in the leg. Horik's warrior cried out and fell to the ground where Rollo killed him. He waited for another to take the man's place, but the warriors from Hedeby were reluctant. They had lost their jarl on the first day and now Ketil was dead. There was no one left to drive them forward any more. Rollo glanced at Sven, the question in his eyes clear. Sven thought about it as he punched out with his shield. He felt that one hard push would collapse the enemy shield wall, but Guttrom had to give the order. It was his army. But the bastard was not there. Sven wondered if he had been injured, but doubted it. He looked at where Horik had been before and saw the old bastard was still in the shield wall, but he was standing in the third rank, not the first. That had only been for show and as soon as the battle had started, the king of Denmark had moved back and let his hirdmen fight in his place.

Sven growled and decided that they had to push forward. They could end this battle today and he could return to Ribe, to his grandson. He was about to give the order when someone pulled on his brynja from behind. Sven turned, his face creased with annoyance, and was about to shout at the man distracting him from the fight. But the warrior from Ribe did not give Sven a chance to shout at him.

'Sven! Your grandson. He is here!'

'What?' Sven felt his legs weaken, and he looked around, praying he had misheard the man.

'Your grandson is here! Ivor Guttromson brought him!'

Sven's head swam as he tried to make sense of what the man was telling him. Charles could not have been here. It was impossible. He stumbled into Alvar, who pushed him back.

'Jarl Sven, go! We can hold them!' Alvar buried his axe in his opponent's shoulder.

'Go! Alvar is right!' Rollo pushed Sven out of the way and closed the gap where he had been fighting.

Sven shook his head and tried to focus on the man in front of him. 'Show me!' The warrior nodded and shoved past the men in the rear ranks with Sven behind him. Once out of the shield wall, Sven sucked in the air to clear his head, before dropping his shield and making his way to Guttrom's tent. The man who had brought him the news followed as Sven pulled his helmet off his head and let it fall to the ground. He felt the breeze cooling the sweat on his scalp, but it did nothing to calm the apprehension that was eating him inside. Because Sven knew he had made a mistake by leaving Oleg in Ribe. Over the battle song, Sven heard Loki laughing at him as he limped towards Guttrom's tent.

28

Charles tried not to cry out as Ivor threw him to the ground in the large tent. He looked up and shuddered as Guttrom stood over him, his brynja and face covered in blood and dirt, and stinking worse than Charles did. The only part of Guttrom that wasn't red was the part of his face where the eye guards on his helmet were, and this made his skin look even paler than what it was. Charles also saw the surprised-looking hostage who had been staying in Ribe. 'Why did you bring the boy here?' Guttrom asked Ivor, his face creased.

Charles had pissed himself a few times since Ivor and his men fled from Ribe, not just because he was afraid, but also because of the way he had been on the horse, every jolt had made its way to his bladder and, as much as Charles had tried to hold it, he couldn't. That Ivor and his men rode through the night and didn't stop once as they raced to their destination had not helped, either. But Charles did not care that his trousers were wet, and that he reeked of piss. His head ached and if he hadn't had so many emotions raging through him, then he might even have been hungry. As they had ridden into the camp, Charles had lifted his head and seen the battle. He had gasped at the large number of warriors he saw and when he spotted his grandfather's flag flying near the centre of the battle, he had screamed as loud as he could. Ivor and his men had laughed at this and once more told him that his grandfather was dead, but Charles did not believe that. Especially not when one man had stood up from some tents and, after gaping at him for a few heartbeats, the warrior had turned and sprinted towards the battle.

'You were supposed to keep the little shit in Ribe until after the battle.' Guttrom glared at Charles.

Ivor filled a cup with something from a jug, his hands trembling. 'Had no choice. That bitch found out what we were doing and threatened us. Things got out of hand and we had to leave before the town turned against us.'

Guttrom's jaw muscles were clenched under his beard. 'Oleg would have calmed the people.'

'Oleg is dead. The bitch killed him and a handful of my men.' Ivor emptied the cup and refilled it. 'We had to grab the boy and run, especially after the chaos this little bastard had caused.' Ivor kicked Charles over, but Charles forced himself up to his knees and glared at the man his grandfather had thought of as a friend and Ivor. He hated Ivor for killing Thora and he hated Guttrom for betraying his grandfather.

'Looks like there's some fire in the piglet.' Guttrom sneered and leaned closer to Charles. Even the hostage smiled at that. 'I wouldn't be so brave, not when we give you over to the bastard spy from West Francia. The king of West Francia is very keen to get hold of you. Only Odin knows why, though.'

'I'm not afraid,' Charles said and was glad that his voice didn't tremble. Most likely because of the anger and hatred coursing through him, both emotions he was struggling to control. His heart pounded in his ears and Charles had to fight the urge to jump up and bite Guttrom's nose. 'God will protect me.'

Guttrom's face turned red, and he smacked Charles across the face with the back of his hand. 'Where is your god now?'

Charles flew across the floor and tasted the blood on his lips, but then his heart skipped a beat when his grandfather walked into the tent, his teeth bared and his body rigid.

'His god is busy, so you have to deal with me instead.'

* * *

Sven did not need to see his grandson lying on the ground in Guttrom's tent, to know he had been used. He did not need to see the dirt on the boy's face or the fresh blood on his already bruised face. He did not need to smell the reek of stale piss. Sven knew Guttrom had betrayed him, and he knew it was to the West Franks. And Sven knew this because he had heard what Guttrom had said to Charles. Ivor's men had tried to stop him from entering the tent, but one of them lay dead on the ground and the others had fled when some of Ribe's warriors saw what was happening and rushed at them.

'Thor's balls!' Ivor shouted, and Guttrom's eyes widened as Sven roared and barged into him like an enraged boar, knocking both of them to the ground. They rolled around, both men trying to get the upper hand as they punched and head-butted each other. Eventually, Sven ended up on top and he punched Guttrom in the face, breaking the man's nose. He lifted his sword to kill the worm when Ivor kicked him off his father. Sven rolled to his feet, ignoring the pain in his legs and back, in time to deflect Ivor's sword aimed at his chest. He ducked under Ivor's next swing and as he stepped to the side, he dragged the nicked edge of his sword along Ivor's leg. Ivor cried out, and as Sven turned to stab him through the neck, Charles screamed.

'Behind you!'

Sven sensed the movement behind him and twisted out of the way before the axe could kill him. He stepped between Guttrom and his grandson as Guttrom circled him while gripping his Dane axe in both his hands. Ivor limped to his father's side as the blood from his wound soaked his trousers. Gunvald scurried to somewhere where Sven could not see him, but he ignored the runt as he glared at the man who had used him.

'Why is the bastard still alive? Thought you were going to kill him?' Ivor screamed at his father.

'After the battle, you idiot! I need the men of Ribe to fight for me!' Guttrom glanced at his son and Sven attacked. He stabbed with his sword, which Guttrom deflected with the shaft of his axe before elbowing Sven in the side of the head. Sven ignored the ringing in his ears as he turned and swiped his blade at Guttrom's legs, forcing the man to jump back. Guttrom chopped at Sven with his axe and Sven ducked under it and shouldered Guttrom in the stomach with his left shoulder. Both men grunted in pain as Guttrom staggered back. But Sven did not waste any time. He turned and stabbed at Ivor, now within reach, and the younger warrior blocked the blow with his sword, but was sent tumbling back. He was about to attack Sven when his father shouted.

'Forget about Sven, get the boy out of here!'

Before Sven could step in between Ivor and his grandson again, Guttrom attacked with a flurry of axe swings. Sven dodged and weaved as best he could to avoid Guttrom's Dane axe while wishing he had his. But it was by his tent, left there before the battle because he had not thought he would need it. Sven ducked under Guttrom's axe and tried to get closer to Guttrom to use his sword, but Guttrom was fresher and stronger than Sven, and nimbly turned his Dane axe to keep Sven at bay.

'Grandfather!' Charles screamed and Sven glimpsed Ivor carrying his grandson out of the tent before Guttrom knocked his sword out of his hand. Sven watched as his sword bounced on the ground and had to jump back as Guttrom swung his axe in a wide arc, trying to slice his gut open. The tip of Guttrom's axe caught Sven's brynja, breaking a few links and slicing through his skin. Gunvald used the distraction and grabbed Sven from behind and stabbed him in the back with a knife that must have fallen on the ground during the fight.

Sven grunted as Gunvald growled, 'This is for Bjarni.'

Sven roared at the mention of his treacherous brother and reached behind him and grabbed hold of Gunvald's hair. He pulled hard and Gunvald screamed and freed the knife from Sven's back. But before he could stab Sven again, Sven turned and drove his sword into the younger warrior's side. Gunvald's eyes bulged as the sword sliced through his body. Sven pulled his sword free and kicked Gunvald to the ground before stomping on his neck. He screamed as Gunvald's throat was crushed under his boot before he turned to face Guttrom again.

Sven ignored the fresh wounds and launched himself at Guttrom, who got his axe between and tried to use it to push Sven away. Both men gripped the shaft of the Dane axe and tried to force each other backwards. Sven's strength was fading, though. Three days of fighting in the shield wall were taking their toll on him, and the wounds in his stomach and back drained what little energy he had.

'You're getting old, Sven. You can't beat me.' Guttrom pushed Sven back a few steps.

Sven ground his teeth before responding. 'Who are you calling old? You're as grey as me.'

'Aye, but while you've been drinking yourself stupid, I was fighting battles and making a name for myself.'

'Fighting for the Franks,' Sven growled.

'They pay well,' Guttrom said, and head-butted Sven.

Sven stumbled backwards and tripped over one of Guttrom's chests and fell against the wall of the tent, which held as Guttrom rushed at him. The old warrior chopped down with his axe, and Sven rolled out of the way as it sliced through the tent. Sven cried out as he fell through the hole and landed on the ground outside. The sun blinded him for a heartbeat, but Sven ignored it as he struggled to his feet. His left leg could barely hold him and Sven was forced to lean on his right leg as he felt the blood from his stomach wound wetting his trousers. But he could not give up. Giving up meant losing Charles, and Sven was not going to lose his grandson.

Guttrom laughed as he stepped through the gap in his tent. The warriors who were not fighting in the battle jumped to their feet and stared wide-eyed as Sven and Guttrom circled each other.

'So you took money from the West Franks to start this revolt against your uncle? All so you could grab my grandson for them?' Sven hawked and spat the blood from his mouth. He grimaced at the pain in his leg every time he was forced to step on it, but Sven had no weapon, so he had to pick his moment before he could attack.

Guttrom shook his head as he gripped his axe. 'No, they paid me to deliver your grandson to them. Quite a lot as well. They are really eager to get the little bastard. They gave me enough to recruit more men and to convince some of the jarls to fight for me. So I decided that now was the best time to take the crown of Denmark.' Sven glanced around, looking for a weapon as Guttrom continued. 'Although, I suspect they knew I'd make a move for Horik's crown. It benefits them, I guess.' Sven stopped and frowned, which only made Guttrom laugh. 'Sven, as dumb as you are stubborn. With the Danes fighting each other, Louis of East Francia will be too busy keeping an eye on us to fight his brother in West Francia. That was the real reason they wanted me to come back to Denmark.

Although, the gods know, I still don't know why they want that runt of yours.'

Sven did not care about any of that, but the way Guttrom spoke of his grandson reignited the spark inside him, and he charged at the bastard. Guttrom smiled and chopped down with his axe, but Sven twisted out of the way and punched the taller warrior in the side of the head. As Guttrom's head snapped to the side, Sven kicked the back of his leg and Guttrom fell to his knees, but managed to use his axe to block Sven's next punch. Guttrom brought his axe around and struck Sven in his wound with the haft. Sven grunted and twisted in pain, which gave Guttrom time to jump to his feet. Before Sven could react, Guttrom kicked him in the chest and Sven was sent sprawling to the ground. Sven tried to get up as Guttrom snarled at him, but he couldn't. His body had no fight left in it and refused to obey him. His limbs felt like someone had placed boulders on them and there was nothing Sven could do. He looked at the battle, hoping to see Rollo or Alvar rushing to his aid, but no one was coming, just like none of the surrounding warriors were going to help Sven. They just stood there and watched as the two old warriors tried to kill each other.

Guttrom saw the same as he stood over Sven. 'You're all alone, Sven.' Guttrom lifted his axe and Sven felt empty when he realised he had failed to protect his grandson. He looked at the clouds in the sky and thought he could see Odin's face smiling down on him. *Fuck you, old one-eyed bastard*, Sven thought as Guttrom sneered. 'This is the end of Sven the Boar!'

But before Guttrom could bring the axe down, a horn blew, and men started cheering. Guttrom and the men surrounding them looked towards the shield walls as the cry reached them.

'King Horik is dead! King Horik is dead!'

Guttrom, his axe still above his head, took half a step back and smiled when he realised he had won. He lowered his axe as he stared at where Horik had fought before, but Sven refused to let him have this victory. He kicked out and caught Guttrom on the side of his knee. There was a sickening crack as Guttrom's knee bent the wrong way and Guttrom screamed in agony before dropping his axe and collapsing to the ground. Sven summoned what was the last of his strength and crawled on top of Guttrom.

'I am king,' Guttrom was muttering, his face pale for the pain.

Sven pushed himself up, his body heavier than it had ever been before, and shook his head. 'Not while I live.' He punched Guttrom in the face, feeling the anger come alive in him again. Before Sven knew it, he was screaming at Guttrom as he punched him again and again, crushing the man's face with his fists. Sven kept on punching until he was dragged off of Guttrom's body, howling at whomever it was to let go of him.

'Sven! Stop! He's dead!' Rollo's voice broke through the fog and Sven shook his head as his mind cleared. He looked at his hands and saw they were covered in blood and the skin of his knuckles was taken off. Then Sven remembered his grandson.

'Charles! Where is my grandson?'

Rollo frowned and looked around at the men surrounding them, but all they could do was shrug. 'Sven, what happened?'

Sven pushed Rollo away and struggled to his feet before collapsing again. 'Charles. Ivor took Charles.'

'I saw him race out of the camp with his men,' one warrior said.

'And my grandson?' Sven asked, but the man shook his head. 'Where is my grandson!' Sven screamed. His heart was racing in his chest and Sven's head spun from the loss of blood so much he thought he was going to black out. But he could not. He had to find Charles. He needed to go after Ivor, but where had the bastard gone? Sven did not know. He struggled to breathe as panic took over him. Where was Charles? Where had they taken him? Sven had to do something. He struggled to his feet again, this time succeeding. 'Get the horses. Rollo, get the horses!'

'Why?' Rollo raised an eyebrow at him.

'I need to find my grandson!' Sven screamed at him and Rollo recoiled as Sven's bloody spit covered his face. The large warrior nodded and then rushed to do what Sven had demanded of him. Some of Guttrom's men had arrived and their celebrations died on their lips when they saw Guttrom dead on the ground and Sven swaying near him. They frowned as Sven spoke to them. 'Your leader is dead and unless any of you know where my grandson is, I suggest you fuck off.'

The warriors glared at Sven and a few took a step towards him when the warriors who had seen the fight got between Sven and Guttrom's men.

'Get out of our way,' one of Guttrom's men said.

'Why?' one warrior responded. 'You're nothing but Frankish whores, paid for with Frankish gold.'

Rollo arrived with Sven's sword, which he must have retrieved from the tent, and some horses, and frowned. 'What, in Loki's name, is happening?'

Sven struggled to get onto his horse, and Rollo had to help him. 'To Ribe. We must go to Ribe.'

'Ribe?' Rollo's brow creased.

'I must find out where they took Charles.' Sven's bloody knuckles whitened as he gripped the reins. 'That bastard Oleg will know where they took my grandson.'

Alvar came running towards them with some of Ribe's men, all of them confused as they took in the scene in front of them.

'Alvar. Let the men rest and then head back to Ribe. We'll see you there,' Rollo said as Sven urged his horse into a gallop without looking at his men. Rollo raced after Sven, leaving the men of Ribe behind in the hands of Alvar, who stood scratching his head as he tried to understand what had happened.

Sven and Rollo travelled as fast as they could without injuring their horses and only stopped long enough for the animals to rest and for Rollo to deal with Sven's wounds before urging on towards Ribe. He had wanted to race to Ribe as fast as he could and if it wasn't for Rollo, Sven probably would have killed himself and his horse before he was even halfway there. But Sven needed to get to Ribe. He needed to find out what had happened, and he prayed to Odin that he might find Ivor there with Charles. Then he would rip the bastard's head off his shoulders with his bare hands and end the line of Guttrom.

As they neared the town, though, Sven saw the gates were closed and, as soon as the men guarding the walls spotted Sven and Rollo, they rushed to open them. Sven and Rollo rushed past the warriors of Ribe left behind to guard the town and made their way to the hall. Sven jumped off his horse before it even stopped and almost collapsed from exhaustion and pain, but he forced himself towards the hall. He wanted to find Thora and was stopped by her aunt before he could enter.

'Sven! Charles, we tried—'

'Where is he?' he asked, his eyes wild as he scanned the roads and the houses for any sign of his treacherous former hirdman.

Tears ran down Ingvild's cheeks. 'Thora did what she could, but...'

'Where is Oleg?' Sven growled the question, wanting to peel the skin off the bastard's back while he was still alive.

Ingvild blinked and then shook her head. 'Oleg is dead. Thora killed him.'

Sven stared at Ingvild with wide eyes. *Thora killed him.* 'Where is Thora?' Sven pushed past the old woman and made his way into the hall. He needed to know what had happened. Before he entered the hall, he heard Ingvild say something to Rollo, but in his rage he did not hear the words. Rollo cried out in anguish as Sven entered the hall and he forgot about the giant warrior. Inside, he saw some warriors sitting on the benches, drinking ale while avoiding his gaze. He stopped and glared at them. 'And what did you bastards do while Ivor and his men came here and took my grandson?' None of the warriors responded, and Sven felt his anger engulf him. He rushed at the men and grabbed one of them before the man could get away. 'You drink my ale while you did nothing to stop those bastards!' Sven roared and smashed the man's head against the table. He knew he shouldn't have been so surprised. These men were loyal to Oleg, that was why he had left them behind as well. But he still glared at them as he let go of the warrior who slid to the ground and left a trail of blood on the table. The other warriors jumped to their feet and fled as Sven scanned the hall. 'Thora! Thora!'

Audhild, Thora's cousin, came out of the sleeping quarters, her face pale and her dress covered in blood. 'She...'

Sven didn't give her time to finish her sentence as he rushed into the sleeping quarters. But his anger fled like the warriors had from the hall when he saw Thora on the bed, pale and drenched with sweat. She had a bandage around her stomach with a large bloodstain on it. Beside her lay a smaller form and Sven saw that it was Alfhild as he approached the bed. Her face was creased in pain and she turned away from him when she saw him. Thora opened her eyes as Sven reached the bed.

'Sven... I... tried... but...' Her voice was weak as she struggled to get the words out, and Sven felt the tears running down his cheek.

He placed his bloody hand on her forehead and winced at how hot her skin was. 'I know, Thora. I know you did.'

'Th... the cross—'

'The cross is not important,' Sven said, his hands trembling. But he wasn't sure if she had heard him as her eyes closed again, her breathing so shallow, he almost didn't notice it. 'Will she live?' he asked Audhild, who had followed him into the room.

Thora's cousin looked at her feet and shrugged. 'She's in the hands of the gods now. All we can do is wait.'

Sven grabbed the small stool near the bed and threw it against the wall. 'Oleg, you bastard!' He stood there venting when Ingvild rushed into the room.

'There's a ship approaching!'

Sven looked at her. 'Who is it?'

Ingvild shrugged. 'It's a Frankish ship, that's all I know.'

Sven glanced at Thora one more time before rushing out of the hall. Outside, he saw Rollo on his knees and crying into his hands, but Sven had no time to wonder why when he saw the ship docking on one of the wharves by the river. But he frowned when he realised it was no trading ship. He guessed that was why Ingvild had told him about it. Sven pulled his sword out of its scabbard and limped towards the river, determined to kill every Frank on that ship, as some of the townspeople followed him. When he reached the wharf, the last person he expected to see got off the ship whose face paled when he saw Sven, covered in blood and dirt and with a sword in his hand. Sven felt the gods laughing at him as he stared at the thrall that had betrayed his grandson. 'What, in Odin's name, are you doing here?'

Gerold took a step back as a woman disembarked. She was shorter than Gerold and wore a long black dress, with a black hood, and had a large golden cross hanging around her neck. Head high and back straight, the woman scrutinised the people of Ribe before her eyes settled on Sven. Sven knew who she was before she even needed to say a word. She had the same nose as Charles and the same shape of eyes.

'Where is my son?' the woman asked in Frankish.

Sven heard the people murmur behind him, some of them asking those who spoke the language what she had said, as all his strength left him. He dropped to his knees, his sword slipping out of his hands as his exhaustion and age took over. Sven struggled to breathe as he realised he had failed his family. He could not protect his grandson like Torkel had wanted him to. Sven looked up at the woman, his vision blurred with tears.

'Gone.'

ACKNOWLEDGMENTS

That's book two in the series done and I'm sure you're all as nervous as I am about the fate of Charles. Rest assured that Sven will let nothing get in his way to rescue Charles, but that is for the next book. For this book, I wanted to give Sven some closure for some of the events in his past, but unfortunately things did not quite turn out the way he nor I wanted. But just like Sven has people around him for support and guidance, I have as well.

Firstly, I want to thank my editor, Caroline, for all her support and guidance and for helping me spot the obvious that I might have missed. I also want to thank Ross and Susan for the attention to detail that they bring to my novels and for bringing the best out of my stories. To all the amazing people at Boldwood Books who work tirelessly behind the scenes to bring my novels to you, the readers, I thank them as well.

To my wife, Anna, for her unwavering support and somehow dealing with my constant talk of Vikings, bloody battles and people long dead and fictional.

And most importantly, to you, for taking the time to read this book. I truly hope that you enjoyed your time spent with Charles, Sven and Thora. Thank you all.

ABOUT THE AUTHOR

Donovan Cook is the author of the well-received *Ormstunga Saga* series which combines fast-paced narrative with meticulously researched history of the Viking world, and is inspired by his interest in Norse Mythology. He lives in Lancashire.

Sign up to Donovan Cook's mailing list here for news, competitions and updates on future books.

Visit Donovan's website: www.donovancook.net

Follow Donovan on social media:

 twitter.com/DonovanCook20

 facebook.com/DonovanCookAuthor

 bookbub.com/authors/donovan-cook

ALSO BY DONOVAN COOK

Charlemagne Series

Odin's Betrayal

Loki's Deceit

WARRIOR CHRONICLES

WELCOME TO THE CLAN ✕

THE HOME OF
BESTSELLING HISTORICAL
ADVENTURE FICTION!

WARNING:
MAY CONTAIN VIKINGS!

SIGN UP TO OUR
NEWSLETTER

BIT.LY/WARRIORCHRONICLES

Boldwood

Boldwood Books is an award-winning fiction publishing company seeking out the best stories from around the world.

Find out more at www.boldwoodbooks.com

Join our reader community for brilliant books, competitions and offers!

Follow us
@BoldwoodBooks
@TheBoldBookClub

Sign up to our weekly deals newsletter

https://bit.ly/BoldwoodBNewsletter

9 781804 838204